Also by Patricia Potter

Also by Suzanne Robinson

When You Wish

Jane Feather
Patricia Coughlin
Sharon and Tom Curtis
Elizabeth Elliott
Patricia Potter
Suzanne Robinson

BANTAM BOOKS

NEW YORK TORONTO LONDON
SYDNEY AUCKLAND

WHEN YOU WISH
A Bantam Book/October 1997

ISBN 0-553-57643-7

Published simultaneously in the United States and Canada

Bantam Books are published by Bantam Books, a division of Bantam Doubleday Dell Publishing Group, Inc. Its trademark, con-
sisting of the words "Bantam Books" and the portrayal of a
rooster, is Registered in U.S. Patent and Trademark Office and in
other countries. Marca Registrada. Bantam Books, 1540 Broadway, New York, New York 10036.

Printed in the United States of America

WCD 10 9 8 7 6 5 4 3 2 1

CONTENTS

Also by Jane Feather

THE SILVER ROSE
THE DIAMOND SLIPPER
VICE
VANITY
VIOLET
VALENTINE
VELVET
VIXEN
VIRTUE

and coming soon
THE EMERALD SWAN

Also by Patricia Coughlin

LORD SAVAGE

Also by Sharon and Tom Curtis

LOVE'S A STAGE
THE WINDFLOWER
THE TESTIMONY
THE GOLDEN TOUCH

Also by Elizabeth Elliott

THE WARLORD
SCOUNDREL
BETROTHED
and available in March 1998
THE ASSASSIN

*S*HE LOOKED CLOSELY at it. A green bottle with a chased silver top. There was something inside it. Would it work? It had to work. Only magic could enable her to make the right decision.

"What must I do? Must I open it in a certain way? Read it in a certain way?"

"You will read it as it is meant to be read." The smile was there again as he took her hand and placed the bottle on her palm. "As it is meant to be read for you," he added.

Her fingers closed over the bottle. She frowned, wondering what he could mean. A spell was a spell, surely. It could only be read one way.

She sat down on the bank and with trembling fingers opened the bottle. A scrap of leather, carefully rolled, lay inside. She drew it out, unfurled it, held it up to the bright moonlight.

To thine own wish be true. Do not follow the moth to the star.

The girl stared in disbelieving dismay. What did it mean? It told her nothing. There was nothing magic about those words.

The choice was still hers to make . . .

From the Prologue by Jane Feather

PROLOGUE

Jane Feather

PROLOGUE

*T*HE MOON RODE high against the soft blackness of the night sky. The great stones of the circle threw their shadows across the sleeping plain. The girl waited in the grove of trees. He had said he would come when the moon reached its zenith.

She shivered despite the warmth of the June night, drawing her woolen cloak about her. The massive pillars of Stonehenge held a menacing magic, even for one accustomed to the rites that took place within the sinister enclosure. The thought of venturing into the vast black space within the circle terrified her, as it terrified all but the priests. It was forbidden ground.

Her ears were stretched for the sound of footsteps, although she knew that she would hear nothing as his sandaled feet slid over the moss of the grove. She stepped closer to the trunk of a poplar tree, then jumped back as she touched its encrustation of sacred mistletoe.

"Move into the moonlight."

Even though she'd been waiting for it, the soft command sent a thrill of fear shivering in her belly, curling her toes. She looked over her shoulder and saw him, shrouded in white, his hood pulled low over his head; only his eyes, pale blue in the darkness, gave life to the form.

The girl stepped out of the grove onto the moonlit plain. She felt him behind her. The priest who held the power of the Druid's Egg. She stopped, turned to face him. "Will you help me?"

"Are you certain you know what you're asking for?" His voice rasped, hoarse, as if he'd been shouting for hours. The pale blue eyes burned in their deep sockets.

She nodded. "I am certain." With a sudden movement, she shook off her hood. Her hair cascaded down her back, a silver river in the moonlight. "Will the magic work?"

A smile flashed across his eyes and he reached out to touch her hair. "It has the power of desires and dreams."

"To make them come true?" Her voice was anxious, puzzled.

He said nothing, but drew from beneath his cloak a thick-bladed knife. "Are you ready?"

The girl swallowed, nodded her head. She turned her back to the priest. She felt him take her hair at the nape of her neck. She felt the knife sawing through the thick mass, silvered by the moon. She felt it part beneath the blade. And then she stood shorn, the night air cold on her bare neck. "Now you will give it to me?"

He was winding the hank of hair around his hand and didn't answer as he reveled in the richness of the payment. The hair of a maiden had many useful properties but it was a potent sacrifice that few young virgins were prepared to make voluntarily. He opened a leather pouch at his waist and carefully deposited the shining mass inside, before taking out an object of green glass. It lay on his flat palm.

She looked closely at it. A green glass bottle with a chased silver top. Vertical bands of chased silver flowed down the bottle from the stopper, like liquid mercury. There was something inside it. She could see the shape in the neck behind the glowing glass. Would it work? It had to work. Only the magic of a man who held the power of the Druid's Egg could enable her to make the right decision.

She reached out and touched it tentatively with her fingertip. "The spell is within?"

"You will read it within."

"What must I do? Must I open it in a certain way? Read it in a certain way?"

"You will read it as it is meant to be read." The smile was there again as he took her hand and placed the bottle on her palm. "As it is meant to be read for you," he added.

Her fingers closed over the bottle. She frowned, wondering what he could mean. A spell was a spell, surely. It could be read only one way.

When she looked up, the priest had gone.

The Druid's Egg was hatched by several serpents laboring together. When hatched it was held in the air by their hissing. The man who had given her the spell had caught the egg as it danced on the serpents' venom. He had caught it and escaped the poison himself. Such a man . . . such a priest . . . had the power to do anything.

Holding the bottle tightly in her fist, the girl turned her back on the stone pillars. She tried to walk but soon was running across the plain, toward the village nestled in a fold of land beside the river that flowed to the sea. She had never seen the sea, only heard tales of a vast blueness that disappeared into the sky. But the river flowing between sloping banks was her friend.

She sat down on the bank outside the village and with trembling fingers opened the bottle. A scrap of leather, carefully rolled, lay inside. She drew it out, unfurled it, held it up to the bright moonlight.

Runes were scratched into the leather at the top, and at the sight of the magic symbols her heart leaped. She hadn't sold her hair for nothing. Here was the incantation she had bought. She squinted at the strange marks and wondered what she was to do with them. Only when she turned the leather over did she see the writing in legible strokes inked onto the leather.

To thine own wish be true. Do not follow the moth to the star.

The girl stared in disbelieving dismay. What did it mean? It told her nothing. There was nothing magic about those words. She looked again at the runes and knew in her bones that they were mere decoration for a simple truth. She thrust the scrap of leather back into the bottle and corked it.

Be true to her own wish. Was it telling her she must face the consequences of her desires? If she wished for the stars, she would burn like the moth at the candle.

Slowly, she stood up. She held her hand over the swift-flowing water and opened it. The little bottle dropped, was caught by the current and whisked away toward the distant sea. As distant as the stars.

The choice was still hers to make. The road still branched before her. She had sold her hair for the druid's power and she was left, as always, with only her own.

Wishful Thinking

Jane Feather

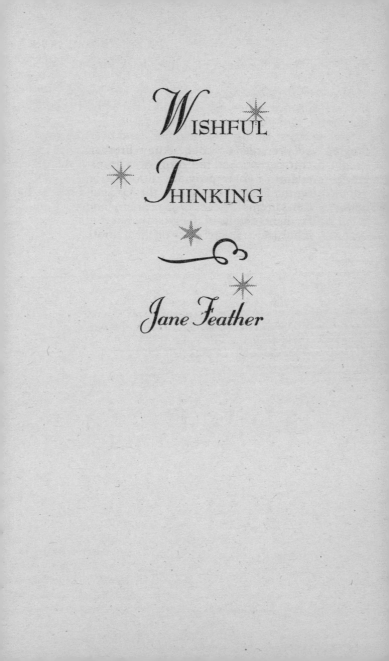

*M*y thanks are due to my brother, Patrick, who at the drop of a transatlantic e-mail provided information on the life to be found in the Lymington salterns in the 19th century, and firsthand details of the gross habits and repulsive characteristics of the axolotl.

CHAPTER ONE

*L*ADY ROSALIND BELMONT strolled up Quay Hill from the town quay, the sun warm on the back of her neck. She was bareheaded, the thick dark hair escaping from its ribbon-tied braids, her feet thrust into a pair of leather thonged sandals. The hem of her gown of sprigged muslin was dark with water, the ruffled edge of her petticoat coated with mud from the estuary. She carried a pail and a net and drew no more than a smiling glance from those she passed. Lady Rosie had become a familiar figure in the little Hampshire town of Lymington during this summer of 1814, where she was visiting the Grantleys in the big red-brick house at the top of High Street.

Rosie's bespectacled eyes were on the cobbles beneath her feet as she scanned the ground for anything that might be of interest to the naturalist's eye. It astonished her mother, her three sisters, and her three brothers-in-law that the youngest member of the Belmont family ever managed to see anything that was more than three inches off the ground.

Her myopic gaze was drawn now to a red admiral fluttering its mottled wings against the white stone wall of a curio shop halfway up Quay Hill. As she approached, it flew up, perching on the sill of the shop's bow-fronted window. Rosie, in her customary spirit of inquiry, bent over it, peering closely at its markings, automatically looking for any difference that would classify this particular butterfly as out of the ordinary. But the insect revealed nothing of special interest and eventually flew off.

Rosie glanced in the window of the curio shop. A collection of silver snuff boxes, a crystal bowl, a decorative assortment of seashells nestled in the window amid an artistic setting of fishing nets and glass weights.

Old Mr. Malone, the shop's owner, peered over the window display and smiled, beckoning. Rosie returned the smile, and opened the shop door, setting the bell clanging merrily. She entered, blinking behind her glasses in the dimness after the bright sunlight outside.

"Good afternoon, Mr. Malone. Have you anything interesting for me?"

"Aye, that I have, Lady Rosie." The white-haired proprietor beamed at her. He hobbled, leaning heavily on his cane, to the back of the shop. "I got offered this collection of insects from some place called Suriname. Old Lady Watson from the Hall sent them over. The butler said they gave her ladyship the creeps."

"Oh, they are most particularly interesting." Rosie set her pail and net on the floor and picked up the display case, carrying it to the window. "How did Lady Watson get hold of them?"

"Found 'em in a drawer in a desk in her late husband's study, apparently. He was something of an amateur naturalist, I gather." Mr. Malone bent over the case with his young customer. "Can't see the appeal, myself."

"Oh, but they're beautiful, fascinating." Rosie gazed, entranced, at the collection of wasps, spiders, fire ants, moths, petrified against a sheet of yellowing parchment. "I must have these."

The shopkeeper nodded, smiling to himself. "Thought they might hit the spot. It'll be three shillings and sixpence."

"I don't have money with me at the moment," Rosie said absently, still scrutinizing the contents of the case. "But I'll bring it when I go back to the quay tomorrow."

"Whenever, my dear," Mr. Malone said with an easy smile.

Rosie's gaze lifted from her treasure. "You're most obliging, Mr. Malone. Oh, what's that?" She reached across a cluttered table and picked up a small bottle of glowing green glass. She held it up to the light from the window, watching the glass become a swirling rainbow of greens and blues. Vertical bands of chased silver striped the bottle, flowing like liquid mercury from the silver stopper.

"What an exquisite thing," she murmured, tracing the silver bands with a fingertip.

"One of the fishermen pulled it up with a crab pot," Mr. Malone said. "Astonishing, but the silver wasn't even tarnished by the salt. Not natural . . . not natural at all."

"It's magical," Rosie said with a laugh. "A magic bottle made of strange and mysterious materials." She was not given to fantasy, but something about the bottle fascinated her. It fitted into the palm of her hand. She made to put it back on the table, but somehow it wouldn't be put down. It was as if it had found a home in her palm, her fingers curled warmly around its sensuous shape.

"How much, Mr. Malone?"

The shopkeeper frowned, pulling at his chin. He was very fond of young Lady Rosie. She was a frequent visitor to his shop, burrowing around in the dusty corners, triumphantly emerging with some forgotten book of plant illustrations or a display case of butterflies. He didn't know whether she had much to spend, but she certainly never gave the impression of wealth. However, the bottle was very beautiful and could well catch the eye of a well-to-do visitor. Business was not so good that Mr. Malone could afford to be philanthropic.

"I couldn't ask less than ten guineas," he said after a long pause.

Rosie looked crestfallen. She could never keep track of her allowance; money seemed to dribble out of her purse. She never knew where it went, but she never seemed to have a surplus from one quarter to the next. Reluctantly, she reached to set the bottle back again. But it seemed to cling to her skin. Her fingers wouldn't uncurl themselves.

"I'll send the money down with a footman as soon as I get home," she heard herself saying. She could ask Mrs. Grantley and then apply to her mother to pay back the loan. Elinor Belmont would not refuse her daughter, but Rosie, conscious of the generosity of the allowance her mother made her, was always embarrassed by her inability to explain her constantly impecunious state.

"I'll wrap it for you, then." Mr. Malone beamed with pleasure as he hastened behind the counter to fetch tissue paper.

"No, there's no need," Rosie said, slipping the bottle into her pocket. It lay heavily against her thigh, and again she had the curious sensation that it was supposed to be there. She gathered the display case of Suriname insects against her small bosom, picked up her pail and net. "I'll send the money within the hour."

"That's all right, Lady Rosie. When you next come past." He opened the shop door for her.

Rosie gave him a brilliant smile. "That was a most particularly satisfactory visit, Mr. Malone."

"Glad to hear it, my lady." He stood in the doorway, watching the slender figure weave a somewhat erratic course up the hill, eyes once again riveted to the cobbles.

Elizabeth Grantley was Rosie's godmother, and an old friend of Lady Elinor Belmont's. Childless, Elizabeth had poured out all her frustrated maternal instincts on her goddaughter over the years and Rosie was almost as at-home in the big red-brick Georgian house at the top of Lymington Hill as she was in the dower house at Stoneridge Manor in the neighboring county of Dorset.

The house was surrounded by a mellow brick wall and Rosie made her way to the side gate, entering the stable yard. A handsome carriage with the Stoneridge arms emblazoned on its side panels stood in the yard. The ostlers were releasing the cattle from the traces.

"Theo!" Rosie said aloud. Her sister had said nothing in her last letter about paying a visit to the Grantleys. She cast a cursory but knowing eye over the horses—blood cattle, as was only to be expected of animals owned by Sylvester Gilbraith, Earl of Stoneridge.

She hurried through a gate into the walled garden behind the house. "Oh, you're all here!" she cried, carefully depositing her insect collection, pail, and net on the grass, before running across the lawn to where three elegant young women sat under a spreading beech tree with Elizabeth Grantley.

"Theo, Clarissa, Emily! What brings you here?" She was lost in the embrace of her older sisters and for a moment the sound of their laughing voices rivaled the dawn chorus in their joyful greetings.

"Rosie! You are so grubby!" Emily, the eldest of the four, exclaimed when she could stand back for a minute. She was a tall young woman with an elegant figure, glowing brown hair, and clear blue eyes. Her exclamation carried a note of resignation rather than castigation.

"I've been collecting specimens," Rosie said with an impatient brush at her skirt.

"But where?" Clarissa asked, laughing. "In a mud pit?" She was thinner, shorter than her elder sister, with darker hair, but her blue eyes were as large and expressive in a dreamy countenance.

"Along the quay, of course," said Lady Theodora Gilbraith, Countess of Stoneridge. "What are you studying now, Rosie?"

"*Artemia salina,*" Rosie replied to the one sister who would see nothing amiss in her appearance or consider her activities in the least inappropriate. "They're very rare and only found on the Lymington salterns. But I found two this morning. Come and see." She took her sister's hand, pulling her over to the abandoned pail. "They're brine shrimp and they like extremely salty water. Much saltier than ordinary shrimp. I can't wait to put them under the microscope. You can look with me if you like."

"I can hardly wait," Theo responded with a chuckle, knowing perfectly well that Rosie would hear only enthusiasm in the dry comment. Curls, black as a raven's wing, clustered close around her small head. Her eyes were the deep velvet blue of pansies in a brown face. Like her little sister, Theo was only truly happy out-of-doors.

"Is Stoneridge here?" Rosie straightened, squinting

behind her glasses as she looked around, expecting to see the tall, powerful figure of her brother-in-law.

"No," Theo said flatly, walking back to the group under the beech tree. "Neither is Edward, nor Jonathan."

"Goodness, are you grass widows, then?" Rosie asked. "Where are they all?"

"Jonathan is painting the portraits of the duchess of Avonleigh's children." Clarissa took a sip of lemonade. "He had to go to Avonleigh Castle to do it, and since I cannot endure Annabel Avonleigh, I decided not to accompany him."

"She is a trifle irksome," Elizabeth Grantley agreed mildly.

"Still, Clarry, it's a splendid commission," Emily reminded her sister with a grave smile.

"And Jonathan won't notice if she's irksome," Rosie put in, taking an iced cake from the tea table. "Jonathan never notices such things."

Since Clarissa's husband was a singularly absent-minded portrait painter who moved through the world in a dream, guided by his adoring and only occasionally more realistic wife, no one disputed this statement.

"Where's Edward?"

Emily's eyes grew soft. "He accompanied his father to the house in Scotland, to talk with the gamekeepers about the grouse shooting. We're having a big house party for the opening of the season and they want to make sure everything's in order."

"And I suppose you thought they'd prefer to go alone," Rosie observed with her usual blunt insight. "Father and son enjoying each other's company without women around."

"Edward and Sir Charles have always been very close," Emily said a trifle defensively. "It's not that they didn't want me around, I just thought that it would be nice for them to have some time together."

"You are a saint," Rosie declared, hugging her sister.

"Nonsense," Emily said, blushing.

"You're both perfectly saintly with your husbands," Theo stated. "I only wish I were."

"So where *is* Stoneridge?" Rosie asked again, her eyes bright with curiosity. It was clear that wherever Sylvester was, Theo was not best pleased.

"In London," Theo said crossly. "He had business with his old regiment at Horseguards. Something to do with the war in Spain."

"Why didn't you go with him?"

Theo didn't immediately reply. She took a sip of her own lemonade and frowned fiercely at the trunk of the beech tree.

"Oh," Rosie said, correctly interpreting her favorite sister's expression. "Wouldn't he let you?"

"He says it's too hot," Theo said disgustedly. "There's a heat wave in town, and some danger of fever, and the journey would be hot and jolting." She glared.

"Oh," Rosie said again. "Are you—"

"Yes," her sister interrupted. "But I feel perfectly well and strong."

"But you had a very hard time with Peregrine," Elizabeth Grantley reminded gently.

"And even harder with Sarah," Emily put in.

Theo said nothing. Of all the Belmont sisters, she had always believed herself to be the strongest, most robust. Until her first pregnancy, she had never known a day's illness, beyond childhood measles. But where her frailer sisters produced babies with enviable ease, Theo struggled through nine months of nausea and threatened miscarriages, culminating in long and agonizing deliveries. It struck her as one of the most unjust strokes of fate. Not least because it meant that her usually malleable, understanding husband became a veritable autocrat at the first sign of pregnancy. And Sylvester Gilbraith, at his most autocratic, was too strong a force even for Theo.

"So," Emily said, "while the husbands are away, the wives thought to play. We've even left the children behind." Her sunny smile embraced her sisters, and Theo grinned reluctantly, accepting that her grievance at Sylvester was between the two of them. And besides, there was something immensely pleasing at the thought of being alone with her sisters again, re-creating their old intimacy.

"Have you heard from Mama?" Rosie asked, as if she read Theo's thoughts. The four of them were not really complete without Elinor.

"A letter from Baden-Baden," Theo said. "I brought it for you to read. She seems to be enjoying her honeymoon."

They all smiled. Their mother had been widowed eighteen years earlier, while she was carrying Rosie. Her recent marriage to the earl of Wetherby had delighted all her daughters and was the main reason for Rosie's extended stay with her godmother.

"I must go in and speak to Cook about dinner." Elizabeth rose from her chair. "I know you all have much to catch up on." She left them, smiling slightly as she heard their voices change tenor, drop a little behind her, as unconsciously they drew together once they were alone, reverting to the patterns of childhood as they exchanged news.

They were not left alone for long. Wellby, the butler, approached in stately fashion across the lawn, carrying a silver salver and a small crate with a chain-link handle.

"Lady Rosie." He paused discreetly on the edge of the sisterly circle. "The postman has just delivered one of those letters . . . and this." He looked down at the crate with ill-concealed repugnance. "If you'll pardon my saying so, Lady Rosie, this has a most powerful and unpleasant smell." He placed the crate on the grass with an expression of heartfelt relief and proffered the salver.

Rosie took the letter quickly. The familiar bold black writing stared up at her from the wax-sealed envelope.

"Who's Ross Balmain?" Theo inquired, peering over her sister's shoulder at the address on the envelope. "Why are his letters coming to you?"

"I'll explain in a minute," Rosie said with almost a snap in her voice. She thrust the letter into her pocket and her fingers closed over the green glass bottle. "Oh, will one of you lend me ten guineas?" she said. "I most particularly need it." Then, without waiting for an answer, she dropped to her knees to open the crate.

Her sisters gathered round, none of them bothering to

inquire why Rosie needed ten guineas. It was bound to have something to do with her scientific explorations.

"Oh, what a stench!" Clarissa jumped back, her hand pressed to her nose, as Rosie pried up the wooden lid.

"It's only marsh grass and lake water," Rosie said, delicately lifting out a large glass jar, its lid punctured with airholes. "They need their natural habitat to survive."

"Dear God in heaven." Theo stared at the two almost formless objects floating in the jar. "What *are* they?"

Emily retreated to where Clarissa stood at a safe distance, leaving Theo and Rosie, who both seemed unaffected by the stench.

"They're axolotls," Rosie told Theo. "A kind of salamander from Mexico. I read this advertisement in a scientific journal. An expedition had brought some back and was offering them for study." She held up the jar and peered at the creatures. "I hope they survived the journey. They were most dreadfully expensive."

"How expensive?" Emily asked.

"Oh, thirty guineas, I think," Rosie replied absently. "I can't quite remember."

The sisters exchanged glances. It was no wonder Rosie was always out of funds.

"They don't look much like salamanders to me," Theo observed, bending closer. "They don't have any shape."

"No, they're still in a larval condition," Rosie explained enthusiastically. "You see they even have external gills. But you can see that they're quadrupeds, and they have tails, if you look closely. They only metamorphose to mature salamanders if the aquatic environment dries up. Then they develop and move on land. That's what makes them most particularly fascinating."

"I suppose so." Theo straightened, feeling slightly queasy. They were the most repulsive-looking blobs of life she'd ever laid eyes on. "I think the blackish one is marginally less repulsive than the pinky albino. What are you going to do with them?"

"I have all sorts of plans," Rosie said happily. "I must go and put them in the aquarium. I bought it especially. A perfect habitat."

"And how much did that cost?" Emily asked into the air as Rosie hurried away.

"A deal more than ten guineas," Theo responded. "But what on earth is she up to? Why is she getting letters addressed to a Ross Balmain?"

CHAPTER TWO

Dear Mr. Balmain,

I'm very sorry we seem unable to resolve this dispute amicably in correspondence. I had hoped that the spirit of scientific inquiry that binds us both would have led to a mutual understanding. I still feel sure that we can reach such an understanding, however, and in the interests of resolution, I propose a meeting. I will make a journey into Hampshire and wait upon you within five days of your receipt of this. I trust you will receive me and we can meet as colleagues in a joint endeavor.

I remain your obedient servant,
Charles Larchmont.

"Oh, no! Now what am I going to do?" Rosie wailed, crumpling the letter in her fist.

"What about?" Theo asked, still peering at the axolotls now floating peacefully in a large aquarium in Rosie's bedroom. She turned toward her sister. "Ah, the letter to the mysterious Ross Balmain. Explain, Rosie." She sat down on the end of the bed.

"Oh, he is the most odious man!" Rosie paced the room with angry strides. "A fussy, pompous old man. There's only one thing I wish for more than anything in the world. And I *know* I should have it. I've done all the work. I *know* I'm right. What right has he to stand in my way? To stop me getting the one thing . . . the only thing I will *ever* wish for," she added extravagantly.

"You're not being very clear," Theo observed, hitching herself up the bed until she was leaning against the pillows.

"What is it you wish for, dear?" Emily asked tenderly. "Can we help?"

"Yes, of course," Clarissa said. "If it's within our power, Rosie. And you know Mama will—"

"*No!*" Rosie broke in with lamentable lack of finesse. "It's within *my* power. I can do it myself. I already *have* done it myself. I don't need any help. Only this . . . this . . . oh, this *horrible,* self-important, self-righteous old man is trying to steal my discovery."

"I appear to be no wiser," Theo murmured, folding her hands over her still-flat belly. "It might help if we knew who Ross Balmain is."

"He's *me,* of course." Rosie uncrumpled the letter.

"*You?*" exclaimed two of her sisters. Theo merely raised an eyebrow.

"I have to pretend to be a man," Rosie said impatiently. "It's perfectly clear. The Royal Society doesn't elect women to its membership, so I have to be a man."

"Ah, I begin to understand," Theo said.

"Well, I don't," Clarry declared. "And neither does Emily."

"I discovered this new classification of moths, black moths," Rosie said with the same impatience. "I documented my findings, I did drawings, I wrote a paper—a very learned paper—and I submitted the specimen to the Royal Society. Only, because I'm female I had to pretend to be male if they were going to take me seriously. And it was all wonderful to start with, and they said I had discovered a new species, and my research was impeccable, and the specimen was beautifully preserved, and so they proposed electing me as a member of the society. They would vote on it at the next meeting, but they were certain it would pass without dissent."

She clasped her hands tightly over the abused letter from Mr. Larchmont and gazed at her sisters. "Don't you see what this would mean? They would name a species after me and a *woman* would be elected to the Royal Society."

"A seventeen-year-old woman into the bargain," Theo remarked. "What a brilliant thing, Rosie. I always knew you were a genius."

"I'm still confused," Emily said. "But what's this pompous old man got to do with anything?"

"He says . . . *claims* . . . that he found the species first. That while I was putting together my research, he was three steps ahead and so the find belongs to him. And since he's already a member of the Royal Society, of course they took his word over mine." She uncrumpled the letter yet again. "I've been writing to him, trying to prove that I got there first, and he just lectures and patronizes in his answers, and treats me just like some *amateur,* which I'm *not,*" she stated emphatically. "And now he's coming here." She gazed down at the letter. "He's coming to meet Ross Balmain. What am I to do?"

"Well, you must tell him the truth," Emily said.

"Of course she can't do that," Theo protested. "If she does that, she'll lose all chance of being elected to the Royal Society."

Such an ambition would have struck Emily and Clarissa as absurd, except that they knew their little sister. Rosie marched to her own drummer. "Maybe so," Clarissa said. "But even if she managed to get elected, how could she keep her true identity a secret? Don't they have meetings and things?"

"I wouldn't have to go," Rosie pointed out. "I'd do my own research, and submit papers, and engage in correspondence—all the things they do, sharing their discoveries . . ." Her eyes shone behind the horn-rimmed spectacles. "It would be so wonderful to know these people, to be one of them. And no one need know anything about me except that I'm some kind of academic recluse."

"Oh, Rosie!" Emily said with a gurgle of laughter. "An

academic recluse! You're only seventeen. What kind of a life is that for a young girl?"

"A most particularly satisfactory one," Rosie said stubbornly.

"I'm sure it would suit Rosie very well," Theo observed. "But it's not going to happen if we can't circumvent the patronizing old man." She yawned suddenly. "I'm so sleepy. It's so annoying."

"Maybe you should take a nap," Clarissa suggested.

Theo shook her head vigorously. "I'm not such a milksop."

"Stoneridge would say you should," Rosie said.

"Yes, but he's not here, is he?" Theo returned acidly, swinging her legs off the bed. "Maybe if I walk around a little, I'll wake up and start my brain working."

"This is pretty, Rosie. Where did it come from?" Emily's eye was caught by the green glass bottle standing on the windowsill, where it caught the sunlight so that it shimmered and glowed in a swirl of blue and green between the silver bands.

"Oh, that's why I need to borrow ten guineas. I fell in love with it in the curio shop on Quay Hill." Rosie forgot her problem for a moment as she picked up the bottle, cradling it in her palm. "There's just something about it. I don't know what." She held it up to the light to admire it more closely.

"There's something inside." Theo, at her shoulder, reached over and took it from her. "Look, you can see the shape." They all crowded round, examining the bottle in the light.

"Let me see." Rosie took it back and turned the silver stopper. It was stiff and wouldn't move at first, but finally turned loose. "There's a plug of cork inside as well."

"Maybe you can get it out with a hairpin." Emily pulled a long pin from the knot of golden brown hair piled on top of her head.

"Stick it in like a corkscrew," Clarry suggested.

"The cork's not even damp," Rosie marveled. "And Mr. Malone said the bottle had come up in a fisherman's crab pot." She inserted the pin carefully, twisted, and pulled.

The little plug squeaked as it moved, then popped neatly out on the end of the pin. Rosie's fingers were as deft and delicate as if she were handling some fragile insect specimen as she extracted a tightly rolled piece of leather and unfurled it.

Her sisters peered over her shoulder. "Look at those strange scratch marks." Emily pointed.

"Perhaps they're symbols," Theo said.

"Maybe they're runes," Clarissa suggested. "You know, magic symbols . . . a charm or something."

"You are such a fanciful romantic, Clarry," Theo said with an affectionate chuckle.

"There's something on the back." Rosie turned the leather over. "Words. Real words."

"What does it say?" Theo again reached across her sister's shoulder.

"I'll read it," Rosie said. "It's my bottle."

"It's half mine if I give you the ten guineas." Theo's laugh was teasing and Rosie ignored the comment.

" 'To thine own wish be true,' " she read slowly. " 'Do not follow the moth to the star.' " She looked around at her sisters. "What could it mean?"

"It sounds very prosy to me," Theo declared. "Who on earth would bother to put something like that in an exquisite bottle that ends up at the bottom of the sea?"

"It's most mysterious," Rosie said, still fascinated by the message.

"Well, let's turn our attention to the matter of Mr. Larchmont." Theo had little sympathy with mysteries. "There's no time to tell him not to come, so Mr. Balmain most regretfully will have to be away from home. Perhaps we could say he's a cousin of ours and asked us to give Mr. Larchmont his deepest regrets that he couldn't be here but he had to go to a deathbed, or something."

"I would like to meet him," Rosie declared. "I would like to meet him and tell him to his face just what I think of people who go around stealing other people's scientific discoveries."

"I don't see why you shouldn't have that satisfaction," Theo said slowly. "It shouldn't surprise Mr. Larchmont if

Mr. Balmain's cousins know the story and of course they would be on the side of their cousin. We could give him a most uncomfortable time, it seems to me."

"Oh, yes!" Rosie clapped her hands. "We'll make him squirm."

"We might even persuade him to reconsider his position," Theo mused.

"How?"

"I don't know yet, Emily."

"Perhaps we could shame him into it," Clarry suggested. "You are sure, Rosie, that he stole your research?"

"Oh, perfectly," Rosie declared. "The Royal Society had my paper four weeks before this Larchmont toad decided to claim he'd discovered the new classification before I did. If he had, why hadn't he published it already?"

"We shall ask him," Theo said. "We shall prepare an inquisition for the gentleman that'll burn him more surely than all the fires of the Spanish Inquisition."

"We'll need to explain the situation to Elizabeth."

"Oh, she already knows. I had to explain the letters to Ross Balmain."

"Then we have only to prepare a reception for the toad." Theo went to the door. "I'm going to rest before dinner," she announced with a touch of defiance. "But don't anybody dare tell Sylvester how feeble I am."

Emily and Clarissa grinned and followed her out.

Rosie looked at the green glass bottle in her hand. She unfurled the leather again and read the message. *To thine own wish be true.*

She had only one wish, one all-consuming wish. Somehow she would become a member of that august group of scientists who made up the Royal Society. She would share in the excitements of others' discoveries; she would finally have fellow scientists to talk to about all the wonderful things that filled her life. She belonged there. And she would get there despite Charles Larchmont.

Whatever it took—she would be absolutely true to her own wish.

CHAPTER THREE

I CAN'T GIVE ye a private parlor, sir, don't 'ave one. But the snug's quiet enough of a Tuesday. I doubt you'll be disturbed there while ye 'ave a bite of dinner." The landlord of the Green Goose on the Winchester Road delivered his message with arms folded across an ample belly, then waited for his prospective customer's response.

"That'll be fine," the tall, lean young man said briskly, removing his high-crowned beaver hat. "Have the lad take my horse. I've ridden him hard today so he'll need a rubdown and a bran mash."

The landlord clicked his fingers at the stable lad, who came running to take the reins of the handsome gray hunter. "If'n ye'd come this way, yer honor, I'll show you into the snug and the lad'll carry your bag up to the best bedchamber."

It was clear to the host of the Green Goose that his customer was of the Quality. His riding britches were the softest buckskin, the gleam of his top boots spoke of champagne polish, and his coat had the fit of a master tailor.

"Ye'll be glad of a bottle of best burgundy, I dare swear, sir." He flung open the door of the snug at the back of the taproom. The air was still heavy with the residue of the previous evening's pipe smoke. Charles Larchmont glanced

up at the row of pipes of every description hanging above
the bar awaiting their owners as he drew off his York tan
gloves, tossing them with his whip on the bar counter.

"Draw me a tankard of October ale, first," he said. "It
was a hot and dusty ride."

"Aye, quite a heat wave we've been 'avin'," mine host
agreed, drawing ale from the keg. "I 'ear it's powerful bad
in London. Fever an' all." He plunked the foaming pewter
tankard in front of his customer, who bent his head and expertly skimmed off the froth as it flowed over the edge, before lifting the tankard and thirstily gulping the contents.

The landlord regarded this expertise with approval. No
dandified gent this one. Probably one of the Corinthian set,
although he looked too slender to be at home in the boxing
ring. Probably quick, though, the innkeeper amended, and
he rode a prime beast, so it was to be assumed he had a
preference for blood sports.

"Do you know a town called Lymington?"

"Oh, aye. An hour's ride from here," the landlord said.
"Pretty little place. Good fishing in the estuary. Crabbing
an' the like."

"Do you know the principal families there?" Charles
drained his tankard and pushed it across for a refill. "Have
one yourself."

"Why, thankee, sir. Well, now, there's the Watsons up
at the 'All." The landlord busied himself at the keg. "Then
there's Dr. Sterling and Squire Jessup."

Charles frowned. "Is that all?" He addressed his refilled
tankard.

The landlord wiped foam from his mouth with the back
of his hand. "Let me see now. Oh, aye, of course there's
the Grantleys."

A flicker crossed Mr. Larchmont's calm brown eyes.
"They have a visitor?"

The landlord frowned. "As to that, sir, I wouldn't
know. Mrs. Grantley's goddaughter is often there, I believe. But we don't 'ear too much of Lymington goings-on
this far afield." He pushed himself away from the counter.
"I'll see about yer dinner, then. A nice boiled cutlet and a
piece of Christchurch salmon? 'Ow does that sound?"

"Admirable. And you may bring me that burgundy now."

The landlord bowed himself out and Charles Larchmont drained his tankard and wandered over to the small window that looked out onto a cottage garden, massed with wallflowers, purple stock, and foxglove. The rose bushes were in full bloom and honeysuckle clambered thickly up the brick wall. As he watched, a woman appeared with a basket. She disappeared into a thicket of canes on which were massed the flowers of runner beans.

Dinner, Charles decided, would be plain but good. He sat down on the settle, stretching his legs to the empty hearth, and drew out the vexatious letter that had brought him halfway across southern England.

This Ross Balmain was a most intemperate creature. Young, Charles had decided at the very beginning of this irksome business. Only the very young would plunge into streams of invective, unhampered by cool thought. Only the very young would imagine that Charles Larchmont, one of the most prominent biologists in the country, would *steal* someone else's research. He had tried the calm approach. He had tried to defuse the situation. He had complimented young Balmain on the quality of his research, the excellence of his paper. He had assured the young man that although this piece of work didn't qualify him for election to the Royal Society, he had no doubt that it would not be long before such a gifted scientist achieved entrance into that holy of holies. And all he'd received for his pains was a stream of hotheaded, insulting letters, accusing him of the worst offense in academia.

He looked down at the letter in his hand. The impassioned accusations leaped off the page. *Most particularly deceitful. Particularly cowardly. The work of a most particular dastard.* Ross Balmain had a particular penchant for the word *particular*.

Charles wondered why he was bothering to attempt to placate and convince such an offensive youth. But he knew why. Balmain's research had all the marks of the passionate yet meticulous scientist. He had heard the exultation coming through the dry academic phrases as the stages of research had been documented and he knew that here wrote a kindred spirit. Someone with whom he could collaborate, even. This was a talent . . . a gift . . . to be nurtured, despite the immature passions of one not yet able to translate the cool head needed for exacting research into the wider world.

Thoughtfully, he replaced the letter in his pocket. The address he'd been writing to was Grantley House, High Street, Lymington. Presumably the Grantleys had guests other than the goddaughter.

The return of the landlord put a stop to his speculations. He watched with all the interest of a healthy appetite as a serving girl set a round table in the window for his dinner. His host drew the cork on a dusty bottle, held up a glass to the light to check for dust or smears before pouring the ruby wine. "There y'are, yer honor. I think ye'll find that satisfactory."

"I'm sure I shall." Charles sipped and leaned back against the settle with a sigh of contentment. First thing in the morning he would ride to Lymington, put up at a pleasant inn, and present himself at Grantley House. It would probably be a wasted exercise and he'd meet only with confrontation and rudeness but he wouldn't be able to put the whole distasteful business behind him until he'd met face-to-face with his young accuser.

He slept well and awoke with the dawn, lying in the cradling warmth of the feather bed listening to the chattering birds in the sloping eaves outside his window. It was very quiet after the rattling hubbub of the streets outside his London house on Ebury Street. He liked city life, found the cries of street vendors, the rumble of iron wheels on the cobbled streets, the cacophonous music made by a crowded metropolis to be a perfect background to his working hours in the large room that served as both study and laboratory. He needed the sense of a busy world outside his own walls to counterbalance the solitude of research. And for the same reason, he needed his town friends, with whom he rode, fenced, drove racing curricles, and sparred. As a result, the Larchmont estate in Lincolnshire rarely saw its owner except in hunting season.

He breakfasted in the sunny cottage garden, took his leave of his obliging hosts, and rode off down the Winchester Road armed with instructions for a shortcut, as the crow flies, to Lymington. The route brought him to the estuary of the Lymington River and the cluster of fishermen's cottages, boatyards, and chandlers' stores at the base of the steep hill, High Street, that led up through the little town, lined with shops, inns, and substantial houses.

The smell of seaweed, marsh, and the crisp salt of the open sea, into which the river flowed, filled his nostrils as he rode along a narrow, twisting street that emerged on the town quay. The Ship inn was a prosperous-looking establishment, as his hosts at the Green Goose had promised. It stood foursquare on the quay looking up the river. Masts and rigging from the flotilla of boats moored at the quay creaked in the breeze; gulls and curlews screamed shrilly as they swooped and dived over the water. It was low tide and the river was a narrow channel running between the salterns of black marsh mud.

Charles dismounted, looped the reins over a black iron hitching post, and strolled to the edge of the stone quay. His gaze dropped to the fertile mud. He frowned, remembering something. The Lymington salterns were the home of *Artemia salina*. The tiny brine shrimp were not found anywhere else in England. He squatted on his haunches, gazing down, heedless of the curious stares of fisherfolk tending their nets on the quay. An immaculately dressed gentleman in a high-crowned beaver hat almost sitting in the dirt staring at the riverbed was a strange sight.

With an air of resolution, Charles suddenly straightened, turned, fetched his horse, and led him to the Ship. He couldn't paddle in the river without waders and canvas ducks, two items of clothing it hadn't occurred to him to bring on this mission. But then, he hadn't expected any bonuses on what he'd assumed would be a merely tiresome journey. A shopping expedition was in order.

An hour later, equipped with a pair of baggy sailcloth trousers, into which his ruffled white shirt was somewhat incongruously tucked, and thigh-high waders, Charles jumped down from the quay into the river shallows and set out across the tidal marsh to see what he could see.

The first thing he saw was a figure bending close to the mud at the very tide line of the narrow channel. A figure in a yellow dress kilted up around her calves. He stopped to watch her. She was examining the mud around her buried feet with a small rake, every now and again picking something out and dropping it into the pail beside her.

A fisherman's daughter picking clams and mussels, Charles assumed, making his way toward her.

"Is it a rich harvest?" he asked amiably as he drew close. The girl didn't appear to notice him for a minute, then she turned to look at him. He had an impression of a small, serious face dwarfed by a pair of thick-rimmed spectacles, dark brown hair escaping from the brim of a large straw hat that shaded the back of her neck. She seemed slight, not at all a red-cheeked, sturdy fisherman's lass.

She appeared to consider the question as if it had deeper meaning than its mere surface pleasantry before she said somewhat elliptically, "It's a neap tide," then returned to her raking.

The mud would be less rich during neaps than spring tides, Charles reflected. Presumably that was what she meant. She obviously wasn't interested in furthering their embryonic acquaintance, so he nodded courteously to her bent back and walked farther along, keeping his eyes on the mud.

Rosie turned her head to watch him as he walked away. She frowned. For all her myopia, she was very observant and her one quick glance had left her puzzled. He was dressed like a fisherman, except for that shirt. But he hadn't spoken like a fisherman. His voice had a very pleasant timbre to it with the crisp vowels of educated speech.

What was an educated stranger doing probing the tide line? A possible answer came to her in a rush. Charles Larchmont? But her tormentor was an old man, fussy and pompous. This stranger couldn't be more than thirty. Younger than Sylvester, older than Jonathan. More like Edward's age.

She tried to return to her harvesting but her concentration was broken and she felt annoyingly disturbed by her unknown companion on the mud, even though he was not paying her the slightest attention. Crossly, she gathered up her equipment, slung her sandals around her neck, and squelched her barefoot way back to the quay, where she sat on a rock and washed her feet in the clear river water.

Charles turned back to the inn, satisfied by his reconnaissance that he could put his visit to Lymington to good use. He saw the girl dabbling her feet in the river. Her hat was beside her on the rock and he could see that her hair was so dark as to be almost black, fastened in a braided coronet around her head. She looked up suddenly, as if aware of his scrutiny, and he could feel the scorching power of her glare behind the glasses despite the distance that separated them. His interruption must have upset her. Shrugging, he continued back to the inn and by the time he reached the quay, the girl had gone.

He had decided to pay his visit to the Grantleys in the early afternoon, during traditional visiting hours. It would serve to break the ice, and if young Mr. Balmain's animosity was clearly immutable, then he would have every excuse to keep the visit very short.

He walked up the hill, enjoying the atmosphere of the small town with its bow-fronted shops, cobbled lanes, air of busy prosperity. It seemed everyone knew everyone else. Landaulets and barouches blocked the street as their occupants exchanged greetings; pedestrians gathered in small clots on corners deep in conversation. They regarded the stranger with affable curiosity, offering nods of greeting as he passed.

Grantley House was a moderate-sized gentleman's residence, its red brick soft in the afternoon sunlight. A small walkway bordered with sweet alyssum and pansies led to the front door. He banged the shiny brass knocker and waited. The door was opened by an elderly retainer.

"Mr. Ross Balmain, please. I believe I'm expected." Charles handed the butler his card.

Wellby looked at the white engraved square. "If you'd like to step into the hall, sir, I'll inform the young ladies."

Young ladies? Charles stepped into the hall. What had young ladies to do with his business with Ross Balmain? The butler disappeared, leaving Charles to inhale the scents of beeswax and lavender, to note the elegant curve of the staircase, the handsome furnishings, the highly polished wood, brass, and silver. The house was of only moderate size but it was unmistakably the abode of a well-to-do family of impeccable taste. He occupied himself with a series of portraits on the staircase, wondering idly if Mr. Balmain would show any resemblance to the genial, aristocratic faces that gazed serenely out at him.

Wellby hurried, in as far as such a word could be applied to his stately progress, through the drawing room and out onto the terrace, where the four Belmont sisters were gathered.

"Mr. Larchmont has sent in his card, Lady Rosie." He handed the card to her.

"So soon!" Rosie exclaimed, examining the card with an air of acute distaste.

"We're not quite ready for him," Theo said. "One of us should go and tell him we can't receive him at the moment, but invite him to join us after dinner for tea."

"And then we'll roast him," Rosie declared gleefully.

"Over hot coals," Theo agreed with a grin. "What do you think, Clarry?"

Clarissa wrinkled her pert nose. "Emily should see him now. She has the most presence and charm—not that you aren't charming, Theo, but—"

"I'm nowhere near as gracious as Emily, or as poised," Theo agreed cheerfully. "And you'll get too easily distracted, Clarry. So, Emily, you're it."

Emily stood up, smoothing down the skirt of her saffron muslin afternoon gown. She patted the ringlets clustering around her face and straightened the ruffles at the high neck of her gown. "Do I look matronly?"

"No, of course you don't," her sisters exclaimed in unison.

"Well, the way you've just described me seemed to imply it," Emily said. "Gracious, poised. You'll be saying matronly next."

"Oh, what nonsense!" Theo jumped up and hugged her. "It's just that the rest of us are so ramshackle."

"You and Rosie are," Clarissa protested, but without heat. "I don't consider myself to be ramshackle in the least."

"No, but you're a dreamer, and you've become much more so since you married Jonathan," Rosie said bluntly. "You both waft around like rose petals."

Clarissa was much struck with this image. "Jonathan is rather like a rose petal. He's so beautiful and he has such a wonderful scent."

"Clarry!" Theo protested. "We all know you found your *parfit gentil* knight, but there's no need to go overboard."

"Well, I'm going," Emily stated, licking her fingertips and smoothing the delicate arch of her eyebrows.

"Be very cool," Theo advised. "Cool and intimidating and gracious."

"You do ask a lot," Emily threw over her shoulder as she walked into the house.

She was not at all sure that this scheme of Theo and Rosie's would find favor in their mother's eye. Elinor Belmont had no truck with deceptions. But two of her sons-in-law would support it. Sylvester would be amused, Edward entirely partisan. He'd been an honorary member of the Belmont clan since childhood and would no more tolerate an insult or injury to any one of them than the sisters themselves would. And if Edward would approve, then Emily had no scruples.

She crossed the drawing room and entered the hall. "Mr. Larchmont?"

"Ma'am."

Everything about Charles Larchmont was a shock and Emily had to muster every ounce of her famed poise in order to control her reaction. She was facing a tall man of about her husband's age, immaculately dressed in beige knitted pantaloons and a dove-gray silk coat. His cravat was elegantly but simply tied, his shoes were of the glossiest black leather. He bowed with a flourish of his hat and smiled. His eyes were a cool dark brown, his complexion tanned, his hair fashionably cropped à la Brutus.

"Mr. Larchmont?" she said again.

"Your most obedient servant, ma'am." He straightened, giving her a quizzical smile. "I am expected by Mr. Balmain, I believe."

Elinor gathered her wits. "I'm afraid we are unable to receive visitors at present, sir. If you would care to return after dinner and join us at the tea table we should be delighted to receive you." She extended her hand. He raised it to his lips, noticing the slim gold band on the ring finger of her left hand.

"And may I ask whom I have the honor of addressing, ma'am?"

"Lady Emily Fairfax," Emily said, realizing that in her astonishment she'd neglected to introduce herself. "At six o'clock, if that would suit you, Mr. Larchmont."

"I look forward to it, ma'am." He became aware that the butler was already opening the front door for him so he took his leave without further ado, strolling down High Street with a puzzled frown. There had been something most curious about his reception.

Emily hurried back to the terrace to be greeted by a chorus of, "Well? What's he like?"

She sat down and smiled mysteriously at her sisters, keeping them in suspense as she picked up her embroidery frame and began to thread the needle with a new silk.

"Oh, Emily, don't be so provoking," Rosie exclaimed. "Is he old and fat or old and thin? Does he have disgusting snuff-stained yellow whiskers and warts on his nose and—"

"None of those things," Emily said. "He's young and handsome."

"*What?*" Theo exclaimed, glancing at Rosie, who had gone suddenly pale. "What is it, Rosie?"

"I suppose he wasn't wearing waders and canvas ducks," Rosie said.

"No, he was dressed like a gentleman, most elegantly."

"But he had brown hair and brown eyes and he's tall and slender, and he has a nice voice," Rosie recited dully.

"Yes."

All three women stared at their baby sister, who was

now doodling on the sheet of paper on which she'd been drawing the exoskeleton of a crab.

"You've already met him?" Theo asked.

"This morning, along the tide line. He was looking for specimens."

"How do you know that?"

"Why else would a biologist be wearing waders and examining the mud?"

"Did you speak with him?"

"Not really." Rosie pushed back her chair. "I have to go and feed the axolotls." And she rushed off.

"Now what's going on?" Theo asked into the astonished silence. "Why would she rush off like that?"

"Do you think he'll recognize her from this morning?" Clarry frowned.

"We'll cross that bridge if and when we come to it," Theo responded.

In her bedchamber, Rosie ignored the aquarium, going instead to the windowsill where the glass bottle glowed, bathed in sunlight. She picked it up. It was cold, despite the heat of the sun. She gazed down into the swirl of colors, seeing the shape of the rolled leather in the neck.

Why did it seem everything had changed now that she knew that her enemy, the thief of her work, was not some stuffy, decrepit old scientist, his brain tired, dulled with age? Why did it matter that, instead, he was young, fresh, probably brilliant. She knew Charles Larchmont's work, but only from references in learned papers. He was immensely well-respected, but she had somehow assumed that was because he was an old, tired member of the scientific establishment. And now to add insult to injury, it appeared that once again they could be in competition if he too was devoting his scientific attention to small crustaceans.

She turned the bottle around in her hand. *To thine own wish be true.* Why should it matter who or what he was? He still stood in the way of her ambition. He had still stolen her work. And she was damned if she was going to let him get away with it.

CHAPTER FOUR

*R*OSIE, WHAT HAVE you done to yourself?" Theo exclaimed when her little sister entered the drawing room before dinner.

"I haven't done anything." Rosie glared fiercely behind her glasses.

"You look like an owl," Theo stated.

"I can't help that. I can't help wearing glasses."

"You don't usually look like an owl." Theo came over to Rosie. "If you did, of course I wouldn't mention it because it would be very rude and hurtful." She stood back and surveyed her sister with a critical frown. Rosie had scraped her hair back from her face, fastening it in a tight, matronly bun at the nape of her neck. It had the effect of accentuating her glasses so thoroughly that her features were eclipsed. "And that is the most ugly gown," Theo continued.

"I like it," Rosie said stubbornly, sitting down on the cushioned window seat with a decisive thump.

"But it's two sizes too large, Rosie," Emily protested.

"And it's such a dingy color," Clarissa put in.

"I must say, dear, it isn't very becoming," Elizabeth Grantley said. "I find it hard to believe your mother could have ordered it for you."

"She didn't. It was a present from Great-aunt Clara." Rosie flicked at the greeny-brown cotton folds of her skirt.

"Oh, in that case it was one of Cousin Becky's castoffs," Theo said. "Great-aunt Clara always sent them to us. She's so stingy she can't bear to throw anything away."

"Frugal, Theo. Not stingy, but frugal," Emily said with a mischievous chuckle.

"No, she's stingy," Clarissa stated firmly. "But we never wore any of them, so why are you wearing that ghastly thing, Rosie?"

"It was a present."

"Well, since Clara isn't here to appreciate the sacrifice, dear, I don't think it's necessary to make it," Elizabeth pointed out. "And particularly since we're expecting a visitor for tea."

"I suspect it's *because* of the visitor," Theo said shrewdly. "Why do you want to look ugly for Charles Larchmont, Rosie?"

"Oh, I wish you'd all leave me alone! What I choose to wear is *my* business."

"Not when you make yourself into an antidote that will put us all off our dinner," Theo said, grabbing Rosie's hands and hauling her to her feet. "Help me with her," she demanded of Emily and Clarissa as she pushed and pulled the protesting Rosie out of the room. Emily and Clarissa followed with alacrity, leaving Elizabeth placidly sipping her sherry. One Rosie would be no match for her three elder sisters.

Rosie continued her complaints but gave up the idea of resistance as Emily unfastened her hair, brushed it vigorously, and twisted it into a casual knot on top of her head. "You have such pretty hair, I can't think why you hide it all the time." She loosened a few curls at the sides, deftly arranging them over Rosie's small ears.

"It gets in the way. You can't look through a microscope with hair flopping all over the place." She wriggled as Theo unhooked the dingy greenish gown at the back, pushing it off her shoulders.

"This one," Clarissa said, emerging from the armoire

with a simple cambric gown of periwinkle blue. "It's a wonderful color with your eyes."

"You can't see my eyes."

"Yes, you can." Clarissa dropped the gown over Rosie's head. "There, that's so much prettier."

Rosie gave an exaggerated sigh, but endured as she was hooked into the blue dress. "Can we go and have dinner now? I'm famished."

Elizabeth looked up with approval when the sisters returned to the drawing room. "Very pretty, Rosie. It goes so well with your eyes."

"I told you people could see them," Clarry declared.

Rosie was unsure what had motivated her urge to appear at her worst before Charles Larchmont. She wanted to think that it was a perfectly intelligent, rational response to the situation. She was a scientist, even though Larchmont was not to know it, and she had no interest in parading her femininity, dressing up for a man whom she despised. That would have been a rational explanation, but she had a nasty feeling that there was more to it than that. There was another reason why she didn't want Charles Larchmont to notice her as a woman. She had been far too aware of him as a man that morning on the salterns and Rosie was not in the least interested in men. She had no intention of marrying, ever. And was not remotely tempted by the flirtatious games played by the young women of her age and situation.

So why did she keep looking at the clock during dinner? And why, as the hands approached six, did a field of butterflies take up residence in her stomach? Because, of course, she would have to come up with a plausible explanation of why she'd been paddling in the mud that morning. That was the perfectly simple, understandable reason.

She took a seat as far from the door as possible in the drawing room after dinner, half hidden behind a tapestry fire screen, and picked up a periodical. Its subject matter was fashion, something that wouldn't hold Rosie's interest for so much as a minute, but with apparent attention she leafed through the pages. When the door knocker banged, she found herself retreating yet farther behind the screen.

"Mr. Charles Larchmont, madam," Wellby intoned from the door.

Elizabeth rose in a rustle of dark gray silk. "Mr. Larchmont." She extended her hand.

"Ma'am." He bowed over her hand.

A man of considerable address, Elizabeth judged, finding no fault with his evening dress of black silk coat and gray doeskin pantaloons. Emily had not been exaggerating. Mr. Larchmont, elegantly and expensively dressed, was a far cry from the eccentric and somewhat down-at-heel individual they had been expecting.

"You've met Lady Emily, I understand."

Emily gave him a small unsmiling bow.

"The countess of Stoneridge." Elizabeth gestured to Theo, seated haughtily on a striped sofa. The arrogance of her posture was somewhat belied by her gamine features but there was no mistaking the chill in the deep blue eyes.

Charles had the distinct feeling he was not welcome. He looked in vain for the young man, his quarry, but met only another pair of blue eyes, another chilly nod, as he was introduced to a Lady Clarissa Lacey.

"And Lady Rosalind," Mrs. Grantley continued.

Charles bowed toward the figure seemingly hiding behind the fire screen. Then his eyes sharpened. He stepped a little closer and the girl from the salterns met his scrutiny with a distinct air of challenge.

"I'm delighted to renew our acquaintance," he said gravely, taking her hand, raising it to his lips. It was a slim, long-fingered hand, but the nails were brutally short. Presumably it made for easier cleaning after a morning's raking through mud. An unmistakable glare was all he received for his pains, so he turned back to the room. "I believe I was engaged to meet with Mr. Ross Balmain?" he said in a tone of polite inquiry.

"Our cousin is not here." It was Lady Stoneridge who spoke. "He was called away and asked us to receive you in his stead."

"I see." He frowned.

"Do sit down, Mr. Larchmont, and take some tea." Elizabeth gestured to the sofa, then poured and handed him a cup. "If you will excuse me, I have some letters to write. You will be well looked after, I'm certain." She gave him a charming smile, before gliding from the room.

Charles sipped his tea and looked around a trifle uneasily. He was being subjected to four icy stares and he had the unshakeable impression that Mrs. Grantley had abandoned him to the lion's den.

He cleared his throat. "I assume Mr. Balmain acquainted you with the purpose of my visit."

"He acquainted us with your theft." Lady Rosalind suddenly emerged from hiding. "He acquainted us with all the details . . . of how he had submitted his research to the Royal Society, and how they were going to elect him to membership, and then he acquainted us with how you were so dastardly and—"

"Rosie," Emily protested softly, too well-mannered to be able to listen to such a naked attack on a guest, however justified. "Mr. Larchmont is our guest."

"Thank you, ma'am," Charles said dryly, putting down his cup and rising to his feet. "And clearly a most unwelcome one. In the absence of Mr. Balmain, I need inflict myself upon you no further."

"Oh, pray don't leave, Mr. Larchmont. Rosie is dreadfully partisan and liable to let her feelings run away with her." Theo rose fluidly, laying a restraining hand on his arm. "We would dearly like to hear your side of the story. There are always two, after all."

"Theo!" exclaimed Rosie, outraged by this apparent betrayal. "How could you say such a thing?"

"Sit down!" Theo insisted in an undertone. "We don't want him to leave before we've had our fun."

Rosie, still glowering, sat down on the window seat. "Well, Mr. Larchmont, justify your theft, if you can."

"It was no theft," he said wearily. "My own research had been finished for over a year. The timing was documented, I merely neglected to present the paper to the Society as soon as it was completed."

"That's what you always say in your letters," Rosie snapped. "And it's the most lame, feeble excuse for plagiarism that I've ever heard."

Charles's gaze sharpened. "You have read my correspondence with your cousin, then?"

Rosie pinkened. "I am in his confidence," she mumbled. "I help him with his research."

"Ahh. Lucky man to have such an assistant." Charles attempted a little flattery but was met with such an incredulously indignant stare he realized his mistake immediately. "I daresay that was why you were down at the river this morning," he remarked in an effort to break the grim silence. "Collecting specimens, perhaps?"

"You don't think I'd be fool enough to tell you what I was doing?" Rosie stated. "You'd steal my res . . . my cousin's research again."

"Are you married, Mr. Larchmont?" Emily inquired, aware of what a ridiculous non sequitur it was, but she could think of no other way to silence Rosie's invective. A more subtle vengeance had been planned, but Rosie was not known for her subtlety.

"No," he said, making no attempt to hide his surprise.

"I daresay you have found that most women prefer husbands who are known for their rectitude," Theo suggested sweetly.

"On the contrary, ma'am," he flashed. "It is I who find that marriage and scientific research cannot comfortably coexist. Women do not in general have the intellectual energy to tread the paths of learning, and without that companionship there could be no true marriage."

"You are the most particularly pompous man!" Rosie exclaimed. "What gives you the right to say that women are not your intellectual equals?"

"Simple experience, Lady Rosalind." He regarded her across the room, meeting her angry stare with a calm challenge in his cool brown eyes.

"Then you cannot have met very many women," Theo stated, stung as much as Rosie by such a blanket and offensive judgment.

"On the contrary, my lady, in my thirty-one years, I have met many women, of many kinds."

"I am going upstairs." Rosie flung herself off the window seat. "Curiously, I find the company of an axolotl

infinitely more stimulating than that of a patronizing cox-
comb." She stalked to the door.

"Axolotl?" Charles was galvanized. He leaped to his
feet. "You have an *Ambystoma*? I have been wanting to
examine a neotenic salamander for five years. Does it have
all the characteristics of a larval salamander—external gills?
I must see it." He had put an arm around Rosie's waist
and swept her from the room before anyone, least of all
Rosie, could catch their breath.

"Sweet heaven," Theo murmured. "That didn't turn out
quite as we planned."

"No, but we should have known Rosie wouldn't be able
to keep quiet," Clarry said. "But whatever are they doing
now?"

"Drooling over those disgusting prehistoric quadrupeds,
I imagine." Theo shook her head. "Rosie's going to give
the game away in no time."

"Oh, I don't think so," Emily said. "Mr. Larchmont
would *never* believe his rival was a woman, let alone such
a young one."

"Perhaps," Theo said, but doubtfully.

Upstairs, Charles squatted before the aquarium where
the axolotls floated soundlessly. "Oh, fascinating," he
said. "Where did you get them?"

"Mexico. An advertisement. You see the gills?" Rosie
lifted the cover from a glass dish and dropped a piece of
raw chicken into the tank. The two formless creatures became instantly energized, swirling toward the flesh,
jostling, tearing, devouring until it had disappeared.

"Most unattractive creatures," Charles observed. "Do
you have a net? I'd like to take a closer look. There was a
study done on the reproductive capacity of Ambystoma—"

"Marchpane," Rosie interrupted excitedly. "He said the
axolotl can't mate in captivity, but I am determined to
try." She lifted the pink albino axolotl out of the water in
the net. "I haven't had a chance to study the gills, but they
are the most particularly interesting aspect, I believe. I
would postulate that evolutionary pressure causes the gills.
Why would they want to develop lungs like a mature sala-

mander when their habitat is aquatic? Gills are much more efficient."

"Quite possibly." Charles looked around the room. "Magnifying glass?"

"On the table."

Rosie had completely forgotten that she had a grievance against this man. She was so starved of the companionship of fellow biologists that her resentments disappeared in a cloud of shared intellectual fascination. "I have the greatest plan for them," she went on, bubbling with enthusiasm, as he peered at the creature through the glass. "I am going to try to dry out the habitat very slowly and see if they'll metamorphose into land animals, as they do in the wild."

And then suddenly she remembered whom she was talking to and realized with a shock that not once had she attributed this research to the mythical cousin, who was the real scientist. She bit her lip hard, and lowered the net back into the aquarium.

"Go on," Charles said. He was leaning against the table, hands resting on the surface behind him, legs stretched out. His expression was closely attentive.

Rosie shook her head, closing her mouth firmly.

"You're certainly very knowledgeable about your cousin's research," Charles observed, eyebrows lifted over shrewd eyes.

"Yes, well, I told you I assist him," Rosie said brusquely. "And I shouldn't have told you all that because you'll probably steal it."

Charles sighed. "Is it the idea that someone got there first that angers you, or the fact that because of it your cousin was not elected to the Royal Society?"

Rosie took off her glasses and rubbed her eyes. It was not a question she had ever asked herself, but faced with such a blunt choice, she was forced to admit that she could tolerate the idea that two scientists were pursuing the same course of research, even that by some unhappy coincidence they might present their findings at the same time.

"Supposing I put Ross Balmain's name forward at the

next electoral meeting?" he suggested, correctly interpreting the chagrined recognition in the weak, vulnerable blue eyes. "If I could meet him, discuss his present work with him, then I would be more than happy to support his candidacy on the basis of his present scholarship."

"Would you?" Rosie gazed raptly at him, hearing only the last part of his offer. "Could you do that?"

"I believe so. My reputation is such—"

"Yes, I know that you are most particularly regarded," Rosie interrupted, replacing her glasses. "Do you swear you didn't steal my res . . . my cousin's research?"

"I swear it on my mother's grave." Solemnly, he laid a hand on his breast.

"Oh," said Rosie.

"But I can't do anything until I've met Mr. Balmain," Charles said. "You understand that, of course."

"Yes," Rosie said thinly.

"Then I shall remain in Lymington, studying the salterns until your cousin returns. Is that a bargain?"

Rosie nodded, her forehead stitched in a frown. How was she to produce a man who didn't exist?

Charles smiled. Such a grave, clever little spitfire. Without thinking, he stepped closer, caught her chin on his thumb and tilted it up. "Bargains should be sealed, Rosie." He bent his head and lightly kissed her mouth.

Rosie leaped back as if she'd been burned. "Oh!" She touched her lips. "Oh! I *detest* you!"

Charles shook his head. "No you don't. Ross Balmain detests me. You're getting confused, my dear." He caught her chin between finger and thumb. "It's a bargain."

Rosie stared up at him, feeling the warm imprint of his fingers on her chin, the closeness of his mouth hovering over hers. She knew she should pull back, but she didn't move. And when his mouth came down on hers for a second time, she held herself very still, all her senses concentrated in her lips, analyzing the sensation as closely as if she were analyzing an insect specimen.

When he released her mouth and drew back, she still didn't move. "That was most particularly interesting," she said. "I always wondered what it was like."

Charles went into a peal of laughter. "You are a *particularly* adorable spitfire, Rosie." He went to the door. "I look forward to seeing you at the river tomorrow."

Rosie heard his feet, swift and light, on the stairs. She went to the open door and listened as he made his farewells in the drawing room, a bubble of laughter still in his voice. Then she heard Wellby show him out. The front door closed behind him and the house seemed suddenly very quiet. Reflectively she touched her fingertips to her lips.

Charles strode down the hill, laughing softly to himself. Either Lady Rosalind had absorbed her cousin's speech peculiarities together with his research, or something *most particularly* interesting was afoot. Ross Balmain . . . Rosie Belmont. Just a little too similar for pure coincidence, surely? It was an extraordinary idea, but one that explained the concerted attack of the four sisters. And he was a scientist. No true scientist closed his mind to any possibility, however unlikely.

All in all, he decided, his visit to this sleepy Hampshire fishing town was proving unexpectedly entertaining.

CHAPTER FIVE

O IF CHARLES LARCHMONT meets Ross Balmain face-
to-face and talks with him, he will support his election to
the Royal Society." Theo had taken her place on Rosie's
bed, propped up against the pillows. She kicked off her
satin slippers.

"But how can he meet a man who doesn't exist?"
Clarissa pointed out, curling into an armchair beside the
aquarium.

"Precisely," Theo said. "Oh, Emily, is that hot milk?"

"You said you'd like a nightcap." Emily, carrying a tray
with four steaming mugs, carefully closed Rosie's door
with her foot.

Theo pulled a wry face. "Normally I'd mean cognac."
She took a cup from the tray. "But for some reason, this
miserable stuff looks and smells just wonderful."

Rosie, perched on the windowsill, took her own cup
with her free hand. In her other, she cradled the green
glass bottle, absently tracing its shape with her fingers. She
had found herself picking it up without conscious intention but somehow it seemed to calm her, clear her mind. It
was strange, she thought, that the glass didn't warm to the
heat of her skin.

"So, strategy." Theo returned to the subject of this late-night conference. "We can't produce Ross Balmain, so we have to persuade Mr. Larchmont that he doesn't need to meet him to support his election to the Royal Society. Rosie, do you have any ideas? . . . *Rosie!*" she prompted when her sister, instead of responding, continued to stare dreamily out into the night.

"What? I'm sorry." Rosie turned back to the room.

"You seem very distracted, love," Emily observed.

"You were up here with him for a very long time," Theo said, regarding Rosie with narrowed eyes. Her sister's quick flush told a tale. "What happened, Rosie?"

"He kissed me," Rosie said with her usual bluntness. "And I seemed to like it. But I'm not interested in that sentimental stuff," she added, sounding as bemused as she felt.

Theo fell back against the pillows with a peal of laughter. "Oh, little sister. I'm afraid it comes to us all at some point. Look at me."

They all chuckled. Theo's marriage, following a tempestuous courtship by Sylvester Gilbraith, had been a classic case of against-all-odds.

"That wasn't very gentlemanly of him," Clarry said. "To take advantage of being alone with you, particularly in your own bedroom—and on first acquaintance, too."

"Second," Rosie corrected with customary precision. "Although we didn't really get into conversation at the river."

"If gentlemen were always gentlemen none of us would ever have been kissed," Theo commented. "But the issue here, it seems to me, is that if Rosie is developing a *tendre* for Charles Larchmont, then that could tangle this whole business beyond unraveling."

"Of course I'm not developing a *tendre* for him," Rosie denied vigorously. "I only said I liked being kissed—the sensation, that's all. You know what I mean." She threw an almost defiant glare at her sisters.

"Oh, yes, we know what you mean," Emily said with a tiny smile. "But in general, liking the kiss usually means that one likes the man doing the kissing."

"Well, that's not true in my case. I was merely interested

in the sensation, since it's never happened to me before and I know you all like this loving business. I wanted to see what you were talking about."

"Well, if that's all it was, then we don't have to worry about muddling things," Theo said, not for a minute convinced by Rosie's denial, but aware that challenge would not alter her little sister's stated position. "But since you have developed a . . . a . . . rapport with the man, it should help you to persuade him that he doesn't need to meet with Ross Balmain."

"I suppose—"

"Oh, Rosie! This is disgusting! The pink one's eating the black one!" Clarissa, after one horrified glance at the aquarium, recoiled. "It's eating its leg!"

"Oh, Marchpane said that they do that!" Rosie leaped to her feet and bounded across the room. "They're very greedy carnivores, but he concluded that eating bits of one another was usually accidental." She gazed down into the water, adding reflectively, "Although it's difficult to believe one can attribute motive or lack of it to an axolotl."

"Do something, Rosie!" Emily exclaimed.

"Oh, the leg'll probably grow back again," Rosie assured her, taking a piece of meat from the covered plate beside the tank. "Salamanders can regrow their legs and tails." She dropped the raw flesh into the water and the pink blob ceased nibbling its companion and turned its attention to an alternative food supply.

"I couldn't sleep a wink with those things in my room." Clarissa shuddered.

"And I don't think you should keep raw meat up here. It'll attract flies and bluebottles." Emily hastily recovered the plate and picked it up. "I'll take it downstairs on my way to bed."

Theo swung herself off the bed. "I'm tired, too. See you in the morning, Rosie." She kissed her. "It seems that if we can overcome this one hurdle, you'll be in a fair way to getting your wish. Charles Larchmont appears to be quite a reasonable man on the whole."

"Yes," Rosie agreed, kissing them all good-night.

"Not to mention personable." Theo closed the door on this mischievous parting shot.

Rosie returned to the window seat. She flung the window wider and leaned out, breathing the scent of gillyflowers from the garden beneath. The stars were brilliant over the sea and a crescent moon swung like a cradle. *Do not follow the moth to the star.* She caressed the little bottle that she'd automatically picked up again. Was wishing to be an accredited scientist wishing for the moon and stars? For a woman, perhaps it was. A woman blind and driven as a moth in search of the light that would consume it.

But it wasn't fair. It wasn't just. She was as good as any man at what she did. She knew it. Charles Larchmont had responded to her as one scientist to another, until . . .

Until he'd treated her like a woman. A woman who attracted him. And she couldn't be both things for him. A woman to be kissed and flirted with, and a scientist and collaborator to be respected.

Why couldn't she? But Rosie knew the answer to that. Her world wasn't constructed to embrace two such roles in one female body.

She had to make a choice and her choice was clear. If she was to use him to get her wish, then she must forget these strange stirrings. She knew instinctively that if she would be true to her wish, she must be totally single-minded, otherwise she could find herself in the morass of conflicting desires.

She slept badly that night, her mind whirring, her body unsettled. Hot, she kicked off the covers, then, chilled, pulled them up tight again. Her mouth was tingling, as it had done after he'd kissed her. She could see his brown eyes hovering in her mind's eye, the sensuous shape of his mouth, the crisp dark hair waving off his broad, intelligent brow. She could feel the imprint of his hands on her face, and her body burned to feel them against her skin.

It was ridiculous! She tossed and turned, trying to banish the restless images, to concentrate on how she would go about convincing him that he didn't need to meet with the man he would support at the society.

Finally, she fell into a heavy, dreamless sleep just before

dawn and it was past midmorning when she awoke. Her first thought was that it had been low tide for an hour. Charles Larchmont had promised to see her at the river and once the tide started to come in again, he would give up whatever collecting he was doing. And she would miss him.

Rosie leaped from bed. She dressed rapidly in a green holland smock, thrusting her feet into her open leather sandals. She splashed water on her face, plaited her hair roughly, crammed on her wide-brimmed straw hat, then raced down to the kitchen to fetch meat for the axolotls before they turned cannibal again.

There was no sign of her sisters, and Wellby told her that they had gone visiting with Mrs. Grantley. Rosie grabbed an apple and a hunk of cheese in lieu of breakfast, snatched up her pail and rake, and darted out of the house, running down the hill to the quay.

CHARLES HAD started wading through the marshy mud as soon as the tide had begun to run out. He had slept wonderfully well, lulled by the creaking rigging, the call of gulls, the sea breeze on his face. He had awoken smiling and the smile was still there as, equipped now with pail, net, and rake, he followed the tide line. Every so often, he would turn and look toward the fast-retreating quay, hoping to see the slight, energetic figure of Lady Rosalind. As the morning progressed and there was no sign of her, his smile began to fade.

Had he frightened her off? She was clearly inexperienced, an innocent in the games of love, but he had had the impression from her response that he had awoken the sleeping woman. She might maintain that she had permitted the kiss in the interests of scientific inquiry, but Charles, while hardly a rake, was no novice in the arena of love, and he could tell an engaged and willing response from mere endurance.

But perhaps that was the problem: She had been frightened by her own response. But even if that was true, surely she hadn't given up on securing his support for the elusive, if not fictional, Ross Balmain?

When he saw her just before eleven o'clock, he was unprepared for the surge of pleasure. He stood shading his eyes, watching as she jumped down from the quay onto the gravelly beach that led into the marshy mud. She took off her sandals, slinging them by their buckled thongs around her neck, and matter-of-factly kilted up her skirt, revealing her brown calves. A scandalous revelation anywhere else, or in anyone else, he reflected. But Rosie was somehow exempt from the usual rigidities of female conduct.

The smile had returned to his face as he began to trudge toward her. She seemed to skim across the mud, where he sank with each footstep, but he noticed that her eyes were still directed downward. Three times she stopped, bent, stared immobile at the mud, then straightened with a shake of her head.

"I had almost given you up," he said as he reached her.

Rosie flushed, pushed her hat back off her forehead, said abruptly, "I overslept." She turned away from him toward the thick marsh grass edging the tide line.

"What are you collecting?"

Rosie paused, seeming to debate the question. "Guess."

"*Artemia salina*."

"I suppose you're looking for them, too." With that, she dived into the grass and was almost lost to view in the tall waving fronds.

Charles followed her. "Do you have any idea when Mr. Balmain might be returning?"

"Probably not for months," she said, her voice somewhat muffled as she bent to her task. "I'm sure I can tell you anything you need to know about his research."

I'm sure you can, he thought with an inner chuckle, determined now to flush out the truth. "But you must understand that I need to meet the man. There are details of his present research and possible future paths of interest that I will need to know to present to the society. In fact . . ." He was seized with a brilliant inspiration. "It would be best if your cousin was to present his own case to the members—with my patronage, of course."

Rosie was not given to swearing, but she had picked up a large vocabulary of the necessary language from Theo, who was much less reticent about expressing herself at times of stress. Now Rosie mentally ran through every oath she knew, keeping her eyes on the marsh but for once seeing nothing but mud.

"I have no way of contacting my cousin, sir." She moved away from him. "I prefer to collect alone. So if you'll excuse me." She pushed aside a break of reeds bounding a small inlet where a thin trickle of water remained. A sailing dinghy sat high and dry among the reeds, moored to a stake. At full tide the inlet would widen into a significant channel and the dinghy could only be reached by rowboat.

Rosie heard Charles behind her. She struggled to ignore him, but it was impossible, even though he made no further attempt to address her and seemed completely absorbed by the marsh at his feet.

"Well, I'll be damned!" he said suddenly. "I've never seen anything like this."

"What? What have you found?" Rosie straightened hastily.

"I'm not sure," he muttered, his nose almost in the mud.

"Let me see." Excitedly, Rosie plunged toward him, holding her skirts high. She took a step and sank up to her thigh into a deep water hole in the mud, lost her balance, and toppled forward onto her face, the marsh sucking around her.

"Sweet heaven, what are you doing?" Charles came up behind her, grabbed her by the waist, and hauled her upright. He burst into laughter at her mud-plastered countenance and then instantly sobered as she flung her arms out wildly, pushing him away.

"My glasses. I've lost my glasses." She pushed away from him and seemed about to plunge headfirst into the mud again.

"For God's sake, how can you possibly find them when you can't see?" He grabbed her again, lifting her clear of the mud. "Sit in the boat where you can't stumble into another hole, and I'll find your glasses." He dumped her unceremoniously over the side of the dinghy.

Rosie gathered herself together as best she could. Her

nearsightedness was hardly helped by the thick coating of black mud clinging to her face. She looked vainly for a clean patch of skirt to wipe her eyes clear but her dress was as thickly mired as her face. She gave up and knelt, peering over the side of the boat.

"Can you see them?"

"Not yet. Oh, wait a minute . . . what's that? Ah. Success!" He held up the precious spectacles. "They're not much good to you like this." He dipped them into the narrow channel of clear water, washing them clean with his thumb before drying them on his handkerchief. Then he regarded their mud-bespattered owner in the dinghy with a quizzical smile. "What a mess."

Rosie ignored this truth. "What was it you found?" When he didn't reply, she said with enraged comprehension, "It wasn't anything, was it? It was a trick."

"You were so studiously ignoring me it was the only way I could think of to get your attention," he said coolly, soaking his handkerchief in the stream. Rosie blinked furiously at his blurred shape as he came close.

"Hold still." He clasped her chin firmly and scrubbed at the mud on her face. Rosie spluttered.

"A little better," he said finally.

"Give me my glasses." She held out her hand crossly. Rosie was rarely at a disadvantage and her present situation was a most unpleasant novelty.

"In a minute." Charles regarded her still with his quizzical smile, although Rosie couldn't see his expression. "You look quite different without them."

"Less ugly!" she snapped, suddenly close to tears. "Give them to me."

"My dear girl, don't be absurd!" he exclaimed softly. "You are really quite lovely, both with them and without them. And even smothered in mud."

"It's unkind to tease." She bit her lip hard. 'Give them to me, *please*." Her distress was clearly genuine.

Charles swung himself up into the dinghy beside her. "I'm not teasing, Rosie. I find you absolutely delicious."

Rosie was still trying to decide whether he could possibly mean it when she found herself gathered against him, her muddy face upturned to the sun, his own a soft, smiling blur above her.

Charles felt the surprising strength in the slight, tensile frame. He ran his hands down her narrow back, spanned her waist, encircled her throat, stroked the pad of his thumb across her mouth.

Rosie was suddenly rendered dumb as well as blind. She held her breath as his touch moved over her. Her body was alive again with those indescribable stirrings in the pit of her belly, her skin prickling, her lips tingling in anticipation of the kiss she knew was coming. And when his mouth took hers she burned from head to toe. She turned fully toward him so she could kneel up, her arms encircling him, her body pressed hard against his. A wild hunger swirled in her veins, her nipples pressed hard against her bodice, and a liquid warmth filled her loins.

Charles tasted the salt marsh on her lips; her skin smelled of the fresh air and the rich loam of the river mud; her hair was warm and fragrant with the hot morning sun. He felt the burgeoning passion in every lithe contour of her body beneath his hands. It was she who drew him down to the deck of the dinghy, her legs twining with his. The tall reeds closed over them and the deck planking was sun-dappled and warm.

"Rosie, Rosie," he whispered, unsure whether he was protesting this passion or expressing it. He palmed her face, smoothed over her eyelids with his fingertips. She put her own fingers in his mouth, her hips lifting without volition, pressing against his jutting hardness.

And then suddenly she was pushing him away, writhing to free herself, rolling sideways and up into a sitting position as he moved his weight from her. She stared at him, her weakened eyes even more vulnerable, expressing her inner turmoil.

"No," she said, shaking her head in confusion. "No."

He sat back, leaning against the mast, drawing his knees up to his chest. Tilting his head to the sun, he closed his eyes, feeling the heat beating against his lids as his breathing slowed and he took charge of himself again.

"My glasses?" Rosie asked.

He opened his eyes and, leaning over, gently put them on for her. "Now what do you see?"

Rosie shook her head, adjusting the spectacles. "I don't know." She slipped over the side of the dinghy. "Good-bye."

"Rosie?"

"Yes." She stopped, her body turned from him in the attitude of a fleeing fawn.

"I have all the time in the world," he said softly. "I can wait all summer if necessary for Mr. Balmain to return."

Rosie made no reply. She leaped off down the gradually widening channel, careful to step only where she could see the riverbed.

Charles swung himself off the dinghy. Rosie had abandoned her collecting equipment and he picked it up with his own. How was he to get her to tell him the truth? Because until she did, she would always run from him.

CHAPTER SIX

"You look as if you've been having a mud bath, Rosie!" Clarissa exclaimed as Rosie came across the lawn, flushed from running up the hill. Perspiration ran down her face, streaking the mud that remained after Charles's perfunctory scrubbing.

"I tripped in the mud." Rosie flung herself down on the grass. Resting on her elbows, she glared ferociously up at the rich copper leaves of the beech tree.

"And?" Theo prompted.

"What am I going to do?" Rosie wailed suddenly, falling onto her back, flinging a muddy arm across her eyes. "It's all the most dreadful muddle."

"Mr. Larchmont, I suppose." Emily plied her needle in her tambour frame, smiling sympathetically at the prone figure stretched on the grass. "More kisses, love?"

Rosie groaned. "More than that."

"Whatever do you mean?" Emily and Clarissa, shocked, spoke in unison. "What more?"

"Oh, come on, you know," Theo said with a lazy grin. "Chaste kisses are never really enough, are they?"

"Theo, you are outrageous!" Emily declared.

"I know," she said. "I always have been. But at least I'm honest. Don't tell me you and Edward didn't indulge in a little more excitement than mere kisses before your wedding night. Or you and Jonathan, Clarry?"

Both sisters said nothing, but the pink tinge to their cheekbones told its own story. "Belmonts are very susceptible to passion, Rosie," Theo continued, still grinning. "So you've nothing to be ashamed of."

"I'm not *ashamed* of anything," Rosie said, sitting up. "It was wonderful and I didn't want it to stop."

"But it did stop, didn't it?" Emily asked, leaning forward with sudden urgency. "It's all very well for Theo to joke, love, but if things are carried too far, then . . . well . . . things—"

"Emily, I'm a biologist. I know all about the consequences of mating," Rosie interrupted before her eldest sister could get farther into the swamp. "But don't you understand? If I tell Charles who I am, then I'll never be elected to the Royal Society. And if I don't tell him, then I couldn't ever . . ." She paused, sucked in her lower lip, then said with resolution, "I couldn't ever see him again."

"And that would matter?" Emily asked.

"Yes, dreadfully," Rosie replied miserably. "I want to be with him all the time. I want to talk to him all the time. I want to kiss him and love with him."

"That's a bit sudden," Theo remarked. "But it does happen. Clarry knew the minute she laid eyes on Jonathan that he was her only possible husband."

"True," Clarissa agreed with a somewhat complacent chuckle.

"The issue seems to be whether you would rather be a member of the Royal Society, or married to Charles Larchmont," Theo stated.

"I didn't say anything about marrying." Rosie sat up abruptly.

"No, but when you feel so strongly for someone, one thing tends to lead to another," Clarry pointed out.

Rosie contemplated this for a minute. Charles Larchmont for a husband? She could find nothing wrong with the idea at all. Finally she shook her head. "I don't know what I want. If I did know, it wouldn't be a problem. Why, *why* can't I have both. Just because I'm a woman!"

"There has to be a way," Theo said. "Why don't you take a bath before nuncheon while we put our heads together."

Rosie agreed with a shrug and trailed off across the lawn into the house.

"There isn't a way around it," Emily said. "I don't mean to be a wet blanket, but there isn't. Once Charles Larchmont knows that Rosie is Ross Balmain he couldn't recommend her to the Royal Society even if he wanted to, and she could hardly be a member of the Royal Society in secret while married to him."

Rosie was preoccupied throughout nuncheon, leaving the conversation to her sisters and godmother. Elizabeth knew the Belmont girls well enough to know when something was concerning them, but she showed no signs of her curiosity. They would confide in her when they were ready.

A messenger arrived from the Ship inn as they were concluding the meal. He brought Rosie's abandoned pail and rake with the compliments of Charles Larchmont, together with an invitation for Mrs. Grantley and her goddaughter to take tea with him the following day.

"How very civil of him," Elizabeth said. "But I didn't realize you were becoming acquainted with the gentleman, Rosie. I thought you were at outs with him."

"I no longer believe he stole my research," Rosie said, always unable to speak less than truth. "But I *do* believe that if he hadn't already been a member of the Royal Society they would have given as much weight to my paper as to his."

"Ah." Elizabeth nodded. "So should we accept this invitation?"

"Not for me," Rosie said. "I beg you will decline the invitation, ma'am. I don't ever wish to see Mr. Larchmont again if I can help it."

Her sisters looked at her and she met their eyes with a little defiant tilt of her head, a what-would-you-do shrug. She had made up her mind. The green glass bottle had made up her mind. While she had been lying in the hip bath soaking off the mud, the bottle had glowed on the windowsill, the outline of the leather scroll dark at the neck.

To thine own wish be true. Do not follow the moth to the star.

Of her two wishes, she could have only one. To pursue both would risk seeing both devoured in the fire of impossible ambition. So she would become a member of the Royal Society, an accredited scientist. She would accept the life of a recluse, living a double life in exchange for the excitements of science. And she would give up the pursuit of ordinary happiness. After all, only yesterday, she could not imagine a more wonderful existence than that centered on the cloistered intellectual satisfactions of a highly regarded scientist. A fleeting attraction for a personable man had jolted her into a moment of self-doubt, causing her to question what she had always held to be the only possible future for herself. But she had put the moment behind her now, and was all the stronger for it.

No one questioned her decision until after nuncheon, when Theo said, "How will it help not to see Charles Larchmont again?"

"I don't know," Rosie said. "But I do know it won't help to see him, so I'll just have to stay a prisoner in the house until he leaves Lymington. Oh . . ." She looked aghast. "I forgot. He said he had all the time in the world and he was quite happy to stay here until Mr. Balmain returns."

"He can't stay here forever," Clarry said comfortingly.

"He could stay here all summer doing *my* research on the salterns and preventing me from collecting specimens."

"Then we'll have to get rid of him," Theo declared casually. Nothing in her demeanor indicated that she didn't accept her sister's decision.

"But how?" Emily regarded Theo a trifle warily. She recognized the light in Lady Stoneridge's pansy-blue eyes.

Theo grinned. "Rosie shall be Ross Balmain."

"*What?*" They all three stared at her.

"You'll have to meet him after dark in some gloomy, secluded spot," Theo continued blithely. "If the light's really bad, and you wear a cloak and take off your glasses and practice a different voice—"

"But why would Ross wish to meet in the dark?" Rosie was intrigued. Theo could always be counted on to produce a plan, however wild and unlikely. "It would have to be something very convincing."

Theo frowned, then snapped her fingers. "Creditors," she said triumphantly.

"Oh, I see it all." Rosie pranced up from her chair. "He had to leave Lymington in a hurry because he was being dunned by creditors. Then he crept back to collect something, but he had to come secretly so he wouldn't be dunned again . . . then we told him about Charles, and he devised this way of meeting him that would still keep his presence here a secret to save him from unpleasantness. Theo, you are the most particularly satisfactory sister." She embraced Theo in a bear hug. "And once he's met him, then he'll *have* to do what he promised and put my . . . I mean Ross's name up for election to the society." *And I won't have lost quite everything out of this encounter.* But that addendum she kept to herself.

"That's all very well," Clarissa protested. "I know Emily and I aren't given to such flights of ingenuity, but how is Rosie to look remotely like a man, even in the dark?"

"She doesn't have to look like a man, but like a stripling. A youth," Theo said, frowning as she thought this through. "Presumably Mr. Larchmont doesn't know Ross's age, Rosie?"

Rosie, bright-eyed, shook her head. "He doesn't know anything about him. All my letters were about how particularly dastardly it was to steal someone else's research. . . . Where will we get the right clothes . . . and shouldn't I cut off all my hair—"

"*No*, Rosie!" Emily cried. "It was bad enough when Theo did it, but at least she was already married."

"Since I intend to be a bride of science, I can't see that losing my virgin locks matters in the least," Rosie said tartly, sweeping her plaits forward over her shoulder to examine them more closely. "I could just cut them off at my neck, couldn't I?"

"No, you could not!" Clarissa jumped in. "If you're going to cut it, then have it done properly, like Theo did."

"But there aren't any French coiffeurs in Lymington."

"Maggie will do it," Theo said, referring to Elizabeth's abigail. "She's skilled enough with scissors and tongs and curling papers."

"Good, so that's settled. Now, what about clothes?" Rosie was striding about the room, ticking items off on her fingers.

"Emily can buy those. She has a perfect eye for size and for what's appropriate," Theo said. "You can go to Hubbard's on High Street, Emily. They'll have something for a young lad. It doesn't have to be very smart, particularly since he's supposed to be incognito."

"I think this is a very bad idea," Emily stated. "But I know that won't stop either of you."

"No," Rosie agreed. "And you are all the most particularly satisfactory sisters anyone could possibly ever have."

CHARLES RECEIVED a message at breakfast the following morning. It was in a very feminine hand, a far cry from the indignant black scrawl of Ross Balmain. It informed him, however, that that gentleman had returned unexpectedly for a very brief visit. For compelling private reasons he wished his presence in Lymington to be kept a secret. He would meet with Mr. Larchmont in the gazebo at the bottom of the garden of Grantley House at eleven o'clock that evening. Mr. Larchmont would find the side gate unlatched. The message was signed Clarissa Lacey.

Charles reread the message, a deep frown corrugating his brow, his coffee cooling beside him. This he had not expected. Could he be wrong? Was there a Ross Balmain after all? Or were the sisters trying to foist an impostor on him? But they would be aware that no impostor would be able to stand up to the meticulous questioning of a member of the Royal Society.

Well, he would learn the answer soon enough. He put aside the message and sliced into a joint of sirloin, reflecting that he would have expected Rosie rather than Clarissa to have written to him. He had barely spoken to the other sisters.

He could still see Rosie's face as she'd run from him the previous day. Perplexed, even frightened, as if something was happening over which she had no control. And he would guess from what he'd observed about Rosie Belmont that she would find uncontrollable confusions most *particularly* threatening. And people tended to run from what threatened them. Presumably she was still running, and delegating the letter writing to her sister was one way of keeping her distance.

She didn't appear at the river that day, which, while it didn't surprise him, threw a blight over the sunny morning. He had never met a woman like Rosie; in fact, until his visit to Lymington, he would have denied such a creature could exist. A passionate, learned scientist with a brilliant mind contained in an utterly appealing frame. She was as unusual in her looks as she was in her personality. As uncompromising as her spectacles. But he knew that a deep current of warmth and humor ran beneath the blunt exterior.

What a wonderful partner she would make. He caught himself on the mental observation with a swift indrawn breath. Mud sucked at his waders as he stood in the marsh, gazing without seeing at a flock of dabbling mallards. A partner in science? Certainly. A partner in life?

Good God, why not? He laughed aloud and a seagull screeched in response. He had never entertained the possibility of marriage because he had never met a woman remotely interested in his own passions. In London society, bluestockings were anathema, and even if a woman *was* interested in intellectual pursuits she would never admit it. He enjoyed mild flirtations and retreated thankfully to the seclusion of his library and laboratory the minute the spun sugar became too cloying.

But Rosie Belmont was a different kettle of fish altogether.

"STAND STILL, love," Emily instructed through a mouthful of pins. She was turning up the sleeves of the brown worsted jacket that Rosie was wearing.

"The britches seem fine." Clarissa stood back, head tilted to one side as she assessed her sister's costume. "It's good that you're so slight."

"I always knew I'd be glad one day that I didn't have any bumps or curves," Rosie commented. There was a touch of acid in the comment, which surprised them all. Rosie was not given to fretting about her physical appearance.

"Actually, you do have," Theo said. "But they're not as noticeable as some people's." She was picking through the contents of a lacquered box as she spoke. "These are small enough. Put them in your mouth."

"What for?" Rosie stared at the two small marbles Theo held on the palm of her hand.

"To alter your voice. They should make it deeper, plummier."

"Theo, she might swallow one," Clarry protested.

"No, I won't," Rosie said stoutly, taking the marbles. She popped them in her mouth.

"Hold them in your cheeks," Theo instructed. "Now say: The brown cow jumped over the moon."

Rosie obediently repeated the sentence. "They make me sound strange in my head," she mumbled.

"You certainly don't sound like yourself." Emily shook down the sleeves with a tiny domestic frown. "Are you sure you'll be able to talk properly?"

"I'll manage. It won't matter if he thinks I have a speech impediment. I'm sure he'll be too polite to mention it."

"Put on the cloak." Theo swathed Rosie in the folds of a dark broadcloth coat. "It's a warm night, but we'll have to hope he'll put it down to the need for secrecy. Pull up the hood."

Rosie drew the hood over her hair, now cropped to shoulder length and tucked behind her ears, a short fringe wisping on her forehead. Elizabeth Grantley had refused to permit anything more drastic without the consent of Rosie's mother. "Does it hide it?" She rolled the marbles to the sides of her mouth experimentally.

"Yes, perfectly." Theo approached with a piece of charcoal. "Take off your glasses now and let me see if I can darken your eyebrows and give you just a hint of a mustache." Frowning, she applied the charcoal as Rosie stood stock-still, clutching her spectacles. "There. What do you think?" Theo stepped back to examine her handiwork. "I think it's convincing if you don't look too closely. And it will be dark."

"I think the whole idea is absurd," Emily said roundly. "But since there's no persuading either of you, I suppose we have to go along with it." She examined Rosie, then took the charcoal from Theo and adjusted the line of the eyebrows. "That's better."

"It's almost eleven." Theo had gone to the window to look out over the garden. "There's no moonshine. It couldn't be better."

"If it rains, don't get your face wet," Clarissa advised. "The charcoal will smudge."

"And don't swallow the marbles," Emily counseled.

"Fusspots!" Rosie tried to laugh but it wasn't possible with the marbles. "It will all be over in five minutes, I promise you." She had no intention of remaining longer than absolutely necessary in the isolated gazebo with Charles Larchmont, even in disguise. She would concentrate only on convincing him of Mr. Balmain's scholarship, his worthiness to join the hallowed halls of the Royal Society, and then she would disappear into the night and never have to worry about the emotional turmoil and the compelling urges that came over her in Charles's vicinity. *To thine own wish be true.* She repeated it to herself as if it were a talisman.

"You want to get there before he does." Theo pushed her toward the door. "Oh, give me your glasses."

"I'll keep them in my pocket. I can't go without them," Rosie said on a note of panic.

"You must. If you have them in your pocket you might put them on automatically while you're talking. And then you can give up all hopes of the Royal Society."

Rosie handed the glasses to Theo. "I'll probably trip on my way down the path."

"I'll guide you." Theo took her arm and hurried her out of the room.

"Marriage hasn't changed Theo at all," Clarissa remarked, joining Emily at the window, where they could see the dark, hunched shape of the gazebo at the bottom of the garden.

"Did you expect it to?"

"No. And it won't change Rosie either."

Emily looked sharply at her sister. "You think? . . ."

Clarissa shrugged. "I think Theo's playing a double game."

CHAPTER SEVEN

$\int$TAND AT THE back," Theo instructed in a whisper as she ushered Rosie into the dark gazebo. "Wellby hasn't turned out the lamps in the drawing room and they throw a faint light."

Rosie felt her way to the rear of the structure. "I can't see a thing."

"You won't need to," Theo responded in a bracing tone, adding, "besides, you said you never wanted to see him again anyway."

"I don't."

Theo grinned in the darkness. "Then you've nothing to complain about, love. Answer his questions succinctly, don't get led up any garden paths, and you'll be a member of the Royal Society before the year is out." She dropped a quick kiss on her little sister's cheek and slipped from the gazebo.

Instead of returning to the house, however, Theo darted behind the massive trunk of the copper beech and waited. She wasn't going to miss a minute of the upcoming play.

Rosie shivered and sucked the marbles, finding it comforting, like sucking her thumb. She could see nothing, but she heard the squeak of the side gate, the sound of steps on the narrow flagstone path leading to the gazebo. Drawing the cloak more tightly around her, ducking her head backward into the hood, she edged into the corner.

"Hell and the devil!" Theo swore from her position behind the tree as she saw the bobbing lamplight preceding the tall figure of Charles Larchmont. He was dressed practically, in buckskins and riding boots, a caped riding coat draped over his shoulders. And he was carrying a lantern. Sensible for a man roaming around strange gardens in the dark, but it might bring matters to a head sooner than she had hoped if the light banished the night gloom of the gazebo. If Charles saw instantly through Rosie's disguise, she would fly off the handle and into the night, and would never see him again. For Theo's plan to work, Rosie would have to make the decision to reveal her identity herself.

Rosie saw the glow of the lamp filling the entrance to the gazebo. She shrank back as far as she could. "Put out the lamp," she insisted in a fervent whisper. "They might see us from the house." Her voice through the mouthful of marbles sounded satisfactorily peculiar.

Charles held up the lantern, illuminating the small space, his curious gaze on the hunched figure in the corner. "But they know you're here, surely. Your cousin Lady Clarissa wrote to me."

"Mrs. Grantley doesn't know," Rosie prevaricated, keeping to a hoarse whisper. "My cousins are hiding me. She banished me from the house when my creditors started dunning her." Rosie silently begged her godmother's pardon for this calumny tripping off her tongue.

Charles extinguished the lantern and they were in darkness. Rosie breathed more easily. Charles set the lantern on a table and perched casually on the arm of a rattan sofa. He regarded the figure of Mr. Balmain with a quizzical smile. The young man appeared to have a most unfortunate speech defect. It made him quite difficult to understand, but not in the least difficult to know.

"It's a pleasure to meet you face-to-face, Mr. Balmain. Although, face-to-face is something of an overstatement," he added.

The listener behind the tree stifled a laugh at this

pointed comment and prayed hard that if Charles Larchmont was a step up on Rosie's game, he would be patient.

"I must keep in hiding," Mr. Balmain mumbled.

"Oh, yes, so I understand. Creditors . . . such inconveniences." He extracted a snuffbox from his pocket and flipped the lid. "Do you take snuff, Mr. Balmain?" He extended his hand across the space that separated them.

"Thank you, no."

"It's a very fine mixture, made up for me by Lord Petersham himself," he coaxed.

"I don't indulge."

"Ah." He took a pinch himself. "Prudent of you, I'm sure." He replaced the box in his pocket and folded his arm with an air of decision. "So, to points, Mr. Balmain. I trust your cousins . . . *particularly* Lady Rosie . . . have convinced you of my integrity. Such a splendid assistant she must be," he mused. "Astonishingly knowledgeable for a slip of a girl. Don't you agree?"

Mr. Balmain managed a grunt.

Charles was aware of a strange sucking sound. "Are you quite well, Mr. Balmain? You sound a little . . . a little strained."

"Perfectly well, thank you. You have some questions to ask about my present research?" Rosie managed to get out the whole sentence without dislodging the marbles, which evinced an annoying tendency to roll around her mouth of their own volition.

Charles wondered how long he was supposed to participate in this charade. With difficulty he resisted the urge to sweep the infuriating biologist off her feet and demand the truth.

"The experiment with the axolotls," he said carefully. "The change in habitat? Your cousin seemed very excited by such an experiment, but of course she can't possibly understand all the difficulties involved. She sounded as if she thought she was playing a game." He laughed. "A useful little assistant, I'm sure. And most conscientious in her caring for the specimens." He waited, politely attentive, as the silence lengthened.

"She's my right hand," Mr. Balmain finally managed to say. "She understands everything about my research."

"Oh, I see. How unusual." Charles chuckled quietly. "And you trust her to gather your specimens, too? I hope you'll find that she's harvesting *Artemia salina* rather than common or garden crustaceans. They do require specialized knowledge to identify."

How could she ever have even liked the man? He was as pompous and patronizing as she'd always believed. Rosie bit her tongue in her effort to control the surge of indignation. "I thought you wanted to talk about my research," she said finally.

"I beg your pardon. I didn't quite catch that." Charles leaned politely toward her, cupping his ear.

"My *research*. The axolotls and *Artemia salina*." Her voice was strangled with frustration and marbles.

"Ah, yes. But before we discuss that, I would like to be certain that your work is not compromised by your assistant," Charles said gravely. "You understand my concerns, I'm sure. If you're not here to supervise her, I can't in all good faith recommend you for election to the Royal Society in case your findings are tainted by lack of knowledge, general inexperience." He shrugged pleasantly. "It's most unusual for a female, let alone such a young girl, to be involved in such a field. Women are fine in their place, Mr. Balmain." Another amused chuckle. "And we both know what that is."

She'll have your eyes out, Mr. Larchmont. Theo again tried to stifle her laughter. Charles was playing the game as if she'd given him precise instructions.

"But in a laboratory, sir?" Charles shook his head. "I know that my colleagues at the society will be as cautious as I am about—" He got no farther.

Rosie bounced out of the corner, seeing only the shape of this odious, utterly detestable *man* in the dimness. "You are the most particularly pompous *ass* . . ." She tripped over a chair leg as she vented her outrage and stopped dead, hand clutched to her throat. "Oh, heavens! I've swallowed it!"

"Swallowed what?" Charles grabbed her as she swayed off-balance.

"A marble. I've swallowed one of them." She spat the other out into her palm, staring at it in disbelief. "How could I have been so stupid!"

"I can't imagine," Charles said dryly. "But what goes in has to come out eventually."

Rosie turned on him again. "You are the most insulting, offensive, dastardly *bastard*! What do you know about my research? How dared you cast aspersions on my methodology, my knowledge. I could run rings around you in a laboratory any time I pleased, Mr. Larchmont." Her hood had fallen back and her eyes, usually weak and vulnerable, sparked with a fiery brilliance.

Charles peered closer. "Sweet heaven," he muttered. He turned aside, struck flint on tinder, and relit the lantern. He held it up. "What have you done to your hair, Rosie?"

"What business is it of yours," she snapped. "Get out of here. I never want to lay eyes on you again."

"Is that a mustache?" He ignored her, holding the lantern higher. "It *is*. Oh, Rosie, you are the most absurd creature." He began to laugh.

Your first mistake, Theo thought, peering around the tree trunk in time to see the lantern crash to the ground as Rosie flailed in a shortsighted but nonetheless ferocious assault on her tormentor.

Charles wrestled with the lithe frame. Her speechless fury lent strength and he found it hard either to get a proper grip on her as she aimed painful kicks at his shins or to swing his body sideways.

"Spitfire!" he exclaimed, finally managing to lift her off the ground. "Why on earth would you try to play such a trick on me?"

Rosie stopped writhing in his hold. "Put me down, please," she said dully. She had lost everything, including her self-respect.

He set her on her feet, but kept hold of her waist.

"You wouldn't take a woman seriously. None of you would. You've just admitted it," Rosie said with bitter resignation. "And now you've amused yourself, Mr. Larchmont, I'd like you to leave."

"As it happens, I haven't amused myself in the least," he

declared. "It doesn't amuse me to be made game of. What kind of fool did you think me that I would be deceived by such a transparent deception?"

"A fool who would never imagine in a millennium that a woman could be a respected scientist," she flared. "Fools like that can be deceived by any trick." She tried to twist away from his hands.

"But if I am not such a fool as to fall for such a trick, then it follows that I'm not such a fool as to believe that a woman couldn't hold her own in my field," he said softly. "Doesn't one premise follow from the other, my lady scientist?"

"But you said—"

"But you said you were Ross Balmain's assistant," he interrupted. "Sauce for the goose." He moved a hand to capture her chin, licked his finger, and rubbed at the charcoal mustache. "I seem to be making it worse, but never mind. You're still wonderfully kissable as well as brilliant and a match for any male scientist. And I do most earnestly beg you to do me the honor of becoming my partner." He kissed her before she could respond.

Theo, with a little nod of satisfaction, slithered away into the darkness toward the house, content that they could manage the rest of it on their own.

"Your partner?" Rosie said, when she could draw breath. "In what?"

"In marriage and everything else."

"In your research?"

He nodded.

"And you would be my partner in mine?"

He nodded again.

"That would be particularly satisfactory," Rosie said thoughtfully. "But I would have to be credited. I won't be a silent partner, just because I'm a woman."

"Of course."

"And the Royal Society? How can I be a member of that?"

"You can't. But Ross Balmain can." He drew her toward him again. "My dear little love, if you think you can play the role rather more convincingly than you did tonight, you can be known in the scientific field as Ross

Balmain. I see no reason why that should conflict with your position as Lady Rosalind Larchmont."

"And no one need ever meet Ross Balmain," Rosie said with a gleeful clap of her hands. "It's exactly as I always intended it to be."

"Exactly?" he queried.

"Well, I hadn't thought of marriage," she said. "But we could publish together, couldn't we?"

"Among other things," he agreed solemnly.

"I wish Theo hadn't taken my glasses," Rosie grumbled. "I can't see your face properly. Are you laughing at me again?"

"No. Now, you've agreed to be my partner in research, but you haven't yet said that you'll marry me."

"Oh, I thought I had." Rosie beamed. "Of course I will. And since everything's been resolved in such a particularly satisfactory way, perhaps we could go back to where we were on the sailing dinghy. There's a lot I need to understand, and I do abominate not understanding." She bent to pick up the fallen lantern and blew out its still-flickering flame.

HER SISTERS had long given up waiting for her when Rosie finally let herself into the house. She felt her way upstairs to her room, where a candle burned on the table, her glasses beside it. She put them on with a sigh of relief and bent to examine her reflection in the mirror. Her face was smudged with charcoal, her lips kiss-reddened, her skin aglow. The green glass bottle on the windowsill was reflected in the mirror.

Dreamily, Rosie went over and picked it up. She held it up to the candlelight. It glowed.

"Well," she said. "I've just won the moon and the stars. Where does that leave your prosy prescriptions? *Wish all, dare all, win all*, little bottle."

She set it back on the windowsill, absently tracing the delicate silver bands.

Smiling that same dreamy smile, Rosie turned to drop raw flesh into the aquarium for the axolotls.

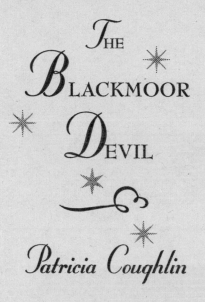

The Blackmoor Devil

Patricia Coughlin

CHAPTER ONE

London, May 1815

He was the unluckiest man alive.

Awareness of his ill-starred fate hovered over him as he lunged, once again, for the chamber pot. When would it end! he wondered as his stomach heaved all over again.

Groaning, he managed to yank the cord beside his bed that would summon the footman. He would replace the soiled pot with yet another fresh one. Surely this next one would go unused, he told himself, hope laced with desperation. Surely this last debilitating episode would be the end of it.

The footman entered and withdrew in silence, having learned during the long night that even a single word of sympathy or offer of assistance would unleash an uncharacteristically harsh tongue-lashing from his master, who lay sprawled on the bed, his usually powerful body as weak as a kitten's.

It was an intolerable state. Weakness of any kind was anathema to Christian Lowell, the newly ensconced eighth earl of Blackmoor, renowned rake, legendary war hero, idiot.

Christian turned his head and scowled at the small green

bottle on the nightstand. Now empty, it had recently held a potion that cost him an amount damn near equal to Napoleon's plunder. And worth every shilling, he'd thought as he'd eagerly gulped it down.

Belatedly it occurred to him to wonder what the hell the potion had contained. Perhaps nothing more lethal than tree bark, turnip juice, and mint water, if he were lucky. Which he clearly was not. In which case he might well have ingested a costly concoction of minced lice, dragon's blood, and cobwebs. Whatever had been in the potion prepared on his behalf, it was no worse than he deserved for resorting to a folk remedy in the first place.

He was not by nature a superstitious man and it was only through discreet inquiries that he had been put in touch with Lillith, the aging sprite who called herself a magician healer and whom some considered to be a sorceress, others a quack. It mattered little to Christian what she was. She was his last hope, and while he had expected her to respond to his dilemma by issuing a spell of some sort, he had been willing enough to accept the potion she sent him. What choice had he?

He was hardly about to consult his personal physician about such a matter. Not unless he fancied a long stay at Bedlam, which was doubtless what he would get if he appealed to a member of the modern scientific community for help in reversing a hex.

He sighed with relief as his stomach quieted and the dizzying rush of nausea passed without incident, surely a sign that the worst of it was over at last. Cautiously he straightened and reached for the damp cloth on the washstand, running it over his face and neck. The effort cost him and he had to grip the solid wood stand with both hands to steady himself. *Damn,* he thought, despising the weakness and everything that had brought him to it.

His gaze narrowed and his vision blurred until he saw neither the porcelain basin nor the oiled oak washstand, but rather, the narrow, hawkeyed, beak-nosed face of the old French crone who was the cause of all his troubles. Now, as when he had first set eyes on her, he found her to be a most unpleasant and unwelcome intrusion into what, until then, had been his rather charmed life.

The crone's visage was soon joined by that of a beautiful young woman. On that fateful afternoon three months ago, the voluptuous seductress had been writhing beneath Christian in the candlelight.

Fresh from the latest battle between Wellington's forces and Napoleon's, he had been flush with victory and restless with excitement, and the enticing French flirt whom he'd encountered on the way back to camp had been eager to help him celebrate.

He had just lowered his weight onto her when a high-pitched shriek tore through the hayloft.

He rolled to his back and reached for his saber in one motion, prepared to defend himself from a stray French soldier bent on revenge.

There was no soldier in sight, however, only a withered old woman dressed in layers of swaddling black who stood poised at the top of the ladder. Their eyes met and a shiver danced up Christian's spine.

"What the hell?" he muttered.

"*Ma mère,*" cried the woman beside him, clutching her dress to her full bosom.

"'*Ma mère*'? This is your mother. *Mon dieu.*" He kept his eyes on the spot where the old lady's hand disappeared inside the folds of her skirts, hoping she wasn't going to pull a weapon on him. You never knew with these peasants and he wasn't about to be done in by an avenging mother.

Slowly, still holding his gaze, she lifted her hand, but there was no weapon, only her crooked crone's finger, which she pointed at his naked chest as she invoked her curse.

Christian's French being more of the Parisian than peasant variety, he didn't understand every word she screeched at him, but he was able to decipher something about a pox on his descendants and a dearth of luck forever.

He didn't believe in hexes, and since he had no plans to marry and spawn descendants it hardly seemed to matter in any case. But why spoil the old hag's fun by saying so?

He simply stood, fastened his breeches regretfully, and laughed.

He wasn't laughing now.

In the months since that fateful day he had learned to take seriously the power of all sorts of things at which he had once scoffed. First had come the dizzy spells that forced him to leave his vaunted position at Wellington's side. Relegated to a desk at the support base near Gijon, he had promptly found himself challenged to a duel, of all things, by an irate husband. Worse, he'd lost, or at least had feigned defeat sufficiently to satisfy his opponent's honor. Even so, the ridiculous skirmish over the lady's non-existent virtue may have cost him his right eye. He fingered the black patch. The doctors had told him it would be six months before they could remove it and ascertain if the damage was permanent.

It was shortly after the duel that he received word of his older brother's death. In one swift blow fate took from him the only family he had left and passed to him the title earl of Blackmoor, with all the duties and responsibilities it entailed.

If Christian had not already been convinced of the power and legitimacy of the crone's curse, he was then.

He'd immediately returned to London, and ever since, his life had been a continuing deluge of bad luck that had him constantly looking over his shoulder and wondering what would go wrong next. He was unwilling to risk something as innocuous as picking up a deck of cards or crossing a busy street, much less getting on with his life as earl of Blackmoor.

Aside from the fact that such an excess of caution made for a hellishly boring existence, it was bloody inconvenient to be always losing things and tripping over his own feet and being trailed around town by black cats . . . when he dared to venture from his house, that is. He, who had never encountered a risk he wouldn't take, was becoming a prisoner of his own fear, and he didn't like it one bit.

Clearly something had to be done. Lillith had assured him she could remove the curse, he had paid her handsomely to do so, and by God, he was going to hold her to it.

And this time he wouldn't send a servant on his behalf, Christian decided, reaching for the empty bottle. This time he would go himself.

THE DOOR of the small stone cottage on the city's northern outskirts was bolted from the inside and the windows were dark. Christian gave the door handle a final jiggle, knowing that it was useless. Lillith was gone. He contemplated waiting, reasoning that her absence might prove to be brief, but given his luck of late, it made more sense to expect the worst. There was no telling where Lillith might have gone or for how long.

Frustrated, he started back to his waiting carriage, barely fitting his six-foot-two frame beneath the vine-covered trellis that sheltered the path. Tall, prickly shrubs bordered the stone walkway on both sides; stray branches snagged his sleeves and scratched his face as he passed; ghostly vine fingers clung to his shoulders and dark hair.

The whole place made him shudder and want to get away as quickly as he could. Between the overgrowth and the heavy spring fog, he couldn't see a foot in front of him and he was lamenting the fact that he hadn't brought along a lantern when he nearly collided with a cloaked figure hurrying along the path from the opposite direction.

The figure was too tall to be Lillith, about five foot seven, Christian judged, but he could tell from the willowy build beneath the cape that it was a woman.

"Pardon me, madam," he murmured and stepped aside to let her pass, his right foot landing between stones and sinking ankle-deep in mud. Christian didn't curse. He didn't even flinch. He was growing accustomed to such mishaps, he observed with disgust.

"Thank you," came the voice from beneath the hood.

It was a uniquely clear, feminine tone that tripped something in his memory, making him strain for a closer look as the woman turned sideways to squeeze past him. There was just enough moonlight filtering through the trellis to reveal a flash of gold hair and a slant of green eyes and reconfirm what Christian already knew.

He really was the unluckiest man alive.

And she was the last woman in all of London whom he wished to run into unexpectedly this way, or any other way, for that matter.

She was well-named, he'd give her that. Delilah. Lady Delilah Ashton Moon, to be precise, and as he stood there, inhaling the cool night air spiced with her scent, Christian felt a new kinship with that poor Biblical sap Samson. He contemplated escape, retreat, call it what you would, discretion was the better part of valor and all that. But by the time he'd yanked his foot from the mud and lurched back onto the path beside her, it was too late.

CHAPTER TWO

"CHRISTIAN?" THE HOOD of Lady Moon's ivory cape fell away as she tipped her face up, exposing a dazzling amount of blond hair and flawless porcelain skin. "Is it really you?"

Christian was suddenly thankful for the heavy shadows. He never blushed, never, but damned if he didn't feel his cheeks heating now. And well they might. After all, Lady Moon represented an exquisitely mortifying moment in his past. His *distant past*, he reminded himself, resisting the urge to cringe from her searching gaze. Just because the memory made him wince was no reason to let his discomfit show. Why, for all he knew, she had forgotten it ever happened.

Not bloody likely, spoke the voice of reason.

Regardless, at such moments a rational man had but one possible course of action: feint and parry.

"I beg your pardon, madam," he said, as if struggling for a clear view of her in the dim light. "Are we by chance acquainted?"

He watched as she absorbed the deflection, regrouped, and rearranged her front line, all in a matter of seconds.

"It appears it is I who must beg your pardon, sir," she replied, mimicking perfectly his tone of polite detachment.

"I spoke impulsively and on first impression, but on closer perusal I can see that I mistook you for a much younger man and one who, if I may be so outrageously blunt as to say so, does not wear a patch over his right eye."

A much younger man? Christian bristled, insolently examining the lady for similar evidence that seven years had passed since their last meeting and finding none.

"Why, Christian Lowell, it is you after all," she exclaimed with mock amazement. "I'd know that sinister scowl anywhere."

"Lady Moon," replied Christian as if recognizing her for the first time. "And I would know your charming manners and ladylike restraint anywhere."

She smiled, revealing gleaming white teeth that were perfectly even but for a small chip at the back of one that you couldn't see. You had to find it with your tongue. That chip was only one of the myriad of small, fascinating details about her that Christian had never quite managed to forget.

"I was so very glad to hear that you had returned home," she blurted, then bit her bottom lip and quickly added, "I mean to say I was happy to hear you had returned safely. So many men do not. You're very fortunate."

Fortunate? Him? It was all Christian could do to keep from snorting. "Appearances are sometimes deceiving."

She sobered instantly. "Please forgive me. I don't know what I was thinking of. Naturally I was terribly dismayed to learn of Charles's tragic demise."

"It was tragic," Christian agreed, "for all concerned. A little cough turns into pneumonia and suddenly Charles, the rightful and fitting master of three centuries of Blackmoor tradition, is gone and I'm left a bloody earl."

"I understand how you must feel," she said. "A title is no recompense for the loss of a brother."

Among other things, thought Christian. Charles was not only a brother, but also his closest friend and a safe port in times of trouble. Beyond that, however, Charles's death meant the loss of freedom and irresponsibility and living for the moment, the only way Christian knew how to live. He'd lost it all. And on top of all that, he was cursed.

"You're right," he said to Delilah, "a title is no recompense at all. But I'm not the only one who has suffered a grievous loss since last we met. I was equally saddened to learn of the deaths of your father and husband. Please accept my deepest condolences."

"Thank you," she said, her eyes downcast.

"Your husband died at Coruna, did he not?" he inquired, naming a battle that had taken place nearly three years ago.

"Yes. He slipped from his horse in the thick of things and was trampled."

"What rotten luck."

"What a senseless waste is more like it," she countered with all of the impulsive intensity he remembered so well. "He never should have been there in the first place. He was far too young and inexperienced."

Christian responded with something about the horrors of war in general and the Peninsula struggle in particular, ending with a small, rueful smile.

"Forgive my manners," he said, "I shouldn't keep you standing here on a damp night discussing such melancholy matters. If you've come to see Lillith, I'm afraid you're as out of luck as I am. She's gone."

Delilah frowned and glanced down the path to the unlit cottage. "Gone? But that's impossible. I need her."

Christian nearly chuckled out loud. Her belief that the whole world turned on her whim was something else he remembered. He fully expected her to pout and stamp her foot over Lillith's disappearance and was taken by surprise when instead she sighed and squared her shoulders.

"Oh, well," she said. "I shall simply have to try again tomorrow."

"My thought exactly," he responded, eyeing her with new curiosity. Since returning home he'd been so preoccupied with his own dilemma that he'd paid little attention to gossip, but he vaguely recalled hearing something intriguing about Lady Moon. He wished he could remember what it was.

"Well," she said as he stood searching for a polite way to question her more closely. She was toying with the ties on her cape with an awkwardness that struck him as most unlike her. "I should be going."

"Of course."

"It's just . . . I wonder . . ." She let go of the ties and her chin came up. "Enough beating about the bush. I shall ask you outright. That is, if you'll forgive me for posing a terribly indelicate question?"

Christian braced himself behind a careless shrug. "I can't pledge forgiveness until I hear the question. Ask it anyway."

"All right." Her sheepish expression gave way to curiosity. It sparked in eyes the bright, clear green of a summer meadow, illuminating her whole expression in a way Christian remembered all too well. Delilah had always been far too curious for either of their sakes. "How did you injure your eye?"

"Oh, that," he said, touching the patch. He wasn't sure what he had expected her to ask him, only that he was greatly relieved. "I received a slash wound and the doctors said that six months of resting the eye and surrounding muscles might restore my vision."

"How horrid. So it is a battle wound. I had heard . . . rumors."

"It's more or less a battle wound," he replied with a shrug, which only served to revive that damn glint of curiosity in her eyes. "Oh, all right, if you must know, it happened during a duel."

"Why on earth were you fighting a duel?" she asked.

"Because I'm an idiot," Christian retorted.

She chuckled and that was it. No prying, no silly feminine display of shock or disapproval for him to endure. She was, and always had been, one of a kind.

"I see," she said. "And if six months' rest doesn't revive the eye? What then?"

"Then I suppose the ton shall grow weary of seeing me at every masquerade ball dressed as a pirate."

She laughed outright at that, a bright, infectious sound that captivated him now as much as it had the first time he'd heard it.

"I rather doubt they will weary of you anytime soon,"

she assured him dryly. "Your heroics are legendary. And the patch adds a rakish touch. I daresay there will be any number of ladies who prefer you this way to the devil's disguise you used to favor."

"That wasn't a disguise," he retorted.

"No, I suppose it wasn't. You made a splendid, utterly believable devil."

"Thank you."

Their gazes held, like the locked blades of two swordsmen taking each other's measure, until she blinked and they both spoke at once.

"I should . . ."

"May I . . ."

"You first," she said with a sweep of her hand.

"I was going to ask if I might escort you back to your carriage."

"Thank you. I would be most appreciative."

As she turned something fell from inside her cape, hitting the mossy ground with a small thud.

Christian bent to retrieve it, surprised to see that what she had dropped was a bottle identical to the one in his pocket, right down to the silver chasing on the cork.

She thanked him for retrieving it. "I shouldn't want to lose this before I have a chance to return it to Lillith."

"Now it's my turn to ask an indelicate question . . . if you will permit me?"

She nodded.

"Why are you returning it?"

"Because I believe Lillith gave it to me by mistake." She hesitated, then shrugged and went on. "You see, I came to her for a special nostrum and instead was given this bottle containing only a useless scrap of old leather with scribbling on it. There was another man at the cottage when I arrived and a great deal of confusion ensued when Lillith's cat leaped onto the table, knocking things about and—"

"Was it a black cat?" he interrupted to ask.

"Why, yes, it was black. How did you know?"

"Lucky guess," he muttered. "This scrap of leather, could the scribbling on it be a spell of some sort? An incantation?"

"I suppose it could be. It says something about wishes

and moths." She shook her head impatiently. "I only know it's not what I paid for, nor what I need."

"When did Lillith give you this bottle?"

"Last evening. Why do you ask?"

"Because last evening is also when my man visited Lillith and was mistakenly given this bottle with a quite pungent liquid inside." He withdrew the green bottle from his pocket and held it in his outstretched palm.

"Why, they're exactly alike," she exclaimed, holding hers next to his.

"Yes. Perhaps our coming here tonight will not be a total waste after all."

"Are you suggesting we have the bottles intended for each other?"

"I am. And since we have no way of knowing when Lillith might return, I suggest we take it upon ourselves to right the matter."

She hesitated only a second before nodding and holding out the bottle. "That seems sensible."

Christian took the bottle from her and handed her his with only the faintest twinge of conscience. Fairness demanded he tell her his bottle was empty. But survival might well depend on saying nothing to prevent her from handing over the spell he was convinced Lillith had intended for him.

His survival instinct won out and a sudden rustling in the bushes spared him any further remorse. An instant later a figure in a long dark coat emerged from the shadows and charged toward them, stopping a few feet away, a coiled whip in one hand.

"There you are," the figure exclaimed. "Is yer ladyship all right, then?"

"I'm fine, Esmerelda. I've run into an old friend here and we've been chatting." She turned to Christian. "My coachman," she explained, a trifle inaccurately.

Esmerelda was a woman's name, and it was a woman's voice that had called to Delilah, and, as he squinted in the darkness to get a better look, Christian realized it was definitely a rotund woman's figure blocking the path. Who on earth employed a woman as a coachman?

Delilah. Now he remembered the gossip he had heard about her, about how she employed an entire household of women and children and had even organized the women into some sort of business, making . . . what? Toys? No. He couldn't recall, only that the unorthodox venture had made her the talk of London and scandalized her family.

"I really must go," said Delilah before he had a chance to ask her about it. "Esmerelda will accompany me to the carriage. Thank you for returning my bottle. Good-bye, Christian."

"Good evening, Lady Moon," he replied, bowing and watching as she and Esmerelda disappeared into the darkness, leaving him with dozens of unanswered questions, and a fascination he thought he'd left behind years ago.

CHAPTER THREE

D ELILAH SAT IN the moving carriage, fingering the pretty little green bottle Christian had traded her. The pretty little *empty* green bottle.

The man had done it to her again. Duped her. Used her. Misled her and then sauntered off, leaving her to deal with the consequences.

Christian Lowell really was the devil, she decided. Seven years hadn't changed that.

She had once vowed to remember what he was in every fiber of her being. And she would have, she told herself, if running into him so unexpectedly hadn't jostled her nerves and stirred up all sorts of silly feelings. In those few moments they were together she had succumbed to a flurry of emotions: surprise, embarrassment, excitement, amusement, and—as much as she hated to admit it even to herself—a flicker of renewed interest.

At the moment, however, all she was feeling was a controlled, low-burning, slow-spreading fury. Aiding her control was a sense of relief that the worst was over. For weeks, ever since learning of Christian's return, she had been braced for their initial meeting, prepared for the inevitable awkwardness, at least on her part, and determined to impress upon him that she was no longer the silly little girl she'd once been.

In spite of the impact of encountering him so unexpectedly, she was satisfied she'd recovered and performed admirably. Next time she would do even better. Next time she wouldn't be taken by surprise or played for a fool by him in any way.

Delilah felt an instantaneous surge of indignation. Next time wasn't good enough. He couldn't be allowed to get away with his little stunt *this* time.

She was no longer a gullible, love-struck sixteen-year-old with limited options. Her lips curved upward at the thought that the Blackmoor Devil didn't know it yet, but he had met his match.

Leaning forward, she yanked on the cord to signal Esmerelda to stop and called to Dare, the boy riding postilion, to join her inside the carriage. He appeared quickly, and as usual, with an added touch to make the black-and-gold livery she provided his own.

"Lovely scarf, Dare," she commented, eyeing with some suspicion the long black-and-white checked scarf looped with characteristic insouciance around the twelve-year-old's neck. It was hard not to be suspicious from time to time, since she and Dare had first met on opposite sides of her reticule as he attempted to relieve her of it against her will.

"I won it fair and square, Lady Moon," he responded, his tone far more earnest and less belligerent than it had been when he first joined her a year ago.

She sighed. "Poker again?"

Dare nodded, his quick grin sheepish and irresistible. "But not with the younger boys. I remembered what you said about a gentleman not stooping to easy pickin's. You don't have to worry about me breaking your rules. I've put the life of crime behind me."

"I know you have, Dare," she said, her own conscience rumbling a reminder of how fine a line she was about to walk. "In a way that's what I need to speak with you about. Please have a seat."

As he settled himself across from her, she called new directions to Esmerelda.

"And as quickly as possible, please," she concluded, pulling the door closed.

Delilah gripped her seat as Esmerelda shouted and the well-trained horses took off.

Turning to Dare, she said, "Dare, in the year I've known you, we have spoken at great length about rules, and you have done an admirable job of following them to the letter. But sometimes there are exceptions to the rules. There sometimes arise unusual situations, what we refer to as extenuating circumstances. Do you know what that means?"

Dare shook his head.

"It means," Delilah said, "that I need you to do a very big favor for me, one that will require breaking, or at least bending drastically, one of the rules we've established."

"Which one?" he asked, leaning forward.

"The one about picking pockets. Do you remember what I said about that?"

"You said I must never do it again, no matter how easy a bloke makes it. You said it's wrong to take something that doesn't belong to me."

"Exactly. So it is very important that you understand that the item I am going to tell you about really does belong to me, and that if I could think of any other possible way to get it back from the gentleman in question, we would not be having this conversation. Understood?"

Dare nodded, his blue-black eyes narrowing with an awareness beyond his years.

"Good," said Delilah. "Here's what we're going to do."

DELILAH WAS primed and ready the following afternoon when Christian arrived at the elegant Mayfair townhouse that was hers by virtue of the fact that she was the widow of Sir Andrew Moon. She kept him waiting just the same, allowing him to simmer and suffer for a change before joining him in the drawing room.

"Hello, Christian," she said, pausing just inside the airy and sophisticated room done in shades of gold and white.

He turned abruptly to face her.

"Very clever," he said without preamble. "Now give it back."

"I'm fine, thank you for inquiring. Yourself?"

"I'm angry as hell."

"Oh, dear. Would a cup of tea help?"

"No," he said between gritted teeth.

"Then perhaps a sherry? Port? A seat?"

"I won't be here long enough to sit or drink sherry. I want my bottle, Delilah, and I want it now."

"Which bottle? There are two, as you may recall, remarkably alike in detail, and one belonging to each of us."

"I want the one you stole from me last night."

"*I* stole from *you*? How exactly did I do this?"

"Don't give me that innocent look. You know bloody well how you did it. You picked my pocket."

"Me?" she countered, hand on chest.

"Yes, you. Not directly, of course. You're much too devious for that. But you arranged it, I'm certain. You somehow beat me home, orchestrated that little altercation on the sidewalk out front, and while I was distracted you had the bottle plucked from the coat pocket where you saw me put it."

Delilah arched her brows in a delicate expression of amazement. "My, my, that was clever of me."

He smiled smugly. "To a point. Your little ploy may have succeeded, but for one fatal mistake. It was very sloppy of you to send a pickpocket dressed in livery I could easily trace back to your doorstep."

"Oh, do you really think so?" she asked, her tone as careless as her movements as she retrieved her fan from the velvet duet seat and toyed with it. "I was beginning to fear I should have been a great deal sloppier, seeing as how it took you all night and half of today to figure it out."

That wiped the smile from his face very nicely.

"You wanted me to know," he said, his voice pitched low enough to alarm a less intrepid woman.

"Of course. That was half the fun."

"And the other half?"

"The other half will come from returning it to you." He

looked so relieved at the news that she couldn't resist letting the moment drag out a bit before adding, "After extracting my pound of flesh, of course."

"What does that mean?"

"It means you owe me, Blackmoor."

"You dare to say that I owe you when you're standing there in possession of both bottles?"

"Wrong. I tossed your bottle, the *empty* bottle, into the Thames. Leaving me with only one in my possession, the one I was given by Lillith."

"Mistakenly."

"Irrelevant."

"And one, I might add, that is of no use to you, as you yourself admitted," he reminded her.

"That was last night. It's very much of use to me at the moment."

"Simply by virtue of the fact that I desire it?"

She smiled. "I'm glad to see your wits improve as the day progresses."

"Unfortunately my temper does not keep pace. Tread carefully around me, Lady Moon. I am in no mood of late to be toyed with."

"And I am in no mood to be hoodwinked. Twice now you've played me for a fool, so it's really two scores I'll be settling for the price of one." She shrugged. "I'd say you're still getting the best of the bargain."

"This is nonsense," he declared, not asking the nature of his earlier transgression. Nor denying it.

So he did remember, thought Delilah. Good. And he had the common decency to feel some remorse over the way he'd taken advantage of her, if the dark red flush creeping from his neck to his sun-browned cheeks was any indication. His *gaunt,* sun-browned cheeks. Daylight confirmed last night's suspicion. While still the most annoyingly handsome man she had ever seen, the years of war had taken a toll. He looked exhausted and edgy and . . . desperate, she decided with satisfaction. Under the circumstances, she found it a very encouraging combination.

"Where's the bottle, Delilah?" He glanced around, then strode across the room, examining the desktop and the corner curio cabinet, his agitation evident. "Don't make me turn this place inside out."

"I wouldn't dream of it. I am more than willing to tell you where to find what you seek. Better yet, I'll show you."

"Please do. And quickly."

"It's right here."

Watching him, she smoothed a palm over her hip and down the front of her thigh to a spot just above her left knee, where the outline of the bottle was obvious beneath the delicate fabric of her ivory batiste skirt.

"I've attached a gold silk cord to the neck of the bottle and tied it around my waist, beneath my chemise," she explained, deliberately painting a word picture for the benefit of his imagination. Judging by the reflexive tic in his right cheek, it worked. "There it is and there it stays, until you earn it back."

Slowly, his dark gray gaze lifted from the concealed bottle to meet hers. At that moment, Delilah counted his eye patch a blessing. She wasn't sure she could have endured twice the fiery outrage in his glare. She waved her fan, as if that idle motion could cool the air between them.

At last he spoke. "What, precisely, madam, shall I be required to do to earn back the bottle?"

"Nothing too strenuous, or outside your field of expertise." The fan fell still. "I want you to ruin me, Blackmoor. Feeling up to it?"

No, screamed everything inside Christian as he struggled not to appear dumbstruck. After two sleepless nights in a row, he was barely up to crawling into bed and pulling the covers over his head. *His own bed,* in spite of what she seemed to be proposing.

It was a trick. It had to be. The way his luck was running, if he accepted her offer he'd no doubt stumble on his way to her chamber and break his neck. He paced the room, trying to figure out what she was up to. He'd learned the hard way that with Delilah, things were never as uncomplicated as they first appeared.

There was nothing to do but call her bluff.

He turned back to her, casually checking his watch. "All right. I have an hour or so to spare. Let's get on with it, shall we?".

"An hour or so?" She laughed. "Sorry, Blackmoor, my challenge will not be so simply met, nor, I'm afraid, was it intended to be taken quite so literally."

He shrugged. "Then you're blackmailing the wrong man, Delilah. This poor, ravaged soldier knows of only one way to ruin a lady."

"Ha. You're hardly poor, or ravaged, nor are you any longer a soldier," she pointed out. "I'm also in a position to know that you are eminently knowledgeable and practiced in the art of compromising a lady." She ran her gaze over him. "Perhaps that's why you appear to be in such dire need of a good night's sleep. Tell me, have you been making up for lost time, Blackmoor?"

He managed a suitably smug grin, not about to admit the truth—that at present, he, the rakehell of Wellington's army, was reduced to a cowering jinx who would no more dare a clandestine rendezvous than he would poke out his other eye.

"I see my paltry attempt at modesty is no match for your insight," he told her. "So if you will be a bit more *literal* in your request, I'll do my best to accommodate you."

"I suppose what I should have said is that I want you to ruin my reputation . . . or at least sully it enough around the edges so that the duke of Remmley will refuse to marry me."

CHAPTER FOUR

Remmley?" Christian frowned, as he managed to place a face with the name. "Why, he must be sixty years old."

"Sixty-three," she corrected.

"Why on earth would you want to marry a man old enough to be your grandfather?"

"I don't," she snapped, tossing the fan aside. "That's the point. The problem is that my brother is having a hard time getting that inconvenient little fact through his thick skull."

"Roger?"

"Yes, Roger. With my father gone he thinks it's his solemn responsibility to see me safely wed. As if one trip down that primrose path weren't enough," she grumbled.

"But why Remmley?" asked Christian. Her disgruntled remark had inspired numerous questions about her marriage.

"Because he's available and respectable and willing . . . which a surprising number of gentlemen are not. I seem to have developed a reputation for being difficult," she said with obvious satisfaction.

"I can't imagine why," he drawled. "So Roger has deemed Remmley a suitable mate for you?"

"Roger wants me married, as quickly and with as little fuss as possible."

"Even if you're opposed to the idea?"

"*Especially* because I'm opposed to the idea."

"But why?" he pressed.

She quirked a pale brow at him. "The usual reason a woman is married off against her will—to bring her under control, tame her, break her spirit."

"I see," he countered. He'd like to meet the man with enough time on his hands to try to tame Delilah.

He didn't doubt her claim, however. He and Roger Ashton had been at Eton together and Christian knew firsthand how protective the other man was of his baby sister, and how sensitive he was to public opinion. People were talking about Delilah and that was bound to make Roger unhappy.

"But Roger is not going to have his way in this," Delilah declared as she flounced defiantly into the chair beside her, gleaming like a rare jewel against the gold brocade high back. "He can push as hard as he pleases. I'll push back harder."

"Perhaps you're judging him unfairly. Has he told you his reason for wanting you to wed Remmley?"

"Has he told me?" she retorted, coming out of her seat again. "Does the man ever speak of anything else would be a better question. Roger is convinced a woman requires a husband to look after her and manage her affairs and since I've seen fit to toss in his face—his words—every suitable candidate he's put forth, he had no choice but to issue the Remmley ultimatum, and now he won't give in. He insists it would be an insult to the duke to back out at this late date and that he can't afford that politically. Just as *politically* he can't afford a sister who lives alone and makes her own decisions and chooses for herself the company she'll keep."

Ah, thought Christian, sensing that they were growing closer to the heart of the matter.

"And," he added, "one who sets tongues wagging by hiring women to drive her coach and tend her gardens and who dares to intrude on a God-given male domain by running a successful business of her own?"

Her beautiful eyes were no less beguiling when narrowed to angry slits, he discovered.

"You sound just like Roger," she said, folding her arms stiffly across her chest. It was clearly not meant as a compliment. "I take it you share his ludicrous opinion that a woman needs a man to manage her affairs?"

"I'm not sure," he replied honestly. "I'd have to know more about the woman, and the situation in question."

She waved her hand impatiently. "The situation is that I want to be left alone to do what I want with my life. I am financially independent and have asked Roger for neither assistance nor advice. On the contrary, I have been most considerate of his sensibilities and conducted all my business affairs with the utmost discretion."

Christian quirked a brow.

"That is to say with as much discretion as possible while still being competitive. I have even tolerated Roger's endless meddling and matchmaking attempts. Until now. I am a busy woman, with others depending on me, and I no longer have either the time or inclination to indulge his fantasies for my future."

"So you don't deny the rumors? You are running your own business and employing women exclusively?"

She tossed her head. "I am."

"Why?"

"Because I have this revolutionary idea that women have as much need—and right—to eat and keep a roof over their heads and care for their children as men do."

"Some would argue that it's a man's responsibility to feed and care for his wife and children."

"Then men will just have to cease running off to war and getting themselves killed, won't they?" she retorted. "The women who work with me are all widows, war widows most of them, with young children and no other means of putting food on the table. Neither my brother nor Remmley nor any of their fine, upstanding gentlemen friends were willing to take a chance on these women, so I did."

"And in the process you get to thumb your nose at an overbearing brother and make yourself the center of a great deal of attention."

"Is that what you think of me?" she demanded, hands on her hips, a warrior's gleam in her eye.

He shrugged. "I am not sure what to think. Aren't you the one who once told me she enjoyed shocking people and wanted to dedicate her life to doing things others didn't dare?"

"Yes, but I was sixteen at the time, a child . . . barely out of the nursery, to quote you."

"It appears you haven't changed much."

Delilah pressed her lips together and folded her arms stiffly in front of her. "Think whatever pleases you," she said.

With a toss of her head she began to pace restlessly, whirling to face him from the far corner of the room. "But even if you share Roger's asinine opinion about women, do you really believe that the punishment for wanting to live my own life should be a loveless marriage, shackled to a man who creaks when he walks and drools when he chews and whose hands are so cold they make me shiver? Do you?"

No, he thought, meeting her impassioned gaze. *God no.* Though he could well understand why a man, any man, even one as old as Remmley, would want to put his hands on her. The beauty that had been only a promise at sixteen was in full flower now. The coltishness was gone from her movements and the wary innocence from her gaze . . . to devastating effect.

With her full breasts, narrow waist, and gracefully curved hips, she might have stepped out of one of the fantasies he'd woven during the long, lonely nights between battles. Her eyes, angled beguilingly and smudged with dark lashes, reflected a tantalizing sensuality. Her cheekbones were high and her full lips rosy and provocative, souvenirs of a Hungarian Gypsy ancestor. Or so she'd told him on one of their long, rambling, clandestine walks years ago. With Delilah, he was never quite sure. Of anything. That was part of what had attracted him to her so strongly and in utter defiance of common sense.

The idea of her youth and beauty being sacrificed for the sake of politics, or appearances, revolted him.

"No," he said at last. "I don't think you should be forced to marry Remmley. Not for any reason."

She breathed a sigh of relief and looked hopeful. "Then you'll help me?"

"I might," he said. "You still haven't explained exactly what you have in mind."

"Nothing too complicated, since I have only a week before Roger intends to make the formal announcement of our betrothal. I'd first thought to avoid the inevitable by making myself so sick at the last minute that I would be unable to attend the ball Roger has planned. That's why I needed Lillith's nostrum."

"Let me get this straight. You intended to drink something you knew would make you sick?"

"Yes, and there would be nothing Roger could do about it." Her eyes sparkled. "Brilliant, isn't it?"

"Idiotic is more like it," Christian retorted. "For once, couldn't you have just thought to do what any other female would and plead a simple headache?"

"You obviously don't know Roger as well as you think. Nothing short of a disgusting and violent display of illness would prevent him from dragging me there to make an appearance. Obviously that's no longer an option, though I still don't understand what happened to the contents of the bottle."

"Spilled," he said. "Hellishly clumsy of me, I know."

"You might have told me that instead of trying to pass off an empty bottle on me."

"I might have," he allowed. "But would you have been so amenable to handing over the other bottle in exchange for nothing?"

"We'll never know, will we?" Her small smile gave way to a look of consternation. "Why are you so eager to obtain the incantation in the bottle?"

Christian briefly considered telling her the truth. Then sanity returned. "I'm helping out a friend," he said.

"Now you'll be helping another old friend at the same time. Me. Things have a way of working out for the best, don't you think?"

"For you, perhaps," he said. "You're not the one being bled to get back something he's already bought and paid royally for."

"Stop grumbling. You'll get your bottle back in plenty of time to help your friend."

"Provided I succeed in ruining you to your satisfaction?"

"Yes, but that shouldn't be a problem for you, of all people. All you have to do is be seen with me, frequently, and in ever-so-slightly compromising situations. I know for a fact that Remmley is not particularly fond of you. The mere suggestion that you are my special confidant will taint me by association and render me forever unsuitable in his eyes."

"Thinks that highly of me, does he?" he asked dryly.

"I'm afraid so. As do most proper members of society."

"Hypocrites."

"And thank heaven they are or my plan would never work." She smiled. "Now then, we should begin immediately. I've made plans to attend the theater with friends this evening. You can stop by our box and insist on speaking privately with me and then—"

"No."

"No?"

"No. *If* I agree to do what you ask, I will not be given instructions and fed my lines like some sort of puppet on a string. I'm perfectly capable of compromising a woman."

"Yes," she said. "I know."

Christian cursed silently. He'd handed her the needle and she'd wasted no time pricking him with it. His hide would no doubt resemble a pincushion by the time she was through with him. If he went along with her plan.

"So," she prodded. "Will you do it?"

"If I do, will you promise to relinquish the bottle—with the incantation intact—on the night of your brother's ball, regardless of the outcome?"

She paled at the possibility of failure, but nodded. "I promise."

Christian considered his options. They weren't encouraging. He was damned—quite literally—if he surrendered the incantation and walked away. On the other hand, if he agreed to her scheme it would mean spending time with Delilah, and something warned him that could present a different sort of danger.

It was, he realized suddenly, a new twist on a quandary he'd faced countless times in his reckless life. Flames were licking at the back of his heels and up ahead Delilah was holding the frying pan, waiting for him to jump.

Old habits die hard, he thought, sighing and steeling himself to do what he inevitably did at such moments.

He jumped.

CHAPTER FIVE

A GENTLEMAN WOULD have given Delilah advance warning of how and when he intended to tryst with her. That was precisely why Christian had not done so. He wasn't a gentleman, not much of one, anyway. Besides, he thought, taking care to stand in the shadows by the side of the road, their association had less to do with courtship rituals than blackmail. At least that's what he kept telling himself.

He had discovered that old habits weren't the only thing that died hard. The last seven years might not have existed for the way he reacted when he was near Delilah. The restless anticipation that tightened the muscles in his chest, and lower, was the same he had felt that long-ago night as he strode across the ballroom at Greenwall, her family home.

He hadn't wanted to be there. Country house parties were not his preferred venue, but a more alluring invitation had fallen through when the lady's husband returned home unexpectedly. He'd arrived at Greenwall feeling moody, regretting he'd let himself be talked into coming. Then he saw Delilah and he was transfixed.

"Dance with me," he'd said without preamble when he reached her side.

It wasn't a request. What it was, as evidenced by the

shocked murmur that passed like a dark cloud across the elegant assemblage, was a flagrant violation of all that tonish society held dear. Delilah was sixteen, a pure-as-the-driven-snow innocent about to experience her first London season. And he was twenty-four, the Blackmoor Devil, a man of vast and unholy experience who ought to have known better than to let his interest be waylaid by a pair of wide green eyes flirting outrageously with him across a dance floor.

He did know better, of course. It had been years since he'd prowled within ten feet of a virgin. That's why he could offer no rational explanation for his actions that evening, nor afterward. Not then. Not now.

To his credit, he had never actively pursued Delilah during the week-long springfest comprised of picnics and parties and balls. Not that her family would have permitted it had he tried. But neither had he discouraged her furtive pursuit of him. She'd called the tune, but he had danced, and he'd been infinitely more knowledgeable about the steps.

He'd made himself available, he'd fallen into each of her inexpertly laid traps, and so they had spent many hours alone together, walking along cool, shady forest paths, rowing across the secluded cove she had shown him, and talking, always talking, more openly and naturally than he had ever been inclined to converse with the countless more glib and sophisticated women of his acquaintance.

He had understood what was happening, of course. She had developed a crush on him. Her very first, he suspected, hatched, not in spite of his wicked reputation, but rather *because* of it. And in the process of indulging her infatuation, which was what he'd steadfastly assured himself he was doing, he had fallen madly in love with her.

Mad as in insane. It wasn't rational. Hell, it wasn't even real, as it turned out, though it certainly felt real at the time. It was, however, the only explanation he could come up with for his behavior that week.

Lovesick. The word alone made him cringe, but he was honest enough to acknowledge, if only to himself, that that's what he'd been. After years of sidestepping the maneuvers of more experienced women, he had been felled by a mere slip of a girl. He was bedazzled by her honesty and her enthusiasm; enchanted by the brash way she looked at the world and, even more, at the fresh, new way the world looked to him when he was standing by her side. He couldn't explain the spell she cast on him any more than he could deny it.

Douse one lovesick fool with a liberal number of after-dinner brandies and you get a man reckless enough to dare anything, even a sixteen-year-old's challenge to climb to her bedroom window and steal her away for a late-night ride on the swing hanging from the massive oak tree down by the summerhouse.

It was there that Roger had found them, drawn by the sound of Delilah's laughter as Christian pushed her higher and higher in the air. Of course, Roger had to climb from his bed and make his way to the summerhouse, giving Christian ample time to progress from pushing her to holding her, ample time for them to move inside the small shuttered bungalow, time for his passion and her eager curiosity to overtake whatever common sense either of them possessed.

The laces of her white nightgown had been loosened and one strap had slipped off her shoulder. Her head was tossed back and his face was buried in her throat, his hands on her breasts, when the door had been flung open. Delilah gasped. He remembered that, too. Mostly, however, he remembered how she had looked, her pale gold hair unbound, her face flushed, her lips bee-stung from his kisses. She was, at that instant, the most beautiful sight he had ever seen, and part of him had wanted to kill her brother for intruding.

"I'll kill you," Roger had uttered, evidently sharing the sentiment. He looked as if he'd dressed in the dark, in a hurry, and his sandy hair was tousled.

Christian felt Delilah stiffen and released her immediately, turning slightly so his shoulder blocked her from view as she hurriedly righted her nightclothes.

"Calm down, Rog," he said, striving for nonchalance,

not an easy feat for a man who was breathless and flagrantly aroused. "It's not what it seems."

Roger Ashton laughed harshly. "What kind of blind fool do you take me for, Lowell? You mean to say you weren't just pawing my little sister? Putting your filthy hands all over her? Rearing to take full advantage if I hadn't gotten here in the nick of time?"

"I would never take advantage of Delilah."

"Ah. So you intend to marry her, then?"

Marry her? Roger's scornful tone made it clear he wasn't serious, but the challenge held a certain appeal nonetheless. He could marry her, Christian thought, his newly awakened heart and the brandy working in unison. Hell, he *would* marry her.

"No, Roger please, not that," Delilah exclaimed, moving to stand in front of him.

Before she put her back to him Christian had a fleeting glimpse of her face, washed of all color and frozen in horror. He came instantly to his senses. And he realized that for the first time ever, he, a master at playing a woman's heartstrings, was the one who had been played for a fool. People had warned him that it would happen sooner or later, but he hadn't believed it. And he didn't like it.

Of course Delilah did not want to marry him. She only wanted to play. Their long conversations had revealed that she was heady with anticipation of the season ahead and in no rush to have her wings clipped before she'd had a chance to spread them. She was riding a wave of burgeoning feminine power and cutting her teeth on the safest male heart available. Everyone knew that when it came to being shackled, women were eminently safe with the Blackmoor Devil. He never fell in love.

"Marry her?" he countered, slanting Roger a look of sardonic amusement. "Really, Rog, she's barely out of the nursery. Seems to me you'd be the one taking advantage if you forced that issue."

"But . . . you . . . you kissed her," her brother insisted, his expression reflecting a decent man's struggle to do the right thing. Which was why decent men were always at a disadvantage at such moments. "You touched her."

"Roger, please," pleaded Delilah. "I beg you not to—"

"Not to make more of this than there is," Christian interjected to spare the further humiliation of hearing her beg her brother not to force an alliance she clearly found offensive in the extreme. "I intended only to tweak you a bit, as payback. You do remember that time you and a few others nailed my boots to the floor of one of the upstairs rooms at Madame Cosseau's?"

Roger's face puckered. "But that was years ago, a schoolboy's prank."

"Yes, well, some men outgrow such pranks and some of us never do. At any rate," he continued, yawning as he sauntered to the door, "now we're even. Good evening, Lady Ashton. I trust your brother will see you safely back to your door. 'Night, Rog."

He'd left before the household awoke the following morning. Three weeks later he was back with his regiment, still nursing his wounded pride, and she was betrothed to Andrew Moon, a pleasant enough, totally innocous young man, as Christian recalled, who no doubt couldn't believe his luck that such a spirited beauty had fallen head over heels in love with him so quickly.

If indeed she had. Delilah's hasty marriage had always been a puzzle to him. Perhaps the coming days would provide him with an opportunity to solve it. Perhaps, he speculated, the days ahead would provide him with a second chance at other lost opportunities, as well.

He glanced again at his watch. Either the theater was running late or Delilah had taken a different route home. His growing concern was alleviated a few moments later as the carriage traffic along Haymarket increased suddenly, signaling that the performance had at last ended. He watched for Delilah's carriage with its four distinctive white horses. When it pulled into view, he stepped from the shadows, leading his own horse.

"Halt," he shouted, signaling the driver to stop, then quickly leaping back as the carriage wheels kissed the toes of his favorite boots.

"Devil take the woman," he muttered, spitting gravel.

Furious, he swung into his saddle and galloped after

them. As he drew abreast, he again called for them to stop, this time backing up the command by wresting the reins from a feisty Esmerelda and steering the team to the side of the road.

"Are you deaf, woman?" he demanded.

"My aunt hears fine," responded the boy riding postilion. "We just don't take orders from you."

Christian recognized the little bugger as the one who'd picked his pocket the night before. He honed his gaze on him. "Would you care to wager on that?"

The kid didn't flinch, which was more than many grown men who'd been on the receiving end of Christian's icy glare could claim.

"Gentlemen don't bet with suckers," the boy retorted.

"Why, you little—"

The carriage door opened and Delilah leaned out.

"What is it, Esmerelda?" she asked. "Why are we stopping . . ." She caught sight of Christian and frowned. "What are you doing here?"

The boy cried out, "He's accosting us, Lady Moon. I can run for help, if you want."

Christian edged his horse closer, coming within reach of the boy. "You move and I'll—"

Delilah cut him off. "That won't be necessary, Dare. I can handle Lord Blackmoor. Well?" she prodded, turning to him once more.

He draped one hand carelessly over the saddle pommel and smiled at Delilah. She looked ravishing in sapphire silk. "I was in the mood for a romantic moonlight drive," he said, surprised to find that the idea held tremendous appeal.

"Are you daft?"

"Obviously. As are you," he added dryly as he dismounted and hitched his horse to the back of the carriage. "Move over."

She complied by sliding as far away from him as possible, her arms stiffly folded across her chest, her mouth arranged in a soft, utterly distracting pout.

"Drive on," he called.

Nothing.

"Please proceed, Esmerelda," Delilah said.

"By way of the park," Christian added. He cut off Delilah's protest by adding, "You do want this to appear an amorous assignation, do you not?"

"By way of the park," she called to Esmerelda, and like magic there was forward movement.

"I waited for you to come to my box," she said as he stripped off his gloves and tossed them on the seat opposite.

"I told you I don't take directions."

"I still thought you'd come."

"If it's any consolation, I tried, but I was detained by Lady Hoppinworth. She was intent on catching me up on every last detail of the time I've been gone."

She rolled her eyes. "Old Lady Hoppinworth, what awful luck you have."

Christian just smiled.

"Still, you could have made some excuse and stopped by just for a moment. Everyone was there this evening and the news that we shared a private moment in my box would have quickly reached my brother and Remmley."

"I decided to take a more direct route."

"You call this direct? Who can see us here?"

"No one. And everyone. That's why it's so perfect. Rest assured, someone will have noticed me climbing in and my horse is adorning your rear flank like a flag of occupation. It will be all the more tantalizing because they can only imagine what's transpiring behind these curtains," he said, drawing them.

"Which is nothing."

"Is it?"

Their gazes met and clung. The air inside the carriage heated and stilled.

"Don't do that," he warned quietly.

"Do what?"

"Look at me."

"Why not?"

"Because. It gives rise to an overpowering urge to do this."

• • •

HE WAS going to kiss her. The realization exploded inside Delilah as she watched him slowly lower his head, giving her time to protest if she wanted to. She didn't. Then his mouth was claiming hers in a kiss that was exciting and familiar.

Familiar because it was the kiss she had dreamed of countless times, asleep and awake, during that long-ago spring when she had believed in him and in love and in happy endings. She recognized the rough scrape of his jaw, where dark whiskers shaved that morning were already beginning to reappear. She recognized the smell of his skin and the warmth of his open mouth. Most acutely, however, she recognized the hunger in him, in the urgent thrusts of tongue and the fierce possessiveness of his embrace. It was exactly like her dreams.

She leaned into him, letting old memories stir and old hungers awaken and stretch. Her fingers moved through the thick waves of his hair and over his face, relearning the curve of his ear and the hard angle of his cheekbone, her fingertips brushing gently over his eye patch.

His lips moved slowly across her cheek, heating a path to her ear and nibbling gently on the lobe. Just as she was adjusting to that jolting new sensation his tongue began to trace the curve, exploring each tender crevice, until she trembled from the waves of tension radiating through her. As soon as he felt her response, Christian's arm tightened around her, while his tongue thrust boldly into her ear.

The excitement he sent rushing through her was almost unbearable. As if knowing that, he curled his hand around her nape, holding her still for his fiery caress, then scattering kisses down her throat and back again. His warm breath rustled her hair and his whisper was achingly gentle as he brought his mouth close to her ear once more.

"Oh, Delilah, you have no idea what you do to me."

Delilah rather suspected that she did. A very good idea at that, since his touch aroused a blinding desire in her. They would have to be blind, and dumb, to fall into each other's arms again after what had happened last time.

On second thought, perhaps their desires were not so similar after all, now or in the past. The difference last time was that her need had been both physical and emotional, whereas everyone knew that Blackmoor was interested only in easy conquests of the flesh. The difference now was that she was old enough and wise enough to see through him.

"Perhaps I don't know what I do to you," she said, disengaging herself from his embrace. "But I do know what I am *not* going to do. I am not going to toss my heart under your bootheel a second time."

He gave a bleak, tight-lipped smile. "I suppose I deserve that."

"And worse."

"Damn it, woman," he muttered, shifting restlessly, as if the padded seat were a bed of tacks. "You make me ache."

Delilah applauded, her smile teasing. "Bravo, Blackmoor. You do give a wonderfully credible impression of a man intent on compromising a lady's reputation."

"What if I told you it wasn't an impression?"

"I'd ask if you're always so easily overpowered by your urges."

"Where you are concerned? Always. Regrettably."

In spite of her good intentions Delilah's heart leaped as he once more reached for her and bent his head. His mouth had barely brushed hers when the carriage rocked to a halt with a violent wrenching sound.

She grabbed his arm as they listed sharply to the right. "What's happening?"

"It would seem you've lost a wheel."

"Oh, no. What now?"

"Putting it back on is the usual approach."

"I'm not certain Esmerelda and Dare will be able to manage that on their own."

"An excellent reason for employing a male coachman," he pointed out.

Ignoring him, she reached to open the door. "Is it the wheel, Dare?"

"Yes, ma'am. Fell clean off the axle for no reason I can see. I checked all four before we left, same as always."

She climbed down to inspect the damage for herself and

Christian followed. "Why on earth would it just fall off that way?" she wondered out loud.

"Fate," Christian suggested, eyeing the stripped axle with surprising contempt.

"Maybe there was a rut in the road," she said, glancing around without seeing any ruts.

Christian sighed and ran his hand through his hair. "No. It was fate. Mine. The least I can do is fix it for you, if you have tools."

"You'll ruin your clothes," she protested.

"I have other clothes. You don't have another carriage handy."

"There's a toolbox in the back," Dare volunteered.

"Good. I'll also need you to lend a hand," Christian said to him.

Dare nodded. "I'd do anything for Lady Moon."

"Yes, I'm in a unique position to vouch for the extremes you're willing to go to on your mistress's behalf," Christian said dryly. "All right, let's have at it, young man. This will give you a chance to make amends for last night."

Delilah held his jacket as he went to work. To her surprise, he seemed to know precisely what he was doing and exhibited more patience than she would have expected in showing Dare what to do each step of the way. In preparation for future mishaps, he explained, though it would be years before Dare had Christian's strength, she thought, mesmerized by the play of muscles beneath his sweat-dampened shirt as he strained at the lever in order to lift the carriage enough for Dare to slide the wheel into place.

This was certainly a side of Blackmoor she had never seen before. She'd venture to say few people had. His reputation as a rake, a blackguard, and a debaucher preceded him through life and—in Christian's own words— he had always done his best to live down to it. Delilah had to admit that it was his infamous reputation that had first attracted her, appealing to her reckless side.

It was later, as they wandered the meadows and woods near her house alone, that his guard had slipped and she had gotten to know his gentler, more vulnerable side, the part of him that yearned for more out of life than swashbuckling across continents and winning wars. She had gotten to know *him*. Or thought she had, she reminded herself ruefully. How naive she had been. She certainly had not known, or liked, the Christian who had emerged that night in the summerhouse, tossing her aside as carelessly as if she were a penny novel he had started, but had no interest in finishing.

He was truly a chameleon. No, she thought, a chameleon changed as a matter of survival. The reasons for Christian's shifts of personality had more to do with manipulation and self-indulgence, and that made him far more dangerous. She would do well to remember that when he was near, she reminded herself, touching her lips where his kiss still burned.

"A job well done," he said at last, slapping Dare on the back as they admired the results of their labor. "You were an extraordinary help. Are you sure you've never before mounted a carriage wheel?"

"I'm sure. Though I've helped to lift a few off in my time."

"No doubt," Christian responded, his expression sardonic.

Delilah hurried forward before he could explore Dare's colorful past too deeply. "Dare, see if you can find a rag for Lord Blackmoor to wipe his hands on, will you? I'm afraid you have grease everywhere," she said regretfully.

"Which, I suppose, means our romantic ride is over for the night." He lifted his hands as if to touch her, caught sight of the black grime covering them, and dropped them to his side with what sounded like a growl. "Delilah, I . . ."

The sound of an approaching carriage drew their attention. It pulled up beside them and the door, with its elaborate Hoppinworth crest, opened.

"Lady Hoppinworth," Delilah said, nodding deeply. At her side, Christian bowed in greeting.

"I saw your predicament from the top of the hill. I'd offer my man's assistance, but it appears you have the situation under control."

"Thank you," said Delilah. "My carriage lost a wheel, but luckily Lord Blackmoor happened by and was able to fix it for me . . . much to the detriment of his evening clothes, I fear."

The elderly woman turned to Christian. "You are a good, decent gentleman, Blackmoor. I don't care what everyone else says. You stopped to help Lady Moon out of sheer, unselfish concern for her safety and I shall make it a point to see to it that everyone understands that. Anyone who dares to suggest otherwise shall have to answer to me." She winked at Delilah. "Rest assured that your reputation is safe, my dear."

"Thank you," replied Delilah, her teeth clenching as Lady Hoppinworth's carriage pulled away. "Wonderful. The dragon lady herself, the biggest gossip in all of London, happens by and sees us together. It's an absolutely perfect opportunity to launch all sorts of juicy innuendo and speculation about our relationship and what does she decide to do instead? Why, defend my reputation, of course. What wretched luck."

"I tried," Christian said with a shrug.

Delilah paused on her way into the carriage and patted her skirts where the bottle was hidden. "Try harder, Blackmoor."

CHAPTER SIX

THREE DAYS LATER Christian was summoned back to Delilah's drawing room. He checked his watch again. He'd been wearing a path in the rug for over a half hour and couldn't decide if his annoyance had more to do with her lapse in manners or his own impatience. Since leaving her last evening he had thought of little else but seeing her again. Her early-morning note requiring a meeting to discuss strategy had spared him from having to come up with an excuse of his own.

He told himself he was simply eager to put an end to this, retrieve the bottle, and get on with his life. It was an eminently reasonable explanation for his mood, even if it didn't quite explain why he couldn't get thoughts of kissing Delilah off his mind. To his own surprise, since inheriting the title, a sensible and hitherto totally unknown side of him had slowly begun to emerge.

His new responsibilities and obligations had a sobering, even calming effect that he was gradually coming to terms with and finding not as distasteful as he'd once feared. At odd moments he even found himself thinking of the future in terms of possibilities rather than duty alone. Currently the family lands and holdings were being managed by trusted solicitors, with orders to maintain the status quo established by his brother. But that might change, he thought. Who knows? He might someday become as ambitious and accomplished a gentleman as Charles had been. Once this hex business was behind him, that is.

In large measure the curse stopped him from living, but it hadn't stopped him from thinking and he found himself forced to contemplate a future quite different from any he had ever imagined or desired. While once he'd thought never to marry, convinced it was as lethal to a man as a noose around his neck, he now conceded that it might have its advantages. In fact, from time to time, the notion quite intrigued him.

What would it be like to have one person with whom you could share everything and care for unconditionally, and who would care for you the same way in return? What would it be like to have someone waiting to welcome you when you came home? What would it be like to come home to Delilah?

He grinned, thinking of Delilah's headstrong, often impulsive nature. It would be interesting, that was certain. Not to mention unpredictable.

He shook himself. What was wrong with him? He was mad even to include her and marriage in the same thought. The woman was spoiled and scheming and obviously dedicated to being outrageously unconventional at any cost. In short, she was exactly what he didn't need and shouldn't want in a countess. And yet, he couldn't deny that ever since he had kissed her and held her in his arms again, he wanted her desperately.

The sudden sound of laughter and clapping was a welcome intrusion on his conflicted thoughts, drawing him to the window that overlooked a pretty side garden with a birdbath and an ornate white iron bench. Seated on the bench was a small girl with dark hair and the biggest blue eyes he had ever seen.

Or perhaps, Christian amended, they just appeared unusually large as she gazed in wide-eyed wonder at the performance being given for her benefit alone. He joined her in watching as Dare tossed three red balls in the air and juggled them. Suddenly, with no explanatory movement that Christian could spot from his vantage point at the window, there were two red balls and one yellow. A few seconds later there were two yellow and one red, then all yellow. It went on like that with colors coming and going until Dare was juggling all six balls at once. This time when the girl broke into applause, Christian joined in.

Immediately Dare stopped and turned, snatching the balls from the air.

"Bravo," said Christian. "That's quite an impressive feat, Dare, even for someone as nimble-fingered as I know you to be."

The boy had the grace to look sheepish at the subtle reference to his handiwork in Christian's pocket a few nights ago.

"Least I left you your gold snuffbox," he offered defensively.

Christian paused, digesting the fact that in order to know the snuffbox was gold Dare must have managed a look at it while he was lifting the bottle. He laughed out loud.

"Yes, you did, and I can see now that I should be grateful for that, and probably for the fact that I made it home with my straps intact as well."

Dare shrugged. "They weren't gold."

He laughed again, liking the little beggar in spite of himself. "May I ask who your young admirer is?"

"My sister," Dare replied. "Her name's Jane." He tugged on the little girl's sleeve until she stood beside him. "Jane, this here is Lord Blackmoor. Curtsy," he prompted in a whisper, helping her along with a little shove from behind.

"Don't push," Jane said, shooting her big brother a fierce look. "I 'membered all by myself."

"Did not."

"Did so."

Dare bit his lip and took the high road, letting it end there while Christian savored a bittersweet memory of Charles doing the same during similar squabbles when they were growing up.

"I'm pleased to make your acquaintance, Jane," he said. "Do you juggle as well?"

She stuck out her lower lip and shook her head, sending

her glossy dark brown curls dancing. "Dare says my hands are too small to hold the balls," she explained, offering them for his inspection.

Christian nodded. "I see. Well, that's something time will remedy. How old are you, Jane?"

"Five."

"Almost six," added Dare.

"Not until tomorrow," she corrected.

"That's what *almost* means," her brother retorted. "Tomorrow."

Jane smiled. "Oh."

"I predict that by the time you're eight you'll be juggling with the best of them."

"As good as Dare?" she asked, her eyes widening with anticipation this time.

Christian nodded. "If you can persuade him to teach you his secrets." He turned to Dare. "Who taught you to juggle so well?"

"Lady Moon," he replied.

Christian's brows shot up. "Really?"

Dare nodded. "Least ways she taught me to juggle the first three balls. I added more on my own. The magic, making them appear and disappear, I learned that on my own, too."

"You're a very resourceful young man. I'm sure that took a great deal of practice to perfect."

"Some. I like it, though. Lady Moon says juggling is good practice for life. She says if you're lucky you'll have lots of different things going on in your life all the time and that juggling teaches you to focus on what's most important at the moment."

Christian nodded, struck by his careful recitation. He wasn't sure which impressed him more, that Delilah indulged in philosophical discussions with her postilion or that the boy had committed her words to memory.

"Lord Blackmoor."

He glanced over his shoulder to find Mrs. Tibble, Delilah's housekeeper, at the door.

"Lady Moon will see you now," she said.

He'd expected Delilah to join him in the drawing room,

as she had last time. Evidently that was not to be the case. Curious, he nodded to Dare and his sister and followed Mrs. Tibble from the room and down a short hall. She paused at a door left ajar and announced him. Stepping into the room, Christian glanced around at the book-lined walls and heavy burgundy drapes that kept out the sun and provided a somber aura very unlike the bright, airy drawing room.

Delilah remained in her high-backed leather chair without glancing up from the papers on the desk before her. A tall, severely dressed woman stood by her side, accepting each paper as Delilah affixed her signature to it and handing her another one to examine.

"Please have a seat, Christian," said Delilah. "I'll only be another moment. These orders really must be placed today or work will come grinding to a halt."

He remained standing, examining open maps on which various shipping routes had been traced in colored ink, and several framed prints of sailing vessels.

"Your husband's office?" he inquired.

"*My* office," she replied with a vehemence that made him smile.

"There," she announced at last. "That's that. Thank you, Gretchen. That will be all for now." Dismissing the woman, she remained behind the solid barrier of the massive cherry desk and added, "I am sorry for keeping you waiting, Christian."

"Are you?" he challenged, taking a step around the desk. He might permit her to summon him at will and keep him dangling in the drawing room, but he'd be damned if he'd be kept at arm's length as if he were some Cheapside merchant there to talk business.

"Of course I am," she said, smoothing her hair with a quiet laugh. "It was so kind of you to drop by to see me."

As soon as Christian heard the undercurrent of nervousness in her laugh, he knew. He knew that he was not the only one who had been taken by surprise by their kiss in the carriage, or who was still feeling its impact today. Excitement surged inside him at the realization. And confidence. He continued circling the desk until he stood close beside her and held out his hand expectantly.

After a second's hesitation, Delilah placed her hand atop his open palm. He bent and kissed it. She wasn't wearing gloves and her skin was so soft and smelled so sweet that he was tempted to open his mouth and taste her, running his tongue over her palm and the inside of her wrist and undoing the endless row of tiny buttons along her sleeve so he could lick all the way to her shoulder.

It was with great reluctance that he released her hand and straightened to meet her gaze. "I didn't drop by. I was summoned. I got the distinct impression from your note that this visit was not optional."

"How astute of you," she shot back, visibly gathering her mantle of self-assurance. Christian might have been fooled into thinking she was as nonchalant as she pretended if not for the way she clasped the back of her hand where he had kissed it. The lady was not quite as immune to him as she would like to appear.

"I meant my note to be taken seriously," she continued. "We need to talk, Christian."

This time when she waved him toward the seat across from her, he complied.

"Our campaign is not going at all well," she said.

"I'm excruciatingly aware of that fact, madam. First, Lady Hoppinworth decided to champion our reputations, then our timing was off at the opera, and yesterday the blasted rain was so heavy I probably could have ravished you when we met in Grosvenor Square and no one would have taken notice of us."

"Don't make excuses," she snapped.

"Don't chastise me," countered Christian. "I'm not one of your lady lackeys."

"Lady lackeys?" she echoed, standing and leaning on the desk with both hands as she glared at him. "That is just like you, to make a joke of something you don't know anything about."

He shrugged. "Educate me, Delilah."

"Hah! I wouldn't know where to begin."

"Begin by telling me about this business of yours," he

suggested, far more interested than he was willing to appear. "What exactly is it you do that has raised male hackles and has the ladies of the ton whispering behind their fans?"

"As if that's such a feat," she scoffed. "Most of those ladies would whisper just as savagely if my slippers didn't match my ball dress."

He chuckled. "True enough. I still think there's more to this than mismatched slippers. Are you running a ring of pickpockets, perhaps? Selling women into slavery? Printing subversive literature?"

"Are you through?" she asked at last.

"I think so. I've exhausted my repertoire of dastardly deeds."

Silently she stood and crossed the room, returning with a small wooden box, which she handed to him.

"Open it," she directed.

He did so, noting the intricate craftsmanship as he lifted the dome lid with its mother-of-pearl insets in the shape of a butterfly. The rest of the box was mahogany and when he turned the handle inside it played a lilting French melody. A music box. Belatedly he remembered being told that Delilah was manufacturing jewelry boxes and not being especially impressed. He was now.

"That's it," she said. "No slaves, no pickpockets, no subversive literature. What you're holding is what has everyone talking. That is my dirty deed, the offense that enrages my brother, challenges the social order, and threatens to topple civilization as we know it."

"The music box," he said.

"The music box," she confirmed. "How does it feel to be so close to a purveyor of wanton destruction?"

"I have to admit that I am impressed. No, amazed. How in the world did a woman with no business experience and a group of war widows manage to produce this?"

Her offhand shrug did not disguise her pride. "We simply took stock of our talents and went from there."

The look he gave her challenged the notion that there was anything simple about what she had accomplished.

"One of the women was the daughter of a watchmaker

from La Vallee de Joux, a region of Switzerland near the French border. Did you know that's where the music box originated?" she asked.

He shook his head.

"Neither did I," she confessed. "Elise worked side by side with her father and uncles for years and she was able to teach the craft to several of the other women. As we went along we discovered that another woman had worked in her father's cabinetmaker's shop and another had been married to a jeweler. We shared what we knew.

"Those who have neither knowledge nor an aptitude for the creative process do whatever they are suited for, cooking or teaching or bookkeeping, pitching in wherever they're needed from day to day."

"Keeping all the balls in the air," he murmured.

"What did you say?"

He shook his head. "Sorry, just thinking out loud."

"Anyway, somehow, miraculously, everything gets done. And women who were once reduced to begging for handouts are able to look after themselves and their children with dignity."

"Teaching, cooking," he repeated, still coming to terms with the magnitude of her undertaking. "Did you open a factory or found a bloody city?"

She smiled with amusement and satisfaction. "Actually it's more of a workshop than a factory. The word *factory* conjures up such a grim image. We have curtains on the windows and teatime and children running in and out. But to answer your question, I suppose I did a bit of both. I founded the Widows' Memorial Cooperative, and if orders and production remain on course for the next two months, we will show our first profit before year's end."

"Your first profit?" His eyes narrowed. "Do you mean to tell me that for years now you have been supporting all these women and children and pouring money . . . Of course, you have," he murmured, his gaze softening as he opened his eyes, and heart, to a side of Delilah he hadn't bothered to notice until now.

"It was an investment," she insisted, evidently accustomed to defending herself on this point—to Roger, no doubt. "I invested in a business venture, just as men make investments every day of the week, and it's about to produce a return, a very handsome return, if my projections are correct, and I'm sure they are."

"So you are the sole owner of this business of yours?"

"Well, not exactly," she countered with an awkward lift of her shoulders. "I knew it would be an uphill struggle and it just made sense to me that everyone would work harder if they had a personal stake in the outcome. So each woman was allowed to purchase a share of the company based on her ability to pay."

He looked astounded. "Based on her . . . Is this in writing? Is it legal?"

"It's honorable. That's good enough for me," she declared, lifting her chin in preparation for an argument. She didn't get one.

Christian was too busy dealing with the sudden lump in his throat. Inexplicably, he felt as proud as if he had been the one to work a miracle, changing people's lives and teaching them to make something beautiful and valuable out of what little they possessed. Delilah was not the woman he had thought her to be. She was much more, more caring, more generous, more daring . . . daring in ways that mattered, in ways that made a real difference, in ways that inspired hope and restored pride and enabled a little five-year-old girl to sit in the sunshine and laugh.

"I see I was wrong," he said lightly, unwilling to let her see how moved he was. "They're not your lackeys at all, they're your partners. On second thought, Roger and the others might have cause to object. You really might be in danger of overthrowing civilization as we know it."

She snatched the music box from him and put it aside. "Mock me all you want," she retorted. "I don't know why I tried explaining anything to you in the first place. You're as cynical as ever, utterly beyond redemption, and I certainly don't owe you any explanations."

Her comments stung. The truth had a way of doing that. "I suppose not," he retorted. "You do, however, owe me the return of my bottle, Saturday night, regardless of the outcome of this little scheme of yours."

"I'm beginning to regret that I ever agreed to that stipulation. Making the bottle's return contingent on success might have provided you with greater motivation."

"Perhaps it's your own motivation you should question," he advised, standing and approaching her. "Not to mention the consequences of success. If I do manage to cast aspersions on your reputation, however discreetly, Remmley won't be the only man scared off. No matter how fulfilling your work seems now or how successful you are at it, the allure will fade in time. Trust me. I know. Are you prepared to live the rest of your life alone?"

"Yes," she said, stalking away from him. "I'd prefer to, actually."

"You'd prefer to?" he echoed, startled by the fervor in her reply. "Prefer not to have the support and protection of a man who loves you? Prefer not to have children?" His expression dark, he grasped her arm and turned her to face him. "Why are you so opposed to marriage? Did something happen? Did Moon mistreat you? Scare you? Did he—"

"No, no," she said, shaking loose of his hold. "Nothing like that. Andrew was . . ." Regret softened the tense lines of her expression. "Andrew was a very sweet man who deserved far better than I could possibly have given him."

"I'm sure that's not true. I'm sure you were a wonderful wife and that Moon considered himself lucky to have you." *What man wouldn't?* he thought.

"Lucky to have me," she echoed softly. "If he ever truly did. We were together only a few weeks before his regiment was activated. Did you know that?"

Christian nodded. He knew. For no particular reason that he could name, he'd made it a point to stay abreast of the milestones in her life. He knew everything there was to know that was public knowledge. There were, however, things not commonly known, the things hidden in the turbulence of her eyes at that moment, that were a mystery.

"And during those weeks I wasn't much of a wife, I'm afraid."

"You were young . . . inexperienced."

"For God's sake, I was pretending," she blurted, and

immediately looked trapped by her honesty. "We were husband and wife, but I felt as if I was playing a role, constantly having to think of what I ought to be feeling when he spoke to me or touched me, instead of just feeling. I kept telling myself that it would change, that I would grow accustomed to being his wife and my feelings would become genuine, in time. But we never had time."

"Did you love him, Delilah?"

"I tried to," she said, looking away. "But deep in my heart I always knew the truth, that what I felt for Andrew wasn't love and that I had married him for the wrong reason."

"Why did you marry him?"

She lifted her gaze to his. "I married him to punish you, of course."

CHAPTER SEVEN

C HRISTIAN FELT LIKE a rag doll with the rags knocked out of it. "Me? You married Moon to punish me?"

Delilah sighed and nodded.

"Why?" he demanded.

"Because I was in love with you." Christian's heart lifted into his throat, then quickly sank as she added, "Or rather, I thought I loved you, silly chit that I was at the time."

"I had no idea."

"Oh, please. Don't pretend you didn't know. I may have been green and gullible back then, but no longer. How could I not have fallen in love with you? You were so handsome and charming and reeking with all the excitement and glamour I longed for and that was missing from my life. I couldn't believe my luck when you danced with me. Me, gawky, inexperienced, tongue-tied me."

"You were never gawky," he said softly. "Or tongue-tied, either, as I recall."

"Not with you. You made it so easy to talk with you and be with you. And you were such a . . . such a . . ." She lifted her outspread hands, grasping for the right word.

"Bastard?" he suggested.

"Man. Such a man. So powerful and . . . sensual," she said, hurling the word at him. Less defiantly, she added,

"And you made me feel like a woman, powerful and sensual, too."

"God, Delilah, you will never know how—"

"No, *you* will never know. You'll never know how desperately I felt about you. That night you came to my window and carried me off to the summerhouse was like a dream come true. Oh, I knew you were simply amusing yourself with me."

He shook his head. "I wasn't."

"But I didn't care. I *loved* you. I wanted you to love me. The last thing I wanted was for Roger to barge in and force your hand or twist your arm or shove in your face just how unsuitable a choice I was for you. I had it all planned, you see, I knew I would continue to see you in London that season. I thought that in time—" Delilah cut off the thought and squelched the small, bereft smile that accompanied it. "I know now it doesn't work that way. You can't learn to love someone."

Arching her brows, she added, "Especially not someone barely out of the nursery."

He grimaced. "Delilah, believe me, when I said that I was—"

"You were speaking the truth," she broke in. "I *was* too young and foolish to be involved with a man . . . especially a man like the Blackmoor Devil." Her sudden laugh had an edge of self-disgust. "If my behavior that night didn't prove that beyond any doubt, I certainly proved you right a few weeks later when I insisted on marrying Andrew in order to show you that I was not a child, that I was a woman." She laughed again, wearily this time. "Instead, all I managed to do was cheat and confuse a man who deserved much better."

"Moon bragged about you all the time," he told her. "I know because we had friends in common. If it's any consolation, I don't believe he felt cheated in the least."

"Thank you, but it's no consolation. I know the extent of my deceit even if poor Andrew never did. If I didn't realize it fully while he was alive, I had it driven home to me when I attended the memorial service to accept the medals he was awarded posthumously."

Delilah swallowed, her throat aching at what was still a painful memory. Oh, why had she ever gotten into this with him? What good were explanations and recriminations now? Was she trying to punish him at this late date? To make him shoulder some of the guilt and responsibility for what had happened? Or did the reason she was opening these old wounds have to do with what had happened when they were alone together the past three days?

She reeled inwardly. Good God, did she want a second chance with Blackmoor? Was that what this was all about? She thrust the thought away, ignoring the feelings of excitement sweeping through her. It was too late. She might have changed, but he had not. Men like Blackmoor never changed. Even if he were to offer her a second chance, Blackmoor was a risk she could no longer afford.

She felt his hand settle lightly on her shoulder.

"Talk to me about it," he urged softly. "Don't hold it all inside."

"Talking about it won't change anything," she replied, sliding away from the warm temptation of his touch. "I stood with all those other widows, women who were grieving the loss of their husbands, the fathers of their children, poor women, most of them, women with little hope of making a decent life for themselves and their children on their own, women who'd had their entire worlds annihilated by a gunner's blast. Marriage hadn't been merely a game or a petulant whim to those women. It had been real, just as their losses were real. My situation seemed to make a mockery of theirs and I vowed then and there that . . ."

"What?" he pressed, his voice deep and solid. "What did you vow, sweetheart?"

She flinched from the endearment and met his gaze with a defiant toss of her head. "I vowed I would never enter into a sham of a marriage again. I married once for all the wrong reasons. Never again. Do you hear me? I will only marry if I love the man too desperately to live without him and I am absolutely certain he loves me the same way."

"I assume it's safe to say that's not the case with Remmley," he said dryly.

Delilah shuddered. "No, and truthfully I don't expect to

feel that way ever again." She saw the glint that appeared in his eye at the word *again* and hurried on before he could question her. "And since you started all this, you owe it to me to help me, Blackmoor."

"Very well," he replied. "Do you have plans for this evening?"

"Yes, I'm to attend a dinner party at the Vallinghursts'."

"Fine. I'll see you there."

"Impossible. It's in honor of Howard's birthday and the invitations went out months ago. You'll have to come up with something else."

"The hell I will. It so happens Evelyn Vallinghurst and I were once very close."

She rolled her eyes. "Yes, I'm sure you were."

"I'll be there, count on it, and rest assured, madam, this time no one will prevent me from ruining you to your heart's content."

DELILAH SMILED and nodded at whatever Miles Haverhill, the pale, overeager youngest son of the marquis of Wilton, had just said, and continued to think about Christian.

She'd warned that he would not be able to attend the Vallinghursts' party this evening and it appeared she was right. The satisfaction that brought her did not come close to equaling her disappointment. Irrationally, she had taken seriously his cocky boast and had half-expected to find him lounging in the drawing room when she arrived, sipping champagne and eyeing her with smug superiority.

More irrationally still, she had actually dressed for the evening as if he would be there to see her. The shimmering lavender gown she was wearing was her favorite and most flattering, and before donning it she had primped and preened and powdered and dabbed with the diligence and enthusiasm of a woman preparing for a most important romantic assignation. Which was utterly ridiculous. Christian Lowell might well be the most handsome, sensual, and intriguing man she had ever met, but she had no interest in him beyond his usefulness in discouraging Roger's matchmaking attempts.

Did she?

Miles Haverhill's right elbow suddenly jutted danger-ously close to her chest. "I believe this dance is ours," he said, the zealous glitter in his eyes the polar opposite of her own feelings at that moment.

Suppressing the urge to touch her temple and plead a sudden migraine, she flashed him a game smile and placed her hand lightly on his arm. They had barely reached the edge of the crowded dance floor when Delilah felt another, more commanding touch at the small of her back and she glanced over her shoulder to find Blackmoor standing there, wearing precisely the expression she had anticipated.

"Dance with me," he said.

The silky command was every bit as improper as it had been the first time he'd uttered it to her seven years ago, and Delilah discovered that she was every bit as unable to resist it. She was vaguely aware of him murmuring some-thing insincere and apologetic to Haverhill and then she was in his arms and they were swept into the whirl of other waltzing couples.

"I don't believe you did that," she said, tipping her head to gaze up at him, unable to stop smiling in spite of the fact that she knew a reprimand was in order.

"Why not?" he countered. "It's not the first time it's happened."

"No, but it's still every bit as ill-mannered."

He moved effortlessly with her, taking advantage of a turn to pull her imperceptibly closer. "And you're still every bit as happy that it's me you're dancing with and not whatever insipid partner I dispatched. Why not admit it?"

"Why should I?" she challenged, laughing, exhilarated by the music and the movement and his closeness. She'd been there for over an hour, but she'd had no idea that the orchestra was so fine or the air so sweet and the crowd so agreeable.

"Because it's the truth," he said. "And it seems to me that our relationship is overdue for a little truth."

"Really? I wasn't aware we had a relationship, Black-moor, merely an agreement."

He grinned. "As in you agreeing to torture and blackmail me and generally drive me mad?"

"No, as in you agreeing to act in a manner guaranteed to cast our association in a questionable light."

"If you'll look more closely, madam, I think you'll see that that is precisely how I am acting at this very moment."

His words were as effective as boulders in her slippers for bringing Delilah back to earth with a thud. The tingles that had been running up and down her spine sputtered and ceased. Of course that's what he was doing, she reminded herself. He was acting, playing the part she had cast him in, doing exactly what she herself had maneuvered him into doing.

It had simply felt so wonderfully real that for a moment she was the one taken in by his laughter and his undivided attention and the look of utter adoration he was bestowing on her. *Of course it felt real, you ninny,* she chided herself. It felt real because he was perfect for the role. The very best.

Some men painted masterpieces, some designed great monuments, Blackmoor seduced women. It was his gift, his calling. And success was contingent on his talent for making a woman feel that she was the center of his universe and that pleasing her mattered more to him than his next breath. There was no way a woman could ever trust such a man, no matter how right it felt.

Was there?

"You're frowning," he observed. "Shall I interpret that to mean you are displeased with my performance this evening?"

"Not at all," she said, tossing her head and arranging a bright smile. "Your performance is as accomplished as I would expect from one of your wide and unseemly experience. Insofar as it goes, that is."

This time when they turned the tightening of his hold on her was very perceptible, to Delilah and, she surmised, anyone else looking on.

"I apologize for my restraint. Tell me, Lady Moon, just how far would you have me go this evening?"

Delilah glanced around to see if any nearby couples had overheard. "Will you please lower your voice?"

"No. What I will do is drag you outside to the terrace for a more private dance, if you like. Or perhaps we ought to abandon any semblance of discretion and head straight upstairs to the master bedroom. Do you suppose the Vallinghursts would mind?"

"I'm sure Evelyn wouldn't," retorted Delilah. "Unless she takes offense at the fact that she is not the one you chose to dally with after she rearranged her dinner plans at the last moment to accommodate you."

"Can I help it if the lady takes seriously her patriotic duty to wounded soldiers?"

"And former lovers?"

"I'm here, aren't I? Is there no pleasing you, madam?"

"I'm easily pleased by those who do what they've promised to do."

The music ended, but he did not release her. "Does that mean you're prepared to cooperate by accompanying me upstairs?"

"That is too ridiculous a proposal to merit a response," she said, glancing around with a frozen smile, aware that they were beginning to draw attention and not sure she wanted to garner more by going to the extreme of struggling to be free of him.

"I see," he said with a look of mock consternation. "You desire even more forthright action. I have it, we'll elope."

She stared at him, aghast. "I want my brother to free me from this engagement, not kill me." By moving suddenly she succeeded in putting space between them. In a quiet voice, she added, "I said I wanted a hint of scandal, a *hint*, Blackmoor. Does that mean anything to you?"

"Everything," he murmured, lifting her hands to his lips and kissing them lovingly. "Trust me."

ALONE IN the Vallinghursts' library, Christian recalled some advice his father had once given him. He'd said that the surest path to regretting something you've said is to put it in writing. That was the reason Christian had never poured his heart out in a love letter. Until now.

He would pen a letter to Delilah, he decided, a letter

ardent enough to turn her eyeballs blushing pink. Only it would not be Delilah's eyes reading his scorching declarations. This time he was going to ambush his own plan and spare fate the trouble. A misdirected missive was certain to ignite gossip without requiring the sort of blatant impropriety that could come back to haunt him. Bottle be damned, he had no intention of shredding Delilah's reputation beyond salvation.

The only problem with his plan was that years of practice *not* putting his feelings into words rendered him ill-equipped for the task. *Concentrate,* he ordered himself, finding it difficult to string two syllables together with the sounds of chatter and laughter filtering past the library door.

The harder he pressed, the more words eluded him. What the devil did lovers say in letters to each other?

Dear Delilah.

Too formal.

My Dearest Delilah.

Better.

My Dearest, Darling Delilah.

My Dearest, Darling Delilah. No matter how slowly he read it, it wasn't enough. He had a sudden insight into what Delilah had meant about trying to create feelings toward her late husband. In desperation, he stopped trying to make up sentiments and instead concentrated on what he actually felt in his heart. To his amazement, the words came.

Flowed.

Gushed.

He could have gone on for pages, but the sound of the guests moving to the dining room forced him to stop. He tossed the pen aside, wondering if he should reread what he'd written and deciding against it. He had no time to waste, and besides, it wasn't as if Delilah herself would be reading the letter. Lady Diana Hanover, who had conveniently worn a dress in a similar shade to Delilah's this evening, would have that singular pleasure.

Any woman's curiosity would be piqued beyond control by such a note. Christian was counting on Lady Hanover to avail herself of the first opportunity to excuse herself to read it privately. When she did, he would be right behind her, waiting to retrieve it as soon as she was finished, apologizing profusely for the mix-up. She would be left with only her own recollection of the sentiments expressed and a tale of how the Blackmoor Devil had written a torrid letter to Lady Moon, on the very eve of her betrothal to one of the most important men in England.

He hurriedly sealed the letter and left the library, singling out the brightest-looking footman in sight.

"Please give this to the lady in the lavender gown," he directed, nodding in the general direction of the Hanover woman as she swept from the room. "And see that you are discreet about it."

The footman bowed and slipped the note into his sleeve.

Christian had to hurry to locate the lady he was to escort upstairs to dinner and was barely seated at the table when he observed the footman enter the room and survey the seated guests. The man's expression grew progressively more perplexed. Puzzled, Christian followed his gaze as it rested first on Lady Hanover, then Lady Rumplescore, then, in quick succession, Ladies Billingly, Babson, and Dillinger, all of them dressed in lavender gowns.

Any one of them would do, he supposed. Any one as long as it wasn't Delilah. That would defeat the entire purpose of his scheme, not to mention leaving him open to abject humiliation when she read what he had written.

Just thinking of it brought on a rush of heat that had him tugging on his neckcloth as he endeavored to watch the footman without appearing to. At last he managed to catch the man's eye and he darted his gaze in the direction of Lady Hanover. *That one,* he thought, alarmed enough to attempt to send the man a psychic message. *Just give it to her, for God's sake.*

Finally, the great liveried lout seemed to discern his intent. Giving Christian a none-too-subtle wink, he moved in the direction of Lady Hanover, stopped, bent and, to Christian's silent horror, discreetly deposited the letter into the lavender lap of the woman to her left.

Delilah.

CHAPTER EIGHT

*I AM WEARING your kiss, the one I tore from your lips.
It is a brand, a scar, a treasure.*

Delilah's hands, still clutching the letter, fell to her lap.

She considered pinching herself to see if she was
dreaming.

No.

If this was a dream, she didn't want to wake from it, not
yet. Soon enough she would have to face reality. She
would have to put aside the feelings roused by Christian's
words. She would have to put *him* aside and forget the
magic spell he'd managed to cast over her heart during the
past few days.

But not yet, she thought, her gaze once more roaming
over the sheet of parchment, now creased and smudged
from her damp grasp. She had not let go of the letter since
the footman dropped it in her lap, not even when Christian
cornered her later to explain his bungled ploy and demand
its return. Especially not then. Ruse or not, she wanted to
see for herself what he would write in a love letter to her.

*If I were noble enough, just loving would be sufficient.
It would be as good as seeing and tasting and touching.
But I am not noble and we both know it.*

She smiled, savoring the slow, warm wave of pleasure

that moved through her. No, he was not noble, not in a conventional sense. He was brash and demanding and, she realized, utterly, infuriatingly dear to her.

I want to love you every way a man can love a woman . . . properly, improperly, quickly, endlessly, wildly, gently. Like a devil, like an angel, like myself.

Like myself. Those words touched her deeply. They captured best the vulnerability that ran just beneath his clever, fervent prose. They brought back to her the man her heart remembered, the man Christian had shown himself to be during the spring they'd spent getting to know each other through easy conversation and the sometimes even easier silences.

Like myself. Those two words were the most revealing of all, suggesting that the letter was not merely a ploy and the sentiments expressed not simply hurried, hollow musings intended to mislead. Was it possible? she wondered. Could these words be heartfelt, written by a man to the woman he loved?

Was Christian in love with her? And did this breathless feeling of excitement mean she loved him, too?

She folded the letter abruptly.

No. It was not possible. Not even remotely, slightly conceivable. Unless . . .

Her grip on the letter loosened. Unless Blackmoor had changed. Unless she was not the only one who had grown up during the last seven years. People could change after all. She had.

The prospect was dazing. And bittersweet. There was a time when Christian's love would have answered all her prayers and fulfilled all her dreams. But those had been a young girl's dreams. She was no longer that impulsive, carefree girl, ruled by her own whims. She was a woman, a woman with promises to keep and to whom others were looking to have their prayers answered and their dreams fulfilled.

And Christian was a man she didn't dare trust with her heart, much less her dreams.

If only . . . too late . . . The words chased one another

around inside her head, just as feelings of wonder and hopelessness did battle in her heart.

It was too late. For both of them. Sooner or later Christian would be required to apply himself to the duties that came with his new position as earl of Blackmoor, not the least of which was producing an heir. He would make a political match, and a convenient one. He would want a woman to bear his sons and stand silently by while he played fast and loose with half the so-called ladies in England. She was not that woman.

A noise outside the window brought her upright in her chair. A slight breeze lifted the curtains and she eyed them warily. It was at moments such as this that she regretted just how thorough she had been in replacing male servants with females. A household of women and children had its drawbacks, and Dare was still a child, no matter how colorful his past or strenuous his claims to the contrary.

She held herself very still and listened, hoping the sounds had been only her imagination at work and quickly realizing they had not. She felt the letter drop from her hand. Silently, she slipped from her chair and moved to stand out of sight beside the window. The sounds were closer now. In desperation she snatched the paperweight from her desk as a dark shadow rose above the windowsill.

"Delilah?" whispered a familiar voice.

"Christian." She lowered the paperweight to her side with relief. "You scared the—"

She was cut off as he vaulted into the room, accompanied by the loud crunch of splintering wood. It was followed by a crash somewhere below and a muttered oath.

He grimaced and rolled to a sitting position, gingerly patting his ribs.

"Are you hurt?" she asked, leaning over him.

"No, damn it, just fond of making an entrance."

"Well, rest assured you succeeded. What happened?"

"The trellis broke. I should have known something would . . ."

"Broke?" she asked as he trailed off. She glanced out the window and back to him. "But now how are you going to get down?"

"Good question."

"I have an even better one. What were you doing climbing up here at this time of night in the first place?"

He shrugged. "I was in the neighborhood."

"Very funny. A pity you weren't so clever earlier this evening."

"I might have been if you had returned the letter in time for me to right matters."

"Wrong matters, you mean. I was merely trying to prevent you from botching things further. Doing so seems to be your avocation. Besides," she added, ignoring his glowering, "the letter was delivered to me. That makes it mine to do with as I please."

"The hell it does," he countered, glancing around and on his feet in one fluid movement as he caught sight of the letter where she'd dropped it.

He was fast, but Delilah was faster.

"Give it to me."

"No," she said, holding it behind her as she backed away from him. "I think you should leave."

"I came for the letter and I'm not leaving without it."

"Then I hope you're prepared for a siege."

He laughed. "A siege? A rout is more like it. Now do as I say and—" He stopped abruptly, his big, hard body going still as he succeeded in trapping hers against the wall. The impatience in his gaze abruptly gave way to something else, something far more dangerous.

As dangerous, Delilah thought uneasily, as the feeling surging inside her. A feeling both urgent and unfamiliar.

He ceased grabbing for the letter. Instead he placed his palms flat on the wall on either side of her head, making escape impossible even if she'd wanted it. Shamefully, Delilah realized she didn't. She wanted something else entirely.

"Did you read it?" he asked, his deep voice sending a thrill along her spine.

"Every word. Did you mean it?"

"Every word," he said.

Happiness washed through her. She could feel his warm breath on her face and sense the waves of heat and nervous energy coming off him. *This is madness,* she told herself. *Mad and unthinkable and impossible.* At the same time she couldn't stop thinking about it, thinking that it wasn't only possible, it was real. Breathless, she ran her tongue across her bottom lip.

Christian groaned and bent his head.

She whispered once. "We can't."

"We won't."

They did.

IT WAS like the first time for Delilah in many ways.

The first time she had stood in the candlelight and allowed a man to remove her clothing . . . all her clothing.

The first time a man had lavished her with touches and kisses in tender, hidden places on her body that until now had been unknown even to her. The soft underside of her breast and her inner thighs and the hollow at the small of her back all learned the power of Christian's touch.

It was the first time a man had spoken to her in bed—words of desire, words of love, hungry, urgent, reckless words that made her pulse leap. The sound of Christian's voice, blessedly familiar and at the same time possessing a rough new urgency, lent a sense of intimacy and rightness.

This was Christian . . . kissing her, touching her, turning her in his arms and covering her with his aroused body.

Christian . . . telling her she was beautiful, so beautiful he ached, so soft and hot he couldn't wait. He couldn't wait, he murmured it against her throat and breast, over and over, even as he held his desire in check and waited for her passion to rise and meet his.

Christian . . . the only man she had ever loved, loving her . . . twisting with her amidst a tangle of sheets . . . making her weep with inconceivable pleasure at the fury of her climax and finally his own.

"OH, MY," said Delilah, still breathing heavily as Christian shifted his weight to his side. It was as eloquent a remark as she was capable of that moment.

"My sentiments exactly," he responded.

Their gazes met and quickly skittered away. They rolled to their backs at the same time.

Christian stared at the ceiling and wondered what she was thinking. Possibly the same thing he was? That what had just transpired was incredible . . . unprecedented . . . inevitable. Destiny. He'd never had much use for the word, but damned if he didn't suddenly like the sound of it.

WHAT WAS he thinking? wondered Delilah. That is, if he was able to think. She was certainly having trouble stringing her thoughts together. Every phrase, every sentence fragment that filtered through her mind, seemed to lead back to Christian. It was as if even though his body had withdrawn, his spirit filled her still. She felt bedazzled, invigorated. Terrified.

HE COULD always come straight out and ask her what she was thinking, he supposed. But Delilah was very good with words, too good. She might very well turn the question around to him and then what would he do? What would he say? No, he wouldn't ask, that much was certain.

SHE WISHED he would say something. Anything. No, not anything. The right thing. The thing she wanted most to hear, that this night felt as wonderful and as right to him as it did to her. And that if she surrendered her heart to him as she just had her body, he would treat it with the same tender care. *Say something,* she willed him.

CHRISTIAN SLANTED her a look, mesmerized by her profile in the candlelight. "I never . . ."

"Nor I," she said softly.

"That is, not often, at least . . ."

"That's what I meant."

"Of course."

"Of course."

Silence settled over them once more.

Damn, what was wrong with him? He'd felt a great many ways after lovemaking, but never at a loss for words. He was a little old to be tongue-tied around a woman.

He cleared his throat determinedly. "At least we've finally managed to solve your dilemma," he ventured, more intent on the feel of her hip pressed to his than what he was saying. "If this does not sully your reputation around the edges, nothing ever will."

"You're overlooking one little detail, aren't you? There were—thank heaven—no witnesses to our lapse into madness."

He rolled to his side and succumbed to the urge to run his lips over the curve of her shoulder. "If this is madness, lock me away forever. As for the other little detail, it's easily enough remedied."

She reached for the sheet, eyeing him warily. "What are you suggesting?"

"Nothing bizarre," he said. "Simply that we could always announce our attachment. I've been giving it some thought and it seems to me that no one in his right mind could expect you to become Remmley's wife when you are pledged to be mine."

"*Your* wife?" She gasped.

"It makes sense," he said, managing to shrug as if his entire future were not riding on her response. "I have compromised you most outrageously after all and I am willing to do the honorable thing and marry you."

"Oh, you are, are you?" She tossed off the sheet, flounced from the bed, and reached for her robe, her gaze an angry blaze. "Well, it so happens I am not *willing*. I have no intention of marrying a man simply because of a quick tumble and because he declares himself *willing*."

"What are you saying?"

"I'm saying I refuse your proposal, that's what I'm saying."

"I feel obliged to point out that I didn't actually propose."

"No, you didn't. Perhaps if you had, my answer might have been different."

"Are you saying that if I do propose you'll accept?" He reached for his breeches and fumbled his way into them. "Are you?"

Delilah folded her arms and turned away. "Oh, I don't know what I'm saying at this point."

"All right then, I'll say it. Marry me, Delilah."

She tugged on the sash of her robe with a small sob. "I can't."

Christian reeled. "Why the hell not?"

"Because . . . because you're you, damn you."

"That's not a reason. I'm the perfect man for you and you know it."

"Ha! The perfect man to ruin me, you mean, not marry me. It would never work."

"It worked fine tonight."

"Marriage is more than falling into bed together."

"I know that. I want more."

She seemed not to hear him. She paced, her hands clenching and unclenching. "I've already explained to you that I vowed never to marry again."

"Wrong. You said you vowed never to enter into a sham of a marriage again. I'm not proposing a sham. You have to know how I feel about you."

"No, I don't know, not really."

"My letter—"

She cut him off. "A ruse. You said so yourself. I don't want to hear otherwise," she cried, covering her ears with her hands. "I can't. It will only muddle matters more without changing anything." There was a note of pleading in her voice, but her jaw was set as she dropped her arms to her sides. "I can't marry you, Christian. Leave it at that, please."

"You'd rather marry Remmley?" he demanded, his fury explosive. He knew that determined tilt of her chin all too well. It filled him with both an urge to shake some sense into her and a gnawing sense of impotency.

"I won't marry Remmley," she replied. "I'll think of some way out of it. I always do." She moved to her dressing table and turned back to him holding out the green bottle tied to the silk cord. "Go on, take it. You've earned it."

"No. I haven't. Not yet." He ignored the bottle, desperation pressed like a blade against his throat. "You still need me, Delilah. Nothing has changed."

"You're wrong," she replied. "Everything has changed. *I've* changed. I'm not a little girl any longer. I know what I want from life and I know how to get it. Do you recall what you said to Roger that night at the summerhouse?"

He shook his head impatiently. "No. Whatever it was, I didn't mean a word of it."

"You said to him, 'Now we're even.' " She tossed him the bottle. "Now we're even, Blackmoor."

CHAPTER NINE

THIS WASN'T THE first time he'd stalked from Delilah's house in mortification and anger, nursing a heartfelt desire never to set eyes on the blasted woman again. That was as far as the similarity went, however.

Last time, despite the humiliating sting of her refusal, he had accepted that it was best for both of them and refused to regard it as a rejection per se. He'd escaped feeling both humbled to have been taken in by the little brat and relieved not to have blundered his way into a parson's mousetrap. In time his embarrassment had faded, leaving only a memory that was like a loose thread, an unfinished sonnet, a possibility.

No longer.

Four simple words had put an end to all that sentimental rot. *I can't marry you.*

Will not, she ought to have said. That was the truth of the matter, he thought, abandoning his bedchamber for the library, cognac bottle in hand. He drew the drapes tightly before sitting, in no mood for sunshine. He'd be willing to bet that her brother would not share her compunctions. Old Roger would be happy enough to see her wed to any reasonable prospect . . . even the Blackmoor Devil.

But she did not want to marry him. There was no possible way for him to interpret her words as anything other than pure, out-and-out rejection. *I am not going to toss my heart under your bootheel a second time,* she had said to him several nights ago. Then she had gone and trod all over his instead.

His eyes burned and it felt as if he'd been ripped with a blade from his throat to his gut. It hurt to breathe and to swallow, to sit and stand and move from one empty room to another. Hell, it hurt to live, he thought, dropping into a fireside chair and tipping the bottle to his lips. The glass had disappeared during his restless nightlong safari in search of a place in his own home where he might be free of Delilah's memory. How was it possible, he wondered gloomily, for the woman to haunt a place she'd never set foot in?

The answer, of course, was sickeningly obvious. Delilah was not stalking his home, but rather, his heart. He was in love with her. It was that simple. And that hopeless.

Groaning, he rested his head against the high chair back and closed his eyes. Through the dark web of his lashes his attention was snagged by a glitter from the mantel. Lillith's damn bottle. He'd been so self-absorbed he hadn't even bothered to look inside. Not that it mattered any longer. It was a little late for luck when the woman he loved wanted no part of him.

Still, he stood and reached for the bottle, uncurling the scrap of leather inside. The marks on it were faded and ornately scrawled and his vision at the moment could best be described as blurry. He had to squint and hold it close to the candle to make out the words.

To thine own wish be true. Do not follow the moth to the star.

"What the hell is that supposed to mean?" he muttered. A worthless purchase if ever he'd made one. He raised the cognac bottle in the air. "To Lillith, who knows a sucker when she sees one."

The scent of the fine fifty-year-old brandy made his stomach roil, a sure sign he'd had enough, he decided, putting the bottle aside and shaking his head to clear it.

To thine own wish be true. The words followed him around the room. *Do not follow the moth to the star.*

What was magical about that?

To thine own wish . . .

The only thing he wished for was Delilah, to have her love him the way he loved her. Madly. Completely. Desperately. Exactly the way she claimed she wanted to be loved.

He loved her, and he'd never even had the chance to tell her so.

But he would, he decided suddenly, and with a surprising degree of clarity and determination for a man who'd had too little sleep and too much brandy.

He could do that much, at least. He would tell her he loved her and no self-doubts, no old crone, and no silly hex were going to stop him.

THE DINING room of Delilah's townhouse was a whirlwind of noise and color, with bright streamers strung everywhere and a sign reading HAPPY 6TH BIRTHDAY, JANE hung over the sideboard. Nearby sat what remained of the cake Cook had prepared for the occasion. Neighborhood children, accompanied by their nannies, mingled with Jane's playmates from the days before she and Dare and their aunt Esmerelda had come to live there. Everyone Delilah had expected to come was there. Everyone but Blackmoor.

Not that he'd been invited, of course. It was simply another of her irrational notions to hope that in spite of their angry parting last night, he might come back. If he did, it would prove . . . what? Delilah wasn't sure, only that it would prove something very important and that it was not going to happen.

She had spurned Christian and he had retreated with all the grace of a bear with a wounded paw. No doubt by now he'd found some pretty bird of paradise to soothe his injured pride. That, she told herself, was what men like Blackmoor did. A smart woman would not care. She would put him from her mind and get on with her life.

Apparently, Delilah brooded, she was not quite as smart as she liked to think.

She was wise enough to recognize Blackmoor for the scoundrel he was, but not nearly wise enough to keep from falling in love with him. Not once, but twice. Once with a sixteen-year-old's impulsive näiveté, and now with a woman's passion and strength. And that kind of love, she discovered, was not so easily denied.

In spite of her own dismal mood, Delilah had been determined that Jane's party be a success and it appeared it was. All that remained was for Delilah to give Jane her final present and the children would spend the rest of the afternoon playing games. She might even steal a moment alone to give her poor smile a rest.

At a signal from her Dare left the room, returning shortly with a large bundle swathed in pink satin. Delilah moved aside the velvet hair ribbons and colorful toy tops Jane had been given to make room for him to stand the bundle on the table in front of his wide-eyed sister.

"Is this for me, too?" she asked softly, looking overwhelmed by the unprecedented fuss being made on her behalf.

"It certainly is," replied Delilah. "Climb up on the chair so you can untie the ribbon and see what it is."

Jane scrambled to obey, standing on her toes on the needlepoint chair seat to reach the ribbon.

"Now close your eyes," Delilah told her, "and wish for something very special."

"You wish with me," Jane urged.

Delilah laughed. "All right. I'm wishing . . . I'm wishing . . . one, two, three," she said, whipping the satin wrapping in the air with a dramatic flourish to reveal . . .

Blackmoor.

Exactly what she'd wished for. Not beneath the pink satin, but standing in the doorway, one broad shoulder propped lazily. His mouth was slanted in a familiar wry smile, but his gaze was open and warm and trained on her alone.

"A doll," Jane squealed as she finally opened her eyes. "A doll that looks like me."

"She does indeed look like you," Delilah agreed, forcing her attention back to the child. "That's how I knew the instant I saw her that she must be yours."

"She can be my sister," Jane exclaimed. "We can play together."

Delilah smiled and bent to press a kiss to the little girl's silky head. "That sounds perfect. Happy birthday, sweetheart."

"Say thank you," prompted Dare, standing by his sister's side.

"Thank you," Jane echoed. Then, with much more sincerity, she threw her arms around Delilah's neck and hugged her. "I love you, Lady Moon."

"I love you too, sweetie. Now, since all the presents have been opened, we—"

"Not quite all the presents."

The comment came from Christian as he strode across the room. "Good afternoon, Lady Moon," he said, bowing his head, before including the others in his greeting. "Good afternoon, everyone." He smiled at Jane. "Happy birthday, Jane. This is for you."

Delilah looked on in surprise as he presented Jane with the small green bottle.

"But it's not wrapped," Jane announced.

Dare elbowed her. "Jane, don't—"

"It's all right," Christian assured him with a smile. "You see it is wrapped, Jane. The bottle is the wrapping and my gift to you is inside it."

Pleased with that arrangement, Jane uncorked the bottle and withdrew the scrap of leather. Dare read the words written on it to her and she wrinkled her nose in bewilderment.

"Do you remember our conversation yesterday?" Christian asked her. When she responded with a nod, he bent and whispered in her ear so that only Jane could hear.

Whatever he said tickled the little girl's fancy, thought Delilah, observing Jane's gleeful expression.

"Truly? All six of them at once?" she asked him.

Christian straightened and nodded. "All six. If you want it enough."

"I do," Jane said. She carefully replaced the scrap of

leather in the bottle and held on to it tightly. "I'm going to put it under my pillow right away, just like you said."

"You watch, she'll lose it," Dare predicted as she ran from the room, his look of superiority unique to big brothers. "Whatever it is, she'll lose it."

Christian clapped him on the back. "Don't worry, Dare. This is something that can never be lost, no more than it can be bought or sold," he added, finding Delilah's gaze and holding it. "It can only be found, and only then if you are willing to open your eyes and look for it." He circled Jane's empty chair. "A word alone with you, Lady Moon?"

Delilah smiled.

THE BRIGHT sunroom that overlooked the back gardens was as different from the dark, quiet office as it was from the elegant drawing room. Each of the rooms represented a different aspect of Delilah and Christian loved them all, the sophisticated noblewoman, the resourceful entrepreneur, and the girl who'd picked daisies and run barefoot through the grass with him. With all the reasons she had to mistrust him, he only hoped he could convince her of that love.

He did not sit in one of the overstuffed chintz-covered chairs and she did not offer. It was obvious this was not the sort of conversation you conducted with your feet up.

"On the way here," he began, pacing back and forth among the baskets of ferns, "I thought of at least a dozen ways to say what I have to say to you. I could flatter you and try to sweep you off your feet. I could invoke the past or play the penitent lover and appeal to your soft, generous heart. Instead I'm just going to say it outright and you can deal with it as you will."

He stopped and faced her. "I love you, Delilah. I love you with every breath I take and with every fiber of my being. I don't know when it started, only that it's burning me up and that it will never, ever stop. I love you."

"I know," she said.

He drew back. "How can you know when I only realized it fully myself an hour ago?"

"I didn't say I'd known long," she confessed, a smile tugging at her lips.

"How long?"

"Since I looked up and saw you standing in the doorway."

Christian ran his fingers through his hair in exasperation. "How did that prove to you that I loved you?"

"Because you came back," she explained, her small smile becoming a beam of satisfaction. "Even after we made love and after I hurt you and sent you away. The fact that you came back proved that I wasn't merely a conquest or a whim or, worse, a chance to get revenge for that night in the summerhouse. It proved that you loved me enough to try again."

"And again and again . . . as many times as it takes until I get it right," he told her in a smoky tone, pulling her into his arms and kissing her. She kissed him back with wild, indescribable sweetness and he fell a little more in love with her.

"There is something else," he said, drawing a steadying breath. "Something I have to ask you."

"All right," she said, anticipation flaring in her green eyes. "Ask me."

"Delilah, will you please teach me to juggle?"

He felt the shock that rippled through her and suppressed the urge to laugh.

"Juggle?" she echoed.

He nodded with the utmost sincerity. "Yes. Dare told me what you said about juggling being good practice for life. I want my life to be filled with bright balls in the air . . . us, your work, my responsibilities and, eventually, a few children of our own."

"That's a lot of balls, Blackmoor."

"Not too many for four hands—and two hearts—to handle, do you think?"

"No." She shook her head. "Not too many."

"Are you willing to try?"

"Yes," she said, grinning. "Again and again and again, until we get it right."

This time she initiated the kiss, winding her arms

around his neck and tugging his head down, running her tongue over his lips and in-between. Christian's heart slammed against his ribs and the blood roared in his ears. He still had no trouble hearing the sunroom door being slammed off its hinges.

With Delilah arching against him, he lifted his head to see Roger bearing down on them. It looked, Christian observed, as if he hadn't combed his hair since the last time they met.

"Brace yourself, sweetheart," he murmured to Delilah, who had stiffened in his arms. "Afternoon, Rog."

"So, it's true," Roger shouted, his voice like thunder in the glass-walled room. "I wouldn't have believed it unless I saw it with my own eyes. I warned you once before to stay away from my sister, Blackmoor. This time you won't walk away from your obligation."

"Believe me, Roger, walking away is the last thing on my mind."

"By God, you'll marry her."

"I will. Today, if possible."

His conciliation was lost on Roger, who was shaking with anger. He turned to his sister. "And you, you'll marry this time and I won't hear anything else."

"I will," said Delilah, smiling happily.

Roger's red face puckered in confusion. "You mean you're willing to marry *him*?"

"Yes. Today, if possible."

That seemed to drain all the anger from her brother. His chest flattened and his shoulders sagged. "Well then," he muttered, looking from one of them to the other. "Well and good. All I can say is you deserve each other."

They managed to hold their laughter until Roger had stalked from the room, kicking the broken door on his way past. The way, Christian surmised, the man would dearly like to be kicking his future brother-in-law.

He took Delilah's hands in his. "I had hoped to imbue the request with a bit more romance than Roger managed, but it's done now. Did you mean it, Delilah, will you marry me?"

"Yes, Christian, I will marry you. I love you. Part of me always has. All of me always will."

Delilah felt giddy, as if it were champagne bubbling in her veins, as he claimed her mouth with a kiss that was slow and deep. At the same time she felt safer than she had in a long time, believing in Christian, and in the power of love.

When he lifted his head, she ran her hands over his chest, aware of his racing heart. She laughed softly.

"What's so funny?" he murmured, his lips in her hair.

"I was just wondering if marrying you will make me Lady Blackmoor Devil?"

"A singular title, to be sure," he responded dryly. "If it pleases you, it is yours, my love, along with everything else that is mine to give. I only know what this makes me—the luckiest man alive."

PATRICIA COUGHLIN

PATRICIA COUGHLIN is the award-winning author of over twenty-five novels. Her first historical romance, *Lord Savage,* was chosen by *Publishers Weekly* as a Notable Book of 1996 and was praised by *Romantic Times* as "an utterly engrossing, fast-paced debut historical romance by a skilled storyteller."

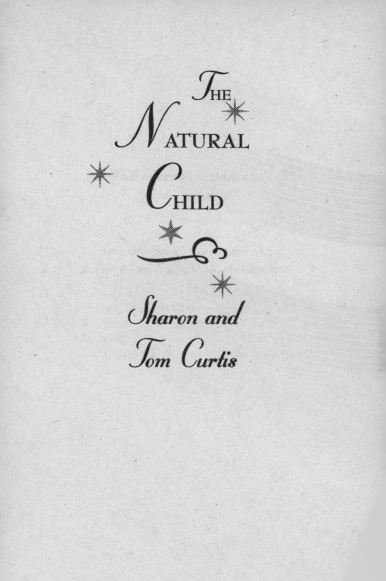

THE NATURAL CHILD

Sharon and Tom Curtis

For Kathleen Peterson Blakslee
Miss you, Mom

Let your hook be always cast;
in the pool where you least expect it,
there will be a fish.
— OVID

CHAPTER ONE

$\backsim\!\!\!\!\backsim$

London, 1818

*I*T BEGAN THE afternoon she went with the Justice Society (Or Club) to Human Bone Creek to fish and plan a kidnapping. In fact, it began while the Society members were arguing about whether or not they ought to call it a kidnapping.

As a group, they were the essence of democracy. They argued constantly.

Lucy had settled on the gently humped grass bank, propped her back against the ragged bark of a crack willow tree, and cast a baited line into the brook rilling sweetly through a cluster of warm, flat stones. When the sun's dipping angle cast a glare into her eyes, Elf had wordlessly handed her his dusty tricorne, which she pulled over her eyes. She was *this* far from falling asleep.

She had been meeting here with the others for ten years since the summer she'd turned seven when the group them had met one another at a street riot.

Just to her left, juggling seashells and oranges, Elf saying, "You can't introduce a Subsidiary Motic change the wording from 'kidnapping Lord Kend' 'taking action to bring Lord Kendal to a sense responsibilities.' Once a Principal Question has been acted on, you can't bring it up again in the same session unless you enter a Motion to Reconsider. And once you've acted on a Motion to Reconsider, you can't renew the question unless the question was amended when it was previously reconsidered."

Although George Pennington, fifth earl of Rydal (currently seated with his thin, hairy legs sunk to the knees in the muddy creek bed), was not, nor ever would be, the parliamentarian that Elf was, he said, "All right, I make a Motion to Rescind the original motion."

Charlotte regarded him with fond exasperation. "George, you can't introduce a Motion to Rescind because I've already made a Motion to Adjourn and an unamended Motion to Adjourn takes precedence over all other motions."

"Except a motion to fix the time to which to adjourn," Elf amended.

Which was not very helpful, as it turned out, because it prompted George to say, "I make a motion that when the assembly adjourns, it adjourns to meet again immediately after the time of adjournment."

In the gloomy silence that followed this pronouncement, Lucy could hear a linnet sing on a branch far above her head. Water trickled in the brook. A breeze feathered the willow catkins. A cloud moved and she felt sunlight spatter heat through the leaf dapples, warming her legs and stomach.

London, dirty, noisy London, was just beyond the park gates but it seemed mute and distant. And she thought, *I want my life to stay like this forever. There's nothing that could make me want to grow up to be a woman.* A fleeting vision of Henry Lamb's astonishing smile—never, of course, directed at her—appeared in her mind, and was swiftly, firmly banished.

Rupa, the last of their band, said, "Fast, vee motta smell eff vee goda nuf boats to add yarn." Because everyone he Society had spent years learning to understand her v accent, they knew what she had said was, in fact, we might as well see if we've got enough votes to
"

The earl gave a snort of cheerful contempt. "You know you don't have the votes to adjourn. Lucy's your swing vote and she never wants to adjourn until she catches some verminous minnow to make into fish-head soup."

An orange-scented breeze fanned Lucy's cheeks. Elf had tipped a corner of the tricorne to peer down at her. He said, "How about it, Luce? D'you want to adjourn?"

Elf had turned out to be the best-looking of them. Even with the eye patch. You wouldn't have guessed it, given the nastiness of his childhood. He had a good smile with a tease to it, clean chestnut hair worn too long for fashion, graceful features, and quick hands. He was a cheapjack's son who looked like an aristocrat while George, born into the peerage, looked like—well, like sort of a clerk.

The earl had been a narrow, blond, hawk-nosed boy and nothing about that had changed as he grew except that his hair had darkened in color and the whole package had gotten more stretched out. George had the look of a scholar and the soul of a scamp. Which, all his life, had proved handy.

Charlotte, a delicate, tidy brunette, was peering down through her spectacles at the record book of Minutes, spread open on her lap, no doubt sorting through the maze of resolutions, motions, amendments, reports, points of order, and votes produced in today's meeting.

Rupa had seized the pause to intercept one of Elf's oranges, which she was eating unpeeled. Orange juice trailed down her chin and into her handsome bodice. George was staring at this.

Charlotte looked up. "You going to vote, Luce, or lay there like a boiled kidney?"

"She's making up her mind," Elf said, "whether she'd get more satisfaction from confounding George's prediction or from curried fish soup."

Rupa said something, and Lucy no sooner figured out that it was, "If it's her pride or her fish, know you she'll want her fish. I'll put a little magic in her bait so she'll catch a fish so big it'll take four people to carry it home. Then we can adjourn," when Lucy felt a tug on her fishing rod.

She tightened her hand on it.

The rod tugged so hard it half dislocated her shoulder.

Holding tightly, her heart pounding like a war drum, she scrambled to her knees.

Before she had time to analyze what was happening, she was yanked forward, landed hard on her elbows, and lay there, winded, prone, astonished, with a tree root gouged in her ribs and a mouthful of turf. Spitting grass, she gasped, "It's a big one, all right!"

So big it required the joint effort of all five of them to subdue and land him. So big they had to haul him to her cottage slung in Rupa's shawl. The fish was longer than the shawl. The shawl was two meters long.

Seven cats followed them home and sat, yowling, outside the cottage door until Lucy's tomcat, Roger, leaped from the parlor window to claw the males, molest the females, and spray scent marker wildly across the green-painted cottage door.

CHAPTER TWO

*T*HEIR KITCHEN WAS a modest one, cluttered with baskets of onions, grain, and potatoes, shelves of preserves, the low ceiling strung with rows of dried garden herbs that made gentle tapping sounds in the window breeze. Once they'd got into the kitchen and deposited the fish on her mother's worktable, they were cramped in like nestlings, and breathless, having argued their way back to the cottage without benefit of parliamentary rules, after their hasty adjournment.

Rupa puffed out what everyone was able to translate as, "What do you think? This is marvelous! Marvelous! A magic fish! You know what we've got here?"

"A sturgeon. And a poached one at that." George had been inspecting the fish's snout and head. "This is a royal fish. If you catch it, the law is you have to turn it over to the Crown. You know, *the king shall have the wreck of the sea throughout the realm, whales and great sturgeons.*"

"The king can have whatever wrecks of the sea he wants," Lucy said. "But I couldn't drag this thing another step and I'm certainly *not* going to lug it to the palace. If the king wants some, he can come to supper. Elf, can you reach my whetstone?"

Simultaneously, Rupa was saying, "No sturgeon! No!

Magic fish!" and George was saying, "They swim from the North Sea into fresh water to breed and that's why sometimes one finds them in the Trent."

"George, Lucy didn't find this fish in the Trent. She found it in a brook! This is magic!" Rupa gingerly plucked at the tail fin. "Inside, Lucy's gonna find a magic gift, just for her!"

"Inside," Charlotte said firmly, "what she's going to find are intestines."

Inside, there was a vilely soiled glass bottle with a silver ornament.

"Holy Mother," Rupa said, "this is a spell bottle. A real spell bottle. Look at this. Lucy, you can make a wish on this! A real magic wish."

Lucy's mother, who had merely glanced up from her strawberry bed with friendly disinterest as they'd dragged an enormous fish into her kitchen, took this unfortunate moment to stick her head in the diamond-paned window. "I see the fishing was successful."

"A big success," said Rupa. "And inside there's a spell bottle that will give Lucy her one true wish."

Lucy's mother frowned. "Oh, no. No wishing. Certainly not. What we need from God, we pray for. What are wishes but desires we are too ashamed to ask of God! No good can come of a wish." Then, smiling all around, "So, who's staying for dinner?"

RUPA WASHED the bottle, studied it narrowly, and tucked it on the sash bar of the window, where it glowed brightly in the afternoon sunlight, ignored until Lucy's mother decided it would be the perfect vessel to root an ivy cutting.

Elf, put to the task of prying off the stopper, said, "Will you look at this! There's some sort of note in here."

"Let's have it out, then." George arrived quickly at his side. "A message in a bottle! It could be anything!"

Lucy's mother offered dryly, "A foot-powder advertisement, for example."

George was not easy to dampen. "It could be from a mariner. A shipwrecked mariner!"

"Yes, indeed." Charlotte didn't look up from the minutes she was recopying. "A fleet might have been dashed to shreds on the pebbles farther up the creek and its company marooned, say, in Hyde Park."

Oblivious to Charlotte, George was continuing, "Who knows where the sturgeon came from. He could have swallowed the bottle anywhere on the high seas. I once read a book about a shipwrecked sailor who used a charred stick to scratch the word *help* on a scrap of lamp shade, and set it adrift in a bottle—"

Lucy could see poor George was setting himself up for one of his grand disappointments. She tried to let him down gently. "What's the good in scratching *help* on a paper and setting it adrift? If anyone found it, how would they know *where* to help?"

"It doesn't say *help*." Elf had succeeded in prying loose the note. "It says . . . Charlotte, can I borrow some of your candle—thank you. It says . . . I think it says, 'To thine own wish be true. Do not follow the moth to the star.' "

In the moment of bewildered silence, Lucy saw her mother hiding a smirk behind her dishcloth.

Rupa appeared as entranced as George. She made a hand-sign to ward off witchery. "It's a spell cast. A *real* spell cast. This is something very ancient. Very powerful. Dangerous."

"No, no," George said. "This is a code of some kind. Obviously, it's a code. You're right, Lucy. No one who was shipwrecked would write *help* on a paper and send it out in a bottle. What would be the sense in that? What's happened is," he went on with rapidly increasing excitement, "he's put his cry for help in a code!"

Charlotte had abandoned the minutes. "Why on earth would he do that?"

"Pirates."

Lucy saw more of her mother disappear behind the dishcloth.

"Just think about it," George said. "You're lost on a desert isle. You put a note in a bottle and throw it out to sea. What then? Pirates might come on it and find you ou and you'd be worse off than before. So you do the thing in code."

"George, how can you be such a stupid?" Rupa said. "This is a spell. This is spell language. What kind of message says, 'Do not follow the moth to the star'? Moths don't go to stars."

The ensuing argument about the habits of moths lasted until Lucy's mother put them firmly from the house.

CHAPTER THREE

CRIMPED STURGEON WITH lobster sauce. Sturgeon à la St. Marcel. Sturgeon pudding. Sturgeon stewed in cream. Sturgeon with caper sauce. It was a week to remember. Every night there were friends to dine and there was still some to give away.

Lucy wished for nothing.

It wasn't until the last delicious morsel had been eaten and Roger tomcat had stolen off with the spine that Lucy recalled her mother's condemnation of wishing. Because she found herself *almost* wishing she could catch a sturgeon every week. She stopped herself just in time.

It wasn't as though she placed any faith in Rupa's belief that she'd fished up a spell bottle. Rupa frequently tried magic of one sort or another, and Charlotte had once designed a formula comparing the success outcome of Rupa's spell casting to the success outcome of pure mathematical chance. It had turned out Rupa's rate of failure was higher than pure chance would have predicted. In other words, you were more likely to come out on top from ignoring a problem than you were by going to Rupa to have it fixed.

So, did she have herself a wishing bottle?

No.

But Safe is a happier fellow than Sorry. As she had s(

many times in her life, Lucy found herself grateful for her mother's profound good sense. Lucy regarded her mother as a woman of courage, resolve, and wisdom. In short, she idolized her.

Lucy's mother, born the Honorable Miss Laura Hibbert, had suffered a Disappointment in her youth. Which meant, without benefit of metaphor, that at age twenty, she had been delivered of a child out of wedlock shortly after the death of her lover, which had occurred in the most scandalous and humiliating manner imaginable.

When anyone inquired about Laura's family, it was her habit to say they had cast her off. This was not strictly true. What had actually happened was that after announcing to her horrified parents and siblings that she was in the family way, Laura had sold off a Botticelli given to her by her grandpapa on the occasion of her confirmation, and had used the proceeds to move to London and buy the cottage in which she had raised Lucy. Because her family continued to try to ensure her well-being by offering her a wealth of unwelcome sermonettes, it was Laura herself who decided to dispense with the obligations of having to please a family with whom she had never seen eye to eye.

This had begun, for Laura, a golden age of freedom. She had introduced herself to her new neighbors by saying, "I am Miss Laura Hibbert, and I am an unwed mother. This is my blameless daughter, Lucinda. You may shun us if you choose, but it would be an Unchristian act."

She then devoted herself to her daughter, to her garden, and to the foundation of an institute to help other women in need. And, in the evenings, to small classes of students who paid her a two-penny piece a week for the privilege of attending. Hundreds of impoverished London children had learned to read, write, and do sums at her knee. Some had stayed with her for years, Elf, Charlotte, and Rupa among them.

Lucy couldn't imagine anyone having a better upbringing then hers, filled with playfellows, sensible encouragement, a sense of mission, and fishing. And now there was the kidnapping to look forward to.

She had no sense that she was being stalked by disaster.

She was pleased to note, as she stepped out on a cool Thursday dawn to walk with her mother, that there was not a thing in the world to wish for.

She strove for a state of blissful contentment. Why wish for relief from the thick morning fog? Fog shrank the city. Made pearls of the lamp globes. Shined the paving stones.

The moist clatter of unseen market wagons and the thud of trotting horses were softer and more secret.

"I'll bet we have Hyde Park to ourselves," her mother said cheerfully.

Lucy thought, *It would be nice if we had the park to ourselves, but I don't wish for it.* She was pleased she was able to make so fine a moral distinction. In fact, she realized she was so pleased with herself in general that she began to feel a little uneasy. She was just beginning to worry she might be growing smug as they turned the gates into the park.

The park was deserted.

She heard only the hushed tap of dripping leaves and the sigh of the wet grass surrendering to their passing footsteps.

When they climbed the south knoll, the fog was so thick she could barely see the newly planted geranium pots that lined the walkway. The poplars ahead were pale, stately, giant.

The world seemed to have tiptoed away and left her floating with her mother in a dense and muffled silver sea. She made a point not to think there was something magical in the vast dancing curtains of opalescent mist. She made a point not to wish they didn't have the park quite so much to themselves.

Then, amidst the haunting quiet, she heard a woman's rich, throaty laughter. Surprisingly close by.

She stopped, twisting quickly around.

Saw nothing but shivering tendrils of fog.

Her mother had stopped too, and stood still as a doe, gazing west. She whispered, "Don't look, Lucinda. What you see will disgust you."

But as though the fog had curled its soft fronds and held her, Lucy could not look away.

The mist opened like a web before a glistening coppice

of holly trees dotted with small white blossoms. Beneath the branches, a young man held a woman in his arms.

The woman was half-dressed in a wet evening gown of gold silk tulle. Sprinkled with grass thatch, fog-drenched, the gown might have tumbled from her bare shoulders if it had not been held aloft by the lady's creamy upraised arms, which clung so tightly to the young man. The lady's hair was loose, damp, dark, lovely.

Lucy did not travel in fashionable circles. She did not know the woman.

Oh, but the man.

Henry Lamb.

No one could miss that face. It was widely regarded as the most captivating in England. Henry Lamb. Enthralling, disgraced, disgraceful Henry Lamb.

Lucy had seen him only once in her life, and afterward it had taken months of serious effort to cleanse him from her thoughts. For once, two Christmases earlier, she had witnessed him engage in one of the most naïve, sweet-spirited, and careless acts of kindness she had ever seen.

It had occurred on Boxing Day, on what was surely the bleakest morn of winter, when she had gone with her mother to the St. Giles slum to help nurse a child with putrid fever. The child's fever had broken about midnight and at daybreak, he slept peacefully. Lucy's mother had fallen asleep too, sitting upright in a parlor chair.

So alone with Mrs. McGrew, the ill child's mother, gazing out through the window frost into the chilly gray of morning, Lucy had seen two begging children approach a young man. Elegant, disheveled, stop-and-stare handsome, Henry Lamb was unknown to Lucy, but not to Mrs. McGrew, who had seen him pass this way once or twice before with a group of young rakehells who came to bet at the fighting-cock dens.

Lucy had stood up from her chair, ready to grab her shawl and run outside to intervene. Young bloods slumming made it a practice to cane the begging children who were so often accomplished pickpockets.

Mrs. McGrew had called her back.

"Here, now, stay. Will you look at that? Will you just look at that?"

Henry Lamb had knelt by the children and was talking to them, emptying out his pockets to them, crumpled banknotes, gold coins, silver ones, bronze ones. Everything. His night's winnings, it seemed. And when he had emptied every pocket, he gave them his watch, the gold ring from his finger, and then popped the gilt buttons off his waistcoat to give them to the children, too. Finally, he blew their noses on his silk cravat and, laughing, tucked it into the little boy's frieze coat. And then he had walked off, his finely etched mouth carrying the slight whimsical smile she would have to work so hard to erase from her dreams.

Henry Lamb.

As famous for his amazing good looks as he was for the shame he had inflicted on his family.

And somehow, in this odd, shocked moment of coming upon him so suddenly, again at dawn, in a mist-hung park, in the obvious act of having compromised a lady, a terrible thing happened.

Lucy felt it happen. A little wish slipped out. A horrid, irrepressible, wicked little wish. Somehow—she couldn't understand how—but *somehow* she felt herself wish she might be the barely dressed lady in his arms.

She immediately imagined the wish in her mind as a fire she was trying to stomp out. Stomp that wish. Stomp it. Crush the life out of it.

But a strange tingling sensation was beginning to spread through her body. Hot prickles. Cold prickles. She felt light-headed and rather sick.

She practically ran from the park.

Her mother caught up with her near the park gates.

"Oh, poor Lucy. I'm so sorry. What a thing to have to see. And before breakfast, too. If it's any consolation, I saw they were so engaged with each other they didn't even know we were there."

Lucy found that was no consolation. None whatsoever.

CHAPTER FOUR

$\mathcal{L}$UCY SPENT THE balance of the morning violently weeding her bean garden. Chickweed and docks lay around her in ragged piles of slaughter.

Could you unwish a wish?

She alternated between unwishing and the certainty that the unwishing was as frivolous and ignorant as wishing. Superstition was a bane to humanity.

She tried to enforce the idea in her mind that there was nothing real about magical spells. For heaven's sake, stick to science. Ban the uncomfortable memory of the day Rupa had miraculously cured the Misses Hoskinses' lame pig.

Lucy had struggled to understand how Henry Lamb could have taken such hold of her thoughts on her first view of him. What had captured her? The uninhibited act of generosity or the astounding sweetness of his smile? Or merely the novelty of his undeniable good looks and blackened reputation?

There could be nothing so absurd on her part, nothing so utterly ludicrous, as to feel even a small shred of distress because she had seen him kiss a lady. Henry Lamb had no part in her life. And furthermore, if there was truth in common gossip, kissing women was the thing Mr. Lamb spent the better part of his time doing. That women *paid* him to do this.

Could anything be worse?

Sometimes she worried she had inherited her father's unsteadiness of character.

She wished the sun would come out so she could go back to Human Bone Creek and fish. And then she thought, *Have mercy, Lord, I've wished again.* What was the matter with her? What was she becoming? An addle-brained wish wisher?

She was losing her serenity. Or even her sanity.

As she shifted between the weed piles, her glance fell on her gray stone cottage, nestled in honeysuckle and jessamine and clematis that climbed to the eaves. Above the bluebells in the window box, the sash held the vexing glass bottle, now filled with a nodding runner of ivy.

"I know you're only an old bottle," she said. "You have no power whatsoever. *But* if it were to happen that by an undiscovered quirk of nature or science you have a sort of power, I want you to understand what happened this morning was not a wish. I am not interested in being in the company of any ramshackle gentlemen for—for any purpose. I know about those sorts of men from my poor mother's Disappointment. I am a contented person. I wish for nothing. My life is exactly the way I want it to remain. As is."

She felt utterly stupid. She was talking to a bottle.

A lone shaft of light sliced the heavy cloud cover and fell like a spent arrow upon her cottage window, striking the bottle with a bright glint. It was so lucent, so merry. It looked like a wink.

CHAPTER FIVE

*L*UCY WAS RELIEVED that afternoon when the weather turned to rain. No fishing today. The bottle had shown itself unable to command the elements.

At two, the Justice Society (Or Club) was meeting for the last time before the kidnapping, which was now called "the provision of an opportunity for Lord Kendal to initiate an act of compensation for his lechery."

Forced indoors by the rain, the assembly convened at George's, a rare treat. George's parents were not fond of the lot of them. George's parents had, in fact, said if they caught any members of the Justice Society *near* their home, they would have them arrested and whipped.

But, fortunately, George's parents were spending the week with George's married sister in Kent, and had left George with his grandfather and a skeleton crew of staff. Since George had sent most of the remaining servants on ˌoliday, keeping around only those he could bribe, and ˌ ce George's grandfather spent the afternoons napping, ˌ mansion became a perfectly safe meeting place.

ˌhey gathered in a snug drawing room, with walls hung ˌ e textured silk, and rosewood furnishings detailed in ˌ Rain rattled against the windowpanes but a large fire crackled in the grate, a luxury this time of year that only George was used to.

George had raided the larder of a pair of roasted woodcocks with lobster sauce, some sausages cooked with Spanish chestnuts, a substantial pigeon pie, asparagus points dressed in the French fashion, brandied cherries, apple tarts, a compote of peaches, and a bottle of burgundy. It was splendid. They could have stayed there until midnight, debating resolutions.

In the friendly hubbub before the meeting was called to order, Lucy felt a light pressure on her wrist, and turned to see Elf had taken her arm. He drew her aside to join him on a silk-upholstered settee.

"Lucy, my dear girl, what's the matter?"

Shocked that her painful unease might be visible, she blurted, "Why do you think there's something the matter?"

"Your cheeks are flushed. Your eyes look unhappy and I hardly ever see you look unhappy. And you've been tying nymph-fly lures. You always do that when you're upset."

Astonished, she said, "How did you know I was tying nymph flies?"

"Because you've left one strung to your hair ribbons. Don't close me out, Luce. What's happened?"

"Nothing. Really nothing. It's just . . ." She looked toward the fire, where Elf's ancient terrier, Mr. Frog, lay rolled over, basking with his feet in the air. "This is so ridiculous. . . . Elf, you don't think there's any chance Rupa could be right about that silly bottle, do you?"

"What bottle? The one in the sturgeon, do you mean?"

When she didn't answer, he began to laugh. "Lucy, Lucy . . . what did you do, wish for an eye in the back of your head? I'd better have a look."

When she had finished smacking his hands out of her curls, he pinched her chin affectionately and began to untangle the nymph fly from her hair.

He said, "I know what you wished, I'll bet. You wish your hair ribbons would turn to fishing lures."

By the time the meeting began, Elf had teased her o▪ her feeling of unease. She felt so much more cheerf▪ was able to enjoy the meeting and vigorously ac▪

opinion to such questions as whether Lord Kendal was to be rendered insensible by a blow to the skull or by a sleeping powder (furtively administered).

They had begun to tackle the list of demands to be made of Lord Kendal when George's grandfather ambled into the drawing room in embroidered mules and a plum-colored banyan, his hair whisped like floss under a tipsy nightcap. It was clear where George had got his hairy legs and hawk nose.

The old duke gazed crossly around, glared at George, and demanded, "Who on earth are these persons?"

It was abundantly clear they were not going to be able to pass themselves off as young men and women of fashion. George stood petrified like a waxwork, fumbling for inspiration. His grandfather was the one person capable of unnerving George.

Charlotte leaped to her feet, curtsied clumsily, and said, "If it pleases Your Grace, we have come to inquire about the position."

The duke looked bewildered. "Have we a position open?"

"Yes, sir," George said, finding his tongue. "I've been conducting . . . interviews."

"Interviews, eh?" The duke looked them over fiercely while they tried their best to appear ingratiating and submissive. His Grace observed the ink on Charlotte's nose, Elf's eye patch, and the fact that Rupa was trying to eat one of the wax apples from the table decorations. "Damnation, they're a disreputable-looking bunch." His gaze lit on the telltale scattering of wineglasses, in various stages of emptiness. He thundered, "By God, you haven't been giving them spirits, have you?"

"No, sir. Certainly not." George was fighting to achieve a lord-of-the-manor posture. "This was . . . I was . . . I had ~~l~~aid out the glasses to test them. To see how well they ~~co~~uld do, cleaning up after a—a soiree."

~~G~~eorge's grandfather had screwed up one eye to squint ~~at~~ the empty burgundy bottle. "I don't see that you had ~~to w~~aste the ninety-seven on it. I carried it back myself ~~from t~~he Continent." He seemed to warm to the recollection. Mellowing slightly, he pointed to Charlotte. "The spindly one might clean up to advantage, I suppose." When his gaze reached Lucy, he said severely, "You're not thinking of this one, I hope?"

"No, sir!"

"See that you don't. Your father's got a weakness for blue-eyed redheads. Your mother'd never have her in the house." Looking down his nose at her, he said, "Weren't thinking to come here and ensnare my grandson, were you?"

"Oh, no, sir." She tried for a cockney accent. "Oi'm a good girl, oi am."

"Humph. No better than you should be, I'll wager." He turned his attention to Elf. "And you, sir. Get yourself to a good barber next time before you go looking for a post." Then, waving vaguely in George's direction, he continued, "You might as well carry on, but stay out of my wine cellar. I'll see you at dinner." He frowned at the clutter of dirty dishes. "Which you appear to have begun already."

The shuffle of slippers faded down the hallway.

George looked at Charlotte. "You're hired. The rest of you can leave." And got a shower of pillows lobbed in his face.

They had just voted to adjourn when Charlotte pointed out the rain was over and the sun had come out.

"Look," Rupa said from the window, "there's a rainbow. It seems it's rising straight out of Human Bone Creek."

IN SPITE of the sunny weather, and in spite of a late-afternoon catch of two very fine pike, Lucy found she was able to put the glass bottle out of her thoughts. She was even able to laugh at her previous bout of nerves. Temporary delirium.

Tomorrow, they would kidnap Lord Kendal.

Lucy spent the evening designing some promising new fly patterns, reread "Observations of the Eel, and Other Fish that Want Scales; and How to Fish for Them" in her tattered copy of The Compleat Angler, said Gentle Jesu with her mother, and slept like a schoolchild.

CHAPTER SIX

IN THE MORNING, Lucy trimmed her straw hat with violets and bluebells, watching fondly as her mother ate a breakfast of bread and tea while poring over the newspaper.

"I'll be off soon, Mama. You shouldn't expect to see me till late."

"Umm-hmm" sounded from behind the paper.

"I'll be on a mission, with Elf and everyone. For Justice, you know."

"Justice. Excellent," came the absent reply.

"Do you know anything about Lord Kendal, Mama?"

"Umm? Kendal? A Whig. And a bigot." She peered around the corner of the paper and said, "It's wonderful to see you're taking a greater interest in politics," and disappeared again. "Please endeavor not to put Charlotte's father to the trouble of having to collect you from the police magistrate again. You do remember what it did to George's father's dyspepsia."

"Yes. Absolutely. He chased us across Piccadilly with a horsewhip."

"That kind of exertion can't be good for a man of his ￼e."

"No. Absolutely not. But he's out of town, you see. So there can be no objection."

"None in the world," her mother said. But Lucy noticed her tone was somewhat sardonic.

Lucy took a sip from her cooling teacup and watched the scattered tea leaves tumble over themselves like glitter in a snow globe.

She plucked another bluebell from her garden basket and studied the pedals. "Mama?"

"Umm-hmm?"

"Do you remember yesterday—"

"Despite my advancing years, I *am* able to remember yesterday, yes."

Lucy laughed and kissed her mother on the top of her head. "I was going to say, do you remember yesterday when we saw the man in the park?"

"You're spilling pollen on my toast. Yes, I remember the man in the park."

"That was Henry Lamb, you know."

"I did know. But I'd rather hoped you didn't."

Examining her hat, finding a place to add the bluebell stem, Lucy said casually, "He was attractive, I thought."

"Yes."

"Notably attractive, I thought."

"He is as handsome as hell is wicked."

"But bad, though," Lucy added. "I mean he doesn't look bad, but I hear he is bad."

"Very bad." The newspaper sagged, rustling as her mother released a hand to pick up her teacup.

"Women *pay* him?"

Without a trace of expression, her mother answered, "I'm happy to report I have no personal knowledge of his obligations in that area."

"Don't you find it interesting, Mama, that a profession that excites one to so much compassion when it is engaged in by women excites one to so much revulsion when it is engaged in by men? How did Henry Lamb come to be so bad?"

Lucy's mother readjusted the newspaper with a snap. "He was unkindly treated as a child."

"Why?"

"His mother had a liaison and in time, gave birth to a child who had clearly not been fathered by her husband. Her husband is a hard man with an unforgiving nature and he sent the baby to the country, where it was raised under extremely harsh conditions. The husband did everything in his power to make sure neither his wife nor her child had a moment's happiness until the day she died."

"But how cruel. How barbaric."

"It was. But the husband had been deeply in love with his wife and his sense of betrayal was very sharp. It must be some small comfort to Henry Lamb that his present way of life gives a maximum amount of embarrassment to the proud man who is not his father and who should have been."

Lucy waited for more, but her mother had evidently said all she had to say on the subject. It was clear she had gone back to reading the newspaper because in a moment, she turned the page.

"Mama?"

"Yes, dear."

"When I was born, thank you for not letting something like that happen to me."

Lucy's mother set down her paper, leaned forward to clasp her daughter's hand, and held it.

Just held it.

CHAPTER SEVEN

*L*AW-ABIDING CITIZENS MAY be surprised to learn that the greatest difficulty in a successful kidnapping is not the abduction. The average metropolitan resident can be plucked from the street in broad daylight in the wink of an eye. (The Justice Society acknowledged that it was a sad comment on our times. But useful, in this case.)

No, the greatest difficulty in a kidnapping lies in finding a place to stow the victim. This is especially true if the abductors still live with their parents.

Even as liberal a parent as Lucy's was not likely to let her store one Lord Kendal in the family linen cupboard.

In this case, the Society was in debt to George's grandfather, who owned a small property George discovered in the Inventory of Rents Owing ledger under the heading Properties Untenanted. The keys, neatly labeled Property #32, were discovered in the key closet. An urchin, paid five shillings a week to pass the house twice daily, reported that it was completely abandoned.

The history of Property #32 was obtained from the duke's valet, mellowed by the gift of expensive sherry. The stone-and-red-brick structure dated back more than two centuries. Conveniently barricaded with a tall sticky-bush and blackthorn shrubbery, it had been used as both dowager house and bachelor digs; and, if you could believe anything said by a drunken valet, back in the days of hair powder and skirt hoops, George's grandfather had employed it as a love nest.

Most recently, Property #32 had been pressed into service by the Crown. During the Napoleonic Wars, it had become a secret facility to hold highly sensitive political prisoners—French spies, who would have been executed if their powerful familial connections had not made it impossible to do so. Following the peace, they had been shipped home with invitations never to return. The alterations to the property necessary to make it useful as a prison had made it unattractive as a rental home, so it had not been let since.

Perfect.

At noon, Lucy met George and Charlotte at Dudley's bookshop in Pall Mall, and from there they made their way east, along the Thames.

They arrived at Property #32 and found their key ring opened nothing. This was a setback, since they planned to meet Rupa, her brothers, and Elf here with a wagonload of Lord Kendal.

After trying each key in the kitchen doorlock, George said, "Elf could have this open in a second."

Charlotte struggled with a stubbornly shut rear window. "We can't waste time. I'll take my cousin's hackney carriage and look for Elf and Rupa."

"They're shadowing Kendal. They could be anywhere."

"That makes it simple. I'll look for Kendal. When I find them, I'll bring Elf back here, and he can pick the locks if you haven't had any luck."

Charlotte left quickly.

It seemed that the house was locked up tighter than a mint. But eventually, by standing on George's shoulders, Lucy was able to pull the board off a high window, smash the glass, and wriggle inside. George tossed her up the nub of a candle.

Cleaned and inspected twice a year by the ducal staff, the house was in respectable order, smelling faintly of stale varnish, cold ash, and cedar. It was rambling, dark, and quiet, with room after empty room, and the uneven floors of a building that had settled slowly over time. The windows were barred and sealed. The interior doors, however, were of modern origin and grimly reinforced.

Only one room retained its furnishings. In a remote corner of the attic, at the end of a narrow, twisting corridor, was a small room with spotless, whitewashed walls, a feather bed with a dimity bedcover patterned with tiny violets, and a delicate basin stand and table carved in walnut to the same pattern. Two tiny circular windows let in a smear of diffused light. The room door was solid iron, the lock like the jaws of a beast.

When she let George inside by a ground-floor window, she led him back to the attic room.

"What do you think, George?" She set down the candle. "Was this a cell or wasn't it?"

George tested the feather bed. "It was a cell, all right."

"For some great lady?"

"Not as I understand it. She was a commoner but she'd made a powerful friend, if you know what I mean."

"Someone in the government?" Lucy was mindful of her mother's encouragement to show an interest in politics.

"Someone so high in the government, you have to call him Your Highness. I don't know what secret she pried out of him, but it must have been good because they kept her locked up here four years. He wouldn't let them execute her, I guess. Of course, when Grandpa's valet said all that, he was so intoxicated he was guzzling soap from his shaving mug."

"In any case, there was a key in the lock. You'd better take it, I suppose."

"All right. Let's go explore the cellars. We don't want to keep Kendal up here. It's too comfortable. He won't have enough of an inducement to give in."

They located the locked cellar door in a windowless stillroom, and it proved as inaccessible as the rest of the house. Even the key from the attic chamber was useless.

Lucy opened her tackle box and began to gouge at the lock with her pocketknife and her bodkin. George went off to map the perimeter and watch for Elf and Charlotte.

Lucy knelt on the cool kitchen tiles, the quietude broken only by the screech of her bodkin in the lock. Candlelight made a flood of bobbing shadows on the drab wall paneling. Damp, chill air crept beneath the cellar door, carrying with it a whiff of arsenic. Someone had laid down rat poison, below.

When she heard a muffled commotion from their entry window, her knees were too stiff to stand. By the time she was upright, Rupa had hurried into the room, smiling and winded.

"We've done it," she said. "We've got Kendal."

CHAPTER EIGHT

APPARENTLY, LORD KENDAL's abduction had been no amble in the park. It had taken three men to cudgel him into submission. One of Rupa's brothers had lost two teeth. The other had a cracked rib, a black eye, and a nose-bleed. Elf's right hand was broken. The three seemed to be in excellent spirits.

The cellar being still unavailable, the decision was quickly made to haul the unconscious viscount to the attic. There was consensus among his three assailants that it would be better if he was behind a locked door when he awoke.

Lucy showed Elf the cellar door while Rupa's brothers puffed their way upstairs with his lordship's deadweight. Lucy left Elf armed with the tools in her tackle box and joined the others in the attic.

She met Rupa's brothers on their way downstairs, and said good night, because they were leaving until morning. Rupa and George were standing outside the open iron doorway. They had already worked out a plan of action.

George said, "I'm going to be downstairs to see if I can lend Elf a hand. Rupa's going outside to keep watch for Charlotte. It seems they missed each other, so Charlotte'll probably show up here any minute. You keep an eye on Kendal. The first sign he shows of waking up, shout."

Alone once more in the attic gloom, she tiptoed into the whitewashed chamber, where Lord Kendal lay as they'd dumped him, facedown on the bed, covered in his greatcoat.

The chamber and hallway seemed dimmer than they had been when brightened by candlelight, and the overcast daylight from the windowlets gave the room a fragile haze. Kendal could have been a mound of clothes. Beyond, the corridor was a somber, gaping hole.

The aged house had an eerie way of swallowing sound. She could no longer hear George or Rupa and certainly not Elf. She began to wonder if they would hear her if she did shout.

Far down the corridor, she heard a faint creeping sound . . . a footfall. Quickly, she stepped to the doorway. And saw nothing. It was so quiet, you could have heard the spinnerets of a spider.

Lucy wished her nerves weren't so on edge. She shut the iron door and began to feel better.

There was no place to sit so she stood against the wall and designed lures in her head. She was relieved to see Kendal shift slightly once or twice. At least they hadn't murdered him.

She was even more relieved when she heard footsteps in the corridor and Elf call out, "Luce? I'm sorry we've been so long, but we had an accident belowstairs." He tried the door handle. "Open the door, will you?"

"What sort of accident?" She tried the door herself. "Elf, it doesn't seem to be opening."

"Oh, hell, Lucy, what possessed you to shut it? Is Kendal still out cold?"

"Yes. Elf, this won't open! George has the key, though. What accident?"

"When we got into the cellar, George fell headfirst in a cistern. I've only just got him out. He smells like a cat box. Stay put. I'll be right back with the key."

Lucy found her shaky feeling of security retreat with his running footsteps. The minute he was gone seemed like a lifetime. The clothes pile on the bed slept on.

She was grateful to hear two sets of running footsteps echo in the corridor.

"Elf? George?"

"Lucy? Are you all right? Any change in Kendal?"

"No, Elf. But could you get me out of here immediately, please?"

George's overexcited tone came through the door. "We've got a problem, Lucy. I don't have the key."

"Don't have it? What do you mean, don't have it?"

George's voice lowered, as though he'd got a *sotto voce* stage command. "Elf, she's getting hysterical. I told you she was going to get hysterical."

Elf said, "Gently, Luce. We're not going to let anything happen to you, I promise. Take a deep, slow breath. George lost the key in the cistern but I'll pick the lock. I'm working on it now, can you hear?"

"Please hurry, Elf," she encouraged shakily.

"I will. Try not to worry."

Considerable time passed. Elf said, "All right, Luce. Try the door again."

She tried. Nothing.

"Damn it to hell, Lucy." George's voice was taut with frustration. "What made you shut the damn door?"

"Damn it to hell, *George*," Elf snapped. "What made you lose the damn key? Will you stand back out of my light? And don't pace. You're making the candle flicker."

Lucy glanced fearfully at the greatcoat on the bed, which didn't seem to be quite in the same position it had been in before.

"Elf," she moaned softly. "Elf, please . . ."

"Luce, I'll get it open. I promise."

Moments slipped by. Lucy could hear distant footsteps. Then voices. Rupa. And Charlotte.

Charlotte was saying, "I can't understand where you and Elf disappeared to. When you two shadow someone, you vanish completely. I've been following Kendal all afternoon and I didn't see you once. Ugh! George, you smell like a privy. What on earth, Elf? Rupa tells me Lucy's got herself locked up in a cell?"

"She's in here." Elf spoke without interrupting his work. "With Kendal."

"No," Charlotte said. "She's not."

"Charlotte? I am," Lucy said miserably.

"No, you're not. I just left Kendal a quarter hour ago. He's at his haberdasher on Bond Street being fitted for a 'chapeau.' "

Activity outside the door ceased.

Lucy heard Rupa say, "Charlotte, you've been following the wrong man this afternoon. Because believe me, we put Lord Kendal in this room."

"I was not following the wrong man." Charlotte spoke with careful patience. "Lord Kendal was identified for me by the apprentice of his tailor, by the shop assistant in his cravat shop, and by his coachman. How did you identify Lord Kendal?"

Rupa volunteered, "We climbed the rose trellis near their bedchamber and saw him undressing Lady Kendal." Then, in a puzzled tone, "Are there two Lord Kendals?"

"No." This from George. "There's only one Lord Kendal."

Elf said, "You've known him for years, George. Did you take a look at the man we dragged up here?"

"No. I didn't think I had to. Rupa's brothers had him rolled up in his greatcoat and—"

"Elf, please—" Lucy's throat was tight. "He's moving. Open the door."

"I don't know who you've got in there," Charlotte said, "but it's *not* Lord Kendal."

"Elf, he really is moving. . . ."

"I'm sorry, Lucy. This lock is a lot more complicated than I thought. I need time. You're going to have to knock him out again."

Weakly, Lucy repeated, "Knock him out again?"

"You can do it, Lucy." This from Rupa. "Give him a good whack. Pretend he's a fish."

"Have a little sense, you two." Charlotte sounded thoroughly exasperated. "Lucy's never struck anyone on the head in her life. She won't be able to bring herself to do it. Don't tell me you didn't bother to bind him! Lucy! *Who-*

ever he is, he's going to be in a pretty ugly mood when he wakes up. You need to tie his hands. What have you got on you? Pull off your sash. Do it now."

"Charlotte," Lucy said in a helpless whisper, "he's awake."

With a sense of icy foreboding, she watched the man she had thought was Lord Kendal roll over. Pull off the greatcoat. Sit up. Rest his head on the cradle of his outspread palms.

Lucy felt the world heave under her feet.

Henry Lamb. Of course it was Henry Lamb.

Her pulse beat like a wren's wing.

She thought, *The Bottle.*

CHAPTER NINE

*H*E HAD OBVIOUSLY taken a powerful blow. Minutes passed before he was able to lift his head. He gazed blindly at the room for a time before he seemed able to take it in.

She had nothing else to do but to study him at leisure.

One remembered, instantly, that he was famous for his looks. "After God made that face," the queen once had said, "he rested for a week." It was a sculpture made by an immaculate hand, a face undoubtedly, explicitly male but beautiful in a way few men get to be after they attain manhood. It was not, however, the countenance of a choirboy. There was no describing his mouth. You saw it, you wanted it to kiss you. That was all.

His coloring was striking also, his skin pure and light-colored, his hair dark as jet, and his eyes . . . For the first time, she was able to see the color of his eyes—sea-green with dark brown circling the irises. Hold fine colored glass to the sunlight and you'd get a sense of the brightness of his eyes.

Lucy realized with despair that she was taking pleasure in looking at him.

She was acutely aware of the moment his gaze began to

focus on her. After a pause, a quizzical smile tipped the corner of his exquisite mouth.

"Hullo," he said. "Have we met?"

She answered, "No." But the obstinate lump in her throat made it a two-syllable word.

He stood up, wincing, one long, elegant hand pressed to the back of his neck. "I don't suppose you happen to have any brandy?"

"Not"—gulp—"at present."

He was rubbing his neck, his eyes shut in a brief point of agony. She tried to stop herself—but instead she felt herself longing to feel that light, sure touch against her own skin. Against her own neck. Perhaps lower, perhaps caressing her shoulders, her uncovered shoulders.

She thought, *I am really in very serious trouble here.* But she had apparently said some part of it aloud because he opened his eyes and focused again on her. Taking in, it was clear, far more than she would have wished him to.

"I'm sure," he said, "when you find yourself able, you'll explain why you're in here with me." His tone was pleasant. His undertone, however, was anything but. "Which are you, by the way, victim or perpetrator?"

"To be completely honest with you—"

When she stopped to swallow, he said, "Complete honesty. Now there's a novelty. Keep trying. I'm sure the words will find their way out eventually."

"Perpetrator."

"Well, well." He examined the room, the small windows, the fearsome iron doorway, the puddle of her on the floor, all with an alarming degree of intelligence. He indicated the door with a gesture. "I suppose it's locked?"

She nodded, watched him check the pockets of his greatcoat, consult his pocket watch, withdraw a small handful of banknotes.

"Evidently," he said, "not a robbery."

He returned the notes to his coat, dropped it on the feather bed, and approached her, studying her from a much nearer vantage. "So what have we here? I must be here at someone's behest. Let me guess—extortion?"

"Oh, no!"

"Act of vengeance? Debt collector? Stop me, darling, if I'm getting warm. Jealous husband? Good God, not my father!"

Shaking her head, holding a hand to her increasingly sick stomach, Lucy could hear that outside in the corridor, the Society had predictably, infuriatingly, called an emergency meeting.

Henry Lamb said, "Do you know what, my dear? You *really* are on the wrong side of this lock." He banged the door once, vigorously, with the side of his fist. If Elf had been faceup to the lock, it would probably have made him deaf. With every veneer of patience wiped from his voice, Lamb said, "Are you idiots ready to have a conversation?"

Lucy heard Rupa say, "He's not going to get any more wide-awake than that!"

George said, "In any case, from his accent, he's clearly a gentleman. We may brush through this with no harm done, after all." More distinctly, obviously to Henry Lamb, he spoke. "Sir, we would be most appreciative if you would be so obliging as to inform us whom we might have the honor of addressing?"

Lamb, rather carefully, replied, "Do you mean you dragged me into an alley, knocked my head half off, locked me up, and you don't even know who I am?"

George addressed the door with painful diplomacy. "Sir, my comrades and I have shown an unpardonable lack of discernment in this case that we most freely admit. Please be assured we will do everything in our power to compensate you for your inconvenience. I think I speak for—"

Diplomacy, apparently, had its limitations. Lamb interrupted. "Open the door, you twit. This is becoming more inconvenient by the minute."

Daunted, but game, George persisted. "It is our goal to oblige you in every particular, sir, however—"

"Oh, heavens, George, stuff it," Charlotte interrupted. "If that's the way you gentry talk to each other then God knows how you get a thing said." Louder, addressing the door: "Look, you inside. Here's the truth. We've kidnapped you by accident, locked you in a room with one of our friends, and lost the key down a cistern. My friend *here* has been trying to open the lock but you broke his hand and he's having a rough time of it."

Lamb digested this, his forearm resting on the door. It was obvious to Lucy he had a monstrous headache. He said, "You with the broken hand. Believe me, that is not the last bone in your body I'm going to break if you don't come back to the door and get it open."

Elf said simply, "It's a very complicated lock. You'd better give us your name so we can send someone to tell your family you've been delayed."

"There's definitely no one I want you to inform of it, but my name is Henry Lamb."

"Cousin Henry?" This from George, sounding astonished. From the amplification of his voice when he spoke again, Lucy could tell he'd approached the door. "Are you my cousin, Henry Lamb?"

"Don't tell me—George Pennington? I haven't seen you since you were in short skirts. Here I thought I was the bad seed of the family and you've fallen in with a gang of Gypsies."

"They're not a gang of Gypsies and—well, actually, some *are* Gypsies—but—my God. Henry Lamb."

"Yes. Social pariah. Expunged from the family Bible. Outcast, wastrel, and slut." Lucy could see the reunion with his kin was affording Mr. Lamb no enjoyment whatsoever. "Tell me, do you take part in abductions frequently or is this your first time?"

George sounded defensive. "What we're trying to do here is to accomplish a great deal of good."

"Are you? What do you do when you want to make mischief, burn Rome? Listen to me, George. I've got"— he struck the door—"to get out"—he struck it harder—"of this room." The final blow was so loud it set Lucy's ears ringing like sleigh bells.

Elf tried for the next quarter hour to pick the lock, to break the lock, to dismantle the lock, to pry the lock out of the door. It was useless.

George said, "I suppose we'd better have a meeting to decide what to do next."

"Yes," Charlotte rapped out. "That's just the ticket. Let's have a meeting so we can introduce a motion to send Mr. Lamb a note of apology. Let's form a committee to debate the wording of it! And in the meantime, I'd like to add to the Orders of the Day a resolution to censure George Pennington for losing the only key to this room down a storm drain!"

Henry Lamb listened to the ensuing row, one shoulder propped against the wall, and from his expression, Lucy could see the last of his patience had evaporated. His gaze fell upon her in a considering way she didn't much like, under the circumstances.

After an uncomfortable moment, he said, "Take off your hat."

"My . . . hat?"

"Yes. I'm going to kiss you. It's in the way." He pounded his fist once on the door, and got their immediate attention. "George, let me help you with your priorities. Shortly, I have to be somewhere else. This is an appointment I absolutely cannot miss. Are you taking this in? You have two hours to get me out of here. Two hours. That's all. If you don't get me out of here in two hours, I'm going to deflower this—this girl in the hat."

An alarmed outburst started behind the door.

Outrage lifted George's tone an octave. "Oh, no—you wouldn't—"

"Since clearly you know me by reputation, then you know very well I would. Why don't you explain to your felonious cronies what I'm capable of."

"Cousin Henry, if you lay so much as a finger on her, I swear I'll kill you."

Lamb said, "You're going to have to be on this side of the door for that, aren't you?"

"Sir, you were at least born a gentleman! This is an innocent girl!" George was banging on the door. "You can't possibly—"

"I can," Lamb said, "and I'm going to." Lamb's attention found its way back to Lucy. "My love, you haven't taken off your hat."

Lucy felt the world shudder to a halt on its axis. It must

have done. What else could explain the fact that she could no longer feel the floor level beneath her feet? It was terrible to search in the desolate sea of his eyes for the sweetness she had seen in him with the two street children. And find it was still there. It was a tragedy, that life had ruined this man.

She felt the cool room air tickle through her scalp as he slowly withdrew her hat and set it behind him on the table. He stood before her, so close her quick breath disturbed the white fabric of his shirt.

"This," he murmured, "is what happens to kidnappers."

Gasping and fearful, she put out a hand, to stop him or to steady herself. It landed heavily on his shirt, and she could feel him beneath the fabric, the unexpected warmth and strength of a male chest.

He took her hand in his, touched a kiss to the tip of her middle finger, and tucked her hand back against his chest. She shivered, receiving the light touch of his fingers on her skin, and shivered once more as he began an unhurried exploration of her, learning her cheekbones, the curve of her jaw and, moving lower, the line where her gown opened at her throat.

She thought, *I really, really have to stop wishing for things*. Her breath stuck around a swallow. She closed her eyes.

And felt the touch of his breath, and then, as softly, the pressure of his mouth. A touch only, and then more. A faint, questing pressure.

The soft pressure of his mouth increased, withdrew, teased. Pressed hard. Tasted.

His lips left hers and found the side of her neck, brushed her collarbone, the base of her neck. Again, her mouth . . . her mouth. More than she could ever have imagined, it was wonderful and disturbing, unfamiliar and intimate.

Beneath her palm she felt the slight quickening of his breath and became genuinely frightened.

Against his lips, she said, "I might fall down, I think."

His mouth left her and he drew her into his arms, steadying her until she felt the world reappear beneath her feet with a jolt. She opened her eyes.

Looking down at her, he just said, "Hmm."

Gently releasing her, he returned to the door, and said, "You might as well give it up, George, and try something else if you haven't made it through yet. While you've been wasting time, I've kissed your lady friend and she's fainted dead away."

"Lucy!" Charlotte called. "Is he telling the truth?"

"Well"—she made an effort to recover herself—"partly."

Lamb looked at his watch. "You now have one hour and fifty-five minutes."

Lucy heard Elf's voice. "George, stop throwing yourself at the door. You're not doing any good. Look, I've been thinking this over. There may be a way to get the key out of the cistern."

George, utterly furious, commanded through the door, "Don't you touch her again. Do you understand? This whole mess is half your fault anyway. Rupa never would have taken you for Lord Kendal if you hadn't been have-at-you with his wife to begin with."

Rupa said, "George, you idiot. Don't make him any madder than he is already."

Which Lucy was fairly sure Henry Lamb could only have heard as, "Gorge, chew eat yet. Donna mock hymn matter tin hiss oil ready."

"Rupa, take George downstairs." This from Elf. "No, George, you have to go. Rupa is absolutely right. Find rope and buckets so we can start bailing the cistern."

George was anguished. "We can't go and leave her alone with him."

"The faster we find the key," Elf said, "the faster we can get her out. For God's sake, George, get downstairs and start to work, will you? All you're doing up here is giving the man an audience. If we're not here he's much more likely to leave her alone. Charlotte, you also. I'll be right down."

"Lucy—" Charlotte sounded helpless.

Elf said, "Charlotte, just go."

Charlotte called out, "Lucy, hang on. Whatever it takes, we're going to do."

Over the swiftly retreating footsteps, Elf spoke through the door. "Sir, as angry as you are about this, don't harm her, please. You can't imagine. She really is the gentlest girl."

Henry Lamb said, "One hour and fifty-four minutes."

Elf took off at a run.

Lucy noted that Henry Lamb looked a shade less wrathful. "Finally, I think they're motivated," he said. "Don't you?"

CHAPTER TEN

FINE-BONED, SLENDER, ENGAGINGLY disheveled, Lamb stood with a shoulder hunched against the wall. A thin line of pewter light from the window traced out the breathtaking architecture of his face, the careless grace of his posture.

He was a man who owed no part of his appeal to the hand of fashion. His russet jacket was worn loosely across the breadth of his shoulders; his dove-colored buckskins were soft from long use. His riding boots, she saw, had never been solaced with a smudge of polish.

It took no more than a single uneasy glance at his face to see he was still thoroughly out of temper.

Desperately, she wondered whether he planned to do as he had said, and whether he had kissed her only to scare George.

She wondered, also, if she should put back on her hat, since it appeared hats got in the way of kisses. This, she had never realized. Was this the reason that when she left the cottage with George and Elf, her mother always said, "Don't forget your hat"?

Not able to lift her gaze higher than his buckskin kneecaps, she asked, "Do you think they'll be able to get us out of here in one hour and fifty-four minutes?"

"Not if they have to empty a cistern."

His tone was so unpromising she seized her hat from the table and thrust it over her curls. Plucking up spirit, she hotly addressed the bruised toe of his riding boot. "I want you to know I think *deflower* is an odious word. What could be more medieval? It sounds like something that would be done by a"—she cast shakily for a historical example—"by a Visigoth. I think it's entirely hypocritical for men who have no intention whatever of remaining virgins themselves to comment in a fulsome way about the virginity of women."

"You," he said dryly, "are eloquent on the subject. You should consider writing a pamphlet."

She bravely persisted. "Look at the worry you've put my friends to!"

"It grieves me." His voice dripped irony. "Your friends are so incompetent, the need to rescue you promptly is the only thing I can see that will galvanize them to do anything effective." He shouldered off the wall. She fled behind the table. "Did you not think if you participated in a kidnapping something bad might happen to you?"

"It never has before," she answered.

"*Before?* Are you saying you've actually made a habit of this?"

His tone was so incredulous she decided the question was better left unanswered. For a long, harassed pause, she stared at his shirt buttons. Then she whispered in a suffocated voice, "And if we haven't managed to open the door in one hour and fifty-four minutes, do you mean to do with me as you've threatened?"

Cool-voiced, and with extreme deliberation, he said, "You can depend on it."

Softly spoken though they were, his words seemed to bring her entire capacity for thought and action to a shuddering halt. She gripped the edge of the table with her hands and hung on for dear life. The knot in her stomach nearly bent her double.

She wanted to touch her lips, which felt as though they still carried the burn-print of his mouth.

She wondered suddenly if there was a chance Henry

Lamb's kiss had satisfied the bottle. Good God, it ought to have! She went to the door and rattled the handle. When it wouldn't give way, she shook it savagely, like Roger tomcat with a mouse in his teeth. She gave it a kick, for good measure.

Breathing hard, she stared at the door.

"You've got to admire the engineering," he said. "An ordinary door would've been in splinters by now."

She stared at her hands, at the floor. She unwished, and unwished.

She couldn't believe it. That hateful bottle.

It was actually willing to have her ravished.

Her mother was so right. Wishes were a poor counterfeit for prayer. God knows whether or not to answer a prayer. God screens out the folly.

The bottle didn't care. She had wished to be in the arms of a notorious rakehell and the bottle had arranged it, willy-nilly, without the slightest compunction. It was utterly literal. A juggernaut.

The most eerie aspect of the whole thing was that the bottle had overcome her expressed aversion to what she'd asked for by creating a situation where she could not escape her own wish. It was as if the bottle had brought her here by the scruff of the neck and said, *Here's what you've wished for. You're going to have it whether you like it or not.* The bottle's malevolence stunned her.

Henry Lamb thought his only avenue to leave this room in a timely way was to carry out his threat. And he was so right. But it was not because he had to galvanize her friends. It was because he had to appease The Bottle.

She sank to the floor and sat on the circle of her yellow chintz skirt with the heels of her hands covering her eyes. The plank floor was cold as a frozen pond.

The room was so quiet, she could hear the unsteady pattern of her breath. At length, she said, "Mr. Lamb?"

"Rest assured, I haven't gone anywhere."

"If you wouldn't consider it importune, could I ask you a personal question?"

"I consider everything you and your hooligan friends do importune. Don't let that stop you."

When she tipped up her head to meet his eyes, the cool room air hit her hot cheeks like windburn. "What will happen to you if you don't keep your appointment?"

"I'll lose a large sum of money."

"Why?"

The green eyes considered her. Then, abruptly, he said, "That floor must be colder than hades. If you'll come sit up on the bed, I'll tell you."

"I'm not ready to sit on the bed yet."

"Fair enough," he answered.

Now that she matched his gaze directly she saw something in his eyes she had missed previously. She saw in them a warm gleam of humor.

She tried again. "Why would you lose money?"

He stirred restlessly. Exhaled. "It's a long story."

"Well," she said. "I've got one hour and fifty-four minutes."

That made him laugh. Which changed him completely. All the sweetness time had not torn from him was evident in his face, as though laughter was its only repository. She felt a strange tickling sensation inside the hard lump her stomach had become, as though something had touched her there.

"I would like to know," she told him.

"Why not?" he shrugged, half smiling. "As it happens, last month, a wealthy man from Italy visited London, where he had the misfortune to meet a man who cheated him at cards." Lamb drove both hands into the pockets of his breeches, dropped a hip on the edge of the table, and sat there, swinging his foot. "In this game, the man from Italy lost a small castle he owns, near Florence. Even though the man from Italy has other houses, he is particularly fond of the little castle because his mother is buried there. He also doesn't like being cheated. So he offered me a small fortune to find proof the British man had won by cheating. It wasn't easy, I promise you."

She had previously thought her stomach had gotten about as tight as it was going to get. She'd been wrong. Dismay building in her, she said, "I can imagine it wasn't."

Still with the faint wry smile, he continued. "It took me

a month to find the proof I needed, but this evening at six the Italian man will sign over the deed to the castle to the man who cheated him and after that, my information will become worthless. Which is unfortunate because I owe a lot of money."

She felt terrible. Absolutely terrible. Because of her wish, people who were owed money would not be paid. Because of her wish, a man would lose a castle to a cheater. A castle where his mother was buried!

Miserably, she asked, "What will you do then?"

"I'll have to go after the deed." A note of asperity entered his voice. "Which will undoubtedly cause me to get my skull broken for a second time in one day." Then, "Oh, no, don't hang your head again. I'm getting tired of looking at the top of that damn hat."

She took off the hat, held it across her knees, and faced him squarely.

"That's better," he said. "Now look, I don't know how long you've been up here before I woke up, but you look to be chilled to the bone." He levered himself off the table and offered his hand. "Come and sit on the bed."

His hand was so beautiful, it could have been painted on the Sistine Chapel. She stared at it. "I think I ought to stay here so I won't be ravished."

"Much you know about it." Then firmly, "I've ravished dozens of women on the floor."

"That doesn't seem likely to me. With all the fuss you've made about how cold it is."

His eyes were alive with amusement. "Up with you. Before you grow icicles from your chemise. Don't be stupid."

" 'Don't be stupid'?" she repeated. "What sort of thing is that to say? I thought you were a famous seducer. Is that what you say to women?"

He laughed again and she felt her heart turn over and over.

"Actually, no," he admitted. "But allow me to point out you've been misled by gossip if you think I go around *seducing* people. I'm completely nonplussed by resistance."

She hugged her knees nervously. "I don't see that you're remotely nonplussed. But that you're *unaccustomed* to resistance, I do believe." His smile began to burn her, as his lips had done. "If I'm to have my resistance overcome, I want to be read sonnets."

Never once breaking contact with her eyes, he said, "I don't know any sonnets. But come to me anyway. You're tired and frightened and cold and I can make you warm and happy."

"Yes, well—" The color was flooding her face at the memory of the pressure of his mouth against her. "I've already been made 'happy' by you once and I don't know how much more 'happiness' I can bear in one day." She placed her hand hesitantly in his, allowing him to haul her to her feet. "But I suppose I'd rather be made happy than ravished."

"That's the spirit," he said encouragingly, the green eyes vivid. "Would it help if I promised not to treat you unkindly?"

"I doubt your definition of *unkindly* matches my definition of *unkindly*."

He had retained her hand, and she would have stared in fascination at the pale, long-boned fingers enclosing hers, but with his free hand he cupped her chin and brought her gaze back to his. Softly, he said, "Then teach me yours."

CHAPTER ELEVEN

$\backsim\!\!\backsim$

$\mathcal{S}$HE COULD NOT negotiate with the bottle. But perhaps she could with Henry Lamb.

"Sir? If you're quite intent on this"—and she knew he would be because that horrible bottle would somehow make sure of it—"could you engage to behave . . . I don't know how to put this . . . with finesse?"

He studied her face intently for an extended time. At length, he said gently, "My dear, I understand you're trying to convey to me something important, and something you find it difficult to express, but I'm afraid you'll have to narrow this down. I don't have a clue what you mean."

"I know there are arts. Between men and women, I mean." She could see he was keeping his expression meticulously empty, though something flickered in his eyes that was no longer humor.

"Arts," he repeated.

"Yes. I don't know what they are but I'm sure you must." She saw that his eyes had widened slightly. "Can you see what I mean?"

"No."

"To prevent the creation of a child. Can you do that? It would be wrong for you to make a child you would not love as a father. I know how such a child would feel, you understand." Then, with simple dignity, she said, "I am my mother's natural child."

She had never seen a man keep his expression so carefully washed of emotion. And yet somehow, she could see she had dealt him a body blow. His hands withdrew from her slowly; his gaze, more slowly still. Finally, she heard him exhale.

He took a step back, and gently lifted one of her curls, which slipped, glinting like holiday tinsel, between his long, pale fingers.

It seemed to her as if a long time passed before he took another breath. With a slight rueful smile that made mincemeat of her pulse, he said, "We have something in common." His smile became so gentle she felt briefly as though it had stopped her heart. "I can only explain myself by telling you that I'm not used to very young women. Yes, there are arts. And yes, I would have employed them. I apologize both for making you fear it, and for making you say it."

Enthralled as she was with gazing into his magnificent green eyes, it took her a moment to realize that he had said *would have*. Aloud, stupefied, she said, " 'Would have'?"

Mistaking her expression, he said reassuringly, "Please don't look so stricken. I know it's taken a while but I have come to my senses. You'll take no further hurt from me, I swear it."

She thought, *Oh, dear God, that bottle will keep throwing us together till Judgment Day.*

Frantically, she crossed the space he had made between them and grasped him by the lapels. "Sir," she said, "you *must* make love to me. Because I have *wished* it so."

She could see she had startled him speechless. Having left everything so much up to him before, it was difficult for her to know where to begin now. But even standing on her tiptoes, she couldn't reach his mouth, so she pulled hard on his coat, dragging him down toward her, and slid her hands up his chest and neck, into the midnight of his curls. Grabbing two thick, satiny handfuls, she tugged him by the hair down to her. She heard him say, "Jesus!" just before his mouth met hers.

Touching her mouth to his, she felt at first no response, so she tried awkwardly to imitate the kiss he'd given her earlier, light at first, then harder. She pressed slow kisses along the length of his mouth. She nuzzled him with her lips. She slid her lower lip along his.

She could feel his confusion in the taut resistance of his body, felt the resistance turn to indecision as she took one hand out of his hair and grabbed his wrist, placing it low on the small of her back. She felt him try to lift his head, to say, "No. You don't want—" She smothered his response with her mouth, twisting her hands deeper into his hair, feeling the vibrant strands work between her fingers, stroking the sides of her fingers, her palms.

She felt his mouth melt open over hers, and his warm breath quicken against the moisture on the inside of her lips. And then, because she'd wanted to so badly earlier and had not, she pressed herself against him, all of her, from her knees up to her chest, and rubbed herself lazily against him, learning for the first time the unyielding warmth of a man's chest, the flat plane of his stomach, the sinews of his thighs.

His resistance had by now evaporated. His hands closed on her back, crushing her closer, into the hot bone-cradle of his body. His mouth, urgent and nuzzling, opened hers, and his tongue slipped inside, tasting her gently, a caress tracing the inner edge of her lips. Chills moved like dancing fingers down her spine but the rest of her was fire.

It was at that moment that he put her from him, disentangling her fingers from his hair, drawing back from her body, and when she tried to stop him, whispering breathlessly, "No, no, no. No, my dear. Really."

He scooped her up in his arms and deposited her on the bed, where he pressed a single soft kiss on her lips. And giving her a smile of heart-lifting charm, he retreated from her, until he was stopped by the wall, where he propped himself, his hands braced on his knees, laughing and breathing hard.

After a moment, she said, "At least this time after you kissed me, you didn't say 'Hmm.' "

She could see it cost him to get the words out, but he

said, "I only said 'Hmm' because it surprised me you didn't seem to realize your role was to move things along by crying out to your friends for help. I wasn't thinking 'Hmm.' "

She said, "What *were* you thinking?" but unaccountably, her teeth had started to chatter, so the question came out sounding rather strange.

Nevertheless, he had understood, because as he came toward her, he said, "I was thinking I wanted to tell you your hair smelled like violets."

The intimacy of the observation shocked her. It hadn't occurred to her that her hair had a smell, or that anyone might notice what that was. She hadn't given much consideration to how she smelled. Most of the time, probably like fish bait. Was this how it was to have a lover? That he noticed things about you as if he were your mother?

When he lifted his greatcoat from the bed and began to tuck it around her shoulders, she covered her nose with his collar and inhaled. It smelled of brandy, of the outdoors, of street fog and pine trees and, faintly, of him.

Looking up into his face, she said, "Could you try to open the door once again, please?"

Quizzical but unquestioning, he went to the door and tried to rattle it open. Nothing.

That bottle. What on earth could it expect?

Lamb was watching her, assessing her in that way he had. After a moment he said, "In the company you keep, I can't imagine how you've remained so untried. George never tried to kiss you? Or that handsome boy who broke a wristbone on my jaw?"

She studied him right back. "Never. Probably, it was because of my hat."

On the way back to the bed, he swept up the hat from where it had fallen, looked it over, and tossed it onto the table. "It's the only thing I can think of to explain it."

He sat at the base of the bed and began to untie the lash in her sandal.

"What are you doing?"

"I'm going to warm up your feet. Try not to let it worry you." He drew off her sandal and dropped it on the floor.

"It doesn't worry me at all. I've been raised with a lot of freedom." His touch, even in this simple chore, was making her light-headed.

Working on the other sandal, he said, "Yes. I can see you're the fruit of a progressive parent." He tossed the other sandal off the side of the bed, and then gently began to rub her stocking-covered feet, starting with her toes. "No one has suppressed the high spirits that move you to make your way around London locking up strangers." While he spoke, he separated each toe, massaging them one at a time. "See where this freedom has gotten you. Not in an enviable position."

"Absolutely I'm not. No one could envy the position I'm in right now."

He glanced up quickly, in time to catch her bashful grin, his gaze lingering on her mouth. She said, "I'll bet my feet don't smell like violets."

"Actually, they do."

She was about to tell him she'd been picking violets that morning in her stockings when she heard running footsteps in the corridor.

Then Charlotte called out anxiously, "Lucy, my poor dear, are you all right? What's happening to you?"

Lucy replied, "He's warming my—" and got Henry Lamb's hand clapped over her mouth.

"Warming?" Charlotte asked.

"She said *warning*," Lamb answered. "I'm warning her of the terrible things that will happen to her if you don't release me in time."

Charlotte said ferociously, "I want you to stop that at once! Tormenting her won't get you out of there any faster. And things are well underway downstairs. It turned out there was no need to waste time draining the cistern. We've discovered that by turning a wheel in the side wall, a hatch opens and dumps all the water out through the grate at the bottom."

Henry Lamb said, "For God's sake then climb down and retrieve the key."

Charlotte responded, "There's been one small problem with that. When we opened the hatch, the key dropped through the grate along with the water." She hastily interrupted Henry Lamb's uncomplimentary rejoinder. "There's no need here for profanity, sir! Every contingency has been planned for." With triumph in her voice, she announced, "Elf has gone home for the ferrets and Mr. Frog." Finally, with menace, "But know, sir, if you continue to terrorize Lucy, we will deal with you later!"

Removing his palm from her mouth as Charlotte's footsteps quickly retreated, Lamb placed a light kiss there.

"How in the world," he said, "did you become mixed up with these bandits anyway?"

She watched him sit down again and draw her feet onto his lap. "We have a Society (Or Club) together."

"A society or club?"

Misunderstanding his expression, she explained, "Rupa thinks the word *club* sounds elitist. But George says if we call ourselves a *society,* we sound like dilettantes. So our name is a compromise." She remembered his earlier question. "We met at a hanging ten years ago."

His hands had gone still on her feet.

She tried to explain. "I hadn't really *gone* to the hanging, as such. I spied the crowd from afar when I was out with my mother comforting prostitutes."

After a moment, he said, "Words fail me. . . ."

She tried again. "It was a large crowd. A very large crowd. My mother said, 'Why don't we go and see what that's about?' and once we got there, she said, 'Now that we're here, we might as well stay.' There were a great many ladies there for her to offer aid to and she planned to take me home before the prison carts arrived. Rupa was there with her brothers and aunt selling cures for warts and bladder troubles. She's a Gypsy girl, you know."

"My cousin George must have been what? Five?"

"Eight."

"He was the most protected whelp on the face of the planet. I can't believe his parents let him attend a hanging."

"No, you're right. He'd bribed a nurserymaid to take him. And Elf—you know, whose hand you broke—was there to pick pockets."

His thumbs were moving warmly over her stockings,

slowly opening the space between each toe. "Did he lose his eye to one of your previous victims?"

"No, that happened long ago. He was the youngest of ten children and when he was four, his mother sold him to a chimney sweep, who starved him to keep him small, and drove him naked up narrow, burning chimneys by holding a torch to his feet. Once a hot brick exploded and blinded his eye. After that he ran away and joined a gang of boy thieves. Oh, and Charlotte—from the hallway just now?— She was there because her father was the hangman."

Since once again she appeared to have deprived Henry Lamb of speech, she continued, "Before the hangings began, a riot broke out in the crowd and I was separated from my mother. I crawled under one of the waiting hearse wagons to cry and found Rupa was hiding there already. The others joined us one by one, because we were all small enough to fit. When it was over, the others saw me home safe, because I am the youngest. That's when we formed our Society (Or Club). We protect children, you see." Then, "We protect natural children."

She found herself hefted, greatcoat, stocking feet, and all, onto Henry Lamb's lap. Embracing her gently, his breath tickling her eyelashes, he said, "My darling girl, don't tell me that's why you were trying to kidnap Lord Kendal? Because he's fathered a child out of wedlock?"

"He has. With a dustman's daughter. And he's refusing to provide for the little baby." Earnestly, she added, "We *only* kidnap as the last resort."

He brushed the backs of his fingers along the curve of her cheek. "Promise me you'll give up any idea of pursuing Lord Kendal. You have no idea what you're getting yourself into. He's a very powerful man, and a vindictive one, too. Believe me, I know this from experience. You and your friends will be in way over your heads."

The tenderness in his voice made her eyes sparkle. "Our motto is 'We risk all.' "

With some asperity, he said, "Then you ought to change it to 'We can't do a thing right.' "

She tilted up her head, caught the softness of his exhalation on her smile. "Not one thing?" she inquired, resting her mouth, barely touching, against his.

On a quickly indrawn breath, he conceded, "Maybe one." Taking her shoulders, he drew her gently backward until he could see her eyes. "I am serious about Kendal. You're really going to have to let it alone."

She rested her elbows on his shoulders. The sleeves of his greatcoat were a good half-foot longer than her arms and they dripped off her hands, tapping him lightly on the back. She put herself eye to eye with him. "Does this mean you've decided to join our Society?"

"No, it does not." He kissed the tip of her nose. "Who the devil are Mr. Frog and the Ferrets? Or is that something else I'm going to wish shortly I didn't know."

She answered readily, "Mr. Frog is Elf's terrier. And the ferrets—well, they're two small weasels."

"I know what ferrets are."

"They love to explore tunnels, and they catch rats. Actually, I don't know that they catch any but they scare them out of their dens and when they do that, Mr. Frog—the terrier—kills and eats them. Elf used to be a ratcatcher. It was the profession my mother got him into to get him out of thievery. That was quite a while ago. Now he's at Lincoln's Inn and he pleads law in the Chancery."

"Are you telling me the boy with the eye patch is a *barrister*?"

"He was called to the bar last month. It's come in handy for us already."

"I'll just bet it has."

She decided to pick at his neckcloth, which was falling loose anyway, and shook down the enveloping sleeve of his greatcoat. "What you perhaps don't understand is that ferrets love shiny objects. They'll run off with Elf's keys in a flash if he doesn't watch them every minute."

Henry Lamb's dark-lashed eyes closed for a brief, pained instant. "So in their effort to free us, your friends intend to send down the cistern a pair of key-stealing weasels?"

Tugging at his neckcloth, studying the beauty of his mouth, she resolved herself to get on with pleasing the bottle. "It doesn't matter what they do downstairs. They could take a cannon and blow it off at the door, and it wouldn't open. It just"—she kissed him bashfully— "won't"—she kissed him again—"open." Abandoning the neckcloth, she wrapped her arms around his neck and applied her mouth fully to his.

His strong arms responded immediately, hauling her close. An unsettling discomfort grew in her chest, a feeling of weakness, of frustration. She tried to find relief by twisting herself against him and pushing herself up into his kiss.

She could feel his smile form against her mouth. He said, "I no longer give a damn if it opens or not."

"Then why did you say, 'No, no, no,' and stop me at first when I kissed you?"

Warm and relaxed, his palms were smoothing back the feathering of curls that had strayed onto her cheeks. "It was so unexpected, I was losing my control."

Turning her face slightly, she was able to drag her mouth along the underside of his wrist. "What's wrong with that?"

"If I have no control," he murmured, between the slow, light kisses he pressed along the line of her hair, "you won't get any finesse." He bent his head to touch one light kiss on either side of her smiling mouth. "And it's not good for things to happen quickly if you're not accustomed."

"Why not?"

"Because when you're not experienced"—his mouth moved softly, nuzzling the underside of her chin—"it takes longer for your body to—"

She could tell he was searching for a word. She prompted, "To—?"

Tilting her head with his palms, he traced the side of her throat with his mouth. In time, he murmured, "To find completion. No matter how ready you think you feel, it still takes your body a while."

"I don't know what completion is, but I don't give a fig about it."

"If we keep on like this"—he passed his face over her hair—"trust me, you will."

"What's completion?"

His mouth returned to hers, pressing, searching, opening. "Did your progressive parent who gives you all the freedom never discuss this with you?"

"Not so much." Her voice was beginning to sound odd to her, as though it belonged to someone else. "She's guarded about this kind of th-thing." Her breath shifted momentarily as his palm massaged a deeply responsive nerve path on the nape of her neck. "Having s-suffered a Disappointment in her youth."

She felt her lips part under the altering pressure of his kiss, felt his hand cup her head and drop her slightly backward, preparing her for the penetration of his tongue. Gathering up loose handfuls of his coat and shirt beneath in her hands, she clung to him as his tongue stroked her inside, and his hands, knowing and gentle, moved her languorously against his mouth, against his body.

It continued forever. Forever.

It continued until her shyness and shock over the intimacy had faded and a heart-pounding wonder had taken its place. Until each subtle alteration of his kiss made her breath catch, and the tightness in her chest was close to pain. Until she could feel the regular cadence of his breath alter as hers had and feel, against her cheek, the heat that has risen in his.

The ache in her body became so intense she whimpered and lifted herself harder into him. When he raised his head to look down at her, she said, "My chest."

He said, "I know."

"It aches, inside me."

"I know."

"Can you make it feel better?"

He had been slowly caressing her cheek with the side of his thumb. His hand became still. She could see on his lower lip the faint sheen of moisture she knew had come from her mouth.

His hand left her cheek and slowly separated the folds of the greatcoat where it covered her chest. His eyes were hot and vivid, and brighter than Welsh poppies. He said, "If I make it feel better, it will ache worse. Do you want that?"

When she nodded, he laid his hand very lightly on her breastbone, barely touching her, a large, warm, alarming presence.

He said, "Are you sure?"

"I *wish* you to," she said.

CHAPTER TWELVE

*H*IS HAND STAYED as it was, accustoming her. From time to time, he placed a light kiss on her brow, her hair, on the curve of her cheekbone. When at last his hand moved, it was to smooth over her shoulder under the greatcoat, and then travel lazily down the side of her body, from nearly underneath her arm to her waist, to her hip and then back upward. Where his hand passed, her skin prickled.

Her stomach felt like warm lead and he explored her there too but more lightly, with the back of his fingers, following the line of her ribs, and then, as a sharp little respiration escaped her, the curve of his hand rubbed lightly against the place on her chest just under her breasts.

As the tips of his fingers discovered the outer swell of her breast, he drew her close. The clever fingers left her chest and touched her face, a brief, reassuring gesture.

He softly kissed her, nudging open her mouth. She responded by kissing him back hard, her mouth hasty and clumsy against his and this time it was his breath that became quick and uneven. Driving her lips farther apart, his kiss deepened and his whole palm found and covered her breast, and lightly pressed.

The burst of sensation inside her was so intense, it drew

from her throat a shaken moan. And as his hand made a soft nest to enclose her and tighten over her, she moaned again.

Shivering, drifting, with her body melting into the stroke of his fingers, when his mouth left hers briefly, she still remembered to ask again, huskily, "What's completion?"

"About the opposite"—he kissed her chin—"of having a Disappointment in your youth." His hand abandoned her breast to lift a strand of damp hair from her cheek. Then returned to encircle her breast. "When you're inexperienced, it's not so difficult to feel stirred. It's getting relief from it that's more complicated. At first, your body doesn't know quite what to do."

Tightening her grasp of his coat, she pulled herself upward until her mouth was touching his ear. With the dark silk of his hair tickling her nose and her lips, she whispered, "Show me. *Show me.*"

Far down the corridor, she became aware suddenly of the percussion of running footsteps. She thought, *Bottle, if you've arranged a rescue right at this instant, I'll smash you to dust.*

To Lamb, she gasped out, "That's Charlotte, I think. That's the way she runs."

He had lifted his head to listen. When he started to remove his hand from her breast, she held it there fiercely.

He laughed, though he said, "If she's brought up a key, you'll be sorry." His hand slid to her hip, where it remained, absently stroking her through her gown.

Charlotte's thoroughly winded voice came through the door. "Those stairs are fatal! Lucy, are you all right?"

When he saw Lucy was still unable to compose herself to answer, he said, "No. She's being ravished even as we speak." But he made his voice sound sarcastic and bored. "Why don't you worry less about what's going on with us and more about what you've got to accomplish downstairs?"

Charlotte wheezed enthusiastically, "You can't imagine the time we've had! When George climbed down a rope into the cistern with the first ferret, it didn't bring up the key, but it sure did chase out the rats. I'll bet they could hear George scream all the way to Parliament. Mr. Frog must've killed dozens!"

Lamb said ominously, "You haven't mentioned the second ferret."

Charlotte's tone became faintly apologetic. "Well, the second one brought up the key and he's carried it off."

Lamb said, "As anyone could have predicted."

Charlotte was stung. "Don't you take that ironic tone with me, sir! Not after all the effort we're extending on your behalf, including my having to run up and down these hellish stairs until I'm ready to drop."

"I'm moved when I think of the help you've been to me today."

Charlotte came right back at him. "I don't see that *you've* produced any brilliant ideas. All you've had to add is to sit up here threatening Lucy in what I consider a most unoriginal and even dastardly manner and getting George so upset that his judgment is even more impaired than usual."

"Oh, dear," Lucy said. "What's happened?"

Charlotte answered, "You'll hardly believe this but George's grandpapa has shown up! He found the keys missing and thought something was afoot so what must he do but come tearing over here in his carriage. George tried to convince him that we'd come to set up another test of us as servants, but his grandfather's having none of it. *He* thinks George has come here to try to set up a—well, an assignation house where George can tryst with his mistress."

Lucy was stunned. "George has a *mistress*?"

Charlotte said fondly, "Honestly, Lucy. You never could follow a story. Of course, George doesn't have a mistress—that is, he may, for all I know. It's not like he'd make free on the subject to either of us! That's not the point."

Lamb interrupted in a honeyed tone. "Charlotte, would you be so good as to tell me where George's grandfather is at this moment?"

Charlotte asked with real curiosity, "If George is your cousin, is George's grandfather yours also?"

"Yes."

"That's awkward. Because George thought his grandfather might have an extra set of keys so George told him you were upstairs—"

Lamb interrupted again. "Did he use my name?"

Charlotte answered, "I'm afraid, sir, that he did. He told his grandfather you'd locked yourself in a chamber where you were attempting to dishonor a maiden. When George's grandfather rushed to the carriage for his blunderbuss—"

"His *what*?"

"—George realized he'd made a mistake so while George's grandfather was in the garden pouring shot into the gun, Elf went outside and convinced him you'd escaped. So George's grandfather has taken off to try to track you down at your lodgings."

Sweetly, Lamb said, "I'm so obliged to George for his endeavors. In fact, please tell him for me that as soon as I get out of here, I'm going to—"

Charlotte was laughing now. "Oh, he knows, he knows. He says as soon as we catch the ferret and put our hands on the key, we have to give him a ten-minute head start before we let you out." Then, "Lucy, I'm off to help search out the ferret. It's Elf's belief Lamb won't be able to bring himself to do you any harm. Is Elf right, do you think?"

And Lucy, her cheek tucked warmly into the curve of Henry Lamb's throat, said, "Yes."

As soon as she was alone again with Lamb, she said, "Do you know your grandfather?"

"I've never met him, if that's what you mean. My father hid me from my relatives when I was a child because he was busy pretending to them I was a hawk-nosed blond. Since I've left home—well, you know who I am."

"Yes," she said. "I know who you are."

She saw again in her mind the bleak winter morning, the snow-covered pavement, the young man emptying his pockets to a pair of ragged children.

Her hand found his cheek, as her lips, lifting, found his mouth. She kissed him long and deeply, and, in time, his hands rose and twisted in her hair, guiding her mouth. And she pulled at one of the hands entwined in her curls and dragged it back urgently to her breast, and sighed as his hand closed over her there.

She said, "You've got me in this terrible condition. Don't leave me this way."

With tender amusement, he told her, "Honesty compels me to admit that if we stop what we're doing, you'll find yourself returning to normal."

"I don't think so," she said. "I think if we stop doing this I'll ignite like a firework."

Her hand, discovering his chest, moved lower, and he gasped, "Oh Lucy, Lucy . . ."

"You know my name."

"Yes. Since people have been shouting it at me all afternoon coupled with the command to unhand you." He inhaled sharply, catching her wrist. "Darling, no. Not now. Not here. I'll give you ease but you can't touch me that way." He kissed her fingers. "Remember you don't want me to behave like a Vandal."

She laughed. "A Visigoth. Oh, yes, please *do* give me ease."

"I will, darling. Just please first kiss me, again." His voice, finally, had become as shaky as hers. "You're so very sweet. I—" His words halted as his mouth took hers in a long kiss.

After it, she said, "You—?"

"I adore you," he said, hazily. "I really adore you. Lucy, are you certain you want to experience this? Be certain. Be very certain."

"Stop fussing, Lamb. Accept your fate."

"I can't undo this, if it happens. You need to—Oh, *Sweet*heart—" He closed his eyes as her hand touched open a shirt button and slid inside, stroking his chest. "I need to be sure you understand—"

She interrupted him desperately. "For God's sake, Lamb, yes, please."

This time when he laughed, it made him breathless. "I'm sorry. It's just hard for me to believe"—he stopped to gasp—"that you trust me. I'll help you feel better, Lucy. Truly I will."

Pressing her dry, swollen lips, her feverish cheek against

his ear, she whispered, "I'm getting more achy. Not just in my chest."

His hand had moved under the greatcoat he had wrapped around her, under her skirt and her linen petticoat.

More softly, her lips hardly moving, she whispered, "Do you know where I'm achy?"

"Yes."

She gasped. "When you touch me under my—my skirt, it feels so . . ."

"Do you like it?"

"Yes. Oh yes."

Stroking her thighs through her stockings, he murmured, "This will be more intimate."

"Just do-o-o it, Lamb," she ordered with sweet, husky determination.

"I will. I promise, I will. Love, can we move you a little—"

His gentle, experienced hands shifted her on his lap, made her face him, and then, soothing her with soft kisses, drew apart her knees until they enclosed his body.

He paused to cup her face in his hands, to lightly kiss her mouth. Again, she felt his hand search under her skirts, this time higher.

He murmured, "What do you have underneath all of this?"

"Nothing." Then, shyly, "But do you not mean to undress?"

His smile curved against her cheek. "Most emphatically I don't."

She felt his hands move upward from the tops of her stockings, felt his fingers discover her bare skin, his palm warm the curve of her hip.

Ever so tenderly, he said, "What we need to do is to bring the achy part of you closer to the achy part of me." His hands were under her, on her bare skin, guiding her forward until the low hot ache of her body came into hard open contact with him. She gasped so hard she hiccuped. She dropped her burning face against his chest.

His breath lightly stirred the curls at her temple. He said, "Is it all right, Lucy?"

"Yes," she breathed. His lips were tracing the outer curl of her ear. "Just for a moment I felt a little bit . . . a little bit sick."

His mouth lingered on the pulse of her throat, on the curve of her jaw, on her nape. Softly, "That happens sometimes. It goes away."

His fingers slipped beneath the garter on her thigh and drew it slowly downward until it rested just below her knee. And, as slowly, his other hand lowered her other garter.

His mouth found hers again and filled her with deep, lazy kisses while he rolled down her stockings. Under the greatcoat, she was naked against him, bare hot tingling skin against the cool roughness of his buckskins.

Swallowing air, she whispered, "Lamb, I don't think—" Then she couldn't remember what she didn't think because his grip altered under her gown, his strong hands sliding upward on her naked back to give her support while he kissed her bare throat, and then, over her gown, kissed the tip of her breast. And gently wet her there with his tongue.

One hand left her thigh and came around to cup her, and he drew the peak of her breast into his mouth, damp gown and all, and gave her the long delicious caress of his tongue.

Her breath caught hard in her throat.

His thumb replaced his mouth on the heavy delicate ache he had created as he took her mouth in a deep, plundering kiss. She felt his hand glide back beneath her skirt and caress her bare thigh, and slide underneath her, cupping her bottom, dragging her into tight contact with his body, guiding her against him until she was shivering, light-headed, opened to his kiss, his touch, the hypnotic whisper-soft pleasure words he said to her.

In time, she heard him say, "Your trust . . . it's just so sweet. . . . It does something to me inside."

She clung to him, clung hard and whispered, "Do something to me inside, Lamb." And his mouth came back to her, no longer gentle, kisses like long, turbulent, fiery dreams.

Without breaking the contact of his mouth, he rolled her backward onto the bed, until she lay briefly under the startling warmth and weight of his body. And then he lifted himself away from her. She felt his fingers stroke her belly, her inner thighs, then, with terrible gratitude felt his touch where she burned for it to come.

She dragged free her mouth, and said, shudderingly, "Lamb? . . . Now what?"

"Your body will figure this out." He nuzzled her cheek with his face. "I promise it will."

The complex and knowing stroke of his fingers drove her into a new world. In time, nothing looked real above her.

She clung to him so hard she tore off his shirt buttons. She kissed him so hard she cut her lips on her teeth. She pushed herself against his hand until finally she felt on fire there, and in her breasts and in her swollen mouth and she heard herself whisper, "Lamb, please, help me, help me."

Then he said, "Lucy, my poor love," and slipped a long careful finger gently inside her.

And at last, she learned what he meant by completion. It felt more or less like galloping on horseback and getting hit in the gut by a tree limb.

She thought, *This is better than fishing.*

When she could—which wasn't soon—she gazed up into his breathtaking green eyes and whispered, "Thank you."

His beautiful mouth turned upward at the corners in a smile. He said, "Pshaw. It was nothing." And collapsed laughing.

She laughed too, although the effort almost made her swoon, so it was difficult to prop herself up on her elbows when she heard a faint scritching sound by the floor-boards. Sitting woozily, she stared at a tiny mousehole in the baseboard, invisible to her until that moment. And saw Elf's small brown dappled ferret peek his nose through the aperture with something gleaming between his teeth. The little weasel trundled toward her, humpity-backed, and with a small clink dropped the room key in front of the iron door.

The bottle, she'd learned, was reliable as a Swiss clock-work.

As the ferret disappeared back down the mousehole, she retrieved Henry Lamb's pocket watch from his greatcoat pocket, where it had been digging into her kidney, and handed it to him. He was taking, she could see, quite a while to recover himself. Which made her wonder if the completion had been a little one-sided.

She could see he was forbearing comment on the ferret.

His gaze stayed fixed to her while she picked up the key and unlocked and hauled open the iron door.

She said, "You need to hurry."

As he considered her, his smile faded and a slight frown entered his eyes. He said, "Lucy, if I provide for that child, will you give up your plan to interfere with Lord Kendal?"

She pulled off his greatcoat. "I suppose I could bring it up for a vote."

"God forbid," he said. He left the bed and relieved her of the heavy coat. He placed a final tender kiss on her lips, still so thrillingly raw from the heat of his passion.

She said, "Are you going off to find your Italian?"

"Yes," he said, smiling. "And to learn sonnets."

ANOTHER GROUP of young people might have been daunted by the events of the day. The Justice Society merely assured themselves of Lucy's safety, cooed over her briefly, and then traipsed off with untarnished enthusiasm to kidnap the real Lord Kendal.

Henry Lamb, it seemed, had in no way exaggerated Kendal's malice. Even Elf could hardly remember a time when he'd heard a man use *that* kind of language around girls. Everyone was glad Rupa had thought to borrow a pair of shackles from Charlotte's father to truss Kendal up in.

The Society had their hands full dealing with Kendal until George's grandfather returned from his abortive hunt for Henry Lamb. Charlotte was acknowledged by all to be just about brilliant when she had the idea to tell the old duke that George had been mistaken. It had been Lord Kendal attempting to try a maiden, not Henry Lamb.

George's grandfather kicked Kendal into the cistern.

Elf sent the ferrets into the ratholes, which again abundantly disgorged their vigorous, scabrous specimens.

When they pulled Kendal back up, he was white as a shroud.

He signed every document Elf set in front of him.

CHAPTER THIRTEEN

SEVERAL DAYS LATER, Laura Hibbert was seated at her desk inside the modest office from which she ran her charities.

She had let the same space since her arrival in London, and it had changed little over time. When women needed her, she wanted them to know where to come.

The sign, of course, had caused her considerable expense. At first, in her naïveté, she had had it painted to read REFUGE FOR LADIES OF FALLEN VIRTUE. An unfortunate choice, for it had caused to gather on her doorway a retinue of hopeful young loiterers who had to be shooed off daily. Changing the name to THE SOCIETY OF REPENTANT LADIES improved nothing, and altering it to THE HOMELY LADIES' CLUB fooled no one.

She had settled finally on THE SOCIETY OF LADIES IN SEARCH OF POLITICAL DISCOURSE, which scared off most of the dawdlers, and when she finally had the inspiration to insert the word *stern* before the words *political discourse,* she was able to rout the last of them. The only disadvantage lingering from the name was that from time to time some deluded gentlewoman would stop by and Laura would be compelled to discourse sternly with her for an hour or two about tariffs or the latest Privy Council committee report.

This late in the afternoon, she expected no more visitors, so Laura spent a moment with herself, contemplating her daughter.

Lucinda had seemed unlike herself for several days. And she had tied over seventy nymph flies. To a mother, these were worrying signs. To top it off, this morning, Lucy had suddenly asked her, "Mama, is it complicated too for a man to find completion in an act of love?"

"Heavens, no, Lucy," she'd responded. "A man can find completion fondling a grapefruit."

Laura had just decided that if George had been engaging Lucy in an improper conversation, she was going to box his ears, when she heard a strong knock on her street door.

She opened it quickly, expecting some late-day emergency, and was astonished instead to find herself looking up into the startling green eyes of Henry Lamb. The most gorgeous piece of man-flesh in the kingdom.

Up close, she saw he was considerably younger than she'd imagined. Surely he was no more than a year or two older than Elf. He must have been busy, building the reputation he had by his age.

The only thing that occurred to her was that he must have gotten himself lost in this unfashionable quarter of town and was seeking directions out.

He said, "I know this won't come as welcome news to you but I've fallen in love with your daughter."

It would have been stating the case too mildly to say she was stunned. She couldn't imagine where her chaste daughter had even managed to meet Lamb, who was surely one of London's more exotic creatures.

Answering her unspoken question, he said, "I became acquainted with her when that nasty band of cubs she calls her friends kidnapped me by accident."

All she could think of to say was, "How careless of them." The discussion she would have with the nasty cubs was another matter entirely.

She stared at him for a full minute before she found herself able to continue with, "Well, come in, then, and let's see what's to be done with you."

She could see the wait had stripped his nerves to the fiber, and that moderated not at all the inquisition she put him to. It was one no man who was not profoundly in love with Lucy would have tolerated. She grilled him for two hours, even on subjects that made his cheeks burn with color.

She said, finally, "You're remarkably easy to embarrass for a man of your stamp. I somehow expected you to be more artful."

She saw him wince at the word. "I have no arts. I did what people asked me to."

She said, "What *women* asked you to."

He met her eyes steadily, but, she observed, with effort. At length, he said, "Yes."

"And what is it you find in my innocent child that you did not in those women before her?"

He answered her simply. "Joy."

It was Lucy's most lovable trait, her joy in life. And this damaged man had soul enough to recognize it immediately.

Laura studied him, clear-eyed.

Although he would tell her little about his time with Lucy beyond the fact that he had lost his heart to her, he had borne her questioning with a palpable stoicism that exposed to her how inured he was from childhood to hostile treatment.

She had expected to find him conceited about his appearance, and it took her aback that he was not. She decided it might be because his looks had cost him the love of both parents.

He had a sense of humor, which was a necessity for anyone in long-term contact with her daughter.

She found him dishonored but not dishonorable.

She said, "What would you be willing to do to win her? Would you be willing to work for your bread like an honest man?"

"I would."

After a moment's contemplation, she said, "I've heard

you can train a horse to do just about anything." She paused. "I'm thinking racehorses."

For the first time, then, she saw his full smile. He said, "Thank God for that. I thought it might be two weasels and a terrier."

And she understood then why women had paid him. That smile alone was worth ten golden guineas.

CHAPTER FOURTEEN

*T*HREE MONTHS LATER, George and Elf spent the evening following Lucy's wedding getting pleasantly drunk over a fine bottle of port at Elf's lodging house.

George had propped himself against a chipped and dusty stone mantel, which, like the rest of the small flat, was cluttered with the paper debris of a checkered legal career. George shook his head as he replenished his glass. "I can't believe the cod's head I made of myself the day we kidnapped him, worrying he was going to rape her. The man dotes on her. He wouldn't have hurt a hair on her head. *You,* I noticed, were remarkably cool about the whole thing."

Elf was tipped back in his chair, his bootheel resting on the scarred table. He shrugged. "He has a reputation, true, but never for meanness. And Lucy has a way of wrapping every man she meets around her little finger. I thought either that would happen or she'd start talking about fishing. There's not a man alive who could maintain his arousal when she starts talking about bait and tied flies and how you can tell he-eels from she-eels."

"God, no," George said. "Although you should have seen Henry Lamb last week in the evening when Lucy was reading to him from *The Compleat Angler*. I swear to

God, you would have thought it came from the quill of Eros. Did you finish your study of the family papers I got you?"

"Yes. And you're right. The estate is entailed. In time, Henry Lamb will inherit his father's fortune. His father's tried to break the entail many times without success."

George took a long pull from his glass. "Is Lamb aware of how rich he's going to be?"

"He hasn't a clue. He's kind of a naïf in some ways. Charlotte's been through his accounts and she says he's hopeless with money. He's always giving it away."

"To whom?" George said curiously.

"God knows. To whoever asks for it. He says, by the way, he won't accept your grandfather's offer to settle what's left of his debts."

"Bother about that. Grandfather's taken rather a shine to him. We'll figure some way around Lamb's pride. We have to protect Lucy, after all."

"We'll need to be subtle." Elf said. "Henry Lamb has a mind of his own and he won't take to our running his life. It's not as if he's too fond of us already."

"Yes." George grinned. "I'd say calling us the imps from hell doesn't indicate any particular fondness. I hear he's still mad as fire that we took Lucy along to kidnap Kendal after he had specifically said he thought it was too dangerous."

Elf lifted his left boot from the floor, and crossed it comfortably over the other at the ankle. "Laura says we'll have to be patient with him. Think on it. He was raised thinking life was a place you could barely tolerate and then he meets Lucy and the sun comes out. It'll be a while before he believes he deserves any happiness." He tipped back his head and shook his long hair back off his shoulders.

"Here's to happiness." George lifted his glass. He pulled away from the cold hearth and stepped carefully over the spot where the ferrets and Mr. Frog were curled asleep in Elf's court wig. You got more than you bargained for if you disturbed Frog once he'd decided to go down for the night. He clunked the bottle back on the table. "Speaking of happiness, do you and Rupa still . . ." He waved his hand vaguely.

"From time to time," Elf admitted.

After a pause, George said, "Did you ever think about it with Lucy?"

"Oh, God, am I dead? Only about twice a day my whole life. Why? Have you?"

George hooked an arm through a chair top and dragged it to the table. "Yes. I mean her eyes—and that hair like a sunset." He straddled the chair, facing his best friend.

Elf said, "Ever do anything about it?"

"You can't be serious. I'm terrified of her mother. Why?" Incredulously, he said, "Did you?"

"Once, I almost did. When I was sixteen." Elf closed his eyes. "I was sitting watching her fish and she had her mouth—you know the thoughtful way she has—"

"Damned if I don't." George folded his crossed arms on the chair rail. "It looks like a cherry you want to suck."

"Precisely. So I thought, *Oh hell, why not? I've loved her for years. It's not as if I would do her any harm beyond stealing a kiss.* So I draped my arm around her shoulders—at which point, if she'd been Charlotte, she would have guessed what I was up to and would have been possessing herself of a sharp stick—but Lucy just smiled up at me trustingly."

"Christ, you ought to have been ashamed, the way that girl idolizes you."

"I was, a little. But I was also in the grip of a profound sixteen-year-old's lust. So I said, 'Lucy, dear, what are you thinking over so seriously?' And she said, 'With the weather as it is, I'm thinking whether I ought to switch to live bait. Have you any thoughts on it? I could use dung worms, or maggots, or dew worms, or flag worms. But maybe if I want salmon, I ought to try lob worm?' And then damned if she doesn't pull an assortment of worms out of her pocket—mind you, her skirt pocket—and thrust a handful of them embedded in moss into my face and say, 'What's your opinion?' "

George screwed up his face. "Ah, Gawd! I hate how she

does that! It's like a bucket of cold water. What? You're smiling. What else?"

"When I got up," Elf said, "I had one of her fly hooks dug about an inch into the right flank of my buttock."

The revelation interrupted George taking a large gulp of port. Unable to laugh and swallow at the same time, he spat half and inhaled the rest.

Getting to his feet to thump his friend companionably on the back, Elf toasted the air with his glass. "Here's to Henry Lamb, who'll spend a lifetime pulling fishhooks out of his rump."

CHAPTER FIFTEEN

AFTER THEIR WEDDING, Henry Lamb took Lucy to the Lake District and there in a country inn covered with rose vines, he lay with her on herb-scented sheets and kissed and loved every inch of her, and brought her to pleasure again and again and again. And when he had caressed her to peacefulness, and gently bathed her hot sweaty body, he lay down again at her side and said, "How do you like matrimony so far?"

"I feel as though I've been to the stars and back," she murmured, gazing into the warmth in his eyes. "But what can I do for you?"

"All you ever have to do for me," he said, "is smile."

And so she did.

CHAPTER SIXTEEN

*T*HE SECOND SHE returned from the Lake District, Lucy was determined to be rid of The Bottle.

Her mother found Lucy in the garden with her new husband, shoveling out a hole so deep only her dirty, determined face showed above the edge.

"Lucy," Laura said, "What on earth—"

Lamb, looking unconsciously picturesque, as always, was watching Lucy with soft eyes from where he reclined on the grass on his elbow. Smiling up at his mother-in-law, he explained. "She says she wants to bury this bottle." He indicated it calmly with his hand. "She won't say why except that it's dangerous. She won't let me touch it. She won't let me help her dig." Henry Lamb lifted a moss-filled bucket at his elbow. "My job is merely to superintend the grubs she digs out of the ground."

Laura shook her head. "She was always a whimsical girl."

Rupa, Charlotte, George, and Elf, with Mr. Frog trotting at his heels, arrived at that moment, typically two hours early for the dinner to which they'd been invited.

Elf said, cheerfully, "Hullo, Lamb." Then, "Why, Lucy, that's a great big hole in the ground."

With a raised eyebrow, Lucy's mother pointed to the glinting glass bottle. "She's burying that bottle."

"Why?" George asked. "Is it dead?"

Charlotte said, "Maybe she's growing a bottle tree."

But Rupa looked wise and mysterious. She said, "It's a good thing to bury that bottle. It's *very* dangerous. You can *wish* on it."

Lucy's mother, amused, picked up the bottle, turned it over once in her hand, and said, "Then I wish we might learn in every detail what Lucy has so against it."

Lucy looked aghast at her mother, at the beloved friends of her childhood, at her smiling, handsome husband. At the bottle.

And wryly said, "Oops."

SHARON AND TOM CURTIS

SHARON AND TOM CURTIS reside in Wisconsin, where they share their home with a very elderly miniature dachsund. LaVyrle Spencer describes their talent as "immense," while Sandra Brown says they have "a rare knack for converting the mundane into magic."

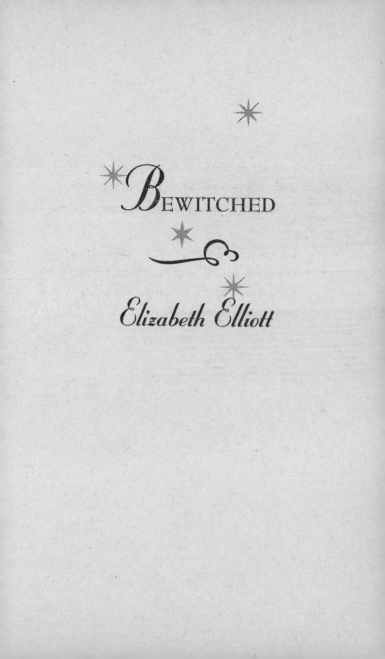

BEWITCHED

Elizabeth Elliott

Rough winds do shake the darling buds of May.
And Summer's lease hath all too short a date . . .

—WILLIAM SHAKESPEARE, SONNETS

To Shauna, a true master of the editor's craft.
Best wishes for all your future endeavors!
With much appreciation for the past,

—ELIZABETH

CHAPTER ONE

Blackburn House, 1820

D O TRY TO smile, dear." Lady Evelyn patted her
dark curls to make sure they were in place, then glanced
over her shoulder to take in the sullen countenance of her
son. "This is a party, after all, and not a funeral."

James Drake, Lord Wyatt, followed Lady Evelyn onto
the balcony that overlooked the long gallery at Blackburn
House, then turned to press a hidden lever. A section of
the bookcases slid closed behind him with a quiet hiss. The
sound was lost amidst the music of a string quartet and
dozens of voices that arose from the cavernous room below them. They stood high above the crowd, even above
the room's massive chandeliers, all but hidden in the secluded shadows of the balcony.

Wyatt moved forward and braced his hands against the
smooth, warm wood of the balcony's railing, a man holding fast to what was his in the face of a mob that had over-
run it. The long gallery stretched out before him, its
burgundy-colored walls covered by gilt-framed paintings
that made the crowd gathered within those walls look like
colorful birds in a gilded cage. Most were female, their
high-pitched chatter punctuated by an occasional shriek of

laughter. "I find it difficult to smile when I specifically asked that you not hold the house party this year. Imagine my surprise when the engraver's bill arrived yesterday morning."

"This party is an annual tradition," she argued. "If you had heard my plans beforehand, I knew you would have put a stop to them."

"Of course I would have stopped it," Wyatt said. "Your annual tradition set me back a thousand pounds last year. There are at least fifty people down there, and I would lay odds that each brought a maid, or manservant, as well as their coachmen and carriage horses. The bill to feed this small army will eat up the household budget for the entire year. The only reason I am here now is to make certain this does not turn into an extended holiday, as it did last year." He braced himself for an argument, resolved to stand firm. "My first step will be to lock the wine cellar. A lack of fine spirits tends to encourage early departures."

"Shame on you, Wyatt. These are my dearest friends, not a group of petty scavengers." One delicate hand fluttered toward the crowd. "This party is also an investment in your future."

Wyatt was instantly on his guard. "What are you scheming this time, Mother?"

"Scheming?" She looked insulted, but the glint of humor in her dark eyes remained. "A mother's interest in her only child's welfare should not be called scheming."

"Do not tell me you have found another one." Wyatt took a step backward. "Not another potential bride."

"You make the poor girls sound like stray cats."

Wyatt thought through the odd assortment of heiresses his mother had paraded past him over the last few years and nodded. "They tend to share a certain forlorn quality."

"Nonsense. You are too fussy. If you are so convinced that a wealthy bride would ease your worries, then why do you find something lacking in every girl I introduce you to?"

"I am discriminating enough to want a wife who doesn't make me cringe when I look at her. Then there is my unreasonable preference for a woman with more intelligence than my horse." He gave her a dark glance from beneath his brows. "I could afford a wife with a few pleasing qualities beyond wealth if you would only learn to economize."

The glint of humor in Lady Evelyn's eyes disappeared. "I will not live like a pauper, Wyatt. You may do your best to convince me that we are poor as church mice, but I know better. Just as I know why you are so determined to keep building your fortune. At some point you must spend a bit of your precious money and enjoy life. I daresay you could afford any wife you pleased, but this constant fretting about a financial disaster clouds your judgment."

"My judgment is based on experience," he reminded her. "The family fortune has nearly recovered from the disaster that befell my father, but a bad investment, or poor crops, or any number of misfortunes, could see us in dire straits once more. A wife with a large dowry will be my final insurance against catastrophe."

A troubled look shadowed Lady Evelyn's face for an instant, then disappeared beneath a bright smile. "Then you may thank me, because this time I have found you the perfect bride. Her name is Caroline Carstairs, a widow just a few months out of mourning. She is a sweet, country-bred girl, but she is well-accustomed to running a house as large as Blackburn. Her parents married her off to a wealthy Irish lord who was old enough to be her grandfather. He bequeathed his young bride an income of ten thousand per year on his passing."

Wyatt's eyes widened over the staggering sum, then quickly narrowed. "She must sport a mustache if none of the bucks in London have snatched her up."

Lady Evelyn rolled her eyes. "If you bothered to attend any parties in London, you would know that the gentlemen find her quite pleasing. Most consider her a great beauty."

"There are men who would consider a goat a great beauty if she came with an income of ten thousand."

"You are too jaded, Wyatt."

"I am realistic." He glanced at the crowd. "Where is she?"

Lady Evelyn looked out over the gallery and nodded toward one corner. "She is standing next to Mrs. Newel."

Wyatt followed the direction of his mother's gaze and spied elderly Mrs. Newel at the far end of the gallery. Two young women stood nearby. The one draped in an ice-blue gown caught his attention first, with her inky black hair and dark, almond-shaped eyes. Her lips were curved into the self-assured smile of a woman who knew she was beautiful. The girl next to her wore a simple apple-green frock, her plain features a sharp contrast to the exotic-looking woman in blue. Her ordinary brown hair was drawn into an unembellished coil, and wispy curls framed an equally ordinary face. Still, there was something graceful and unaffected about her that charmed him. Surely this was the shy, country-bred Mrs. Carstairs.

His mood improved considerably.

As he studied his potential bride, a shrill laugh from Mrs. Newell made the girl's eyes narrow into a wince that lasted the duration of the grating sound, eyes such a pale shade of blue that he could tell their color even from this distance. They widened again when Mrs. Newel plunged into a conversation accompanied by theatrical gestures with her hands. He dismissed Mrs. Newel, but he couldn't dismiss the young widow.

She was not a striking beauty by any means, yet Wyatt found himself struck by her just the same. He could not recall the last time he had glimpsed such an expressive face. Her features reflected her every emotion and he found himself guessing at her thoughts. The shy smile was a reaction to some bit of flattery that made her feel awkward and embarrassed. Although he couldn't hear her murmured response, he felt certain her voice would be soft and perhaps a little husky.

Her smile faltered, then returned again, as if she had trouble keeping it in place. She was trying her best to pretend that she enjoyed this party, but he would wager any amount of money that she could not wait to escape it. The look in her eyes reminded him of a cornered deer. He had an irrational urge to swoop down and rescue her from the chattering women, to lead her through the glass doors that opened onto the gardens and take her far away from this crowd.

She seemed the type who would like the gardens, the intimate solitude of hidden paths and promenades. He pictured them there together, how her skin would glow like priceless pearls in the moonlight. He imagined how her smile would change from one of pretense to one of gratitude. But he wanted much more than a smile. He wanted to kiss her.

As he imagined that kiss, his gaze swept over her figure and he tried to picture what she would look like beneath the filmy gown. The modest décolletage did little to enhance her small breasts, and her billowy skirts gave the impression of a sturdy frame beneath them. While he studied the unremarkable shape of her body, he became aware of a most remarkable response in his own.

He wanted her. All of her. Smiles, kisses, caresses . . . long, sensual caresses that would turn into long, smooth strokes of their hands and bodies when they made love.

As if he had spoken the lurid thoughts aloud, she turned her head and looked up at him. Her wide-eyed expression made him believe she could read his mind. Even that wasn't enough to make him recall his manners and look away from her. In his mind he pulled her hair free of its simple anchoring and let the soft mass tumble over her shoulders. His hands untied the tiny ribbons on her bodice to expose more of her lovely breasts until he imagined a glimpse of dark coral.

A strange feeling came over him, a sense of recognition so deep that he felt as if he had known her all his life. He knew exactly what she would feel like in his arms, what she would taste like when he kissed her.

He had never laid eyes upon her before tonight.

His mother's cool voice intruded on his thoughts. "Wyatt, do stop staring."

Filling that request proved more difficult than he anticipated. Every time he tried to look away from the woman in green, he was racked by an irrational fear that she might disappear, that he would lose her somehow.

"You are making Miss Burke blush," Lady Evelyn added, "and it is rude to ignore me when I am speaking to you."

His head pivoted stiffly to meet his mother's gaze. "Miss Burke?"

"The woman in green. The one you were staring at." She looked suddenly nervous. "You are not acquainted with Miss Burke?"

"No." He knew a keen moment of disappointment, but all was not lost. His mother was right about his requirements for a bride. He would appreciate a woman with an income of ten thousand, but it was hardly a necessity. The alluring Miss Burke made him think that a dowry was not that important after all. "Who is she, and why is she here?"

"She is my guest, of course. When I first met Miss Burke, I thought she might be somewhat . . . unusual, but she is the most delightful person imaginable. She has the most amazing talent that makes her popular at every gathering, even though she might be a little quiet at times, but I find her unaffected manner quite refreshing." She paused long enough to search his face, as if she were afraid of what she might find. "You are certain you haven't heard of her?"

"I haven't been about in society of late," he said, "and I am certain I have never met her. Just what sort of 'amazing talent' does she possess?"

Lady Evelyn's gaze became evasive. "I know you don't believe in this sort of thing, but Miss Burke is something of a fortune-teller. She can tell the history of an object by simply holding it in her hand. Just this afternoon she did a reading of Lady Horsham's silver combs. She told exactly where Lady Horsham purchased the combs, and even described the clerk who sold them to her."

"You can't be serious."

"Lady Horsham confirmed the story," she assured him. "Isn't it remarkable?"

"Remarkable, indeed, that you were taken in by such nonsense. I realize that fortune-tellers are part of society's latest craze for the occult, but I never suspected *you* would be duped by such charlatans." Wyatt lifted one brow. "Remind me to lock away the silver as well until this Burke woman leaves the premises."

The sarcasm masked his disappointment. There would be no courtship to while away his time at Blackburn. The lack of a handsome dowry might be overlooked, but fortune-telling? That crossed the line of acceptability by leaps and bounds.

"Miss Burke is no thief," Lady Evelyn said at last. She drew herself up to her full height, but still had to tilt her head back to look up at her son. "She is a respectable young woman from a respectable family. As for her psychic talents, I hardly think you are in a position to judge whether or not she is genuine when you have yet to witness one of her readings. I happen to believe she is completely sincere."

"She is sincere about fleecing you," Wyatt argued. "How much money did she demand to entertain your guests at this party?"

"Miss Burke is a lady, and ladies do not charge wages. She does readings simply to appease people's curiosity. Many insist that she keep the objects she reads for them, but she would never consider payment for her services."

"So she confiscated Lady Horsham's combs instead?" Wyatt asked. "If I know Lady Horsham, those combs are worth at least twenty pounds. Forgive my skepticism, but that sounds like a tidy profit for a few minutes' work."

"You misjudge her," Lady Evelyn insisted. "The duchess of Remmington started that particular custom when Miss Burke read one of her emerald brooches. When the duchess learned that the pin came to her by way of a beheading in the French Terror, she insisted that Miss Burke keep the brooch as a gift, or donate the piece to some worthy charity."

"I will assume that Miss Burke considers herself a worthy charity." Wyatt fought down an almost overwhelming urge to look at the woman in green again. He could scarce reconcile the image of innocent allure in his mind with the charlatan his mother described. He had heard that those involved with the occult sometimes had a mesmerizing effect on people. Perhaps that was the reason for his mother's sudden loss of her good senses, and the odd effect Miss

Burke had on his own. "If she is from such a respectable family, why haven't they put a stop to her exhibitionism?"

"Her parents are deceased. Other than a younger brother, she is quite alone in the world."

He watched his mother toy with her fan, a nervous habit that he recognized immediately. "What aren't you telling me?"

"Nothing," she said, much too quickly. "Would you like to meet Miss Burke? I'm certain you will find her charming."

"Who were her parents?"

"Oh, dear." Lady Evelyn's smile dissolved. "You will not like the answer. I cannot emphasize strongly enough that Miss Burke is in no way responsible for the actions of her father. Why, she was just a girl when that unfortunate business took place between Baron Rothwell and your own dear father."

It took Wyatt a moment to absorb the news. Then he felt as if he had taken a blow to the stomach. "She is Rothwell's daughter?"

Lady Evelyn retreated a step and slowly nodded.

"Baron Rothwell nearly ruined this family, and now you are telling me that you have invited his daughter into our home?"

"Well, yes," she stammered, "although I feel certain Miss Burke is unaware that Edward lost most of our fortune to her father. If you will recall, Baron Rothwell won and lost a great many fortunes in his time. It seems unlikely that he would tell tales of his gambling exploits to his young daughter."

Wyatt made a conscious effort to unclench his jaw. "Is that supposed to comfort me?"

"No, of course not. I simply wanted to reassure you that Miss Burke is nothing like her father. And *your* father knew the risks when he sat down to play cards with Baron Rothwell. Everyone knew the baron's reputation for playing deep and playing well. Edward never blamed Rothwell, as you do, and it would be wrong to shift your blame to his daughter."

"I want her gone."

"I want her to stay." Lady Evelyn's tone suddenly changed. All traces of patience and cajolery disappeared. "I will not insult Miss Burke by asking her to leave. She is a sensitive girl and that would hurt her terribly. You do not have to like her, but I want your promise that you will treat her with the same common courtesy you would show any of my other guests."

"You ask too much, Mother. It is obvious that the apple did not fall far from the tree. One charlatan begat another." Wyatt knew he had made a mistake when he saw the flash of fire in his mother's eyes. Insulting her new-found friend would not sway her opinion. He tried logic instead. "You say that I must attend one of Miss Burke's readings to judge her fairly, and I am inclined to agree."

Lady Evelyn brightened. "I knew you would see reason."

"As it happens, I recently came into possession of an object that would be ideal for one of her readings. The circumstances that led to my ownership are unusual enough that they couldn't be guessed with any accuracy."

"I will ask Miss Burke if your reading can be the first tomorrow afternoon."

"The reading must be tonight," he said, "and I would prefer that the reading be private. There is another who knows how I came to possess this object. Although there is little possibility that Miss Burke will hear the story, it is a possibility all the same. The reading would have to take place tonight for me to be certain there was no prior knowledge."

"Very well," she agreed, "but why a private reading?"

"Consider it a common courtesy." His lips quirked upward in a humorless smile. "I would spare Miss Burke the embarrassment of airing my skepticism before the other guests. There is also the fact that I want to be certain no one coaches her. Even you."

"Me? How could I possibly coach Miss Burke?"

"Some people can tell a great deal from the expression of others. You are very good at reading my expressions, yet you are not very good at disguising your own. Miss Burke would know if her guesses were close to the truth by simply looking at your face."

"I suppose you are right," she mused. "If a private reading will set your mind at ease, then so be it. When she passes your test, you will set aside your animosity toward Miss Burke?"

"Yes," he said, "but if she fails, I will ask her to leave Blackburn. Politely, of course."

Lady Evelyn appeared satisfied. "I have little doubt that Miss Burke will soon convert you into a firm believer."

Wyatt said nothing. He didn't have to. The look on his face was clear. *Do not hold your breath.*

CHAPTER TWO

$\mathscr{A}$ND THEN WE found this key." Mrs. Newel's eyes glowed like dark jet buttons beneath her mop of snowy curls. She held up a brass key that dangled from a slender ribbon. "There are scads of caves in the cliffs near the abbey, and Mr. Newel thinks this key might belong to a smuggler's treasure chest. We have no idea who placed the key in the desk's hidden compartment, but Mr. Newel does have several theories."

Faro Burke smiled politely as Mrs. Newel expounded upon her husband's theories. It took a conscious effort to appear interested in the talkative woman's story. Mrs. Newel was a very cheerful, friendly lady, but she somehow managed to talk about everything and nothing at all. Caroline Carstairs stood next to the older lady, looking ready to pounce into the conversation again at the next opportunity. As far as Faro could tell, the only person who liked to talk more than Mrs. Newel was Mrs. Carstairs, and the young widow liked nothing more than to talk about herself. Faro scanned the gallery for Lady Evelyn. As soon as their hostess made an appearance, she intended to plead a headache and retire to her room for the night. Given much more of her present company, the excuse would be true.

"Tell me you will do a reading of this key, Miss Burke."
Mrs. Newel reached out to place her hand on Faro's arm.

Faro heard the small crack of static electricity even as
Mrs. Newel snatched her hand away.

"Oh, dear! I haven't received a shock like that since last
winter. The carpets must be very dry here by the fireplace." Mrs. Newel lifted her chin and her nose twitched
as if she might sneeze. "How very strange. The house itself
still feels damp from all the rain we've had of late."

"I believe it has something to do with these woolen carpets," Faro said. She gathered the skirts of her gown and
looked at the floor. "What a beautiful rug. Do you think it
is an Aubusson?"

"I believe so." Mrs. Newel gave the rug a dismissive
shrug, then dangled the key toward Faro again. "Say you
will do a reading for me, Miss Burke. I will not be able to
sleep another night without knowing its secrets."

"She did eight readings this afternoon," Caroline cut in,
casting a smile at Faro that did nothing to disguise the bite
of acid in her tone. "We mustn't exhaust poor Miss Burke
by asking her to do too many readings in one day. Perhaps
now would be a good time to give my recital."

Unfortunately, Caroline was the only one who remained
oblivious to her lack of musical talent. She played and
sang to audiences that winced and flinched at the mere
mention of a Caroline Carstairs recital. Mrs. Newel looked
at Faro with eyes that silently pleaded for a rescue.

"I would not wish you to lose any sleep," Faro told
Mrs. Newel. She removed one of her gloves, then held out
her bared hand. "I would be happy to do the reading."

Common objects had little effect on Faro and she could
usually control the visions, images that appeared as if they
were faded memories from her past. The key looked harmless enough, but looks could be deceiving.

Mrs. Newel dropped the key into her palm and Faro
breathed a silent sigh of relief. The warm metal tingled
against her skin, but just a small tingle that traveled up her
arm until the image of a library began to take shape in her
mind. She closed her eyes and saw images from long ago.

"This key belonged to your husband's grandfather,"

Faro said when she opened her eyes again. It seemed that only a moment had passed since the vision started, but then she noticed the empty glass of punch in Caroline's hand, which had been full when Mrs. Newel handed her the key. She dismissed the oddity and continued to relate what she saw in the vision. "He smoked a pipe on occasion, a habit his wife strongly discouraged."

An odd frisson of awareness distracted Faro and she found her gaze drawn to the balcony, toward a man she hadn't noticed before. Their eyes met and he stared back at her for what seemed an eternity. At last his gaze moved lower. She could almost feel him touching her wherever he looked.

No man had ever stared at her so boldly, deliberately and insolently undressing her with his eyes. She should be shocked. Deeply insulted. The only thing she felt deeply was a blush that heated her cheeks. Despite her embarrassment, she couldn't seem to look away from him.

Although his dark hair and clothing blended too well with the shadows to make out many of his features, a narrow shaft of light from one of the chandeliers slanted across his face to reveal eyes the color of molten gold. The image reminded her of a painting she once saw of a moonlit jungle, and almost hidden amidst the lush setting, a deadly Bengal tiger. The eyes that gazed out from the painted jungle's depths had gleamed with lethal, predatory intelligence. The man who stared at her from the balcony looked no less dangerous. A deep shudder of some unknown emotion passed through her. Fear, she supposed.

"The key has something to do with pipes?"

Faro stared at Mrs. Newel until the meaning of the question penetrated her muddled senses. She handed the key back to its owner. "Yes, the key fits a box that was tucked behind several books in the library, the works of Mr. Shakespeare, I believe. If the box is still in your library, you will find a pipe and pouch of tobacco inside."

The spark of excitement in Mrs. Newel's eyes disappeared. "We had so hoped for smugglers. Newel will be quite crushed when he hears—" She raised her quizzing glass and turned her head. "I don't believe it!"

Faro was accustomed to skepticism, but Mrs. Newel's remark startled her. "The key opens nothing more mysterious than a tobacco box, I assure you."

"Oh, I believe what you say about the key, Miss Burke. You mistook my meaning." She nodded toward the far end of the room. "It is the sight of Lord Wyatt that I find unbelievable. I did not think Lady Evelyn's son would attend tonight. Everyone knows that Wyatt does not care for parties."

Caroline raised her own quizzing glasses. "Is he the dark-haired gentleman on the staircase?"

Mrs. Newel nodded.

Faro's gaze moved across the room and she watched Lady Evelyn and her son descend the staircase that led from the balcony. Both were tall with dark brown hair, Lady Evelyn's touched with silver at her temples. There was no mistaking the relationship between the two. Only their eyes lacked any similarity. Lady Evelyn's were deep blue and wide-set. Her son's were . . . mesmerizing. She would never forget his eyes, but she found herself equally intrigued by the strong, angular features of his face, the dark shadows along his cheeks that reflected the number of hours since he had shaved. He raked a hand through his dark hair, a gesture that gave the distinct impression of a man resigned to a task he found disagreeable.

Faro's heart began to beat harder as he and Lady Evelyn made their way toward them.

"Ladies," Lady Evelyn began, when they reached the group, "it is my very great pleasure to introduce my son, Lord Wyatt." Lady Evelyn turned her smile in Caroline's direction. "Wyatt, you know Mrs. Newell already, these are my dear friends Mrs. Caroline Carstairs and Miss Faro Burke."

Lord Wyatt looked straight at Faro and murmured the usual, "A pleasure to meet you, ladies."

She felt her mouth go dry. He did not look the least pleased to meet them. His sensual mouth curved into a polite smile, but she had the distinct impression that he took an instant dislike to her.

He was not a man she wished for an enemy.

It was an odd revelation to come upon her. She knew nothing about Lord Wyatt beyond the fact that many in London considered him an enigma, too somber and serious-minded to indulge in the endless rounds of parties and social affairs that filled the hours of many noblemen's lives. The somber part looked true enough. This was not a man who smiled easily or often. She supposed it had something to do with his manner. He projected an air of quiet authority, the type of power gained by experience rather than birthright. She wondered how a man born to the comforts of a manor like Blackburn could acquire such a hardened edge.

"Miss Burke has the most unusual talent," Mrs. Newel told him. "She tells fortunes."

"So I have heard." Wyatt's gaze never left her. His voice was deep and resonant, the measured rhythm of his words almost hypnotic. "You have an unusual surname, Miss Burke. However did you come by it?"

"That would be her father's doing," Caroline cut in. "Miss Burke told me the whole story. Baron Rothwell named his children after his favorite pursuits: Faro and Hazard. Can you imagine, my lord? Being named after games of chance?"

Wyatt didn't respond to Caroline's questions, nor did he so much as glance at her. It was rude to ignore the others so thoroughly. Faro realized they must think her manners equally lacking. His unusual eyes held her captive. "Do you share your father's fondness for games of chance, Miss Burke?"

"No, my lord. I do not indulge in gambling of any sort." Her voice sounded far too giddy and girlish for a woman of twenty-three, and she wondered at the ridiculous urge to run. Having met a great many people in London over the past few months, she considered herself an expert at the art of the introduction. Tonight she felt awkward and unsure of herself.

His lashes lowered as his gaze swept the length of her, missing nothing. "Fortune-telling seems something of a gamble."

"There is an element of the unknown," she said, trying

desperately to keep her tone even and controlled. "I avoid weapons or any objects known to be associated with violent events. Most weapons I cannot read at all, but some have very . . . unpleasant effects."

"Faro did the most ghastly reading of a silver candlestick at Mrs. Beauchamp's house party last month." Caroline's dark eyes sparkled with an air of excitement that most men found captivating. Lord Wyatt appeared oblivious to her beauty. "Mrs. Beauchamp didn't tell anyone that the candlestick was involved in a murder, that no one knew the identity of the culprit. Faro thinks Mrs. Beauchamp's underbutler used the candlestick to bludgeon his poor wife to death. Can you imagine?" Caroline didn't give anyone time to imagine anything. "Poor Mrs. Beauchamp. The incident caused quite an uproar. Thank goodness my piano recital made everyone forget that dreadful business."

"Your musical talents must be something remarkable to prove so distracting."

Caroline perked up at this show of interest from Lord Wyatt. "Actually, I mentioned the possibility of a recital just before you joined us. Perhaps you would like to judge my talents for yourself?"

"Actually, I hoped you might like to take a walk in the gardens."

The look in Caroline's eyes reminded Faro of her expression at dinner each night when the dessert arrived. "I am at your disposal, my lord."

"Excellent." Wyatt nodded toward Lady Evelyn. "Mother just mentioned that she would enjoy a walk in the gardens. I daresay she will be delighted to have your company."

"But—"

"I can think of nothing I would like better," Lady Evelyn said, cutting off Caroline's protest. She linked her arm through Mrs. Newel's. "This way, ladies."

"But—"

"Enjoy the fresh air." Wyatt motioned for Caroline to follow the older women. "It's a lovely evening for a walk. Be sure to have Mother show you the arboretum."

Caroline clamped her mouth shut and turned on her heel to march after Mrs. Newel and Lady Evelyn. Faro found herself smiling until she glanced at Lord Wyatt. The predatory look had returned to his eyes. They glittered with a dangerous light that made her instantly wary.

"There is something I would like to show you as well, Miss Burke." He moved toward a door wainscoted and painted to match the wall. He pushed against one side and it sprang open. "Shall we retire to the library?"

"Why must we go to the library?" Faro glanced at the other guests. "It isn't at all proper."

"It is entirely proper. I am your host, Miss Burke, and I have yet to insult any guest in my home by behaving in an improper manner. There are simply a few questions I would like to ask you in a place less public."

He took her arm and led her through the doorway.

Faro let him, mostly because she had little doubt that Lord Wyatt meant to test her. It was nothing unusual. Very few people believed in her bizarre talent without proof. If his hostile demeanor was any measure, Lord Wyatt hoped she would fail his test.

Wyatt closed the door, disguised as bookshelves on this side of the room, then walked toward the center of the library. He came to a halt near an oversized chair and Faro took a seat on a nearby divan upholstered in jewel-green velvet. All the library's furnishings looked heavy and masculine, the unmistakable domain of a man. Bookshelves covered three walls, while a row of tall windows along the fourth wall reflected the evening stars. There were several books scattered on long tables placed before the bookshelves, and a small stack of papers was piled on the desk. Oil lamps flickered from the tables and desk, but the library's dark furnishings reflected little light. The lamps glowed like small, golden oases in the large room. Faro's gaze returned to the door that led to the gallery, almost indistinguishable amidst the bookcases.

"The doors in this house are a little unnerving," she said, for lack of anything better to end the silence. Actually, it was the house's owner who unnerved her. The foreboding look in his eyes didn't frighten her. On the contrary, she found his golden eyes fascinating, but the attraction she felt toward him frightened her plenty. That sort of emotion had no place in her life. She did her best to push it aside and gave him her politest smile. "I never quite know how to make my way from one room to the next."

"The house is riddled with passageways, some secret, some not so secret. They were one of my ancestor's poor ideas of a jest." He didn't return her smile. Instead, he reached into his pocket to remove something, then held it toward her. "I recently came into possession of this bottle and I am curious about its origins. I'm told it might be valuable if I could prove the bottle's age and authenticity. For that I will need to contact a previous owner. Perhaps you could tell me how it came to be in my possession, Miss Burke."

It was not a request, but an order. Faro removed her glove, then held out her hand. "Very well, my lord. I shall endeavor to provide the proof you require."

His lips tightened as he recognized her sarcasm. She knew he wanted proof of her abilities more than he wanted proof of ownership. Or more likely, he wanted proof that her talent was nothing more than a parlor trick. One dark brow rose in silent challenge as he released the small bottle and it dropped into her hand.

It was a very unusual bottle, as deep green as the divan, yet different. Every color of the rainbow shimmered along its surface as if the glass were covered with a sheet of prisms. The untarnished silver that flowed in swirls to the chased silver stopper appeared almost liquid in the soft lamplight, the metalwork far too fine and unblemished to be of any great age.

Her curiosity aroused, she rubbed her thumb along a band of silver. The bottle felt very warm in her hand and that warmth spread through her like liquid sunlight. A flood of emotions followed, all of them stronger and more powerful than any she had felt during other readings. Yet they were not the sensations of violence or anger, but the emotions of lovers.

Her breathing quickened and her heart began to beat

harder. Long ago she had abandoned the notion of suitors and marriage, but she had always wondered what it would feel like to be in love. The bottle gave her the answer, communicating the deepest loves and desires of everyone who had possessed it. And there were a great many of them. She saw fleeting pictures of lovers dressed in clothes that looked almost modern, lovers clothed in styles from centuries past, and lovers who stood in the darkest mists of time. The bottle was not just old, but ancient.

It was also possessed by magic. Very strong magic.

That sudden bit of knowledge made her panic. She opened her eyes and tried to release her hold on the bottle, but her hand wouldn't cooperate. Then the bottle began to glow and she stared at it in wide-eyed wonder. The white light grew stronger, almost mistlike around the edges of her hand. Afraid of what her face would reveal to Lord Wyatt, she bowed her head and closed her eyes again.

What she saw was far beyond any vision she had ever relived. The object in her hand seemed determined to share all its secrets. Sweet, tender feelings of love turned shockingly erotic. Scenes passed before her eyes that were beyond her ability to imagine, an intrusion into moments of lovers' lives that should remain private. She was in the very midst of every emotion and every image the bottle possessed.

Then the visions suddenly changed.

The new images were not of others, but of herself, as if she were somehow a part of the bottle's history. She was in her bedchamber at Blackburn, and a single candle burned at her bedside. In that bed was a man. A very naked man who held her securely in his arms. In the image she didn't seem at all averse to the embrace. The man's face remained obscured in shadows cast by the bed-curtains, but she watched herself rub her cheek against her lover's shoulder and felt adrift in a warm sea of contentment. His hand stroked down her back and she could almost feel his touch there in the library. Then he propped himself up on one elbow and his face was bathed in warm candlelight.

Her lover was none other than Lord Wyatt.

Faro's eyes flew open as the bottle bounced onto the

carpet. She felt dizzy and disoriented. Wyatt reached out to steady her.

"Don't touch me!" The order wasn't supposed to sound so rude. She simply didn't know if she could contain her emotions if he touched her. Wyatt couldn't possibly realize that. His hands fell to his sides and the compassion in his eyes faded to reveal emotionless pools of gold. They stared at each other in silence until she finally willed herself to look away from him.

He reached down and picked up the bottle, then stood up to tower over her. "Well? Can you tell me anything informative?"

Faro struggled to gather her scattered senses. She knew instinctively that the visions were hers alone, but perhaps he too had seen the bottle's strange glow. "Did you see it?"

"See what?" His brows furrowed together in a scowl. "Don't tell me this little bottle has a ghost in residence?"

"Not a ghost. At least, I don't think it was a ghost." She eyed the bottle warily, but it looked perfectly harmless in the palm of his hand. "You didn't see the light?"

Wyatt's lips curved into a humorless smile. "Your performance is most remarkable, Miss Burke. I would venture to say that there is not a better actress in all of England. However, the performance is over. Your charade as well." He held the bottle toward her. "That is, unless you can tell me how I obtained this bottle, or the name of its previous owner."

She shrank away from him. More specifically, from what he held. The bottle was dangerous, a threat of some sort, but one she couldn't determine with her emotions in such turmoil. "I didn't see that part of its history, my lord. The bottle is very old, owned by many people over the course of time. I . . . I could not see anything very clearly." That was a lie, but she felt no compelling need to tell the truth. He would have her locked away. However, she did decide to give him a portion of the truth. "It is very hard for me to read any object owned or handled by many people."

"Would you like another try?"

"No!" She wanted to be as far away from the bottle as possible. Her body felt very strange, as if her blood was thicker and warmer than usual. The light-headed, almost euphoric feeling worried her as well. She watched his mouth and studied the curve of his bottom lip, the slight indentations on his cheeks that might turn into dimples if he ever actually smiled. His black superfine jacket fit perfectly, but she found herself wondering what the muscles beneath it looked like. Especially when he shrugged the jacket open just enough to return the bottle to an inside pocket. It took every ounce of her concentration to comprehend his words when the way he moved proved such a distraction.

"I suspected as much," he said. "My mother believes the little plays you stage are genuine. Of course, she also believes that thieves and brigands wear a black patch over one eye and limit their activities to the king's highways and pirate ships. It would never occur to her that such a pretty package as yourself might be filled with rotten eggs."

He thought her pretty? That astounded Faro as much as her sudden fascination with his hands. Why hadn't she noticed before that he didn't wear gloves? He had his arms folded across his chest in a gesture that displayed his hands perfectly. No, they were perfect hands, placed on display against the stark backdrop of his black jacket. His skin looked much darker than her own, his hands large and his long fingers well-shaped. Deliciously masculine.

Deliciously?

Faro shook her head. Where were these thoughts coming from? She stared down at her own hands and tried to discipline her wandering imagination.

"I am not so gullible as my mother," he went on. "Whatever your reasons for coming to Blackburn House, I am here to see that they fail. You would be well advised to pack your little bag of tricks and return to London first thing in the morning."

She looked up. The bits and pieces of his conversation came together at last. He was insulting her. Threatening her!

"Should you not take that advice and decide to stay," he went on, "know the consequences. If you dupe my mother out of one farthing, one candlestick, one bauble of any sort, I will make certain you never receive another invitation from anyone in polite society. You will be an outcast. In short, I will ruin you."

Faro marshaled her shaken nerves and stood to face him, hoping her wobbly knees wouldn't betray her. "You make yourself perfectly clear, my lord. Now if you will excuse me, I think it would be best if I retire for the evening."

"I agree. Tomorrow promises to be a long day and you will need your rest. I will explain to my mother that you were unwell and wished to retire." He stared at her long and hard, the look in his golden eyes a clear warning. "Good night, Miss Burke."

"Good night, my lord." She hesitated in the doorway, then spoke in a soft tone. "By the way, that is a very unusual scar on your shoulder. Perhaps someday you will tell me how it came to be there."

CHAPTER THREE

WYATT PACED THE length of the stableyard, oblivious to the bright sunshine and blue skies that proclaimed an end to the miserably long week of storms. Despite the fine weather, the scent of rain still lingered in the air along with the smell of mildewed hay. Pigeons lined the rooftops and cupolas of the stable, their low coos an agitated, almost puzzled sound. One of the birds paced along the peak of the roof, a near-perfect imitation of the man below. Wyatt remained unaware of the mockery, his thoughts centered on the woman he had all but ordered off his estate the night before.

He had been more abrupt with Faro Burke than he'd intended. No matter how determined he was to dislike the woman, his thoughts took the oddest turns when she was near him. In the library he had found himself wondering if her skin was as soft as he'd imagined, and if she could possibly taste as sweet as she looked. The urge to experience the answers to those questions plagued him long after she retired for the night.

The attraction he felt toward her annoyed him almost as much as the fact of her identity. Her preposterous claims to the occult only made his desire for her more baffling.

The performance she gave in the library should have soured that desire entirely.

So she had mentioned his old fencing scar. Any number of people could have told her about it. That proved nothing but her cleverness. He was right to advise her to leave. Unfortunately, his mother had argued that the reading was inconclusive. She wanted Faro Burke to stay. After the warning he gave Faro in the library, today he wondered if his mother's sentiments would hold any sway.

The stablemaster inadvertently informed him of the answer to that question when he mentioned that Miss Burke had also ordered a horse made ready this morning. Not a carriage horse that would take her to the village, where she could catch a mail coach to London, but a gentle mare with a ladies' saddle that would carry her to the ruins of the old abbey.

The thought of spending another night under the same roof with her made his palms itch. The last thing he needed was another irksome female in the house. Caroline Carstairs promised all the trouble he could handle. Not that there appeared to be much amiss with the young widow. Indeed, he was hard pressed to find a reason not to like her. She was wealthy, beautiful, and seemed pleasant enough. He should be thankful to find such a promising bride with so little effort. He tried to picture a courtship between them but the image would not form. No matter how hard he tried, he couldn't muster up the slightest desire to woo the lovely Caroline.

Faro was a different matter entirely. He could think of little *but* wooing her. Kissing her. Touching and caressing her. It still seemed a bad jest that he found himself lusting after the wrong woman. Caroline Carstairs was everything he wanted in a wife, everything he needed. Faro Burke turned his blood to liquid fire. Last night he had even dreamed of her, dreams so vivid that he awoke with a start, his body fully aroused. And it had happened more than once. She was like some sort of poison that had invaded him. He had to be rid of her before he did something foolish.

No matter his mother's wishes, Wyatt intended to drive

Faro Burke away. First he would remind her of their conversation of the night before, and he would probably not display much of the common courtesy he'd promised. If that failed to persuade her, he would become her constant, unwelcome companion until she changed her mind about staying. With any luck, she would take one look at him and march right back to the house. To pack.

The sound of boots crunching against the gravel driveway came to him, along with the soft strains of Beethoven's *Pathétique*. His nemesis was humming, her voice light, the tune hauntingly pleasing.

Faro rounded the corner of the stables a moment later and Wyatt was startled again by the same sense of recognition he had felt the night before. His anger faded, replaced by unwelcome fascination. What was there about this woman that made him senseless each time he laid eyes on her?

She didn't see him at first and he took that opportunity to study her, to search for the key to his weakness. Her face was turned toward the sun, her lips curved into a curious half smile. She wore a plum-colored riding habit cut in trim lines that had gone out of style years ago. Either she didn't follow the current fashions, or couldn't afford to. Still, the habit's rich color made her blue eyes look very pale and mysterious beneath the dark fringe of her lashes. Her jaunty velvet cap was the same color as her gown, her face wreathed by toffee-colored curls. A square linen sack rested against her hip with its strap slung over her shoulders. As he wondered at its contents the humming came to a sudden stop, as did Miss Burke. His gaze returned to her face and he watched her lush lips form a perfect circle. She recovered her composure and her expression became a study of cool politeness. "Good morning, my lord."

"Miss Burke," he answered, his tone equally polite. "I thought you would be busy packing this morning."

"The coach I hired will not return until next Friday." She looked him squarely in the eye. "It seems I am stranded here until that time."

"A mail coach runs through the village every day. I shall be happy to arrange a carriage to take you there."

"Believe me, my lord, I have no wish to remain where I

am not welcome. However, talk of my early departure seemed to distress your mother at breakfast this morning. I presented several polite excuses when I mentioned my decision to leave, but Lady Evelyn assured me that her other guests would wonder if I found her hospitality lacking in some way."

His palms began to itch again. "Then you are determined to defy me in this matter?"

"I have no wish to insult my hostess, and she is determined that I stay."

Wyatt gritted his teeth. His mother was really starting to irritate him.

"I hope you will not mind if I borrow one of your horses," she said, with just a trace of uncertainty. "Lady Evelyn assured me that you would have no objection."

"None at all." Who was he to deny an unwelcome guest her entertainment? "The stablemaster tells me that you plan a ride to the abbey. The road to the abbey is difficult to find if you don't know the way. It also passes near the cliffs and the footing is sometimes uncertain after long rains, too uncertain for you to venture there alone. I trust you will not mind my company."

"There is no need for you to inconvenience yourself. I am an experienced rider and shall be fine on my own." She glanced toward the stable. "Or, perhaps a stableboy could show me the way?"

Her frown should have lightened his mood. He wanted to annoy her, at least as much as her presence at Blackburn annoyed him. "The stablehands are too busy with the guests' horses and their own duties for a jaunt in the country. I have nothing better to occupy my time at present. As long as my mother insists that you stay at Blackburn, we might as well make the best of the situation and declare a truce."

She looked wary of the offer, and rightly so. He had no idea where it came from. A truce was hardly the first step toward driving her away from Blackburn. Then again, it could work to his advantage. He might learn something useful that would persuade his mother once and for all that he was right about Faro Burke.

"I know you do not like me, or even trust me," she began.

He sensed a refusal and hurried to reassure her. "Sometimes I tend to form an opinion too quickly. Learning that you were Baron Rothwell's daughter clouded my judgment, and I am a confirmed skeptic in matters of the occult and supernatural. Your difficulty with the reading last night did little to sway my beliefs. Still, my mother likes you and she tends to be a good judge of character. For her sake, I will try harder to keep an open mind about your claims."

It was a challenge few women could resist, the opportunity to change a man's opinions. He waited patiently for her agreement.

She arched one delicate brow. "Your vicissitude is to be admired, my lord, yet I am curious why my father would cloud your judgment of me."

"I would think it obvious." He racked his brain for the definition of *vicissitude*. Was she being sarcastic, or was it some truly admirable trait? He made a mental note to look the word up when he returned to the library.

Faro looked equally perplexed. "It is not obvious in the least. Did you dislike my father?"

"Yes, you could say that I disliked him." Such a tame description for such strong emotions. He had hated Baron Rothwell with every fiber of his being. "Your father relieved mine of a very substantial sum in a game of cards."

"Ah, I see." She didn't look the least surprised, and even nodded as if she had some understanding of his feelings. "Gambling was my father's greatest weakness and his ultimate downfall. Unfortunately, he took a good many men down with him over the years."

Wyatt didn't know what to say. He hadn't expected her to be agreeable on the subject.

"You are shocked," she said, as if she had read his thoughts. "I know it is ill-mannered to speak disparagingly of one's elders, but in truth I barely knew my father. He thought my brother and I were . . . odd. It is very difficult to feel any real affection for a parent who makes his dislike of his offspring so obvious. The last time we saw him was the winter my mother died. That was eleven years

ago." Her steady gaze didn't ask for pity. Only for a measure of understanding. "You are only one of many who
found reason to resent the baron, my lord."

He looked away before the words she left unspoken
could affect him. It was already too late. How could he
hold her responsible for Rothwell's actions when she had
suffered an even greater injustice at her father's hands?
Rather than give in to the urge to make an apology, he
looked up at the pigeons that sat along the peak of the stables and pretended they held great interest.

This truce was an extraordinarily bad idea. The last
thing he needed was to spend the afternoon in Faro Burke's
company. Recognizing his weakness for her didn't do anything to diminish it. Given an hour, she could probably
convince him of anything. Unfortunately, it was also too
late to retreat.

"Perhaps it would be best if we did not speak of your father. It seems he is a sore subject for us both." He glanced
down at her, then motioned toward the stables. "Our
mounts are saddled and ready. The ride to the abbey takes
almost an hour, so we had best be on our way."

HALF AN hour later, Faro still cursed her stubborn pride.
She shouldn't have said a word about her father, but she
always became defensive when someone tried to blame her
for his mistakes, or tried to compare them in any way.
Wyatt didn't know that, and it wasn't the only thing he
found objectionable about her. Admitting that she disliked
her own father had surely sunk his low opinion of her to
new depths. He hadn't spoken more than a handful of
words to her since.

Not that it mattered. She shouldn't care what he
thought of her. She *didn't* care.

The road they followed wound through a thick forest
and she gazed up at the canopy of leaves overhead. At the
same time, her horse stumbled over a fallen branch in the
road and she saw Wyatt glance at her. He probably
thought her equestrian skills were as lacking as her manners. She paid closer attention to the road for a time, but

she soon rolled her eyes sideways to glance at Wyatt without being obvious about it. He seemed to grow more handsome each time she looked at him. She supposed there was little harm in appreciating a man's looks as long as he didn't notice her attention.

How odd that simply staring at a man could bring such guilty pleasure. It was the vision of them together that made her feel guilty, she decided, the way the images came instantly to mind whenever she glanced at him. The vision had seemed so real.

It wasn't, of course. She and Lord Wyatt would never share the sort of intimacies she had envisioned, or anything that would remotely approach affection. He didn't like her. Indeed, he seemed determined that she dislike him as well. Why wasn't it working?

"The abbey is around the next bend," he said, interrupting her thoughts. Their gazes met and she couldn't make herself look away. He really did have the most fascinating eyes, the same gleaming color as old, burnished gold. He cleared his throat, obviously uncomfortable with her scrutiny. "We will soon have a nice view of the sea."

The only response she could muster up was a smile and a nod. He must think her a simpleton. No matter how hard she searched for some topic of conversation that would not strain the fragile truce between them, all she could concentrate on was the steady *clop, clop, clop* of the horses' hooves that marked the lengthening silence.

"Mother tells me your home is near Bath. Do you prefer the bustle of city life in London?"

She silently thanked him for solving the topic problem. "I enjoy the sights of London, but I quickly tire of the crowds. No event is judged a success unless there is such a crush of people in attendance that one can barely breathe. I did not realize how much I missed the quiet of the country until I arrived here at Blackburn."

"You don't return to your country house very often, then?"

"We leased the house to a local merchant and his family soon after my father died." She bit her lower lip and pretended to adjust her reins. Telling him they had leased the family home hinted far too closely at the woeful state of their finances. Her prayer that he didn't make the connection went unanswered.

"I take it your father left a few debts in his wake."

She pressed her lips together, mortified that he had guessed the truth. Not that it was any great secret. "My brother and I manage quite nicely on our own."

"Ah, yes. The fortune-telling. You must have quite a collection of jewels and family heirlooms."

"I would never accept a valuable gift if its owner would suffer from its loss, or even regret it. That is something my father would do, not I." She took a deep breath to calm her nerves. "The baubles and trinkets I receive are rarely worth more than a few pounds, but they do help pay off our family's debts. In return I provide people with an entertainment, a novelty to distract them from the more mundane events of their lives for a time. My collection, as you call it, consists mostly of fans, hair combs, cravat pins, and walking sticks. There is a shop in the Burlington arcade that offers a very fair price for such objects."

"You are paying your family debts by pawning fans and combs?" He sounded horrified.

She couldn't see a graceful retreat from the conversation, so she gave him a curt nod. "Indirectly. My brother, Hazard, invests the earnings and we live off the income. I suppose a man in your position would think that appalling, but I find my situation much preferable to that of a governess, or an unwelcome relative who must live off the charity of distant relations."

His expression changed, as though she had said something that struck him as a revelation. She watched the corners of his mouth turn downward, then straighten again. His hands shifted restlessly on his reins, tightening in reflexive movements. She wondered what sort of internal struggle was taking place.

"Now that I understand your reasons, I find no fault with your methods," he said at last. "You might be surprised at what a man in my position would do to ensure his own survival. After my father lost our fortune, we lived for a time by selling my mother's jewels. Then we mortgaged all the properties. I recently repaid the last of the debts, but I am not always proud of the means I employed to achieve that end. To be perfectly honest, your fortune-telling scheme sounds almost respectable in comparison."

Wyatt glanced over and gauged her curiosity easily enough. His mouth curved into a grim smile. "I captained a privateer during the war, and eventually gained the letters of marque to several others. There is little honor in piracy, even when the government deems it legal and patriotic."

She tried to picture him in pirate garb and succeeded with little effort. There was a dangerous edge to him that lurked just beneath the surface, the dark, brooding countenance of a man who has seen more than he wanted of life. "I am sorry you were forced to take that course."

"I don't want your sympathy, Miss Burke." His curt response was at odds with the strange way he stared at her. It was as if he saw her as some great puzzle he had to figure out. "However, I am curious about the course you feel compelled to follow. The responsibility for your family's debts should lie with your brother, not you. What kind of man is he to let his sister earn his keep?"

"He is a young man now, but only a child when my father died," she said. "Hazard wanted to find work when we realized all our father left us was debt. I convinced him to complete his studies at Oxford. Both our lives will be better for the knowledge he will gain there, and the types of positions he can gain when he finishes."

"If you were my sister, I would not allow you to barter your way through the world, no matter what argument you presented."

He sounded so much like Hazard that she couldn't help but smile. Both men possessed an excess of male pride. "You have not heard any of my arguments, my lord. I can be most persuasive when I set my mind to something."

"That doesn't surprise me." The hint of a smile played about his lips. "What does surprise me is that you are not yet married. You move in the best of circles, and I am sure a number of suitable gentlemen have offered for your hand. Do you not wish for the home and security that a husband can provide?"

She wasn't about to admit that she had never received an offer of marriage, and he wouldn't believe the reasons she would never accept one. She evaded the question with a half answer. "I do not intend to marry. A husband would only complicate my life."

"How so?"

"You wouldn't understand."

"You have my curiosity ablaze, Miss Burke." He pulled his horse to a stop and she was forced to follow suit rather than ride on without him. "You never know. I might prove very understanding."

"You believe I am a fraud, that my abilities are some sort of hoax. How can you understand me if you do not believe anything I say?"

"I am trying harder than you know to understand you, Miss Burke."

His solemn tone made her hesitate. She supposed there wouldn't be any harm in telling him the truth. "Very well. If you must hear it, I can read people as easily as I read objects. When I touch someone I often learn more about them than I ever wanted to know. That is the reason I will not marry. I do not like to touch anyone."

She expected him to laugh out loud. Instead he seemed to mull over her answer. "You held my hand last night during the reading."

"I did?"

"Just for a moment," he clarified, "but your grip was very tight for that moment. What did you read about me? Aside from the scar on my shoulder, of course. Tell me something no one else could know."

He sounded as if he wanted to believe her. He would think her mad if she told him about the vision. A warm blush crept over her cheeks and she lowered her gaze. "Last night was . . . different from my usual readings. I cannot even remember holding your hand."

"I see."

The disappointment in his voice startled her. Perhaps he was not such a confirmed skeptic after all. Not that she had presented any real proof to change his beliefs. "It's rather strange that I spend most of my life trying to convince people that I am not some sort of witch, or possessed by demons. Now I find myself wishing I could fly or breathe fire just to prove myself to you." She met his gaze and forced a lighthearted smile. "Circumstances seem to conspire against me where you are concerned, but never fear, my lord. The time will come when you realize the truth of what I say."

"I almost hope you are right." He spoke so softly that the words seemed more for himself than for her. He cleared his throat and nodded toward the road. "The abbey is just ahead. We should be on our way."

CHAPTER FOUR

THE RUINS OF Halbert Abbey sat on a windswept cliff that overlooked the sea. The breeze blew stronger here than in the forest and carried the distant scents of fish and seaweed. The noisy cries of a gull distracted Faro from the ruins. She watched the bird swoop and career overhead, then disappear behind a square stone tower and over the edge of the cliff toward the sea far below. The tower was all that remained intact of the abbey, six stories tall and made of pale white stone from the nearby cliffs. The stone looked the color of bleached bones in the bright sunlight, a startling contrast to the deep blue sky behind it. The abbey's chapel and outbuildings stood roofless and crumbling, with scattered traces of structures that were now no more than vague rectangular outlines beneath the lichen and sparse grass.

Faro let her horse amble to a halt as she studied the ruins, too fascinated by the desolate beauty of the place to realize that Wyatt studied her just as intently. The gaping windows of the chapel rose upward in graceful arches that vanished into thin air, as if some great disaster had consumed the roof and eaves but left the base in curiously good repair. Time was the disaster, along with some of the local quarrymen, she would wager. She pictured the place in its prime with neatly tended gardens and courtyards, the bustle of people that had lived there as they went about their daily chores. That was the picture she would sketch.

"Most people think this place is haunted," Wyatt said, interrupting her thoughts. "The smugglers do what they can to perpetuate the rumor. They use the caves along the beach to hide their wares, and the tower as a beacon to guide their ships. It can be seen from miles at sea, even at night when the moon is out."

"It must be a beautiful sight." She pointed toward a small hill to their left. A rocky shelf jutted out near the top of it. "That looks like a perfect seat to view the grounds. Is there someplace I could tether my horse?"

"I will take care of the horses," he said, "but don't you want to explore first?"

"Perhaps later. Right now I would rather sketch while the light is still at the best angle." She unhooked her leg from the saddle and slid to the ground, then handed Wyatt her reins and walked toward the hill. He was staring at her. She didn't have to turn around to confirm the feeling, since he had stared at her almost constantly since they left the forest. It was a little unnerving.

The ground was rocky and uneven, and she kept a close eye on her steps as she made her way to the ledge. A dusting of gravel covered the ledge, but after she brushed it away there was a fine seat. She opened her linen sack and pulled out a wooden pencil box, then a worn leather folder. Her drawing supplies were one of the few luxuries she afforded herself and the folder contained stiff sheets of paper separated by smooth parchment to prevent smudges. She leafed through several completed sketches and pulled out a blank sheet of paper. She chose a thin pencil from the wooden box, then started to draw the outline of the tower. Later, at the house, she would complete the picture with watercolors.

Wyatt tied the horses to a low-hanging branch of a tree and started up the hill after her. Her makeshift bench was large enough for two, and he gestured toward the spot next to her. "Will it make you uncomfortable if I watch you sketch?"

"No," she said, without glancing up from her work.

That was a lie. She positioned the sack and pencil box beside her so they took up as much room as possible. He placed the sack on the ground and picked up the pencil box, then sat down next to her. She edged away from him. He moved closer. Her sigh of defeat nearly ruffled her paper. She started to draw again and pointedly ignored him.

He watched her pretend to concentrate on her sketch, his own concentration shattered by her nearness. Her hair held the faint scent of orange blossoms. He placed one hand on the ledge behind her and leaned closer to take a deeper breath of her. The citrus scent made his mouth water, but the hunger it created had nothing to do with fruit. He wanted a taste of something far sweeter.

Faro had made it clear that she didn't want any man in her life, and didn't seem to care what his opinion of her might be. She'd argued against the arbitrary conclusions he had drawn about her, and spoken honestly about details of her life that few would share with a best friend. She was the most unique woman he had ever known. His attraction to her was so complete that he couldn't believe she didn't feel something for him. Sometimes she looked at him with a trace of the same hunger that gnawed at him. Was it enough to make her want to touch him?

It was a challenge, and he always found a challenge hard to resist. What harm could there be in an innocent flirtation?

Disturbed by the direction of his thoughts, he made himself focus on the drawing. The outline of the tower began to take shape, then its depth as she added the side walls and shadows. She had almost finished the chapel when he noticed something unusual in the picture. "How did you know the windows were stone mullioned?"

"Just a lucky guess." She glanced up from her work. "How did *you* know they were mullioned?"

"My great-grandfather had several removed to Blackburn and installed in the south-wing apartments. Fortunate timing, as it turned out. Fire consumed the chapel roof soon after. If you would like to see the originals, I can show them to you when we return to the house." His thoughts skipped ahead to the hours they might spend in the south-wing gardens. He couldn't explain his need to be near her, other than to acknowledge that the stories of her past affected him more than he should allow. They stirred his admiration more than his sympathy, but mostly they showed a side of her that he never would have guessed existed. She had managed to work her way deeper under his skin with no more than a few words.

"I would like to see the originals." She hesitated a moment, then rifled through her folder and withdrew two completed paintings. "Perhaps you could help me make a decision. I did these drawings of Blackburn House yesterday afternoon, and thought I would present one to your mother as a gift. This is the house as it looked yesterday. The other is my interpretation of what the original house probably looked like before any additions, or remodeling. Do you think she will have a preference between the two?"

He held the paintings at arm's length and studied them in silence. Most women he met made a conscious effort to impress him with their accomplishments, or charms. Faro didn't need to make an effort. The quality of her work amazed him. She had captured the essence of the scenes so well that he could almost feel the breeze that rustled the leaves of her painted trees. The image of the original house sent a shiver of recognition down his spine.

Enlarged and expanded through the centuries, he knew that Blackburn House looked nothing like the initial structure. As far as he knew, there weren't any paintings of the oldest parts of the house still in existence. So why did Faro's interpretation look so familiar?

At last he turned the drawing of the original house toward her. "This one, I think. Both are excellent renditions, but this one is unique. It looks as if it were drawn hundreds of years ago rather than just yesterday. The flying buttresses are an especially nice touch. Very Gothic."

"That one is my favorite, too," she admitted. He handed her the drawings and she returned them to the folder. "I saw some very nice frames at a shop in the village. Even framed it isn't much of a hostess gift, but I hope your mother will like it."

"I'm sure she will. I was very set on disliking anything you did, and I like it immensely." It was a thoughtless remark. He admired many of her traits, and admitted there were several they shared, but she also possessed an unexpected vulnerability. He could hurt her feelings without even trying. Her chin rose a good two inches.

"I suppose it's something that you can limit your dislike to my person, and not extend it to my paintings."

That he cared at all about her feelings was a direct measure of his own. He deserved her sarcasm, but she deserved the truth. "I am finding it almost impossible to dislike anything about you, Miss Burke."

He searched for some sign that she might echo his sentiments, but she simply blinked once very slowly. A retreat to safer waters seemed in order. "You should try to sell your paintings, rather than your services as a medium. I know many people who would commission you, especially if I could show them a few samples of your work. Drawing seems to be something you enjoy. I do not think you much enjoy the readings you do for others."

"Your offer is . . . most generous," she managed, obviously surprised by it. She busied herself with the folder and tapped the edges of a few papers to settle them neatly inside. "How did you know about the readings?"

"I don't have any mystical powers," he said, "but I am astute enough to recognize resentment in someone's voice. I hear it in yours whenever you speak of your readings. If circumstances had not decreed otherwise, I doubt you would deliberately set about to become society's latest novelty. You aren't the type who likes a social gathering, any more than I am."

"I really don't like to attend all those balls and parties," she admitted. She slanted him a sideways glance. "Still, I doubt my dabbling talent is enough to impress your friends, and I can scarce count myself among their number. If you will forgive my rudeness for asking, why should you wish to help me?"

"Because I happen to disagree with your assessment of

your talent." He spread his hands. "My offer is made in good faith."

"I didn't mean to insult you." Her expression said she still didn't trust him, but she nodded anyway. "I would be happy to give you a few samples of my work, but only if they would cause no inconvenience. I would not wish to add to your troubles."

"And what would you know of my troubles, Miss Burke?"

"Nothing, really. You just have the look of a troubled man at times."

"I didn't realize my emotions were so readily apparent." He studied her face and the corners of his mouth curved upward. "There are times when I can read your thoughts just as easily, you know."

Her horrified expression made him smile. "You needn't panic. I can't read your exact thoughts. I can only guess at them."

"And what would you guess?"

His smile faded and his gaze lingered on her mouth. She nervously wet her lips. "I would guess that your thoughts at this moment are not all that different from my own."

"What are your thoughts?" She sounded breathless.

He extended his hand toward her, the palm turned upward. "Would you know if you held my hand?"

"Perhaps." She stared down at his hand as if he had offered her a snake.

"You don't have to touch me if you would rather not."

She shook her head. "I'll do it."

Her hand trembled noticeably when she set her pencil aside. She was afraid to touch him. The surge of guilt he felt wasn't enough to make him stop her. He had never known such an overwhelming need to feel a woman's touch, to simply hold her hand.

Her palm brushed against his and he felt a sudden rush of desire, a heady emotion that spread through him like a deep drink of fine brandy. He closed his fingers over hers, careful not to startle her. "Tell me what you feel, Faro."

She lifted her lashes to meet his gaze and her breath caught in her throat. Desire darkened her eyes until they glittered like pale sapphires. "I . . . I don't think I should do this."

"And I think *this* was inevitable." He lifted her hand to press his lips to the sensitive skin inside her wrist. Her shiver sealed her fate. She wanted him. "Do you know my thoughts now, or do you need another hint?"

"I didn't need a hint," she whispered. He started to move closer, but stopped when she leaned away. "You don't *really* want to kiss me."

He didn't answer with words, but reached out and brushed his fingertips across the line of her jaw. The moment he touched her face, he forgot everything but his need to hold her.

"Oh, no," she whispered. But inside she whispered, *Oh, yes*. The touch of his hand was almost unbearable in its tenderness. He cupped her cheek and her whole body tingled from the contact. His touch filled some unknown need in her, then stirred to life yet another. How long had she waited for the man who could awaken her passion, whose touch alone told her that he was the one? Until that moment it had seemed a foolish whimsy, but now she realized it was true.

The force that drew them closer was too powerful to deny, and yet Wyatt tried to resist its pull. He lowered his head inches closer to her, then hesitated, as if to give her one last chance to turn away. She answered by parting her lips, a deliberate invitation. He held her gaze until their lips touched, then he closed his eyes and she heard a sound from deep inside him. It was the sound a man might make if he had denied himself something he wanted very badly, the sound of surrender when he succumbed to his weakness.

Faro knew that feeling only too well, even as she tried to recall why she had attempted to resist this extraordinary experience. His mouth moved urgently against hers, tasting, caressing, plundering. Instinct taught her how to return the kiss, but Wyatt taught her more, fitting his lips to hers intimately, expertly, until her mouth burned with fire. He tasted of sunlight and spices, delicious, exotic places she had never known.

He deepened the kiss and she sensed his impatience, that

he wanted more than just a taste. His tongue brushed against hers in a wet-velvet stroke that made her collapse against him. He repeated the stroke and she suddenly couldn't get close enough.

"You are so soft," he whispered against her lips. He held her chin, then his fingers spread out until his hand covered the smooth column of her neck. "Softer than I ever imagined."

He felt hard everywhere. Her hands moved over the stubbled fabric of his jacket to his shoulders, down his arms, then to his waist and across his chest again. He was also very large, very masculine. She delighted in the differences between them. Wyatt explored those differences in bolder ways than she dared. His hands went to her waist, then higher to skim along her rib cage, then higher still until his fingers brushed against her breasts. The shock of that intimate touch made her gasp against his mouth.

"Let me touch you," he murmured. "You have nothing to fear from me, Faro."

It was true in ways he couldn't imagine. He didn't frighten her in the least. The unpleasant emotions she felt when others touched her were nothing like the emotions he awakened. She felt as if the sun itself shone brightly inside her, coursing its golden heat through her veins. She wanted him to touch her, to fill the dark void made by years of never allowing anyone close to her. She wanted to touch him in return. Everything about him felt exactly right. His body was like a solid wall of strength that surrounded her. She wrapped her arms around his neck and he pulled her onto his lap, held her so tightly that she could barely breathe.

His kiss gave her all the sustenance she needed. His mouth joined hers in an erotic assault that was surely as sexual as any mating. She wanted that kiss to last forever. Once she had thought that the most intimate relations between a man and a woman would be horribly embarrassing and awkward. Now she knew better. He flooded her senses in a sea of sensual longings. She gave herself over to those emotions without hesitation.

The need to hurry toward some unknown goal made her

shift restlessly on his lap, but his hands moved over her with slow, practiced ease. She wondered how he could be so deliberate and unhurried, then he suddenly pressed her hip against him to make her intimately aware of his arousal. A low groan came from deep in his chest and he shuddered against her. Perhaps his control wasn't as complete as she imagined.

His lips trailed to her neck, then lower to the curve of her shoulder. Only then did she realize that he had unbuttoned her jacket and most of her blouse. The thin chemise beneath those garments proved no barrier at all when his fingers brushed over a taut nipple. His hand closed over her breast and hers became fists in his hair. She let out a cry that was half shock and half pleasure.

He kissed her again as he gentled her to the intimate touch. His mouth moved with hers in ways that reminded her of the tide, moving deeper then receding, then returning once more. The rhythmic motions did calm her, enough that she became aware of a need to return the pleasure he gave her. She unclenched her fingers and managed to move her hands down the corded muscles of his neck, then slipped them beneath the lapels of his riding jacket. The heat she felt through the soft fabric of his shirt tempted her, teased her until her fingertips burned. She wanted to touch his bare skin.

The small sound of fabric as it tore had the same effect as a cannon shot. They both broke away from the embrace and stared at each other in horrified silence. Faro's gaze dropped to her hands and she unclenched her fingers to release fistfuls of his shirt. Other than the wrinkles, she could see no apparent damage.

"I . . . Forgive me." Wyatt fumbled with the small ribbons at the neckline of her chemise, but the tear beneath them was irreparable. He gave up the pointless effort and tugged the edges of her blouse together. "I didn't mean to . . ."

He fell helplessly silent and his hands dropped to his sides. He looked worried that she would no longer want him to touch her. She wanted to wrap her arms around his neck while she reassured him that he could touch her all he wanted, but they both needed a moment to think through what they were doing. Another embrace was not a good idea.

"You needn't apologize." She slid off his lap and took her seat next to him. "There was no real damage done."

"No damage?" He gave her an incredulous look, but quickly averted his gaze when she began to readjust her clothing. "There is every need to apologize, Miss Burke. Nothing can come of this. I allowed myself to be carried away with no thought of the consequences. It is my fault for thinking a kiss or two would answer my questions. Now I realize my mistake."

He thought their kisses were a mistake? Her eyes narrowed. "Just what questions did you want answered, my lord?"

He glanced at her, but looked away again when he realized her blouse was still unbuttoned. "They aren't important. Forget I mentioned them."

She thought them very important, even though she could reason them out for herself. This was another of his tests, only this was a test of her character. And she had failed. Only a harlot would allow a man such liberties.

She blinked away tears of humiliation, determined that he would never know of them. By the time she repaired her appearance, she had also regained control of her emotions.

"You are right that there can be nothing between us," she said at last. She couldn't meet his gaze when he turned toward her. Instead she busied herself by packing up her sketches and the pencil box. "There is another reason I will never marry, one you might find easier to understand. The abilities I possess came to me through my mother. The baron knew of them before they married. Like you, he thought they were nothing more than flights of fancy. Eventually he realized the truth, and the truth repulsed him." She clutched the folder to her chest, a shield against the painful memories. "I will not make the same mistake as my mother."

His brows drew together in a thoughtful scowl, but he offered no comment. Not that she expected one.

"If you question whether I make a habit of throwing myself into a man's arms, then the answer is no. I too allowed myself to be carried away in the heat of the moment. It will not happen again." She swallowed a lump of uncertainty. "I think it best if we try to forget not only your questions, but everything that happened this past hour. Are we in agreement on the matter, my lord?"

His only response was the rhythmic tic of a muscle in his cheek. Then he slowly nodded.

CHAPTER FIVE

*T*WO DAYS LATER, a soft knock at the library door brought an end to Wyatt's latest musings about Faro. His mother stepped inside the room, dressed already for dinner in a mint-colored silk gown. "May I join you?"

"Of course." He rose and indicated the seat opposite his at the desk. The rustle of silk followed her across the room, the scent of rosewater in her wake. "To what do I owe the pleasure of your company?"

"I just wanted to make certain you planned to join us for dinner tonight." She eyed his black evening garb as she took her seat and nodded her approval. "We missed you at the archery contest this afternoon. Where were you?"

If she had been with Faro, she would have known the answer to that question. Each day, he followed his mother's guests around the house just to be near Faro. Whenever he did happen to find himself in her company, his heart beat harder and his thoughts raced off in the most lurid directions imaginable. On those rare occasions when their gazes did meet, she looked at him as if he were a stranger. More often than not, she simply looked away. She could stand next to him and be miles away. It didn't matter that she ignored him. He had to be near her.

His mother's expectant look made him recall his answer. "I attended another of Miss Burke's readings."

Lady Evelyn smiled. "I knew you would come around. Aren't they amazing?"

"Amazingly vague," he said. "Each reading I witnessed could be the truth as easily as it could be a lie."

"You can't still think she is a fraud."

"No," he admitted. "Faro actually believes that she possesses some sort of mystical powers. What she possesses is a very active imagination. She is an incredibly talented painter, and I believe the artistic types are often fanciful at heart. When she does her readings, I'd say she associates the object with some image in her mind, probably the same as she must form an image of a completed painting when she looks at a blank canvas. Then she describes the image and believes she is telling the truth."

"I had no idea you were such an expert," his mother said. She shook her head, but her smile didn't falter. "You must be the most determined skeptic in existence. However, I am glad that you no longer object to Miss Burke's presence here. Isn't she a delightful girl?"

Wyatt just stared at her. "Delightful" was not the term he would use to describe Faro. Desirable, perhaps. Bewitching, better yet. Intelligent, ravishing, strong-willed, stubborn, sweet, sensual . . .

"Perhaps you should ask for another reading," Lady Evelyn suggested, "to convince you of her abilities once and for all." She gestured toward the silver-and-green bottle that sat on the mantel. "Maybe another reading of that odd little bottle."

"She won't touch it," he said. "In any event, by now my coachman may have told others how it came into my possession."

"I would like to hear that story for myself."

"It isn't all that complicated. I came across a Gypsy on my way to Blackburn. My coachman and I helped free her cart from the mud. She gave me the bottle as part of her thanks." He didn't feel any need to mention the Gypsy's claim that the bottle possessed magical powers, or anything else the old woman told him that day. The writing on a small leather scroll he found inside the bottle made even less sense. *To thine own wish be true. Do not follow the moth to the star.* The only moths he'd encountered of late were those that took flight in his stomach whenever he looked at Faro; the only stars, the ones he fancied he could see in her eyes.

She wanted him to forget what had happened between them. He could sooner forget his name. Over the past two days he had relived those moments at the abbey again and again in his mind, memorizing each kiss and caress, every soft sigh. And the look on her face when he told her nothing could come of their kisses.

What a liar he was. With his thoughts muddled by lust and a whole host of less-familiar emotions, he had very likely driven away the only woman he wanted in his life. Even worse, he knew why she would never want him in hers. It was yet another reason to hate her father.

"Wyatt? Are you listening?"

He glanced up. "Pardon me?"

"Never mind. It wasn't all that important." Her brows tilted into a considering expression. "You have all the symptoms, you know. An irritable disposition, a brooding countenance, and the attention span of a gnat."

"What are you talking about?"

"The fact that you are behaving like a man whose thoughts are firmly occupied by a woman."

"Do not raise your hopes," he warned. "You may admire Caroline Carstairs, but something about her rubs me the wrong way. Perhaps it is her voice. I didn't realize how high-pitched and whiny it sounds until I heard her sing. She set every hound in the kennels to howling during last night's recital."

"She does tend to fray one's nerves," Lady Evelyn agreed. "However, she has fine manners. That is, if you like a woman who excels at the art of false flattery and meaningless conversation."

"I thought you liked her."

"What is not to like about her?" she asked. "Especially when there is all that money to consider. Surely that makes up for a lack of musical talent? Of course, she makes little secret of her intention to buy a titled husband. Such a marriage is her only means of entrance to the most coveted ranks of society. You just happen to possess a very old and very respected title. I feel certain Caroline considers you perfect for her next husband."

"You have a strange way of extolling Mrs. Carstairs' virtues," he said. "Just a few days ago you thought her the pattern of an ideal woman."

His mother's smug expression made him wonder what trap yawned before him.

"Caroline is *your* notion of an ideal woman, not mine. She possesses everything you want in a bride—wealth, beauty, and I suspect she has her share of intelligence as well. I had the most terrifying fear you would actually like her."

He spread his hands. "If you didn't want me to consider Caroline, then why did you invite her here?"

"To provide a comparison, of course. If I told you whom I actually preferred from the first, you would probably court Caroline in some misguided effort to prove that my plans for you never work."

His mouth dropped open. "You invited *another* potential bride?"

"But of course." She waved the matter aside, then glanced at the grandfather clock. "We will be late for dinner if we tarry here any longer." She rose and started toward the door, then turned to hold out her hand. "Will you escort me?"

WYATT DIDN'T have to ask the name of the other woman. He knew her identity before they crossed the hallway and walked into the dining room. His gaze traveled the length of the table to his place at the end. His mother's choices for his bride were seated within easy comparison: Caroline in the seat to his left, Faro to his right.

He managed to keep his face expressionless as he escorted his mother to her seat, but leaned down to whisper in her ear. "You know I do not like to be manipulated."

She merely smiled and patted his hand, then turned to

greet the guests nearest her. He made his way to the other end of the table, his gaze on Faro. She wore a violet-colored silk gown tonight, her hair in a typically simple upswept arrangement. He wondered how long her hair might actually be, what it would look like around her shoulders, wrapped around his hands.

Caroline called out a greeting. "We were beginning to think you would forgo dinner tonight, my lord. We haven't seen you all day." Vicar Robbins sat next to Caroline and she laid her hand on the elderly gentleman's sleeve. "The vicar just told us what a shame it was that you didn't compete in the archery contest. He says you are an expert archer. Is that true?"

"My aim is no more than fair," he allowed.

"I am certain you are being modest." She gave him a coy smile. "Do say you will attend tomorrow's contest. The vicar says my aim will improve if someone helps steady my bow. Can I count on your assistance? Perhaps an hour or two of instruction as well?"

He gestured toward the man seated next to Faro. "Squire Elgin is the county's champion archer, Mrs. Carstairs. He is the one who should instruct you."

He turned to look at Elgin, but his gaze stopped at the neckline of Faro's gown. The bodice was cut no lower than any other lady's at the table, but he didn't have such intimate knowledge of those ladies' breasts. The dress revealed far more of Faro than he wanted any other man at the table to know. His hands were at the buttons of his jacket before he checked the ridiculous urge to strip off his coat and wrap the garment around her shoulders.

"I would be pleased to instruct you," the squire said to Caroline. "If it were not for my gout, today's archery prize would be in my hand as we speak. Perhaps we would both benefit from a few additional hours' practice tomorrow morning, Mrs. Carstairs."

"Yes, perhaps," Caroline murmured. She did little to disguise her revulsion at the thought of Elgin's pudgy arms wrapped around her to steady a bow.

The spidery maze of purple veins that covered Elgin's bulbous nose, along with his bright shock of red hair, never failed to remind Wyatt of port wine and carrots. Years of rich food and overindulgence in liquor obscured the once-handsome face of his youth, but the squire still considered himself a ladies' man. He misinterpreted Caroline's disdainful expression completely. "Of course, I shouldn't make such a pleasurable pastime sound like such a chore, should I, Mrs. Carstairs?"

Caroline ignored the remark and smiled again at Wyatt. "How did you while away your afternoon, my lord?"

"I attended Miss Burke's readings in the rose garden." He made a conscious effort to avoid Faro's gaze, knowing he would lose his train of thought the instant he looked at her again. Instead he focused on the vicar. "Which reminds me, how fare the parish rose gardens this year, Vicar?"

"There are several new strains that show promise," the vicar answered, "but the peas are the most exciting news of this year's crop. One is a short, compact variety that does well in the poor soil found close to the shoreline. There are new developments in the bean crop as well."

Wyatt breathed a silent sigh of relief. The vicar was an enthusiastic horticulturist. He could speak for hours on the subject as long as Wyatt remembered to prompt him at the appropriate intervals. The first course arrived as the vicar extolled the virtues of bonemeal.

At previous meals Wyatt had noticed that a plateful of food nearly guaranteed silence from Caroline's quarter. Tonight proved no different. Although careful in her manners, she did little to disguise her amazing appetite. She would doubtless be the size of Squire Elgin in a few years. They both appeared to be contestants in a race to see who could eat the most in one sitting.

Wyatt's gaze moved to Faro. She feigned an interest in the vicar's talk, but her fork did little more than rearrange the food on her plate. She ignored Wyatt entirely. If she remained consistent to her behavior over the past two days, she would do her best to avoid any direct conversation with him, and look his way only when absolutely necessary.

She hated this dinner as much as he did. The stiff set of her shoulders and the chilled air between them destroyed the slim hope that she might end their silent battle of wills. He must be the one to take the first step toward surrender.

An apology might smooth the waters between them. Then again, an apology might lead to disaster. He had a very real fear that once he started, he would say anything to have her accept it, make any besotted plea she might wish to hear just to hold her in his arms again. The arguments he repeated against that course of action were almost a litany. *She is the daughter of my oldest enemy. She lacks a dowry. She fancies herself a fortune-teller.*

The first two had lost their conviction the moment he kissed her. Only the third still held any sway in his thoughts. What sane man would want a fortune-teller as his wife? That keen piece of logic never failed to fortify him in the solitude of his library. Why did it sound so inconsequential whenever she was in the same room? Another day and that last flimsy piece of armor would fall away as well. And then what would he do?

Faro lifted her fork for a small bite of roast beef and he watched her movements the way a hawk would watch its prey. There was no doubt about it. Her mouth was made to drive him wild. He remembered to take a bite of his own food, then he noticed her hands. The fishnet gloves she wore tonight were dyed in the same violet shade as her gown and tied at the wrist with slender silk ribbons. He knew what those ribbons would feel like between his fingers. They would be as warm and smooth as the ribbons that held her chemise in place, as soft as the delicate skin beneath those ribbons. His gaze traveled higher along her bare arms and he imagined his fingertips taking the same path. Then his lips. In his mind, he touched her everywhere he looked.

Vicar Robbins cleared his throat. "Did the crop rotations work as I planned, Lord Wyatt?"

"Yes." He wondered if that was the right answer. He reluctantly turned his attention to the vicar. "I hope you will have time to inspect the apple orchards before you leave tomorrow. The trees didn't develop fruit in the numbers we hoped for this year. The gardeners are at a loss."

"The solution is probably as simple as a few bee skeps

to help pollination next spring." The vicar's dark eyes crinkled at the edges as he smiled at Faro. "You are quiet tonight, Miss Burke. All this talk of horticulture must be terribly boring for those who don't share my enthusiasm."

"On the contrary," she said, "I share your interest, Vicar. Unfortunately, I do not share your expertise. The next time I plant roses, I must try that bonemeal you mentioned. Are there different varieties of bonemeal, or will any type work equally well?"

The vicar launched into another long-winded explanation and Wyatt smiled. It seemed she was not above using his ploy to keep the burden of conversation in the vicar's court. She had no more interest in bonemeal than he did.

He watched her lean forward to take a sip of wine and noticed that Squire Elgin also took a sudden interest in Faro's movements. The squire craned his neck to look as far down the front of her bodice as possible.

Wyatt was halfway out of his seat before he realized the scene that would ensue if he smashed his fist into Elgin's face. The guests nearest Wyatt had already turned their puzzled gazes in his direction. He sat back down and hid his clenched hands beneath the table, braced against his knees.

The vicar spoke first. "Is something amiss, Lord Wyatt?"

"Gout," he managed, through clenched teeth. "In my knee. Sometimes one must exorcise one's demons at inconvenient moments."

Elgin finally glanced up, but didn't seem to realize that Wyatt directed his comments at him. "Gout, eh? Vile ailment."

"How dreadful for you, Lord Wyatt." Caroline offered a sympathetic smile. "My own dear papa suffered from gout. I have recipes for several tonics that will restore you in no time."

With the reins of the conversation in her firm control once more, Caroline rambled on about her tonics. Wyatt kept track of Elgin from the corner of his eye. Caroline's voice was definitely the problem. The sound reminded him of an annoying drone of insects. He would give almost anything to hear Faro's soft, sultry voice again. Not here, though. Alone. In the gardens, perhaps. Better yet, in his bed. Would this dinner never end?

A man could only take so much torture. Sooner or later, he had to tell Faro the truth of his feelings. But not here. Nor any other public place.

For a man who didn't frighten easily, the emotions Faro's kisses unleashed disturbed him plenty. He could still hardly fathom the force that had overcome him at the abbey. One taste of her lips had turned his fancy to sample her charms into a full-blown need to possess her completely. He had lost all control of himself. He'd come to his senses only after he had started to tear the clothes from her body. Just a few more moments in her arms and nothing would have stopped him from completing what they'd started. He had wanted her with a need that approached violence.

It was fear for her safety that made him speak too hastily, to encourage her belief that he had rejected her. She would never know the silent war he had fought with himself on that long ride home. Tonight the battle waged more fiercely than ever before, a battle he was bound to lose.

At last Caroline gave him an expectant look and fell silent. He supplied what he hoped was the appropriate response. "I see."

"Then you will help me practice tomorrow?"

Her question met with baffled silence.

"It sounds as if Mrs. Carstairs will receive her instruction from Lord Wyatt," Elgin said to Faro. Wyatt turned in time to see Elgin's hand come to rest atop hers on the table. "Could I persuade you to join me at archery practice tomorrow morning, Miss Burke?"

Faro didn't answer. She stared down at the squire's hand as if she were frozen in place. Her face turned deathly pale.

"I say, Miss Burke. Are you quite all right?" Elgin picked up her hand and began to pat her wrist. "You look a bit peaked."

"Please," she whispered. "Release my hand."

The squire dropped her hand as if she had slapped him.

Wyatt pushed away from the table and came to stand next to her.

"Miss Burke mentioned earlier that she did not feel well," he told the company. He offered her his hand. "A little fresh air might do you good, Miss Burke."

He felt a triumphant surge of relief when she took his hand without hesitation. "Forgive me," she murmured to the other guests. She rose unsteadily to her feet, and her grip on his hand tightened. "I do feel out of sorts. It seems best if I follow Lord Wyatt's suggestion."

Wyatt tucked her hand into the crook of his arm and led her from the dining room, oblivious to the whispers of speculation that followed them.

CHAPTER SIX

~ල~

WYATT TOOK FARO across the hall to his library. His stiff, formal manner disappeared the moment he closed the door behind them. "What happened in there?"

"I . . . I felt ill." She stripped off her fishnet gloves and they fell unnoticed to the floor. The smell of Squire Elgin's wine-soured breath still cloyed at her senses and she felt a need to escape. Escape what, she wasn't sure, but the places Elgin touched her felt branded by something unclean. She rubbed one wrist with the heel of her palm, hard enough to make the skin chafe. "He is an awful man."

"What did Elgin do to you?" Wyatt's hands became fists at his sides. "Was it a remark I could not hear? Did he grope at you beneath the table?"

"He did nothing but touch my hand. What I saw when he touched me was much worse than anything he could do at a dinner table."

Wyatt's arms remained rigid a moment longer, then he slowly relaxed. "What did you see?"

"It doesn't matter." She crossed the room and took a seat on the jewel-green settee to put distance between them. She had spent too much time in his company already tonight. His nearness was beginning to affect her, to wear at her cloak of indifference. "You wouldn't believe me anyway."

Wyatt followed her across the room and sat next to her. "I know you wouldn't deliberately lie to me."

"But I would lie to you unwittingly?" She hoped to hear his denial, but the hope went unanswered. She folded her arms across her chest. "The young women in Squire Elgin's hire would not call what he does to them a lie, unwitting *or* deliberate."

"There are occasional rumors about Elgin in the village," Wyatt admitted, "but the squire is a wealthy man. Money has a way of silencing rumors." He pursed his lips and his expression darkened. "However, none of the locals will allow their daughters to work in his hire. Is it possible that you overheard something another guest said about the squire, then saw what you expected to see when he touched you?"

"No, that is not what happened. The visions were very—" She stood up and brushed the wrinkles from her skirt. He would never understand her. It was pointless to keep trying. "I appreciate your rescue from the dinner, but now I would like to retire."

"Wait, Faro." He took hold of her hand before she could move it away. "There is something I need to . . . We need to talk."

His touch alone was enough to convince her to stay. She recognized only too well the frustration that radiated from him. It would do neither of them any good to relieve that frustration, but she could not make herself walk away. He released her hand when she sat back down. "Very well, my lord. What must we discuss?"

"You don't know?" His lips parted, then he pressed them together again. His gaze went to her hands, folded primly in her lap. "How can you see Squire Elgin's past, yet see nothing of mine when I touch you?"

"You are different from anyone else. With others I receive impressions. Sometimes those impressions are strong enough to form an image. With you I feel . . ." How could she explain her feelings when she didn't understand them herself? She knew the exact moment when he walked into a room, and she could feel his gaze whenever he looked at her. But when he touched her, she didn't know if the emotions she felt were only her own. Along with desire, those emotions brought a sense of comfort and anticipation. And something else she couldn't name. "I feel—"

"Breathless?" he supplied. "As if the air around you suddenly became lighter? As if your heart beats faster than it should?"

She drew farther away from him. "We should not discuss this. We agreed to forget what happened."

"I don't want to forget." He moved closer, taking her hands in a grip so gentle that she could escape if she wished. "If I recall correctly, we agreed that what happened between us was a mistake."

"Yes, a mistake," she echoed, without much conviction. She couldn't think straight when he touched her. It was happening again, the warm, content feeling that made her relax her guard. He was so close that she could feel his breath brush against her neck, just below her ear. She gritted her teeth, fighting the silent seduction.

"It was a mistake because I knew nothing could come of the kisses we shared. Not at the abbey, where anyone might stumble upon us." He rubbed the pads of his thumbs against her palms and she felt his heart race in rhythm with her own. "Once, a very long time ago, my father said I might fancy myself in love on occasion, but somewhere deep inside I would know when the right woman came along. I knew you were the one I waited for the moment I took you into my arms."

The sweet words made her heart ache with longing. No matter how hard they tried, the power of their attraction couldn't be denied. He wanted her to become his mistress. This man who exuded an air of order and stability, loyalty and common sense, wanted a lover who came from a family that possessed none of those traits.

It was an amazing thing to be wanted by a man, to know that the emotions she felt affected him just as deeply. Emotions foreign to her just a few days ago were now her constant companions. She wanted to smile whenever she saw him. She liked the way he followed her around the house each day. Yet she would not, could not, allow her emotions such free rein. The knowledge that his heart would always be beyond her reach was all that kept an icy barrier around her own. Now she felt it begin to melt—against her will, against every instinct of self-preservation. She tried one last time to delay the inevitable, even as she recognized that her words sounded like an admission of guilt. "I thought we could go on as before."

"I cannot go on another day," he countered. "Not like this, pretending there is nothing between us." His grip on her hands tightened, a telling indication of his need to hold her. "Each morning I wake up wondering where you are, when I will see you next, what we will say. Then I wonder what I will do the morning after you leave Blackburn. I want to see you in my home every day. The sound of your voice is the first thing I want to hear each morning. I want to hold your hand whenever I please because it gives me pleasure just to touch you. There is only one way to keep you here, one way to keep you in my life now and always. I want to marry you, Faro. Say you will be my wife."

She felt the color drain from her face. He gave her time to absorb the shock of his proposal, but she knew there would never be enough time in the world to escape its impact. The notion of marriage and a family of her own had crossed her mind just often enough over the years to leave scars in its wake. For an instant at the abbey she had allowed herself to believe that Wyatt was the one man who could turn a fanciful dream into reality. Now she recalled the frowns and hint of doubt in his eyes whenever she performed a reading and realized a frightening truth. Today she faced the same choice that had ultimately led to her mother's destruction.

"I know this is sudden," he went on, "but you may be certain I gave this matter the weight of consideration it deserves. We are alike in many ways, in the ways that matter most in a long-lasting relationship. As my wife, you would be free to spend more time on your paintings. You wouldn't have to perform readings ever again. For my part, you possess the qualities I always hoped to find in a wife. Marriage will suit us both."

He sounded as if he might be describing the benefits of a particular style of carriage; she would be comfortable on that side, he comfortable on his. At least he had enough sense to avoid the subject of lust, although she had no doubt that it played a large part in the reason for his sudden desire to wed. Men wanted most what they couldn't have, and didn't want what they got. They were a mystery to her, Wyatt the greatest of them all.

"Mrs. Carstairs says you wish to marry an heiress." The words were out of her mouth before she could think better of them. It was a logical argument, so she finished the thought before she lost her nerve. "I do not possess that trait, my lord."

"A large dowry would ease my worries," he admitted, "but I can survive without a wealthy wife."

If he said that she was what he needed to survive, that would sway her mind considerably. She waited for a moment, then decided it was best he remained silent. His silence made her decision much easier. "I cannot marry you, Wyatt."

He didn't appear surprised by her refusal, nor overly upset. "Perhaps I spoke too soon. If a courtship will give you the time you need to consider—"

She stopped him before he could make the decision more painful. "A courtship will make no difference. I cannot marry, now or ever."

"Why . . ." His hands fell away from hers and his mouth became a straight line. "I am not like your father, Faro. It is not in my nature to abandon my wife and children for any reason. I accept your belief in your abilities. I even accept that you may wish to do readings on occasion. My hope is that you will not feel obliged to do quite so many of them."

"You are like my father in more ways than you realize." She tried to smile, but it was a pitiful effort. "He too thought my mother's abilities were no more than a figment of her imagination."

"Then prove the truth of your abilities to me now, and I

will prove that it doesn't matter." He glanced around them, plucked at the sleeve of his jacket. "Tell me something simple, such as the name of my tailor. Or even how that bottle came into my possession."

Her gaze followed his to the mantel. Just the sight of the bottle made a tingle of fear trickle down her spine. Then it happened. The image of them in bed together came instantly to mind. She lowered her head to stare at the carpet until the vision returned to whatever dark part of her memory it sprang from.

No, the bottle would not help convince him of anything. She knew instinctively that it would work against her. "If I tell you the name of your tailor, you will assume that a servant or someone else mentioned the name to me beforehand. You will find a similar explanation for anything else I might try. Except for that bottle, and I will not touch it again. That means there is nothing I can do to remove all your doubts. When you finally realize the truth, it will be because of some small incident. Perhaps something so simple as . . ."

"What is it?" He glanced behind him, then his puzzled gaze returned to her. "Why are you looking at me that way?"

"It just came to me." She stood up and walked toward the desk. "It's a trick that Hazard and I practiced as children. Do you have a paper and pen? Perhaps a pen that no one else uses?"

"I suppose so." He moved behind the desk, then took his seat and opened one of the drawers. First he set a sheaf of paper on the desk, then a polished steel pen. "What do you have in mind?"

"A test," she answered, settling into the chair opposite his. "A test so infallible that even you will know the truth of my abilities. Beyond any doubt. Beyond any measure of skepticism. I don't know why I didn't think of it earlier." She nodded toward the pen. "Does anyone else use that to write?"

"No, it is mine alone."

"Excellent. All you need to do is write a word, or even a

short sentence, on the paper. Then fold and seal it so I cannot see what you wrote inside."

He gave the paper a doubtful look. "What will that prove?"

"After you seal the paper, let me hold the pen and I will tell you what you wrote on the paper." Satisfied that he understood his part, she stood up and glanced at the fireplace. "I will stand by the mantel with my back turned so I cannot see what you write. If you prefer, I can leave the room."

"No," he said. "Dinner will be over by now. It would be best if you stayed here." He propped his elbows on the desk and studied her over steepled fingers. "I'll go along with this reading on one condition. If you cannot read the pen, for whatever reason, I want your agreement that we can marry by special license in no more than a fortnight."

She swallowed a twinge of uncertainty. If she backed down now, she would only confirm his doubts. It was needless to worry. She had never failed this test. "Very well. But what if I do the reading correctly?"

The corners of his mouth tightened. "I told you it will make no difference. I will still want to marry you, whatever your terms."

"My terms are a courtship," she said quickly. "A very long courtship."

He gave her a small nod of agreement. A far too easy agreement. He didn't think she could pass his test. He smoothed the paper with the palm of his hand, then picked up the pen. "Let's get this over with."

FARO STOOD by the fireplace and studied the pattern of the brass fire screen. Almost against her will, she found her gaze drawn to the bottle that sat on the mantel. The silver bands gleamed like molten liquid in the soft lamplight, a deceptively pretty object to contain so many disturbing memories. It seemed to beckon her fingers toward the shimmering surface, teasing her to take another peek at what it offered. She clasped her hands firmly behind her back.

The sound of Wyatt's pen as it scratched across the paper came to her. The slow, deliberate strokes seemed to indicate his uncertainty. She heard the rustle of paper, then more scratches. This time the strokes were smooth and sure.

A few moments later, he called out to her. "You may return now."

The cream-colored paper lay neatly folded on the blotter. His elbows rested on the edge of the desk, but he didn't look at ease. "Are you ready?"

He gave her the pen when she nodded. The steel felt warm and smooth in her hand. She turned the barrel between her fingertips. So much depended on this reading. For an instant she felt an urge to refuse the reading, to tell him she could not sense anything. But that would only make her a fraud in his eyes, and a deliberate liar.

Instead she propped her wrist on the edge of the desk and concentrated. A drop of ink splashed unnoticed onto the blotter as the first hazy vision began to take shape. Her eyes drifted shut and she could see the images more clearly. Amazingly, she saw herself, just as she must appear to Wyatt at that exact moment. She turned the pen between her fingertips and the pen in the image turned as well.

Her eyes flew open and the image disappeared. Wyatt stared back at her, one brow raised in question. She looked at the pen, then back at Wyatt. "Did you feel anything . . . unusual happen just now?"

"Was I supposed to feel something?"

"No," she said thoughtfully, "I just wondered if you had."

Mostly she wondered what was happening to her. Certainly nothing that had happened before. The reading wouldn't be quite so easy as she thought. This time she focused her attention on the paper, then turned the pen between her fingers once more.

Kiss me.

Faro's head snapped up and she eyed him suspiciously. "Did you say something?"

"Not a word." He looked as if he was telling the truth. She lowered her lashes, then squeezed her eyes tightly shut. Focus. *Concentrate.* In her mind's eye, she willed the paper to unfold itself, to reveal the writing inside.

It didn't work. Rather than seeing the writing, she kept hearing Wyatt's voice echo again and again in her mind. He said the strangest things. Then she realized why.

The corners of her mouth turned upward and she opened her eyes. Wyatt still watched her, a hesitant look on his face until he saw her smile. He leaned forward in his chair, his tone almost hopeful. "You know the answer?"

"Of course." She placed the pen on the desk, pleased that he seemed anxious to believe her after all. "It was the oddest reading. I couldn't see the words, but I heard them as if you spoke them aloud. It's a rather cryptic little phrase: *To thine own wish be true. Do not follow the moth to the star.*"

His look of stunned disbelief was all the proof she needed. She had passed the test. Wyatt picked up the folded paper and stared at it the way a man might stare at his own death sentence, looking torn between the urge to open it and to shred it into tiny pieces.

"I didn't realize you were such a poor loser, Wyatt." She tried a sympathetic smile, but his scowl only deepened.

"I didn't lose." He held the paper out to her, and she saw something that might be regret in his eyes. "Not really."

"Of course you lost." The bolt of alarm that shot through her belied the certainty of her words. She almost dropped the note in her haste to unfold it. Just two words were scrawled in the middle, written in a bold, masculine hand.

MARRY ME.

"I don't believe it. There must be some mistake. There *has* to be some mistake." She turned the paper over, but the only written words were on the other side. Then she knew there was no mistake. She had lost.

"Don't be upset, Faro. There is more—"

"Of course I am upset." She stood up and the paper drifted to the floor. "No matter what that paper says, I am not a fraud, and I am *not* a liar!"

"I know."

She blinked back the tears that clouded her vision. "You know?"

He opened his desk drawer and removed another piece of paper. There in the middle of the page were the neatly printed words:

To thine own wish

His betrayal washed over her with the force of a tidal wave. She started to back away from the desk. "You meant to trick me. You *deliberately* tried to deceive me."

"That isn't true. If you will just—"

A firm knock at the door interrupted him. Lady Evelyn stepped inside the library, but her smile faded when she caught sight of them. "I . . . just wanted to make certain Faro had recovered." Her gaze moved from one distraught expression to the other. "Whatever is the matter?"

"Excuse me, Lady Evelyn," Faro murmured. She caught a sob behind her hand as she brushed past her hostess. Once she reached the hallway, she started to run.

CHAPTER SEVEN

$\backsim$

$\mathcal{S}$OMEWHERE IN THE house a clock struck midnight. Wyatt took a slow, deep breath, then rapped on the hidden panel that led to Faro's bedchamber. He turned his ear toward the panel, but there was no response from the other side. He released the lever and the panel popped open. Not wanting to startle her, he held his lamp higher and called out in a soft voice. "Faro?"

His gaze moved around the room to take in its feminine luxury, a suite his mother saved for her favorite guests. Striped silk the exact shade of peaches covered the walls and made up the bedding, the pattern repeated in oversized bows that held cream-colored drapes and bed-curtains in place. The painted woodwork glowed the warm golden shade of cream as well. The room always reminded Wyatt of a confectioner's workshop.

A single candle burned by the bedside, little more than a stub. The draft that came through the paneled door made the fragile flame sputter and die. He reached behind him to close the panel and held the lamp higher.

Faro was fast asleep, curled into a protective ball in the center of the bed. A prim white nightgown cloaked her body, enticing curves and hollows sheathed in lawn and lace. He drank in the sight of her. Her lashes lay like delicate fans against her cheeks, but her eyelids looked swollen, evidence that she had cried herself to sleep. He felt a stab of regret even as he noticed the pencil she held in her limp grasp. His gaze moved to the papers scattered all around her. He set his lamp on the bedside table, then picked up two of the papers and held them closer to the light.

The sketches were not of landscapes or buildings. They were pictures of him—so many that he wondered if she had started drawing them the very day he arrived. In one picture he saw himself staring back from the balcony in the gallery, exactly as he must have appeared to her that first night. The sketch of him in the library looked equally forbidding, his black-and-white clothing as stark and austere as his expression. Oddly shaped tendrils curled away from the bottle he held and his hand looked encased in a strange mist. Was that how the bottle had appeared in her vision?

He turned to pick up more of the sketches. There were drawings of him on horseback, at the abbey, at dinners and gatherings. Each captured a different look or expression. It was as if she meant to record them all.

He sorted through the pictures until he uncovered the last drawing, brought to life with her watercolors. The painting made the breath catch in his throat. Unlike the others, she appeared in this picture with him, their legs tangled in peach-and-cream-colored silk.

They were naked.

His eyes widened as his gaze moved along the slender curves of painted hips and thighs to the lush swell of her breasts. In the portrait she lay on her side with her hand resting on his bare hip. He could almost feel her touch upon him. He could most definitely feel the hard stir of lust. The erotic picture left little to the imagination. It fired his all the same. He imagined the heat of her body against his, the touch of their skin. Then he noticed the writing along one corner of the picture. It was a date, the same as the night he had arrived at Blackburn, the same night they met. Next to the date were the words, *Images from Wyatt's Bottle*.

"Good God!" He dropped the sketch as if it had burned him.

Faro stirred at the sound of his voice. Her eyes opened

halfway and she gave him a sleepy smile. That smile faded when she took in his shocked expression. She sat up abruptly and drew the covers to her chin. "What are you doing here?"

"I had to come." He tried desperately to push the vision of her naked body from his mind. That didn't happen. The image would be there always. He focused on her mouth, the bewitching curve of her lower lip. "You wouldn't answer any of the notes I sent earlier."

She glanced toward the door, where a half-dozen notes lay on the floor. He had sent a servant every half hour to slide one under the door. All remained unopened, his wax seals still intact. Her gaze moved next to the sketches. "Oh, no!"

A flurry of white lace soon followed. First she swept the papers into her arms. After one wild-eyed glance around the room, she leaped off the mattress and shoved the sketches under the bed. A blush covered her from the crown of her forehead to somewhere beneath the scooped neckline of her nightgown. He thought it a nice contrast to the chaste white fabric. "There is nothing you need to tell me that cannot wait until morning."

He stared at the outline of her breasts beneath the nightgown, then he noticed the small satin ribbons that trailed from the neckline. It took a concentrated effort to force his gaze to her face. "You rushed out of the library before I could explain what happened. Then you ignored all the messages I sent to you since then. I could hardly present myself at your door when any of the guests or servants might see me." He gestured toward the hidden panel. "No one is about at this time of night, but I thought it best to make my entrance through a more discreet passage. No one will know I am here."

"*I* know you are here!" She took so many deep breaths that he worried she would faint.

He tried his best to reassure her. "I am here to do nothing but talk, Faro."

"In my bedchamber?" She pressed her lips into a straight line. "There is nothing more we have to say to each other. I will not—"

"Faro, please be quiet and listen to me." The firm tone of his voice startled her into silence. She sat on the edge of the bed and folded her arms across her chest. "I never meant to deceive you. The phrase I started to write was so long that it didn't seem a fair test. I didn't realize my indecision would make a difference."

He dropped to one knee at her side and withdrew the bottle from his coat pocket. She immediately edged away from him. "You don't have to touch the bottle. I just want to show you what's inside." He removed the small leather scroll and unrolled it so she could see the message.

She read the words aloud. " 'To thine own wish be true. Do not follow the moth to the star.' " She gave him a sharp glance. "What does it mean?"

"It means you can read my mind. You recited even the parts I didn't write."

Her eyes widened. She opened her mouth to say something, then changed her mind.

"Have you ever done that before?"

"I didn't know that I could." She looked up at him, her expression still dazed. "You know the truth about me now. Why are you here?"

"I told you it would make no difference."

She didn't believe him.

"The Gypsy who gave me this bottle said I would understand its meaning when I understood myself." He gave her a lopsided smile as he stuffed the bottle and its message back into his pocket. "I thought her crazed. Now I realize that what I thought I wanted in my life isn't at all what I need." He took her hands in his and turned them over to gently kiss each palm. "You are my wish, Faro."

Her hands felt stiff and cold; her face was expressionless as she looked away from him. "I am . . . different. You *know* I am different."

"Yes, this pretty much proves that you are the most unique woman I have ever known." His attempt at humor fell flat. She still wouldn't meet his gaze. "Everything about you draws me closer, Faro. Haven't you figured that out yet? You have a true gift, but I will not lie and say it does not worry me. I wonder how you survive in a world filled with skeptics and the likes of Squire Elgin. It makes me almost frantic to think of you alone, even though I know you can manage well enough without me. What I cannot imagine is how I will manage without you."

"You will manage. The truth of what I am will repulse you in time."

"Look at me, Faro. The truth you want is in my eyes." He lifted her chin with the tips of his fingers. "If a long courtship is what it will take to convince you that I am not the same sort of man as your father, then I will court you for however long you desire. Name the test to prove my devotion. Name a dozen tests if you wish."

He cupped her face in one hand and took heart when she rubbed her cheek against his open palm. The movement was so slight that she probably wasn't even aware of her reaction.

"I know what it feels like to be torn by doubts," he said, "to need proof before you can overcome those doubts. We are alike in that way, skeptics to the end. Perhaps that is part of what draws me to you. I will never try to change what you are, but I will do whatever it takes to change your mind about me." He brushed his thumb over the hollow of her cheek, marveling at its softness. His voice became a husky whisper. "Will you tell me what I can do to banish your doubts?"

"There is nothing," she answered, her words just as quiet. Her eyes shimmered, then one crystal tear rolled down her cheek. "You want my heart, and I cannot live without it when you leave me."

"I have your heart already, Faro." He caught her tear on the tips of his fingers, then pressed the trace of dampness to the center of his chest. "Just as you have mine."

Tears turned her eyes to liquid blue. Wyatt knew he could drown there. She took one unsteady breath, then another, then the next gasp turned into a broken sob. He sat next to her on the bed and held out his hands, silently offering the comfort of his arms. She went to them willingly.

"Hush, love. I am here now. I will always be here." He pulled a handkerchief from his pocket and pressed it into her hand, feeling helpless. She didn't believe him, and that meant she didn't trust him. His tone turned desperate. "Stay with me, Faro. You can do readings every day, if you wish. Or, turn your attention to painting, if you would rather. You could be happy here." He stroked her hair while she struggled for control. "Have a little faith in me, Faro. Your heart is safe in my keeping. Let me love you."

She laid her cheek against his shoulder and her hand went to his chest, where she began to draw small, random circles around one of his shirt buttons. "You know the right words to weaken me, to tempt me toward what will only hurt us both."

"You view me as your adversary?"

"No. You are my fate, Wyatt."

She looked awfully grim about it. He tried to reassure her. "The fates will be kind to us. There are too many signs that we were meant to be together." That made no noticeable difference in her expression. He thought about a more obvious sign and chose his words carefully. "I saw your sketches, the picture of your vision when you read the bottle. Is that part of your fear, turning that vision into a reality?"

She lifted her hand to his face and stroked her fingertips over the rough surface of his cheek. "That is what I fear least."

They stared at each other for what seemed an eternity, nothing spoken, yet a wealth of meaning passed between them. Some things could be denied. Others, like fate and destiny, were inevitable.

Wyatt brought his mouth down to hers, slowly, sweetly, savoring the taste of her on his lips. The sweetness lasted no more than a moment, until she returned his kiss with a passion that made his body strain against the need to hold on to his precious control. She opened her mouth and the kiss turned carnal. The hours he had spent dreaming of this moment paled to insignificance until only his longing for her remained a clear memory. The erotic mating of their tongues made his senses reel.

He wouldn't stop this time. He knew that, even as his hand smoothed a course down her neck and beyond. His lips followed, and he kissed her neck and shoulders. She smelled of orange blossoms everywhere. "Do you want me, Faro?"

She didn't answer. Instead she began to nuzzle his neck.

Her fingers worked at a button, then her hand slipped inside his shirt. Such an innocent touch, her hand pressed against the bare skin of his chest. He couldn't recall another caress more provocative. He lowered his head for another taste of her, even as he told himself to be gentle.

He eased her down onto the pillows, his mouth never leaving hers. He memorized the lines of her body with his hands. There were times when his explorations became too intimate, but she made no objection. Nor could he feel any stiffening in her body that would indicate resistance. She was probably too busy unbuttoning his shirt to notice. The way her hands fluttered over his bare chest drove him mad.

"I can take no more, sweetheart." He braced himself on his elbows above her. "Say that you want me, or tell me to leave."

She tried to pull his head down for another kiss, but he shook his head.

"I want to hear the words, Faro. I *need* to hear the words." The sadness in her eyes said he expected too much too soon. "You know that I will always take care of you."

"I do not doubt your sincerity." She smoothed her hands over the muscles of his chest, exploring the planes and contours. "Make love to me, Wyatt."

They were the words he wanted most to hear. Why did they set off a warning in his mind? He decided there would be time to reason that out later. The words were enough for now, especially when her hands seemed so determined to make him crazed.

First she rubbed his chest with the pads of her fingers, a long stroke upward. Then she curled her fingers to let her nails rake a path downward. Over and over. He wanted to grab her wrists to stop the agonizing pleasure. He stared at her hands in helpless fascination. At last she lingered at his waistband to trace the line between the fabric and the taut skin of his stomach. He didn't know if it was relief or disappointment that made his breath come out in a rush when she finally stopped.

"Did that hurt?" She looked concerned, but he managed to shake his head. The tips of her fingers began another upward stroke. "Should I do it again?"

He shook his head harder. Despite his words, he shrugged off his shirt and jacket, then lay down again beside her. He started to push a lock of hair over her shoulder, then stopped to rub the silky stuff between his fingers. "I want you to touch me, love. But there are times when your touch feels too good. Too tempting. You take my control from me."

"There are times when I think you are too controlling, Wyatt." Her brows drew together in a small frown. "Life is not always exactly as you wish it."

"Tonight will be." He gave her a taste of what he planned by placing measured kisses along the line of her jaw, then her cheekbones, over her forehead, down the tip of her nose. He teased her mouth with small kisses at the corners until her lips parted. The tiny trail of kisses across her lower lip made her breathing sound more and more uneven. He rubbed his thumb over her lip to seal his kisses there.

"You see? There is pleasure in control." He traced a line across her chest that followed the neckline of her nightgown, then lower to explore the curve of one breast. Her nipple became a hard bud beneath the smooth material. He teased her deliberately by drawing ever-closing circles around the peak with the tip of his finger. The small, inarticulate sounds she made delighted him. "My intent is to hold fast to my control until I make you lose your own. That is the only way I can be certain to sate all your desires before I sate my own. I want to give you pleasure so intense that you will scream when I release you from it."

"I will not sc—" Her eyes grew round and wide when his head moved toward her chest. His tongue revealed the dusky perfection of her nipple through pale, wet fabric. "Ohhh!"

He drew the succulent bud between his teeth and she moaned, long and loud. Her hands tangled in his hair to pull him away one moment, then hold him closer the next. He wedged his knee between her legs and she curled her hips forward to press herself intimately to his thigh. The moan he heard then was his own.

He stroked the nightgown from her body with caresses that ranged from innocent to sensual, all while he ruined the fabric with his mouth. His fingers skimmed over her knee, where he took a handful of the skirt and dragged it slowly upward, aware of every inch of material that passed between their sensitized skin. She lifted her arms to let him pull the garment over her head and he caught her wrists before she could lower her arms again. He leaned back to look at her.

Viewing the perfection of her body was an experience to linger over, to allow the images to imprint themselves on his mind. First came her face, her kiss-swollen lips, the cloudy haze of passion in her beautiful eyes. Her hair tumbled across the pillows in rich waves the color of roasted chestnuts, a vivid contrast to the pale white of her neck and shoulders. Her skin reminded him of finely powdered sugar against the cream-colored sheets. Perhaps this room was a confectioner's shop, after all.

He started to smile at the thought, even as his gaze drifted to her breasts, to sweet, snowy mounds crested with luscious raspberries. He wet his lips. The slender lines of her waist drew his eye to the curve of her hips, then the dark triangle that covered another small mound. Chocolate came instantly to mind and his mouth began to water. A hint of alarm made him look quickly at her legs, the long, shapely curves the same he could make with his tongue on a stick of hard candy if he ever decided to do it. His eyes traveled a slow path upward again, and thoughts of every sweet confection in existence filled his head.

She pulled her hands from his limp grasp and did her best to shield herself from the intimate perusal. "What is wrong?"

"Wrong?" He focused unsteadily on her face. The worry he saw there was enough to register in his senses, but not enough to shake him from his daze. "I want to eat you whole."

She looked uncertain for a moment, then she gave him a shy smile. "I think I shall insist on nothing more than small nibbles."

"Nibbles," he repeated dumbly. The word alone made the ache in his groin turn painful.

"Your skin feels so hard, yet so smooth." She reached

up to run her hand over his chest and stomach. Her voice dropped to a confessional whisper. "I want to taste you, too."

"My God." He rolled onto his back and squeezed his eyes shut. That only made images of her tasting him leap instantly to life. He tried to concentrate on long, deep breaths, without much success.

"Wyatt?"

"Give me a minute. Or two." He said a quick, silent prayer that she would not pick this moment to act out her wishes. A slight stir of her fingers against his chest and his hand locked around her wrist. He laced his fingers through hers, then held both their hands to his forehead.

"I was a fool to think I could maintain any degree of control with you." He opened his eyes and found her face almost directly above his. "I don't want to hurt you, Faro."

She leaned down to kiss the corner of his mouth. "You could never hurt me."

Under different circumstances, he would have laughed. The tips of her breasts raked against his chest and shoulder, branding him as surely as the scar he bore. Her attention turned to his shoulder and she pressed her lips to the marred skin, more compelling proof that she could read his thoughts.

"You are a man familiar with pain, and I suspect you know how to inflict it. Yet I feel the care you take when you touch me, the gentleness inside you." Her lips moved to the center of his chest and her tongue darted out to take a small, quick taste of him. "When you hold me, I feel cherished."

The sensual kiss didn't turn him into a mindless animal as he had feared. Instead her words had an oddly calming effect on him. The demands of his body faded before the sudden need to fill the void he sensed in her. Had anyone in her life really cherished her?

His arms went around her again and his hand traveled the length of her back. He slowed the caress to explore the indentation of her waist and the enticing curve of her hip. "It seems I have always dreamed of holding you this way, your bare skin pressed to mine. You are so warm, so soft. My skin burns wherever you touch me. Yours must be on fire."

Her brows tilted in silent question.

"When is the last time anyone touched you?" he asked. "I know your father ignored you, but what about your mother? Was she the last to hug you, the last to bestow an affectionate kiss?"

Faro lowered her lashes and caught her lower lip between her teeth. "Mother did not touch us often. She said it gave her headaches."

He stared at her in mute shock, but his expression was enough to set her on the defensive.

"Hazard and I never doubted her love. We were her only compensation for the great mistake she made when she married our father."

Wyatt couldn't believe what he was hearing, didn't want to believe it. The full realization of what he was up against finally struck him. How could Faro conceive the thought of a lasting love when no one had ever truly loved her? Except, perhaps, her brother, although Wyatt would lay any odds that Hazard knew as little about love as his sister.

There wasn't any doubt in his mind about her virginity, yet there would be much more to this night than its loss. He would be her first lover in every possible context of the words. The responsibility overwhelmed him. Even so, fate bestowed him with this gift for a reason. As far as he could tell, he was the only person in her life who would not fail her.

He laced his fingers through her hair and made the most solemn vow of his life. "The children I give you will be the proof of our love, Faro, and one of the greatest rewards of our marriage."

"I cannot—"

He pressed his fingers to her lips, silencing the objection. "I suspect there is nothing in this world you could not do, if you set your mind to it. We shall have a fine argument on the subject in the morning." His fingertips brushed downward, then his hand closed over one soft breast to give her an intimate caress. "You are naked in my arms, love. There is little else I can concentrate upon at the moment."

She gave him a skeptical look, its impact diminished by the small gasps she made as he caressed her.

"Tonight should be perfect for both of us," he went on. "I can feel the desire in you. Give yourself over to it just this once, without hesitation, without fear of what tomorrow will bring." He captured her lips for a long, sensual kiss. When it ended, the light of passion burned brightly in her eyes. "You deserve to be greedy, Faro. Take all the pleasure I can give you. Demand it."

The words seemed to set something free inside her, as if he had just lifted a dark shroud from her shoulders. The shadow of fear that never left her gaze disappeared. For this one night, she would be his. "I love you, Faro."

"I . . ." She gave him a helpless look.

"It's all right," he said, his voice low and reassuring. "I will never be far away when you are ready to tell me." He pressed a kiss to her forehead, then continued to speak around the kisses he rained across her face. "Tonight just let yourself enjoy my love. Wrap yourself in it. I promise to set you free in the morning."

He reached her lips and sealed his vow. The kiss was the sweetest he had ever known. Their hands started to explore each other as reverently as their mouths. Faro gave herself over to his lovemaking with abandon, hiding nothing in her response to his increasingly erotic caresses. Encouraged, he urged her hand to the waistband of his pants, then lower to let her feel the length of his hard erection. It was a delightful torture, yet he felt relieved when she continued to fondle him after he took his hand away.

"I thought you might fear my body," he murmured.

Her eyes glowed with a mischievous smile. "You saw a painting of my vision. Surely you noticed we were naked. How do you think I knew about your scar?" Her fingertips traced the mark on his shoulder. "But I saw much more than your scar, my lord. Your modesty is misplaced."

"You saw all of me?" He arched one brow. "You might have mentioned that sooner."

"It didn't occur to me that you might think I would fear you."

The answer satisfied him, probably more than she knew.

His hands went to the fastenings of his pants, but she wouldn't relinquish control of her territory so easily.

"I saw you in my vision, but I did not get to touch you," she explained. His hands fell to his sides. "You said I should be greedy, even though I have touched you so much already that my fingers tingle. Do yours?"

He simply nodded, beyond explaining that it was a much different part of him that tingled. She sat up and worked the buttons of his pants free from top to bottom, her fingers made clumsy by the unfamiliar fastenings. There were five buttons in all. By the third, he wished there were a hundred. The slow release from the confining fabric and the pressure of her hands at each buttonhole made for intensely seductive foreplay, although Faro seemed unaware of her part in it. He hadn't adopted the custom of wearing drawers beneath his pants, and she stared at his emerging erection with open fascination. "It looks painful. Does it hurt?"

"Only when you stop to stare at me that way." Her expression when she glanced at his face was one he would never forget. Wicked innocence. "Are you drawing this out on purpose?"

The corners of her mouth curved upward and she pretended to concentrate on the last fastening. "You seem to enjoy it."

The simple honesty of her answer was another treasure. No coyness, no artifice he expected to find in other women. She was like no one else he knew, and she would never cease to surprise him. Her transformation from cool reserve to heated seductress made him wonder what lucky star he walked under. Even the dreams that woke him up at night were not this good. Or could this be . . . A quick pinch to his arm dispelled that moment of panic.

She tugged at the waistband of his pants and he lifted his hips, captivated by the range of emotions that played across her face as she undressed him. The hunger in her eyes made him suspect they might share the confection-shop fantasy. She wet her lips and reached out to touch him, hesitant at first, but bold soon enough. Her hand slid down his erection, a single stroke to take in his length.

Then her hand closed around him and she squeezed. Hard. His low groan felt as if it started in his toes.

"Enough play." He caught her hand, his voice harsh. When he opened his arms to her, she stretched out half her weight on top of him. He rolled to his side to reverse their positions. His knee slipped between her legs in the same movement, then his hand caressed a path from her shoulders to the curve of her hip. "I want to touch you first, a little like the way you touched me, only different."

The words made little sense, and it showed in her expression. He didn't even try to explain how he intended to make her body ready to accept him. His hand moved lower, then brushed the downy softness of her inner thigh. Her eyes widened over the intimacy, but her hips arched upward in silent protest when he withdrew his hand. He repeated the small caress and drew a fraction of an inch closer to her heat. This time she also arched her neck, offering her breasts in an unconscious invitation.

"Wyatt."

His name sounded like a plea. He shook his head in a gentle denial. It was far too soon for her to be pleading. Or was it? He caressed her legs again, but this time he fit his hand into the junction of her thighs.

The heat of her desire was incredible. He felt the dampness on his palm before his fingers even parted her. Little wonder she shifted impatiently, her body seeking more from him by instinct alone. She was ready for him already.

That left only one worry about their lovemaking. The knowledge that he would soon feel her soft thighs around his waist made it hard to remember his name, much less any worries. He could hardly wait to feel her warm, wet sheath close around him. That thought made him remember his purpose.

"Put your arms around my neck, Faro." His voice sounded strange to his ears, barely recognizable.

As soon as she complied, he eased the tip of his finger inside her. He withdrew and returned again, this time a little deeper. She buried her face against his neck to muffle her gasps. He repeated the movements over and over, as slowly as he could manage, relieved when he failed to encounter a barrier. That lack of physical proof made her no less innocent. Her body felt so small and tight inside that he suspected there would still be some measure of pain, but there could be no more delay for either of them. She gasped each time his finger moved inside her, but now she bit his shoulder as well. The demands of his own body were impossible to ignore.

Her hips rose to welcome his weight when he positioned himself at the entrance of her body. His hands framed her face and their gazes met to communicate everything that went unsaid. Her eyes reflected her every emotion, doubts and anticipation, uncertainty and desire, then a sense of wonder when he began to slowly ease inside her.

Her body closed around him, resisting the invasion. With one hard, deep thrust, he buried himself within her body. Her nails dug into his shoulders, but she only gasped at the suddenness of his invasion.

"I'm sorry, Faro." He wondered how the words could sound so lucid. He tried to hold himself still until her body could adjust to his, but the incredible sensations of being a part of her made control a thought that came and went. She was small, yes, but perfect for him. Her tight sheath squeezed him in far more seductive ways than her hand, an unconscious invitation that battered at his discipline. Her hands flexed and gripped his shoulders, her toes curled and uncurled against the backs of his legs in the same rhythm. Her whole body beckoned to him. He didn't mean to speak his thoughts aloud, but he didn't regret the words. "You are mine now."

That simple, possessive declaration made it impossible to remain still any longer. He drew away and sank slowly into her again. He tilted his head back and closed his eyes to appreciate the feel of her. His low groan spoke of intense pleasure. The sounds Faro made alternated between shock and surprise, then pleasure as well when she experimented with a small movement of her own. The last of his worries disappeared.

The slow, deliberate pattern he set came as a pleasant surprise, the demand for haste tamped down by the desire to savor each moment. Whenever he sensed her need to slow down, he could even stop to cherish her passionate body, to delight in her wonderful responsiveness. She tried to hold his gaze, but often her lashes fluttered closed. She made the lustiest sounds in the back of her throat. A few more strokes and she arched up to meet each of his thrusts, matching his rhythm, yet at the same time, urging him to increase the pace.

It seemed she took him at his word when he said to be greedy. Soon her legs tightened around him and only her shoulders touched the mattress when he surged into her, then she pressed the soles of her feet down his thighs as she stretched out her legs. She didn't learn how to make love so much as revel in it. She amazed him, her untutored love-making as wild and untamed as it was beautiful. The look on her face each time she met his gaze was one of sheer bliss. It humbled him to think he could give her such joy.

"Always, Faro." He wanted to tell her so much more— how he had never known that making love with the right woman really was making love. How he couldn't recall his life before she came into it, or conceive of his life if she left it. He had promised to let her go in the morning. He would never let her go.

He held her tighter, thrust harder and deeper, anything that would ease the need to somehow mark her, brand her as his own. Possessiveness rushed through him, and a hint of desperation.

It didn't really surprise him when she read his thoughts. She cupped his face in her hands, her expression suddenly solemn. "There will never be another for me. You are . . ."

Her eyes widened and he watched the powerful release take hold of her. He felt it in every inch of their joined bodies. The beauty of her climax took his breath away. Then the same force reached out to take him as well. He felt caught in an undertow, towed deeper and deeper beneath the waves until he thought he would drown. His last breath came out in a shout. His seed flowed into her at the same moment and the tide of passion suddenly thrust him upward again. He closed his eyes against the rush of emotions that hurtled him toward the sunlight, toward the very stars themselves.

CHAPTER EIGHT

FARO STUFFED THE last of her clothing into the worn satchel, careful to make as little noise as possible. The small click of the latch sounded like a cannon shot and her gaze darted to the bed. Wyatt continued to sleep undisturbed, his head burrowed into a pillow, one leg angled to display his backside in all its erotic perfection. The lump of regret she swallowed down went straight to her heart.

Nothing lasted forever. She had known that when she pretended last night would never end. The rose-colored light of dawn that bathed her window mocked the folly of those wishful thoughts. She had to leave now, before anything could mar the memories of their last wonderful hours together. It would serve no purpose to part with cross words. Someday he would recognize the favor she had done them both by sneaking off this way. At first he would be angry, but he would get over that anger in a few days as easily as last night had surely cured his lust for her. He would forget her, and they could both go on with their lives.

Why was it so hard to do the right thing?

One of her sketches peeked out from under the bed and she walked closer. Her gaze went to Wyatt again as she bent down to reach for the drawing. A pair of golden eyes stared back at her.

"Looking for something?" One brow rose as his gaze swept the length of her, taking in the dark blue traveling gown she wore. He rolled to his side and propped his weight on one elbow. "Or are you going somewhere?"

"Today is Friday," she blurted out. "I am supposed to leave today."

It was a ridiculous explanation, but as close to the truth as she wanted to venture. Wyatt didn't seem concerned by the announcement. He yawned and stretched out his body like a big, lazy cat. "Where are we off to?"

"I must return to London." Her voice sounded breathless and she cleared her throat to force out a steadier sound. "Lady Salton invited me to her tea on Monday, and I promised to attend."

"Teas are rather boring affairs," he said, "but I suppose we will manage to live through it."

She watched him rise from the bed to retrieve his trousers, then kept her gaze on the floor while he pulled them on. "I didn't realize you were invited."

"Lady Salton won't mind my presence," he assured her. "Not when she realizes we are courting. Indeed, she will likely be thrilled that we chose her tea to make our first appearance as a couple. It's rather fortunate that her tea is next on your agenda. I must return to London anyway to secure a special license. That will spare us the public nuisance of the banns."

"You promised to let me go this morning." She tried to keep her eyes averted from his face, but found herself fascinated by the way he scratched his chest. The remembered feel of those hard muscles made her fingertips tingle.

"You are not a prisoner here, love. We haven't had a kidnapping in the family for at least a hundred years. While the notion holds a certain romantic appeal, it tends to reflect badly on one's reputation. You may leave Blackburn whenever you wish." He folded his arms across his chest and gave her a stern look. "However, in case you haven't realized, I intend to leave with you. No matter where you go."

"You can't."

"I can," he countered. "A measure of discretion will be in order until you let me announce our engagement. We'll bring my mother along to chaperone. Her presence will ensure that your reputation does not suffer, yet I am certain she will turn a blind eye to *my* presence in your bed at night. She wants us to wed almost as much as I do."

That bit of news came as a surprise. "Your mother wants you to marry *me*?"

"Did I forget to tell you?" He gave her an innocent smile. "I am the reason she invited you to Blackburn. She meant to show me the difference between the type of woman I thought I wanted, and the woman who could make me happy." He looked around the floor, then picked up his shirt and shook out the wrinkles. "I begin to think she is in league with that Gypsy."

He spoke so surely of their future together that she was tempted to believe him, to pretend just a little longer. She shook her head to keep that thought from taking hold. "I cannot marry you, Wyatt."

"Why not?" Such a simple question. His steady gaze demanded an honest answer.

The truth slipped out unbidden. "I am afraid."

He tossed the shirt on the bed and walked toward her. She backed away until her heels touched the wall. Her gaze fastened on his chest, an overwhelming wall of male strength, yet she sensed only security. He stopped just a step away from her, his voice achingly gentle. "Do I truly frighten you, love?"

"It's me," she whispered. "I will do something wrong and you will stop loving me. I . . . I have that effect on people. You know about my father, but I lied to you about my mother. She pretended that she loved Hazard and me, but by the time she died we both knew that she didn't. Even Hazard is starting to tire of me. He scarce listens to anything I say these days. Sometimes I think he defies me on purpose."

"Of course he does." Wyatt caught her hands between his and rubbed his warmth into them. "Your brother is of an age when all young men defy authority. That doesn't mean he loves you any less. It only means he is growing up."

He sounded very certain of his opinion. She wanted badly to believe him. "Do you think so?"

"I know so." The corners of his mouth tightened. "However, your parents are another matter entirely. I want your promise right now that you will let our children love you."

Her brows drew together in confusion. "You cannot control a child's love."

"Yes, you can." He reached out to stroke her cheek, his expression filled with patience. "Don't you see, sweetheart? Rather than avoid your mother's mistakes, you seem determined to repeat them exactly."

"I will not!" The notion terrified her. She wanted to run as far from that fear as possible. "I will not marry you, which means I cannot possibly repeat her mistakes."

"So you would live out your life alone? Deny yourself the love of a husband and family?" He shook his head. "How much different would that life be from your mother's?"

Her eyes widened. Deep inside she recognized the horrible truth of his words. He reached out and placed his hand over the curve of her belly.

"You took my seed more than once last night and may carry my child already. Would you deny that child your love because it would remind you too much of the love you would deny between us?"

"No!" She caught her lower lip between her teeth to keep it from trembling. Did her mother truly close her children out of her heart because they reminded her too much of the love she once shared with their father?

Wyatt read the doubts in her expression. His finger tilted her chin up to meet his gaze. "You will never know the whole truth of what happened between your parents, but you do not deserve to bear the burden of their unhappiness. Let go of the past, love. Make a future with me."

He made it sound so simple. She could not let go of her fears so easily. "I am still afraid."

"No more than I am afraid when I think you might

someday leave me." He drew her into the warm, safe circle of his arms. For a long time he just held her. "Our fears are the same, sweetheart. We can conquer them together. If you accept my love, you will make it invulnerable." He leaned back to look down at her, his voice laced with tenderness. "Do you understand what I am saying?"

The answer came upon her without warning. He would never deny her his love, no matter how vulnerable that made him. She searched his eyes and saw all the love there she had ever craved. A trace of fear as well. Last night he had sworn over and over that he would never leave her. Now he waited to hear the same.

"I love you." The words came out so easily that she said them again, this time against his lips as his mouth closed over hers for a long, sensual kiss. When his kisses moved to the column of her neck, she whispered into his ear. "I will never leave you, Wyatt. I swear it."

"The rest," he demanded between kisses. "I want to hear the rest of your pledge."

She smiled and rubbed her cheek against the warm satin of his hair. "Yes, I will marry you, my love."

EPILOGUE

⟶⟶⟶

$\mathcal{N}$EITHER FARO NOR Wyatt guessed that their love would grow even stronger over the years. Together they truly were invulnerable. Granted, they experienced their share of disagreements, but nothing could shake their faith in each other. Not even Faro's insistence that they name their first child Esmeralda, after the color of the bottle that first brought them together. Wyatt refused to name his precious baby daughter after a rock. Anyone with eyes could see that the child needed a name that would reflect her grace and beauty, something along the lines of Anne or Patricia.

And so it came to be that Esmeralda developed an odd fascination with the silver-and-green bottle. The first time Faro saw a flash of green clutched between her toddler's chubby fingers, she nearly fainted. It took an hour of questions from both parents before they were satisfied that the bottle had revealed nothing of its secrets to the innocent child. They repeated the questions again and again over the years, for it didn't matter where they might hide the bottle. It would only reappear a few days later in Esmeralda's hand.

Although Esmeralda showed clear signs that she had inherited her mother's gift, the little girl swore she saw nothing when she held the bottle, that she sensed only a vague impression of happiness. Edward and Andrew inherited their mother's gift as well, but even when they were babies and bright, shiny objects tended to attract their curiosity, they would not touch Esmeralda's bottle. Eventually Wyatt and Faro decided the bottle was a talisman of sorts for their daughter. If nothing else, it protected her from her brothers' pranks as they grew older. Just the sight of that bottle was enough to make the boys think twice about putting frogs in her slippers, or dipping her braid into an inkwell.

No one realized that Esmeralda was simply the bottle's temporary guardian, until the day she came home from the village fair without it.

"I gave it to the witch," she said, when Faro questioned her.

"The *witch*?" Faro echoed, casting a horrified glance at her husband.

Wyatt set his paper aside. The secretive smile in his daughter's pale blue eyes made her look nine going on ninety. "What witch, Essie?"

"The one at the village fair, the one who tells fortunes." Esmeralda looked across the table at Faro. "She is much better at it than we are, Mummy, but she says I will get better with practice."

"What did this woman look like?" Wyatt demanded. "And why did you give your bottle to a perfect stranger?"

"Because it belonged to her." Esmeralda pushed more of her scrambled eggs under a slice of toast and hoped no one would notice. "She said you and Mummy didn't need it anymore, but she knew someone else who did."

"Essie, look at Daddy." Wyatt waited until he had his daughter's undivided attention. "Was this woman a Gypsy?"

"Oh, no, Daddy. She might travel in a Gypsy caravan, but she is a genuine witch. The good kind, though. You mustn't worry that she meant to harm me."

Wyatt thought about the Gypsy he had met on the way to Blackburn shortly before his marriage. She had looked older than God almost a decade ago. A witch, indeed. The thought of his daughter so close to a woman that mysterious and powerful made him blanche. "What does she plan to do with the bottle, Essie?"

"Oh, I don't know." Esmeralda looked around the breakfast table. Her father turned very pale. Her mother fanned herself with a napkin. Grammsie and the twins just stared at her. She gave them all a bright smile. "The witch said a strange little spell, then she dropped the bottle into a cask of brandy. Isn't that the oddest thing?"

ELIZABETH ELLIOTT

ELIZABETH ELLIOTT is the national bestselling author of three novels and one novella, all published by Bantam Books. Her first novel, *The Warlord,* won Waldenbooks' Bestselling Debut Romance Novel award, and the Romance Writers of America RITA award for Best First Book. *Publishers Weekly* called her second novel, *Scoundrel,* ". . . an exciting story filled with dramatic tension and sexual fireworks," and *Romantic Times* recently nominated her third novel, *Betrothed,* for the Reviewer's Choice Historical Romance of the Year. Elliott's newest full-length novel, *The Assassin,* returns readers to her popular medieval settings to tell a story that the author describes as "A bit like a medieval version of *The Bodyguard* meets *The Saint,*" on sale in March 1998. Ms. Elliott lives on a chain of lakes in Minnesota with her husband and two sons, and for an amazing portion of the year, a lot of snow. She enjoys hearing from her readers, and you can write to her care of Bantam Books, 1540 Broadway, New York, New York, 10036, or online at 72123.1460@compuserve.com

FOREVER

Patricia Potter

CHAPTER ONE

Cornwall, England, 1830

HOLLY HASTINGS SHIVERED in the bitter cold of the night, but the tremors came from fear far more than the icy winds.

Her da and brother were crazy to be out this night. And she was just as cod-headed for disobeying her da's order to stay home with her mother and for being here standing watch.

Honest men both, Da and Paul had been forced to smuggling. A few shipments only, they said, and they would have enough money for passage to America. Tim Bailey, who had arranged for the shipment, had promised to keep the constabulary busy elsewhere.

Holly didn't trust him, nor the man she believed was backing him—John Haford, the earl of Gatwell. She didn't trust any of the gentry. But most particularly she didn't trust the earl.

He'd known they were desperate for money. Her mother was sick and needed to move to a warmer climate, but as tenants they owned nothing to sell, not even the crop Da and Paul worked so hard to cultivate. Their share was scarcely enough to feed them through the winter.

Her da's one wish was to go to America, where they would have a chance to prosper, to own their own land, and to find the climate her mother needed. So despite the fact that a stranger was in their village, and a regiment of the king's soldiers was billeted not far away, her da was determined to meet the smugglers and row in the contraband of French brandy.

Holly huddled inside her cloak as she eyed the bleak landscape, with its twisted trees and rough-hewn rocks. A hundred places could conceal the king's men—or one spy. That could very well be what that tall, dark stranger was, the one who had been dallying at the Kings Cross Arms Inn for the past several days. From the moment she'd first seen him, she'd sensed he was trouble.

She'd run into him as she'd rushed out of the physician's office with medicine for her ma. She'd smiled, amused by her own awkwardness. Then her gaze had moved upward, pausing on an oak-hard chest before resting on a startlingly handsome face with smoky gray eyes and tousled hair so black it could grace a raven's wing. She'd felt a quickening of blood, which gave way to foreboding.

In all her nineteen years, she'd never seen colder eyes or a more expressionless face. Neither had softened even when he'd tried to smile in apology. He had righted her with efficiency, had quickly withdrawn his hands as if he'd been burned, but his eyes searched and weighed her all in a second's time. She couldn't tell whether he approved or disapproved.

"I'm . . . sorry, sir," she'd stuttered.

"No harm done." His words had sounded automatic, devoid of real meaning. "And I bear fault, too."

He was obviously a nob. Though his dark clothes were plain, they were made of fine cloth and his speech was that of the gentry. She didn't see much of his kind in the village, and that made her suspicious.

She'd already heard rumors about him. John Savage, his name was. A gambler by trade, he'd told the innkeeper and thus the village. He was here to collect a large debt from the earl's son, who was away with his father on a hunting trip. No one questioned the reason. Gatwell's son,

Lord Barkley, was a known wastrel and gambler, and both the earl and his son were notorious for not paying their debts. Were all gamblers' eyes so cold, Holly wondered, so dangerous-looking?

Yet she felt something else, too. She was seldom tongue-tied, but she seemed unable to do anything but stare up at a face that was stark and uncommonly interesting. Her breath caught in her throat, and her legs didn't seem to want to move.

"Can I be helping you find someone?" she finally asked.

"No," he said. He then dipped his head slightly, turned, and headed in another direction.

Holly watched his back as he walked toward the inn. She noticed, for the first time, that he used a cane. He moved stiffly, as if each step was an effort.

Despite that, there was something dominating about him, an air of authority and leadership. He was no ordinary nabob, she decided as her throat tightened in apprehension.

She recalled all that now as she stood high above the cliff, near a path that wound down to the edge of the sea, where her father and brother waited with two other men for a signal from the French ship.

Nothing moved except the wind. The sky was black, the moon and stars smothered by heavy clouds. Below her, she heard the heavy crash of waves against rocks. Even without the fear of exposure, the venture was dangerous. The seas were rough, the rocks unforgiving.

In the darkness of the water, she saw a light, then three quick flashes. At the signal, a small skiff left the narrow strip of beach and started toward the light.

Holly glanced around another time. Seeing nothing amiss, she began her descent. Her da and brother would rage to find her waiting for them, but in the end they would relent. Slender though she was, she sometimes worked the farm and carried buckets of water and seed and sacks of food. Tonight she could help unload the caskets of wine. Another hand would mean less time, and less danger.

Just then, she heard a bleat, and groaning aloud, she looked back over her shoulder. Meandering down the

crooked path behind her was Georgette. The goat followed her everywhere, so tonight she'd tied the animal inside her pen with a stout rope. That rope, its end frayed,
now trailed the beast. Georgette, named by her father after
King George, whom he considered no better than a goat,
was an escape artist of note, but tonight was a most irksome time for a demonstration of her talents.

The goat's bleating was plaintive—and loud—and Holly
went over to her and rubbed her ears. Georgette bleated
again. She didn't want affection; she wanted a treat.

"Shh," Holly said. But Georgette was having none of it.
She wanted what she wanted.

Holly sighed. She had hoarded a biscuit from dinner to
eat during the watch tonight. But silence was more important than satisfying hunger. She offered the biscuit to Georgette, who accepted the treat as no more than her due.

"Be still," she whispered to the goat. She couldn't go all
the way home, not the nearly two miles there and another
two back. After consideration, she tied Georgette to a small
oak sapling; the goat had a tendency to butt everyone, including herself, and she wanted no more surprises this
night. Then once again she carefully started her descent.

The path was treacherous, and she slipped several times
before gaining the sandy beach. She thought she might
have ripped her cloak, threadbare as it was.

The beach was deserted, only the slap of waves against
rocks audible in the night air. The darkness was broken by
the flicker of a lantern tucked in a hollowed-out shelf of
the cliff to guide her father, Paul, and the others—a father
and son who owned a rickety skiff they used for fishing.

What would she and her mother do if anything happened
to Da and her brother? If they were caught and died at the
end of a rope? The four of them had always been so close.
Her mother's privileged childhood had, in some subtle way,
isolated them from the other tenants, as had her insistence
that her children receive a sound education. She had worked
in the fields alongside her husband until her health had
crumbled, and Paul had had to end his studies with the vicar.
But Holly had continued hers, at her mother's insistence. She
wanted a better life for her daughter, had hoped she might

obtain a position as a governess. But her mother's sickness had precluded Holly's leaving home.

As long as Holly could remember, every member of her family had sacrificed for the others, all except her. They had not allowed her to take a job as a servant at Gatwell's estate, no matter how much she'd begged. She had tried to do what she could, taking on all the household duties and occasional farm chores.

Tonight, she was determined to do more.

She heard the splash of oars against water. The skiff appeared as a blot against the ocean, its bow barely out of the water. She saw the outline of barrels piled high and realized the danger. The king's preventive men—the law officers charged with stopping smuggling—now seemed the least of the perils risked by her father and Paul. The sea was just as dangerous to those in an overloaded boat.

Her brother and Ted Conley jumped from the boat, splashing up on the beach and pulling the skiff up onto the sand by long, thick ropes. Her father and Ted's father, Ethan, followed, joining their sons in tugging the skiff farther up onto the sand.

Finally satisfied, they dropped the ropes and her father went to a small recess between two jutting cliffs. He dug into the sand with a shovel he'd carried from the boat, then pulled off a wide board covering a vast hole.

Holly stepped out then. Ted Conley saw her first, and he swore before his father cut it off with a sharp reprimand. Then her father and Paul approached her.

"What are you doing here, girl?" her father said harshly. He never called her girl. It was always Holly or daughter or some term of endearment.

She shivered under his withering anger, but then straightened her back stubbornly.

"I thought I could help. You could use more hands, and I'm strong."

"Go home, Holly. Go now. Don't you know how dangerous this is?"

Paul, as always, interceded for her. "Now that she's here . . ."

Ethan Conley shifted on his feet. "We don't have time

to argue. We'll just barely beat dawn as it is. Demmed Frenchies were late."

Her da gave her a long look, which told her she would hear more of this later, then turned away. He started for the skiff and picked up a barrel. The others followed with Holly going last. The keg was far heavier than a sack of seed, but she was aware of eyes on her and she wouldn't be found wanting. Using every ounce of strength, she managed to heft the keg to her shoulder as the others did. Her body bowed under the load, and she staggered to the hole. Paul was inside, taking them and stacking them. One, then another. A third. She thought her body would break.

Just when she was unloading her fourth, Ted Conley stumbled and the keg he was carrying fell, the wood shattering and brandy spilling over the sand.

"Clean that up, Holly," her father said. "Bury signs of the brandy and the staves."

She stooped down, picking up the new-looking staves. Then her hand found something else. A small bottle. What was it doing in a keg of brandy?

"I can use some help down here," her brother called out, and Holly slipped the bottle into her pocket for later inspection. She finished her task of wiping away all signs of the broken keg, then joined her brother in the man-made cave, moving kegs to make room for more. It was easier work, and the hours passed swiftly. When the last keg was stashed away, she helped fit a piece of wood over the cache, then cover it with sand.

"Now it's Bailey's business," her father said before facing her. "You can go back with us in the skiff."

She shook her head. "Georgette is up there. She followed me."

Paul chuckled. "Worse than a dog, that goat. I'm surprised she didn't come down to the beach."

"I tied her up there," she said.

Her father nodded. "The walk back is safe enough, probably safer than the sea," he said. "You go on now, and meet us at the cottage."

She needed no more urging. She was soaked through to the skin, and every bone in her body ached. She turned, but her father's hand caught her. "You *were* a help, Holly, but don't do this again. If anything happened to you . . ."

She nodded, then started up the path, a sense of worth and satisfaction coursing through her. She *had* helped. And *she* hadn't dropped a keg. Pleased with herself, she reached the top of the cliff and headed toward the spot where she'd left Georgette.

She glanced around. The moor seemed as it had been, quiet and deserted. Yet she sensed something was wrong. A crackling tension struck her and ran down her spine like lightning.

Georgette! She wasn't munching happily, but stood with her ears cocked, her body stiff. The wind had stifled bleats of distress but now Holly heard them.

She had a sudden impulse to flee, but she couldn't leave Georgette. Fear made her legs quiver as she took one step, then another, aware now that she and Georgette were not alone.

To confirm that fact, a figure stepped from underneath a tree. "It's a bloody poor night for a walk," he said.

CHAPTER TWO

*I*T SEEMED HE had waited forever.

Justin Talmadge had spent the last few hours stretched out on the rocks above the beach, watching the activity beneath him, planning his next move. Finally, he was close to getting Gatwell.

He had learned to be a patient man over the years, but he'd waited so long for this chance. So bloody long that he was breaking his own code. He was going to use innocents to catch his prey.

The night fit his mood: dark and brooding and menacing. A night for smuggling, a night for deception and fear and, if he was lucky, retribution that was too long in coming.

As one of Prime Minister Wellington's agents, he was seeking proof of criminal acts by the earl of Gatwell. The prime minister wanted Gatwell's hide, but no more so than Justin. He had his own private reasons, and he'd spent almost half his life chasing the bastard. Now, at last, he hoped he had Gatwell by the throat. The earl needed money, badly enough, Justin hoped, to take chances he'd never taken before. Rumors had it that the earl was now engaged in smuggling. The man was careful, never allowing one part of his illegal operations to know what the other parts were doing. What Justin needed was to turn the earl's henchmen back on him. If one person talked, he would lead to another, then another. . . .

Everyone who'd ever worked for, or with, Gatwell had paid heavily for that dubious honor, often at the price of their own lives. He didn't want to see that happen to the young woman who'd nearly knocked him down in the village.

Yet even as he'd followed the sound of the goat, which led him to her, and to the scene beneath the cliffs, he knew he would use her. It was his only chance to succeed. He tried not to think of her large green eyes and copper hair and that smile that had an enchantment all its own.

Holly Hastings. He'd asked about her after their encounter that morning. The question hadn't raised any eyebrows, since she was a pretty thing.

The girl's name had interested him. He'd heard the Hastings name in the tavern, whispered as looking for someone to help with a night's work. And her first name was unusual in Cornwall. The people here had simple Biblical names such as Mary and Sarah, John and Peter.

But Holly fit the girl. It had a lilt that matched the mischief in her eyes and the smile on her lips. Even he, who had trained his heart not to betray him, had been momentarily beguiled.

Now tension curled his stomach. He didn't like the idea of confronting her, of frightening her. But he had no choice.

He watched the girl stiffen, take a step backward as if to ward off a blow. Then she appeared to force herself to relax. Ignoring him, she went directly to the goat. "So there you are," she crooned. "I've been looking for you."

He admired her bravado. He had meant to surprise her into giving him answers he wanted to hear, but she was too quick-witted. He worked at putting sarcasm in his next comment. "She tied herself to that tree?"

She trembled slightly and he realized she wasn't quite so sure of herself. He felt a momentary sympathy. Bloody hell, more than that. He also felt guilt. He tried to brush it aside. He couldn't afford guilt at this point.

"Georgette often gets herself tangled in a tree when she tries to eat its leaves," she said, not looking at him.

"Very good, Miss Hastings," he said. "I'm impressed. I might even accept it, if you hadn't climbed down that path and back again."

"I enjoy watching the sea at night." She untied the goat, rubbed its ears in apparent indifference.

Justin stepped closer, and he could almost feel her fear now. He had to cultivate that fear, even as he despised himself for being a bully.

"How long have you been smuggling, Miss Hastings?" he asked coolly.

Her shoulders slumped, and she turned to look at him then. The clouds slid from the moon and he saw that she was afraid of him, saw that her hands trembled. He found himself wanting to take her in his arms and comfort her, rather than scare the wits from her.

"I haven't—"

He put a finger to her mouth. "No lies, Miss Hastings. They're most unproductive."

She tried to move away, but he clasped her wrist.

"Who are you?" she asked.

"I mean you and your family no harm," he said, then added in a cold voice meant to intimidate, "*if* you'll help me."

Her words had a desperate edge to them. "Are you a preventive man?"

"No," he said flatly and saw her relax slightly.

"Then what? Why are you here? What do you want?"

"Lord Gatwell," he answered. "Help me, and I'll make sure your family isn't hurt."

"I don't . . . understand."

"Gatwell," he said impatiently. "He's behind this venture of yours, isn't he?"

He watched her face, wishing it were light enough to see her eyes.

"What venture?"

"Smuggling," he said. "You know the penalty, I presume. Transportation. Prison. Neither a pleasant future. But I'm not interested in you—or your family. I'm only interested in the earl of Gatwell. Smuggling is the least of his crimes, but we know he's involved."

"Then why don't you arrest him?" Strength crept into her voice. She was beginning to realize she wasn't as defenseless as she'd first thought.

But he wasn't going to allow this bit of a girl to spoil his opportunity to see Gatwell brought to justice.

"He *will* be arrested," Justin said. "One way or another. The question is how many people he'll take down with him. You? Your family?"

She tried to pull away again but he kept her wrist imprisoned. She was seeking time, to think, to consider, and he didn't want to give her that time.

"Are you so loyal then to Gatwell?" he asked softly. "So loyal you'll risk your family? Your father? Your brother? I saw them both."

A tremor racked her body, and his resolve melted under an unexpected, unfamiliar urge to protect. An urge that could destroy everything he'd been working toward these past fifteen years.

Fifteen years since his brother had put a gun to his own head and pulled the trigger. Justin still heard that shot in frequent nightmares. He knew he would keep hearing it until Gatwell paid for betraying Justin's brother and their regiment.

But was he becoming as ruthless as the man he hunted? Was Gatwell's downfall worth losing his own soul?

"You can't prove anything," she said suddenly, "because you won't find anything."

"No?" he asked. "Then I didn't see lights and a boat, and four men and a woman unloading casks?"

A small cry came from her throat, and he knew she had hoped he'd been bluffing.

"Miss Hastings?" he prompted.

"I still don't know what you want," she finally said.

She spoke well, without the heavy accent of the tenant farmers and miners in Cornwall. He'd heard that she was the only daughter of a couple who thought highly of education.

"I want you to listen to me," he said.

"Do I have a choice?" Her small but defiant voice made him wince inside.

"No," he replied. "Gatwell has committed every crime known to God and man. I want him caught and punished."

"You said you weren't a preventive man."

"I'm not. I work for Wellington."

"The prime minister?"

Justin nodded. He shouldn't have divulged that piece of information, but he wanted to assure her that his only target was Gatwell. "He has a debt to collect from Gatwell, too. Our interests, you might say, coincide."

She looked around, as if expecting soldiers to rise out of the rough, rock-strewn cliff.

"The government is offering certain incentives to anyone who will help bring Gatwell to trial," he continued, releasing her wrist. "Unfortunately, the man usually hides behind others, using them to protect himself. Too many seem to die in the process. He doesn't leave witnesses."

Emotions flitted across her face as he talked, then comprehension. "And you want me—my family—to be among those witnesses?"

"We have to catch him in the act," Justin explained harshly. "You will be protected."

She walked away from him toward the edge of the cliff, toward the sea. She looked so alone. He suddenly wanted to go to her, tell her to go home and forget this.

He remembered his brother, a young man not much older than she, and the sad burden placed on him. And he knew he had no heart for terrifying a young lady. He'd wanted to snare grown men who were responsible for their own actions, not an innocent who wanted to protect her family. He had to rethink his plan. Hell, he had to rethink his priorities.

Justin started toward her when he heard a noise behind him. He whirled around to confront whatever danger had presented itself.

CHAPTER THREE

*H*OLLY TRIED TO work things out in her mind, to comprehend what this man wanted from her. But all she saw was disaster.

Her blood was pulsing too fast. She put a hand into the pocket of her cloak and clasped the small bottle she had found on the rocky shore. If only it contained a genie that could whisk her away or make the man behind her disappear. She'd read about genies, just as she'd read about Prince Charming. She was obviously going to be disappointed in both regards.

Then she heard a noise behind her, and she turned.

Apparently feeling her mistress threatened, Georgette, head lowered, was charging toward the stranger. Holly could only watch as the animal rose up on rear legs and crashed into him, knocking him to the ground.

Holly wanted to run, to warn Da and Paul. But it would do no good. The stranger knew her name. He obviously knew her family. And where would they go without money? What would they do?

Run, her mind still argued.

But she couldn't leave the stranger. Her pathetically soft heart wouldn't allow it. What if Georgette had done real damage? A groan escaped the stranger's lips, and his hands massaged his left leg. He tried to move, and she saw his face clench. His pain must be enormous. He was not the kind of man who would give in to it easily.

"Can I . . . help?" she said.

His head turned toward her. She was aware that he was studying her, and she felt herself flush.

"Why would you want to do that?" he asked.

"What?" she replied, startled.

"Help me?"

His voice had a certain intensity that made her pause. She was wondering herself why she didn't run and tell others in the village about the stranger who was a preventive man or worse. They would probably dispose of him, and her family would be safe. The Cornishman had no love for authority.

"I don't know," she said. But she did know. She couldn't bear to see anything hurt or wounded. That was as much a part of her as her love for her family.

She watched as he tried to move again. She heard the quick intake of breath as he started to stand. She offered a hand and, to her surprise, he took it.

A muscle knotted in his cheek and his lips clamped tight, but he slowly got to his feet and stood, swaying slightly. Using her as a crutch, he took a step, then another, until he reached the tree from which he'd emerged several minutes earlier. Then he leaned against it, just barely maintaining his stance.

Holly sensed movement behind her. Georgette, apparently miffed at being ignored, bumped her, sending her against the stranger.

His arms went around her, catching her, and heat radiated between them. Energy swirled like a storm, around and within, wild and hot and irresistible. His body, pressed against hers, was hard, unyielding, and Holly seemed rooted to the spot.

"Devil take it," he said in a hoarse whisper. His voice was no longer impersonal. It resounded with feelings she couldn't identify.

Blood rushed to her face as she continued to cling to him with a need she'd never felt before. The stranger groaned from deep inside his throat, and Holly felt a responding whimper escape her own mouth. She shouldn't be here, she didn't want to be in his arms, but she couldn't force herself to move. It was as if she'd lost all will, all reason.

He shifted on his feet, then looked down just as she looked up, and their faces nearly touched. God help her, but something drew her to him. Fear, she told herself. Only fear.

She pulled away from him then, despair and shame swamping her. Hot tears blurred her eyes. She wanted to stay, to be with him, pressed up against him.

Yet he was a stranger. A member of the gentry who was a threat to all that she loved.

A cry wrenched from her as she backed up, but his hand reached out and caught her, and she felt like a trapped rabbit. Then he let her go and shook his head, as if he too needed to toss off that intensity they'd shared.

She took several more steps backward. "Georgette," she whispered. "I must get Georgette before she wanders off."

"The watch goat?" he asked. "No wonder you don't need anyone on guard." Amusement changed his voice completely, so that it now sounded deep and gruff.

"She doesn't like anyone near me," Holly answered, wondering at his whimsy and tolerance for the offending animal.

He looked toward the goat. Georgette was grazing again, as if nothing amiss had occurred.

"I'll remember that."

Holly's fingers crushed into a fist. She still didn't know who he was, or what he wanted, or what kind of disaster he meant to her family. And yet, for a moment, an odd sense of familiarity, of companionship, passed between them, and with it a hot rush of expectation.

She was afraid of her own reactions to him. He had taken steps toward her, and his face was only inches away. She was aware of the spicy, clean scent of him, the fineness of his clothes. Whoever he was, he was miles above her in station, though the independent Cornishmen bowed to no one.

Despite the awareness between them, the warm humor that had made them equal for a pause in time, she wondered whether he was just another Barkley Haford, the earl's son, who saw a peasant girl ripe for the picking. The thought was like an arrow in her heart, piercing through protective layers she'd built around it.

She recalled the times Barkley Haford had called upon her, the promises he'd made. She'd been but sixteen and honored by his attention. She'd even believed herself a bit in love with him, and him with her. Days after he'd declared undying devotion, she heard of his engagement to the daughter of a marquis. He hadn't ruined her, but it wasn't for lack of trying.

She'd vowed then she would never trust a member of the gentry again. To them, truth was no more than a throwaway word. And this stranger was surely from that class.

He reached for one of her hands, his fingers playing with the back until the tension left and her hand opened. She wanted to close it again. The palm was work-roughened, not soft like those of ladies who had servants to fetch water and wash clothes.

Unlike before, his grip was gentle and carried no threats. The clouds cleared the moon again, and she saw his face clearly, even the deep-set gray eyes framed by dark brows. A muscle moved in his cheek, then he leaned down and his lips brushed hers.

For a second, her lips responded instinctively. Then, horrified by her own behavior, she jerked away.

He straightened. "Bloody hell," he swore softly. "Bloody hell."

JUSTIN WAS appalled at himself. Not only had he frightened a young woman half to death, he had taken advantage of her. He'd never forced his attentions on an innocent before. Never!

"Go home," he said.

"My family?"

"Don't tell them anything," he ordered. "And for God's sake don't let anyone go near that brandy."

"But—"

His finger on her mouth stopped any further words. He wanted to tell her to forget this evening had ever happened. But he couldn't quite do that. She was still the only chance he had. "I'll meet you here this afternoon, after the noonday meal," he said. "We'll talk then."

She hesitated, unsure of him and his intentions.

He needed another threat, though he was loath to convey it. "The captain of the troops in Polperro is a friend," he warned grimly, "and he will have men stationed here shortly. Anyone approaching this cove will be arrested, as will anyone talking about what occurred between us tonight."

She looked dubious. "Why didn't you arrest us tonight?"

"I told you," he said. "I don't want you or your family or the others who are seeking to earn a few pence more. I only want Gatwell, and I'll do whatever is necessary to get him. Now you'd better get home before someone comes looking for you."

She nodded, then turned toward the goat.

"Don't forget about this afternoon," he warned.

"I won't," she agreed reluctantly.

"And you'll say nothing?"

She glared at him. Even in the darkness, he felt her eyes skewering him.

"Nothing," she finally agreed.

Letting her go like this was foolish, but he needed time to map out his strategy. Perhaps he could even earn her trust. Or had he already destroyed that possibility with his threats?

"Go," he said.

She didn't waste time arguing. He watched as she moved over to the white goat, found its rope, and started across the rocky path. He watched until she disappeared, then he found his cane, discovering he *did* need it now.

First time he'd been bettered by a blasted goat.

But then it was also the first time he'd felt this kind of moral uncertainty about his plans, or allowed a pretty face to distract him. And influence him.

He tried to tell himself she hadn't. He still had the control he needed. But he was taking one hell of a chance in trusting her to remain silent, in believing his story about nearby troops. He had no intention of calling in Gavin yet, not until he knew exactly how to trap Gatwell.

He only knew he needed help. *Her* help. He had to lure Gatwell back to Cornwall, into taking overt action, and he couldn't do it on his own. He didn't particularly fear that Gatwell would recognize him; the two had last seen each other only briefly fifteen years earlier. But a stranger would put the man on guard. Even a stranger named John Savage, who had a legitimate reason to be here.

On and off for the past fifteen years, Justin had been playing the role of John Savage, gentleman gambler. It was Savage who held the notes to Gatwell's son's debts. His game leg, he'd told everyone, came from a childhood riding injury, though it had actually resulted from a French ambush on the eve of Waterloo.

Justin placed some weight on his hurt leg, took a step, then another. Steeling himself against pain, and the rumblings of a long-dormant conscience, he hurried to the inn.

AN INCREASING coldness filled Holly's heart as she journeyed home. What if she had condemned her entire family by showing up at the cliffs? What if she had led the stranger to them? What if he was lying about wanting only Lord Gatwell? Would he really care if others were caught in his trap?

Her heart beating hard with uncertainty, she glimpsed her brother on the path, obviously coming to look for her. She had never hidden anything from him before, and now she had to conceal from him knowledge that endangered them all.

He was carrying a lantern, but already the first fingers of dawn were poking through the sky.

"We were worried about you, Holly," he said.

She tugged on Georgette's rope. "She wanted to eat the whole way here. You know how stubborn she gets."

"Serve her right to end up a stew." He too had been the recipient of Georgette's butts.

"You did not see anyone?" she asked.

"No," he said. "It's safe enough. Tim Bailey made sure of that. Paid off the constabulary."

"But the troops?"

"Most likely paid them off, too," Paul said. "Now stop your worrying. Our part's over now, and we have nothing more to do with them. We told you it was safe enough."

"Lord Gatwell—"

"We don't know it's Gatwell," he said. "Be careful how you use his name."

"Will we have enough, then, for America?"

He didn't answer right away, and she knew by his silence they did not. Another night of smuggling, then, or perhaps more. Fear squirmed inside her again.

Cornishmen had never considered smuggling wrong. Most of the families had been involved from time to time, and everyone shared the booty. Kegs of French brandy appeared regularly at grand events such as weddings and births, and from the sly laughter, Holly had known taxes were paid on none of them. This time it was different.

She fingered the bottle in the pocket of her cloak. That bottle was every bit as odd as the stranger who'd accosted her on the cliffs. She couldn't satisfy her curiosity—and apprehension—about him, but the bottle begged inspection.

When Holly reached the cottage, she secured Georgette in the pen. She hoped the animal had had more than enough adventure for one night. She knew that she had.

Da was waiting at the door, his face pinched with anxiety—and anger.

"Mother?" she asked.

"Sleeping, no thanks to you," he said with rare censure. " 'Tis time you chose a husband. Then you won't be running wild."

"I want to go to America with you," she argued.

"That might be years yet," he said, suddenly sounding weary, "and I want to see you settled. Daniel Gray asked

me just last week for permission to call. I told him I would
talk to you."

"But he's . . ." She'd started to say old, but then stopped.
Daniel was her da's age, with three spoiled children. His
second wife had died in childbirth two years earlier.

"He can provide well for you," Da said of the blacksmith. "You won't be finding any lords wanting the hand
of a tenant's child."

He was, she realized, remembering the hurt she'd felt at
Barkley Haford's desertion.

"I know," she replied, "but maybe it is different in
America."

"You are too choosy. You've had some fine suitors.
Love grows, Daughter."

"But you and Mother . . ."

He seemed to age in front of her. He had married a
woman above his station, the daughter of a wealthy merchant. She'd been groomed for a better match, but she'd
eloped with Jonathon Hastings and her father had disowned her.

"Aye, and your mother is the reason I long to see you
settled in a good marriage," he said. "I don't want you to
struggle as she has had to do."

"I don't think she would change a moment." She remembered the way her mother and Da had once laughed
together, the way they'd touched so often, and even now
the way their gazes seldom left the other when they were
together. She wanted the same kind of love, not the stilted
politeness she saw between so many other couples.

"I would change it for her," he said bitterly, and she
saw how the pain had eaten into him. He would never
have consented to smuggling unless he believed it the only
way to save his wife.

And now a new trouble threatened all of them, one she
felt was her fault. If she hadn't disobeyed Da . . .

"You should never ha' come out this night," he scolded.

"She was a help," her brother interjected.

"She was that," Da said, his voice gentling. "But now
it's off to bed with her, with all of us."

Holly rose up on her toes and kissed his cheek. "I love you, Da."

"Get on wi' you now," he said, "and you be thinking about Daniel."

"I will," she promised. And for his sake she would. For a few moments, anyway.

But even that pledge went out of her mind as she lit an oil lamp and climbed up into the loft. She put the lantern on the table, then dug into her pocket for the bottle.

In the flickering light, she studied the object in her hand. She couldn't even begin to imagine how it had gotten in the brandy keg. She turned it over in her hands several times, relishing the cool smoothness of it. Silver climbed up the bottle's neck, and the green glass was transparent enough to reveal its contents.

Contents!

She worked the stopper, finally freeing it, and a leather scroll fell out. Her fingers trembled as she unfurled it and started to read.

To thine own wish be true. Do not follow the moth to the star.

Disappointment swept over her. No genie. No magical potion. Only a cryptic message that offered more questions than answers.

This afternoon she would have to meet the stranger and discover exactly what he wanted. She would have to hide her apprehension from her family. She would have to lie to them, and then perhaps make a bargain with the devil. And all she had to protect her was this small bottle with its strange message.

She examined it again. The bottle was rimmed with silver. Perhaps it would bring a pound or two.

And the message?

Was it an accident that both the bottle and the stranger had appeared this night? Could they be connected in some way? Was fate trying to tell her something?

To thine own wish be true. What was her wish? Safety for her family. Good health for her mother. Hope again for her father. A future for Paul. And for herself? Love. A love that survived time like the message itself.

She clutched the tiny leather scroll. Maybe it *did* mean something. She had to believe it did.

But a demon repeated the other part of the message. *Do not follow the moth to the star.* Was that what she was doing in meeting the stranger again?

No! She refused to consider it. The bottle was good luck, a talisman. It just had to be.

CHAPTER FOUR

$\mathcal{H}$OLLY DIDN'T LIKE lying. She especially hated lying to her mother.

But that's what she did as she sat at her mother's bedside. Forcing calmness, she chattered about Georgette and the weather and a book she'd borrowed from the vicar, a book of poetry by Sir Walter Scott, and she read a passage she particularly loved.

> *True love's the gift which God has given*
> *To man alone beneath the heaven:*
> *It is not fantasy's hot fire,*
> *Whose wishes, soon as granted, fly;*
> *It liveth not in fierce desire,*
> *With dead desire it doth not die;*
> *It is the secret sympathy,*
> *The silver link, the silken tie,*
> *Which heart to heart and mind to mind*
> *In body and in soul can bind.*

A hush followed her words, and her mother's eyes glistened. "Your da and I have that kind of love," she whispered. "I want you to have the same."

Years seemed to fade away and her mother looked

young again and vibrant. She had given up wealth for her husband, and had worked long hours in the fields with him so her children could have an education. She dreamed of a better life for them, dreamed of land of their own and a country and place where her family could control their own destiny.

"Da wants me to consider Daniel," Holly said hesitantly.

"And do *you* want to consider him?"

She bit her lips. She wanted to ease her parents' worry. They had given so much to both her and Paul, unquestioning love, most of all, and she wanted to return the gift.

Her mother smiled faintly. "Don't compromise, love. Don't ever settle for less than that silver link." She held out her hand and clutched Holly's in it. "Promise me."

Holly nodded, wondering if she would ever find that link. She was nineteen, considered on the shelf by many, and since Barkley, no one had excited her heart. No one ever—

The stranger suddenly came to mind, uninvited. He had caused internal chaos but, because of fear and anger, not any tender emotion.

"Holly?"

She looked back at her mother, who regarded her quizzically. "You don't *care* for Daniel?"

Holly shook her head. "I know he's a fine man, but—"

"Then enough said," Celeste Hastings interrupted. "I think I would like to read more of this book."

Holly hesitated. "I could take some eggs into town . . . if you think you will be all right."

"Of course, I'll be fine. My cough is not bothering me, and I feel much better."

"I won't be long."

"Stay as long as you wish," her mother said. "I really am better."

"I can tell." Holly leaned over and kissed her. "I love you," she whispered.

She went to the door. The day was warmer, and she decided not to wear her cloak. The small bottle was already in her skirt pocket; for some reason she didn't want to leave it behind. Summoning all her courage, she left the cottage and started toward the cliffs—toward the stranger who held in his hands the lives of everyone dear to her.

Shivers ran down her back. Dear God in heaven, she didn't know what to do.

Her steps slowed as she reached the meeting place. The cliffs were quiet, most of the people at work in the fields.

Holly saw the stranger before he saw her. She stopped and studied him for a moment. He sat on the ground, looking over the cliffs at the sea. He had one leg stretched out, the other crooked at the knee. His arms rested on that knee and his head on his arms, as if he was infinitely weary. He wore a linen shirt and buckskin breeches. A tan frock coat lay on a nearby rock. The wind ruffled his hair.

In bright sunlight he didn't look like a devil.

"Come closer."

She started at the sound of his voice. He hadn't turned to look at her, and she had been sure he was unaware of her approach. Perhaps he *was* the devil. She instinctively clutched the bottle in her pocket.

He rose in a graceful movement and faced her. "I won't bite." His lips turned up slightly at one corner.

"How can I be sure?" she retorted.

"I'm sorry I frightened you last night."

"Are you?" She doubted that he was ever sorry about anything.

"Aye," he said. "I did not expect a woman."

"But you did expect someone?"

"Perhaps not last night but eventually."

"Why?"

"Rumors," he said. "Casks of brandy showing up where they shouldn't."

"You said you worked for the prime minister?"

"Occasionally."

He was playing games with her, as a cat played with a mouse.

"What do you want?"

For the first time, she saw indecision in his eyes. "I need help," he said finally.

"And you will blackmail me to get it?"

"Yes," he said. "If I must. I would much prefer your

willing cooperation." He hesitated a moment, then continued in a more conciliatory voice. "I didn't expect a slip of a girl to be caught in my net."

At least he wasn't as coldhearted as the earl. At least he had some scruples about using people.

"Will the locals protect Gatwell?" he asked.

"No one here has any reason to like Lord Gatwell," she replied. "But they like preventive men even less. Gatwell might cheat us, but the government has transported men who were only trying to support their families."

"Smuggling's a crime."

"And who does it hurt?" she asked tightly. "Whose mouth does it deprive of food?"

He was silent.

"My da and brother have always been honest men, and where did it get them?" she continued. "My da can barely feed his family, and my mother is sick from overwork and lung disease."

"And so Gatwell made them an offer?"

"No," she said. "Another man."

"His name?"

She stood there silently, unable to give up a Cornishman, even Tim Bailey, who sold unfit horses and beat his wife.

"Gatwell always does business thus," the stranger said. "He always layers himself with protection and allows those beneath him to get caught." He paused. "Or simply disappear."

"How do you know?"

"I've been after him for fifteen years," he said.

Stunned, Holly could only gape at him. *Fifteen years.*

"Why?" she finally managed.

"He traded with Napoleon," he said softly. "And not only brandy. He traded information."

Holly felt faint. She'd only been a tad of a child during the last of the Napoleonic Wars, but she knew of far too many families who'd lost sons, and men who'd lost a leg or arm or eye. The earl of Gatwell a traitor?

The stranger took his coat, laid it on the ground, then eased her onto it and sat beside her. His hand caught hers. She was too startled to try to remove it. Even if she wanted to. Despite his threats, something about him was compelling.

Holly raised her gaze to his. His gray eyes were smoldering, and she swallowed hard.

"If you would chase someone all those years," she said, trying to sneak into his thoughts, even his heart, "then why would you let my family go free? You must answer if I am to trust you."

"You don't have to trust me," he said harshly. "You just have to do what I say."

Resentment flared in her. For a moment, she had almost liked him.

"I have to know," she persisted, her hand reaching in her pocket to clutch the small bottle. "I must."

He sighed and looked away.

"The information he gave the French," he said finally in a neutral voice, "concerned my regiment. My brother was the colonel. I was a lieutenant. We were in Austria, prepared to join Wellington's troops in Waterloo. Gatwell had just delivered a supply of guns to our regiment and gave a party the night before we were to leave for the front lines."

Holly felt the tension in him, heard the pain he was trying to hide.

"We were ambushed the next day," he said. "More than half of the men were killed. My brother and I were wounded, and he was blamed. Someone claimed he'd been drinking heavily the night before and had been careless with his words."

"Had he?" she asked in a whisper.

"He was the one man who didn't drink that night—he never drank before a battle—but he felt responsible because the rest of us had. His name and his career were destroyed. Some even called him traitor."

His anger and grief were palpable.

"That's not the end of it, is it?" she asked.

"My brother killed himself." His jaw set, and a muscle twitched just above his cheek.

She sat there, stunned by the revelation, by his despair. Fifteen years had done nothing to temper it, nor the rage behind it. She shivered as she realized the depth of his determination.

"You are sure it was Lord Gatwell who informed."

"I'm sure."

"I'm sorry," she said softly.

"Are you, Miss Hastings?" he asked, his brows drawing together in a scowl.

"I know what it's like to love a brother."

His gaze met hers, and she felt it burning her. Her stomach fluttered and heat colored her cheeks.

"You know how to strike a blow, Miss Hastings."

"I truly did not mean to do so," she said honestly. "I only answered your question."

"I fired on myself," he said dryly, then raised a finger to her face, looking at her intently. "How did you come by the name Holly?"

The change of subject surprised her. By now she should have expected the unexpected from him. If she hadn't seen a sudden vulnerability in him and understood that he needed to escape wrenching memories, she might not have answered him.

Even feeling she might well be walking into an abyss, she replied, "My mother. She always loved Christmas. I was born on Christmas Day, and she'd insisted on Holly."

He untied the ribbons of her cap and pulled it off. "It suits you," he said, "with your copper hair and green eyes."

His voice had lost its coolness, had taken on a sensuality that frightened her. A new line of attack? She wasn't sure. Yet her breath caught as a flood of new sensations careened through her body.

Her heart pounded faster. Breath came in short gasps. She seemed to be melting and somehow she was leaning closer and closer to the man she'd regarded as a devil only moments earlier.

His head lowered, and she knew instantly what he intended. She wanted it, dear God. She wanted his kiss with every fiber of her being. But she was also afraid. She had to keep her wits about her. She had to be able to think. She had to learn more of this man and his motives.

They touched, his lips with hers, for a second before she

jerked back. Her heart pounded so loudly now that she was sure he could hear it. He was a nob. A nob who wanted something from her, just as Barkley had wanted something from her. He was using her to get what he wanted. Her hand went back and she slapped him, as hard as she could.

He reached up to touch his cheek. In a moment, it would start to redden. She waited for retaliation. But all he did was watch her. Strangely enough, she saw no anger in his eyes.

Then, without a word, he rose and walked to the edge of the cliff. She had the feeling she'd stopped existing for him.

What had she done?

She'd been prepared to do anything to protect her family. But for a few moments, they had been almost like friends. Then came that unguarded moment, when the intensity between them flared. And she'd known raw betrayal. The fault lay with her own body as much as his seductive assault.

She watched him standing alone on the rocky cliff. He looked elegant, his shirt flowing over a broad back and long arms. She saw the pistol then, tucked in his trousers toward the back.

The pistol reminded her of his purpose, of the hard glint in his eyes. The pistol warned her to be careful.

CHAPTER FIVE

*B*LOODY HELL, BUT he'd made a fine mess of things.

His cheek still stung with the force of her blow, but his pride suffered even more.

She'd looked so lovely, so innocent, and something deep inside him yearned to share that innocence. It made him forget who he was. Made him forget the ever-present vision of his brother's face before he had picked up the gun and shot himself.

He'd deserved that slap. And more.

He sniffed the scent of the sea, wanting its cleansing effect. He felt dirty at the moment, as corrupt as the man he wanted to destroy. He was using people as pawns just as Gatwell had. The fact that their motives differed meant little.

"I'm sorry," he said finally, his face still turned toward the sea. He couldn't remember when last he had said those words, and they sounded rusty even to him. "Go home. I'll find another way to take care of the earl."

She should have run. He should have heard the sound of shoes fleeing over rocks. But he didn't. There was only a silence.

He turned slowly. She was standing like a statue. A flush

reddened her cheeks, and her green eyes were like a stormy sea, tempestuous and unpredictable.

He waited for angry words, but they didn't come. Instead she chewed her lip with uncertainty. Then she spoke. "Can you prove that Lord Gatwell sold information to Napoleon?"

"If I could, I wouldn't be here," he said dryly. "Gatwell would be properly hanged by now. One man witnessed Gatwell's meeting with Napoleon's aide the night before our regiment left for Waterloo. And that man died soon after."

The girl had moved closer to him and placed a hand on his arm. The contact took away his breath. He didn't understand why she felt compassion for him, especially after he had threatened her family. He felt small, empty. He felt no better than the man he'd pursued these last years.

"What do you want me to do?" she asked.

"Go home," he said wearily. "I'll have my people comb these cliffs for the brandy and wait until someone comes to pick the shipment up."

"My family . . ."

"I won't involve them." Defeated, he turned toward her. He was giving up years of work, violating his private promise to his brother. But he couldn't blackmail this woman by threatening people she loved.

"Thank you," she replied, but she still didn't go.

"Bloody hell, get out of here."

"You'll never catch him then."

"Why?"

Her fingers tightened around his arm.

"You won't find the cache," she said, "and the earl will know for certain something's wrong if you have a number of strangers combing the beaches. There's already talk about you, but then everyone believes Barkley owes you money. He owes everyone else, since Gatwell won't let go of a pence unless he must. *Does* Barkley owe you money?"

Justin nodded.

She hesitated, her nervousness obvious. Then, "John Savage isn't your true name, is it?"

"John Savage was a young lieutenant who died years

ago." Justin was stunned by his own revelation. That piece of information was something only a few people were aware of.

Yet here he was, babbling away, giving up secrets that could cause his own death. He was appalled at himself.

"Well, John Savage," she said, "I will help you if I can."

Unbelieving, he stared at her. "Why?"

"I might have a goat named for King George," she said, "and I don't like preventive men, but for all that I'm an Englishwoman. I don't like those who prey on their own people."

He realized they had changed sides, and he didn't like that fact one bit. He didn't want to involve her, and now, astonishingly, she was asking him to do just that.

God must have a sense of humor, but Justin didn't appreciate it. He, who had set the trap, found himself saying, "No."

"You've been down there on the beach, haven't you?" she asked.

Justin just looked at her, not agreeing or disagreeing.

"You didn't find anything."

She seemed absolutely sure he hadn't. Why?

"No," he finally said, "but I didn't look carefully."

"You could look for a dozen years and never find anything."

He couldn't trust her, Justin told himself. How could he? Her family smuggled goods, and she would do anything to protect them. He'd known that when she'd appeared this afternoon.

Yet he did trust her, though he couldn't understand why. He'd always been an astute judge of men; he'd spent the last fifteen years perfecting that skill. And he understood her reasoning. Most English hated Napoleon and anyone who dealt with him, particularly at the cost of the lives of their countrymen. Yet as much as he needed her help, he would lose the last shred of humanity in him if harm came to her.

Curiosity, though, drove him to ask, "Why didn't I find anything? There's a cave, isn't there?"

"Perhaps," she said, "but not the kind you know."

Her eyes were suddenly sparkling, full of challenge.

He knew he should pursue the subject of the cave, but he couldn't. He wanted her out of his scheme. "Tell me about your family," he asked, instead. He pulled her down until they both sat on rocks overlooking the Channel sea.

" 'Tis but only four of us," she said. "Da. My brother, Paul. My mother and I. My mother is sick. Consumption, the doctor said. A dryer climate might help, but the mines closed two years ago, and with them any chance of earning enough money to leave Cornwall.

"My da never smuggled before," she continued. "But he was promised he could make a year's worth of good crops in one night. I didn't want him to, but he and Paul saw it as the only way to sail to America."

"America, is it?" he said.

She nodded. "I hear we can get some land there. Da's a fine farmer, but we own nothing, and can earn nothing." He heard yearning in her voice.

"Why do you trust me?" His voice was rough even to his own ears.

"I don't," she replied. "I only know you're the only chance we have. And," she added fiercely, "I don't like traitors."

Should he accept what she was offering? He *could* protect her family from the Crown's justice, but could he protect them from Gatwell? He had the authority to offer rewards to informants, enough to get the family to America, but he knew that wasn't the reason she had offered to help. She would do what she believed was right; she couldn't be bought.

How did he know this? Especially since he had started to think the worst of everyone? A casualty of his profession as spy and spy-catcher.

His throat tightened.

"If Gatwell continues to smuggle," she continued desperately, "he'll draw my father and brother deeper and deeper into his schemes until it is too late for them to get out." She looked him squarely in the eyes. "I think I know a way you can catch him and keep my family out of it. Swear you'll protect them."

"Will you tell them about me?"

"No," she replied. "They wouldn't understand. My da's a Cornishman, and you're a—"

"Outsider," he finished before she could say something less kind.

"An outsider, yes," she said, then suddenly grinned at him.

His heart lurched crazily. After his brother killed himself, Justin had closed off his heart. Now he realized the doors could still be thrown open.

Perhaps he could give her and her family their dream.

And then what would he do? After he brought Gatwell to justice, what would he do? He'd never thought beyond that.

His continued silence seemed to prod her. "I'll show you where the brandy is. You can move it to a cave I know not far away. When Lord Gatwell sends his men for the brandy, they will find nothing. That should bring him down here."

"Won't it endanger your family?"

"I will get to Lord Gatwell first," she said, "and tell him that preventive men were snooping around and my da decided to take the brandy to a safer place."

"And if someone goes to that location, then only Gatwell could be responsible," he concluded. He'd hoped to go a more direct route, find someone who was involved to bear witness against the earl. But there was no direct trail to Gatwell. Her plan was more sure. The Crown would not have to rely on witnesses who might change their minds or just disappear. Gatwell would be caught in the act by the king's own troops.

He hesitated. "It can be dangerous," he warned.

"You could have had us all transported."

"I told you—"

"Next time you might not be here," she said.

She was right. If she couldn't convince her family to quit smuggling, and apparently she'd tried, he could guarantee nothing. But with her plan, he *could* take certain steps to keep her as safe as possible.

She rose to her feet.

He followed her up, marveling at her composure.

But he soon realized she wasn't as calm as she looked. He saw the tension in the set of her shoulders. One hand was deep in a pocket of her skirt, as if clutching something. Several strands of hair had escaped the braid she'd wound around her head, and her green eyes were as alive and turbulent as the sea below. Her cheeks were flushed and her chin set determinedly.

He wanted to kiss her again, but his pride—and cheek—stopped him. He wasn't sure why he was so attracted to her. His eye had always gone to women who, like himself, lived on the edge of society. He'd avoided married women and he avoided virgins. He hadn't needed that kind of trouble.

But suddenly he wanted this girl. Wanted her even more than he wanted the earl of Gatwell.

HOLLY FINGERED the tiny bottle in her pocket as she stared up at John Savage. Perhaps it had been worth more than she first thought, for as she'd heard him speak, the message kept repeating itself in her mind. *To thine own wish be true.*

Her deepest wish was to keep her family safe.

Then the second line: *Do not follow the moth to the star.* Was John Savage the star?

He certainly generated the heat of a star. She still felt the warmth of his lips on her mouth. Heat coursed through her every time she looked at him.

But her mind warned that he might be manipulating her, using a velvet glove rather than an iron one. Even if he was, he offered the best chance her family had. She had no doubt that Gatwell, if caught, would implicate her da and Paul or even try to eliminate them to save his own skin.

She pressed down the warning, wishing instead to believe in the stranger. He'd done his best to free her, and it had been she who refused.

His cheek still bore the mark of her hand, and she let her fingers trail over the lingering redness. "I'm sorry."

"I had no right."

"But I wanted—"

A muscle moved in his throat, and he smoothed back her hair. "Miss Hastings," he said in a voice that made her name sound like a love song. "You shouldn't even be out here with a rogue like me."

"You didn't give me much choice."

A smile tugged at the side of his mouth. "No, I didn't. Which should make you run like the devil's on your tail."

She'd thought that at dawn. What had made her change her mind? His concern? His unexpected gentleness?

Or had it been his tale about his brother, and the grief she'd seen in his eyes?

Was it the odd message in the bottle?

Whatever it was, she was struck by the intensity between them, as if they were alone on an island in a vast sea. Nothing else existed except the fog of inevitability that eclipsed the rest of the world.

He touched her cheek, and she relished the feel of it. She wanted him to kiss her again, and now she would be willing, but instead only his fingers explored her face. Then his lips briefly brushed her lips before he wrenched back with a groan.

As a deep yearning settled deep inside her, she swayed on legs that didn't want to support her. She looked into his eyes. They were intense and scorching. A smile, part incredulous, part accusatory, gentled the hard lines of his lips. His face didn't look so dangerous now.

"You must be a sea witch," he said, his voice hoarse.

"No more than you're a devil," she said, wondering where her boldness was coming from.

"That's no assurance," he replied. As if to confirm her words, a devilish smile tugged on his lips.

She gulped. His charm was wretchedly disconcerting.

But then, like a slate wiped clean of its marks, his face went almost blank. He turned away from her.

Holly struggled for words. "I'll . . . show you . . . where the brandy is."

He turned back to her, and she saw his eyes darken.

"Three nights ago, Da and Paul dug a hole and lined its sides with animal hides and covered it with boards, then sand. Unless you have the exact bearings you could never find it."

"Gatwell has those bearings?"

"The man who arranged the shipment does."

"When will they try to pick it up?"

"Not for several days," she said. "The ship might have been sighted and the coastal patrols alerted. Da said they might not come for a week or more, not until they're sure of safety."

"Then give me the bearings," he said. "I'll have my men come over tonight and move the brandy."

"There *is* a cave in the next inlet," she said. "But Da thought this might be safer. You can move the casks there."

"Can you draw me a map? Here in the dirt?"

"I can show you," she offered.

"No," he said roughly.

Stung, she stepped back at his curt reply.

He put a hand to her face. "You ruin my concentration," he said. "And neither of us can afford that now."

She nodded slowly, found a twig, and in the dirt drew him the location of the cache and then the cave. She looked up to see whether he understood, and found him watching her instead.

When he caught her gaze on him, he merely nodded. "I'll find it. We'll have it moved by morning."

"Be careful," she said softly.

"And you, sea witch."

She stood there, unable to move.

He leaned down and lightly kissed her cheek. "You are a very exceptional young lady."

Then he turned and was gone down the path to the sea.

CHAPTER SIX

$\mathcal{J}$USTIN HAD NO trouble finding the spot indicated by Holly Hastings.

But whether the cache of brandy was below him, he had no way of knowing without a long rod. He would have to bring in the troops tonight and trust that the information was reliable.

He leaned against the side of the cliff. The tide was rolling in, but the water didn't reach into the inlet where the brandy was concealed. In a storm, though, the waves might well uncover the contraband. The kegs must be buried deep.

He looked toward the steep path Holly had scampered up and down with such ease. Pretty Holly. Gallant Holly. His heart had never been touched this way before, never been so totally invaded. The swiftness with which it had happened confused him.

And even more bewildering was his reordering of priorities. Her safety—and that of her family, because it meant so much to her—came first now, not Gatwell's destruction. He'd thought nothing could change his one goal in life. But then he'd never thought a girl could turn tender a heart and soul hardened by an occupation that left little room for compassion.

His gaze moved upward. The sky was bluer than he'd noticed before, the sea more beautiful, the air fresher.

Justin Talmadge was coming back to life, and John Savage, who saw only evil and felt little, was fading.

HOLLY'S MOTHER was feeling better that evening, and smiles replaced worried frowns. Perhaps, Holly thought optimistically, the family's fortunes were changing after all. Perhaps the bottle did have magical properties.

Paul played his fiddle, Holly sang, and even her mother added her weak voice. Holly knew her brother and Da felt safe now that their part in the smuggling was done, and she tried to tuck away the apprehension that clawed up and down her spine. Was she betraying them? Would they think she'd betrayed them?

In a few hours, the stranger and his men would be digging up the brandy. There was still time to tell Da, and let him make the decision. Would he ever forgive her? Knowing her lies of omission were meant to protect them did little to relieve her conscience.

Finally, after all were asleep, she sat on the edge of her small bed, considering the possibility of going to the beach. But someone might see her. Instead she fingered the tiny bottle that somehow connected her with the stranger, with possibilities, with hope. She prayed for her family, and then she prayed for John Savage. His eyes had been so desolate when he'd told her about his troop, his brother, the suicide. He'd lost his soul that day, and that thought made her immeasurably sad.

"CLEVER," GAVIN Karr said. "Very, very clever. We never would have found it on our own."

Gavin was out of uniform, as were four of his most-trusted men. All were swathed in dark clothes and sworn to secrecy about this night's work.

Justin nodded in the dim light of the lantern tucked well within the small inlet. He held a shovel in his hand, having just unearthed the cache of brandy.

Gavin was a friend of long standing, a lieutenant in the king's army. Still, Gavin knew him only as John Savage, one of the prime minister's special agents. He did know, however, that Savage wanted Gatwell's hide.

"You might get him this time," Gavin said. "Who in the hell did you bribe to find this place? Must have cost a king's ransom. Everyone is terrified of Gatwell."

Justin allowed himself a small, stiff smile. It *was* going to cost the government a pretty pence, just not the way Gavin thought.

"Going to keep your secrets?" Gavin probed. "I can use an informant down here. Damned Cornishmen are as tight-lipped as a man cheating on a rich wife."

Justin shook his head. "Sorry."

"You fit right in with them. You always want my assistance, but—"

"Blast," Justin said. "You know you enjoy it. It's a bloody sight better than patrolling the streets of Polperro. And consider the laurels for taking down Gatwell. A promotion at the very least," he added, seeking to take his friend's mind from the informant's identity.

Gavin's face brightened. "A captaincy at least," he said, "if I can haul in a fish like Gatwell." Gavin was well aware that Justin would slip away, unnoticed, once his task was accomplished. He was a man whose anonymity was essential. "Especially if I can bag the whole lot."

"Remember your oath," Justin warned. "Only those caught red-handed at the cave."

"And Gatwell?"

"And Gatwell," Justin agreed.

They both bent their backs then. The kegs would be loaded into a sloop and carried to a cave on the other side of a jutting cliff.

The last keg was transferred and the hole covered again just as the first streaks of dawn stretched across the sky. Gavin summoned a young lad, who looked no more than fifteen. "I'm sending Denny with you," he told Justin. "You can say he's your valet arrived from London. Send him for me when Gatwell returns."

Justin nodded and held out his hand. "My thanks, Gavin. Again."

"One of these days you'll find another man to do your dirty work, and I'll retire into boredom. You keep things interesting, John."

Justin grinned. "I think you'll always find your own amusements."

"If I'm not cashiered first," Gavin said, wading out into the sea before setting foot into the sloop. "Take care, John."

Justin inclined his head in acknowledgement, then leaned against the cliff as he watched the sloop head out.

GATWELL HAD returned.

Holly heard the news when she took some eggs to sell in the village. Her blood started to pulse with excitement. Even a little terror.

A full week it had been since John Savage had moved the casks of brandy, and six days since she'd last seen him on the cliffs.

He'd been waiting as she expected, as if he'd known she would be there, even though they had made no arrangements.

Though he must have been up all night moving the casks, his face held no sign of weariness. As she approached, his arms had opened, and she'd slid into them without words.

He'd held her, and they'd communicated by touch, not by declarations. The embrace was natural, as inevitable as the sun rising at dawn. No doubts pestered her when she felt his arms around her.

"It's done," he'd whispered. His arms had hugged her reassuringly, then hungrily, and again their lips had met, and she'd felt the rush of reckless desire.

But he'd stopped and stepped back. "You are so young and . . . innocent." His eyes had burned into her like hot brands. He had taken her hand and lifted it to his lips in a totally romantic gesture. "And altogether too lovely."

Her fingers touched his stark face. Then they trembled

and she moved them away, lest he realize what was happening to her. He was far above her, too far ever to consider her more than a fling. But these were magic moments, ones she would remember all her life. She was regarded tenderly by a man who made her heart take wing. She would always treasure these days.

"You should not be here," he said.

"I know," she whispered.

Their gazes held. The cool curtain over his was gone, and the gray in his eyes was turbulent.

Finally, he reluctantly released her. "Go," he commanded.

"How do . . . I find you again when . . . the earl returns?"

He grinned suddenly and it changed his face. He looked young and vulnerable. "Georgette," he said. "Bring Georgette into town for something. I'll have someone keeping an eye out for her. I'll meet you that afternoon."

"Here?"

He shook his head. "It will be too dangerous."

"The church," she said. "I sometimes go into the church to pray for my mother."

He winced, and she suspected it had been a long time since he'd visited a house of God. But then he nodded. "Go now," he said, "before I ravish you right here."

She swirled around before the idea became irresistible.

AFTER HEARING of the earl's arrival in Cornwall, Justin waited in the village tavern, setting Denny to watch for a pretty young lady and a white goat.

He played his role as gambler and creditor to its limit. He drank, played with whomever he could tempt into a game. He seldom won, though, reluctant to take money from men who obviously had little.

And he tried not to think of Holly. He wanted to make her promises he had no right to make. He'd seen the hunger in her eyes, but he'd not stooped low enough to take an innocent.

He could never have her.

For one wild moment, he'd thought about asking to call on her, but he was a man with no home, no future, and a past littered with deception. And his was a profession that promised neither security nor longevity.

He was too old, too cynical, too jaded to change. He could only make her life a misery.

But he could give her opportunities she didn't have now. He hadn't used the bribe money available to him, and so he would find a way to give it to her as a reward.

Justin knew Cornishmen. He had fought alongside some. He had lived among them before. She and her family would not take money for helping the government. But he would find a way. He would also find them transport to America.

He just wished the thought didn't cause him so much pain.

CHAPTER SEVEN

*T*HE SMALL CHURCH sat at the end of the village, its doors always open. A cemetery spread its harvest of stones next to the modest building.

A sense of peace radiated from the burial place. Justin paused and studied the plain white stones with their sparse epitaphs. He saw a number with the Hastings name.

Sadness seeped through him. The Hastings family had obviously had its share of grief and tragedy. He wondered whether the other members of Holly's family had her courage, joy of life, and compassion.

It had been a long time since Justin had felt compassion, and he hadn't even realized that fact. That was the saddest aspect of it. When had he ceased to be a human being?

Maybe he was being given a second chance.

After glancing around to make sure no one was paying him any mind, he strode toward the church door with an eagerness that surprised him. That was another feeling he hadn't experienced in a great many years.

The church was empty except for a lone figure in a back pew. Her head was bowed, her body still. Not wanting to startle her, he purposely tapped the cane on the floor. Her head swung around. Her face was solemn, but her marvelous eyes welcomed him. She offered acceptance and trust—such overwhelming trust that he felt reborn. Years of cynicism seemed to fade away.

"Miss Holly," he said softly.

"Mr. Savage," she acknowledged with a smile.

He slid into the pew next to her. "It's Justin," he corrected, wanting her to know, and speak, his true name.

"Justin," she repeated. He was surprised at how lyrical his name sounded on her lips.

Blast, but his heart fluttered like a schoolboy's. He'd almost forgotten the reason he was here. If this continued, he would get them all killed.

"He's back," she said.

He nodded.

"No one has come to Da yet about the missing kegs," she informed him.

"It will take time for Gatwell to find another Tim Bailey."

Her questioning gaze cut to his sharply.

"A friend of mine intercepted him," Justin said with satisfaction. Bailey was now ensconced in a gaol far to the north.

"Did he admit anything?"

Justin shook his head. Unfortunately, the man had not talked. His fear of Lord Gatwell was obviously stronger than his fear of authorities. "Are you sure you want to go through with this?"

"Yes." Her voice trembled slightly, but her chin was set determinedly.

"There's a young man who will accompany you. He will wait outside the gates."

She shook her head. "No. Lord Gatwell will be suspicious."

"You're not going there alone," Justin said. "Denny will accompany you. He's my valet. He's as helpless-looking as a puppy and won't pose a threat to Gatwell. Say that Denny was taken with you and is dogging your very footsteps."

"If he's helpless?"

"I didn't say he was helpless. I said he's helpless-looking," Justin pointed out. "He's a trained soldier for all his youth, and brighter than most." Justin smiled. "And he *is* taken with you. 'A vision of loveliness,' were his very words." He remembered the awe on the boy's face when he'd reported sighting Holly and the goat.

She made a face, and Justin wondered whether she was unaware of how pretty she was.

"If Denny doesn't see you leave within an hour of your entrance into Gatwell's place," Justin continued, "he's to alert me. I have men standing by. But I don't think Gatwell will try anything as long as he knows someone saw you enter."

He prayed to God he was right. He prayed so rarely, he wasn't sure whether his plea would be an advantage or a disadvantage. He thought briefly about canceling the plan, but Gatwell was a danger to her family, to the entire village, and Justin was taking every precaution. Still, uncommon apprehension ran up and down his spine.

Holly put her hand in his. Why didn't he just take her and leave this place? But she wouldn't go without ensuring her family's safety. He'd learned that much of her.

His fingers went around hers. They were long and slender but callused.

"Don't worry," she said. "I have a talisman."

"A talisman?"

She took the bottle from her pocket and showed it to him. He touched the silver filigree. "It is ancient," he said, "and beautiful." He cast a questioning look at her.

"I found it in a keg of brandy that fell and broke open."

"A very unusual keg, indeed. This bottle could be worth much to someone interested in antiquities."

She shook her head. For some reason, she knew that neither the bottle nor its message was meant to be sold.

Curiosity gleamed in his eyes, but she didn't want to talk about the bottle anymore. If she did, she might end up telling him about the message. He might laugh, and she couldn't bear that. "I'll go home and sit with my mother awhile, then go to the earl's," she said.

"Denny will be waiting for you on the road. He has a lock of sandy hair that always falls over his forehead."

"And he looks like a puppy," she added mischievously. "I don't think I'll miss him."

"Don't go into the manor without meeting with him first," Justin warned. "Do you promise?"

"Yes." She looked toward the plain altar in the front of the church. She'd read enough books to believe love could strike like lightning. She felt as if that arrow of light had struck her the first time she'd met Justin on the cliff. Why else was she thinking or dreaming of little else than the tall, dark stranger with agonized eyes?

"Holly?" His voice stirred her from useless musings. He was here for one thing, and one thing only. He might even have a wife and family for all she knew. The thought was excruciatingly painful.

"Where will you go after this?" she asked.

He shrugged. "Where I'm sent."

She hesitated. "And . . . your family?"

"I have none," he said.

"None at all?"

"When my brother was accused of betraying his regiment, my father disowned him. *I* disowned my father. For all he knows, I'm dead."

"You've never married?"

She was still staring at the alter, unwilling to look at him, afraid her eyes revealed too much.

"My occupation is not conducive to marriage," he said, "and I have little to offer a wife."

She could have told him she had no expectations, but she said nothing. She couldn't. He seemed determined to live his life alone, and she couldn't open herself to rejection. Or worse, his amusement that she could even imagine herself a match for him.

She disentangled her fingers from his and rose unsteadily. "I have to go now."

He stood with her, and he held her chin to force her to meet his gaze. He shook his head, as if in wonderment. "You really *are* an amazing young lady," he said.

She wrinkled her brows together, not quite knowing how to reply.

"You have more courage than most soldiers I've met," he explained.

Holly swallowed hard. She was a fraud. She'd sounded brave, but she wasn't. She was terrified. But if she told him that, he probably wouldn't let her go, so she looked down instead.

"No," he said. "Look at me."

She forced her gaze back up. His face was too close to hers. Too attractive. Too tempting.

When his lips joined hers, she relished the feel of them. She felt the warmth of his body, and savored the intoxicating scent of him, an irresistible mixture of soap and leather. The ache inside was like nothing she'd felt before. She couldn't force herself away from the magic that was transforming her from girl to woman.

His arms went around her, and she sheltered in them, her mind whirling with the pure wonder of what was happening to her, to her body. Reason told her she should fight against it, but she didn't want to. She'd stepped into a marvelous, sensation-filled world that was alive with color and energy and life.

His lips explored hers with a tenderness that soon turned into something dangerous. His kiss deepened, his tongue probing her mouth with a recklessness that made her tremble.

He apparently felt it, for he stilled, and his tongue stopped its assault. She didn't want it to stop, though, and suddenly her own mouth responded with a daring of its own. Nothing mattered now except the need each was creating in the other. Then they were feeding on each other, teasing, exploring, reacting, each touch sending her farther away from reality and into a spiral that seemed to have no end.

His lips left her mouth and trailed kisses over her face and her neck, and boldly, Holly found herself returning them, following his lead, knowing from her body's reactions what was happening to his.

When their mouths parted for a moment, she drew back, reveling in what was happening to her. Nothing would ever be the same.

She heard him groan, then heard her own small whimper as he leaned down and kissed her throat. His every touch sent pulsating, heated ripples racing through the core of her.

She didn't know how she could stand more. Her body ached in the most unfathomable ways. She wrenched away, trembling so badly she thought she might fall.

She loved him. She knew that now. She'd found her silver link. The caress, the kiss, the gentle yet fierce passion confirmed it. She loved him. And she was going to lose him.

She was aware of his eyes on her, of his arms still giving her support. Aware of his strength and his tenderness. She never wanted to leave his touch. But she must leave, even as she stored these memories for the future.

"Holly?"

She looked at him.

"You can still forget about helping me. I wish you would."

She shook her head stubbornly.

"Go with God, then," he said. "And know I'll be right behind Him."

With that comforting thought, she slipped out of the aisle and the church.

HOLLY FOUND Denny easily enough. She smiled inwardly as she realized how accurately Justin had described the lad. His face went red as she asked him to call her Holly, and he shuffled in embarrassment when she thanked him for his help.

" 'Tis my pleasure," he said. "I'll not let anything happen to you."

He would, without doubt, risk his life for their mission. It was a burden she did not want, and she wished she could send him on some useless errand. But she'd promised.

As they walked the three miles to the manor, she ran through her speech to the earl. She'd never considered him evil before, only arrogant and unprincipled, but now that she'd heard Justin's tale, she remembered other things: odd disappearances, rumors, even terror. By the time they reached the manor, she was cold with fear. At least Barkley and his wife hadn't returned with the earl; she didn't think she could bear that sneering contempt in his eyes nor the knowledge that she'd once believed his silky words.

She walked to the servants' entrance at the back and rang the bell.

A servant, dressed in black, opened the door and looked at her as if she were dung under his feet. A Londoner, she judged, for she didn't recognize him and the locals would never have behaved with such arrogance.

"May I see Lord Gatwell?" she asked as respectfully as she could.

"What business have you with m'lord?"

"None I need discuss with you," she retorted.

He started to shut the door, but she inserted her foot. "The earl would be none too happy not to hear my news," she said. "Tell him it concerns Tim Bailey."

The door slammed in her face. She sat on the step outside the door, hoping she had not misjudged the butler. He *would* go to Gatwell. He would be afraid not to.

After several moments, the door opened again and she was ushered through the great house. She'd been there once before with Barkley; he'd whisked her through when his father had been gone. She remembered, with some embarrassment, her awe of the interior. Now the grandeur didn't impress her; now she knew it came from the blood of others.

Lord Gatwell was sitting at a desk in his study. He didn't rise as she entered, nor did he acknowledge her presence as she stood awkwardly while the butler retreated behind her.

Finally, Gatwell lifted his head and regarded her with a cold stare. "What do you want, gel?"

"My da's been trying to find Tim Bailey to give him some information, but Mr. Bailey has . . . disappeared."

"And what has that to do with me?"

"Perhaps nothing, sir, and if not I humbly beg your pardon for disturbing you." She turned to go.

"Wait!"

She stopped.

"Explain yourself," the earl demanded.

"I . . . we . . . I mean there was something Mr. Bailey asked Da to do, and he told him where to do it, but . . . then the next day I saw there were strangers about and my da thought it best to move . . . Mr. Bailey's belongings to a better spot. He was going to tell Mr. Bailey, but he just disappeared. Perhaps preventive men . . ." She paused for breath, then continued just as mindlessly, "I'd better go."

The earl's face paled, but still he blustered. "Why do you come to me? I know nothing of Bailey's business."

She gave him an innocent look. "I heard he works for you sometimes, but if he doesn't, then I suppose . . . the goods now belong to Da." She curtsied. "Thank you, sir."

"Wait," the earl said again, his voice almost a roar. "I suppose you're talking about contraband. You know the penalty for smuggling? Perhaps you'd better tell me about these goods, and I'll see to their disposal. No one will be the wiser."

"That is very kind of you, sir," she replied. "But we wouldn't want to taint your good name."

The earl rose to his feet and set his hands on his desk as he studied her face. Had she overplayed her game?

But then he seemed to relax. "Ain't you the gel Barkley trifled with?" Gatwell asked.

Blood rushed to Holly's face. She wanted to throw something at Gatwell. Barkley had not gotten the chance to "trifle" with her, though he'd tried hard enough and, regretfully, almost succeeded. But she was not about to debate that point with the earl, particularly when he had that lustful gleam in his eyes.

Instead, she lowered her own eyes so he wouldn't see the fury in them.

His voice turned soothing. "It's my duty," he said, "to assist my tenants when I can. Give me the location of the contraband, and I will see to its disposal. I would not like to see any of my tenants arrested and transported."

"But what of yourself, my lord?"

He shrugged. "I'll take care of the authorities."

"You're very kind, sir, but what about Tim Bailey, and the fee Da was to be paid?"

"I know nothing about fees," the earl said. "I'm simply

doing you a favor, ridding your family of something that could send you all to New South Wales."

Anger pounded in her. He wanted to cheat her da out of his promised money. He had used her father, and now he'd found a reason not to pay him.

"The location?" he asked.

She shifted on her feet. She couldn't give him the answer too easily.

His voice moderated, became almost seductive. "I just want to help you and your family. They've been good tenants. I wouldn't like to see anything happen to them."

"I'll . . . have to ask Da."

"We don't have time for that," the earl said impatiently.

"The cave at Kell's Point," she said in a low, ragged voice, as if the information had been ripped from her.

"Tell me about the men you saw."

"I was keeping watch for Da and I saw this man at the top of the cliff, looking down, then later I saw him talking to several other men on the road. So Da went the next night . . . and moved everything."

"What did this stranger look like?"

"Short . . . squat," she said, thinking of everything opposite *her* stranger.

He sat back in his chair. "And no one saw you move anything?"

She shook her head. "I was keeping watch again."

He stared at something on his desk. "Get out, gel, and keep your mouth shut. Tell your father to do the same."

"Yes, my lord," she said.

He smiled then. It was a smooth, sly smile. "You and your family need not bother yourselves with the matter any longer. I'll make sure you're all protected."

"But—"

"I want to hear no more of this," the earl said softly. "Get yourself home, gel, and tell your da he should be more careful about his associates."

She gave a brief curtsy and fled, anger and triumph warring with each other inside her.

CHAPTER EIGHT

*D*URING THE NEXT several days, Holly almost told her da about what she had done. But he was apparently living in unconcerned ignorance. His part was over and eventually Tim Bailey would appear and pay him.

She didn't have the heart to tell him differently. Nor could she risk his becoming involved again with the earl. So she kept silent, relieved that it was harvest time and he and Paul spent hours in the field. On their return, they were too tired to ask many questions.

She wanted to see the stranger, but her mother had worsened, and she had to stay at home. He knew what had happened in the manor; Denny would have given him a complete report, and she had little doubt that soldiers would be watching the caves.

She just had to wait, even though she ached to see Justin, to feel his arms around her. But for how long? The thought of never seeing him again filled her with loneliness. She hadn't missed what she hadn't known. But now . . .

"You look different," her mother observed the third afternoon after her visit to Gatwell. "There's no young man, is there?"

"No," Holly replied truthfully. There was no young man. There was only a man old beyond his years who carried burdens she barely comprehended, a man who made it clear there was no room for a woman in his life.

Her mother clasped her hand. "More than anything, I want to see you wedded to a man you truly love," she said. "As I was."

Holly glanced down at her mother, seeing how much that love had cost her. Poverty. Disappointment. And now this wasting sickness. Yet the glow of love remained. And the shine of hope.

And she realized how lucky her mother had been.

She nodded.

"Don't be afraid to take chances for a man you love," her mother whispered. Her fingers clutched Holly's. "Fight for him. Promise me."

It was almost as if her mother knew about the stranger. "I will," she said.

Her mother smiled. "Then go, love. I'll get some rest."

"I'll be in the next room."

"No. You need fresh air. Go to the cliffs. I know you like it there."

Holly hesitated, then leaned down and kissed her mother on her forehead. It was cool. The fever was gone.

When Holly opened the door, she saw the roiling clouds to the east. A storm was coming; the air was alive with electricity.

And then she realized what that meant. Not only would a storm keep almost everyone inside, it also necessitated action on the earl's part. A heavy storm would flood the cave, ruining the casks of brandy, perhaps dragging them back to sea.

Was he so greedy that he would risk retrieving the casks during a storm? She wasn't sure.

She followed the path toward the sea, knowing inside her heart that Justin would be there. She even felt his presence long before she saw the tall figure silhouetted against the clouds that darkened the horizon. He wore no hat, and the wind ruffled his hair. His gaze was directed toward the sea, and he looked stark and lonely, a man apart from all others.

As she had sensed his presence, he had apparently

sensed hers. He turned, then walked toward her. "You shouldn't be out," he said. "A storm is coming."

"I know. I like storms."

He smiled. "I should have expected that." Then his lips thinned, and the smile disappeared as if it had never existed. "Tonight could be dangerous. If he's going to move, it must be now."

"Yes," she agreed.

"I paid him a visit today," he said, "and demanded my money."

"He didn't recognize you?"

He shook his head. "No reason he should. I was in full uniform fifteen years ago. I've changed a great deal, and the cane is more effective than a mask. People often don't see the man carrying it."

Was he warning her, testing her? The cane had never mattered to her, not even when she'd first seen him in the village.

"What did he say?" she asked.

"That I was a notorious gambler who had probably cheated, and he had no intention of rewarding a scoundrel," he replied dryly. "He was very righteous about it all, but he knows he must pay to avoid a scandal. There were too many witnesses to the game."

She noticed that her body was leaning into his. She had no idea how it had happened.

"Denny's even more in love with you now," he continued. "The vision of loveliness also has the heart of a lioness, according to him. Tell me, Miss Holly, are you daunted by anything?"

"I was terrified," she said.

"That's the test of true courage, Holly. Not lack of fear."

Her heartbeat quickened, and then she wondered if he was talking about himself. He had a strange expression on his face and his gray eyes were smoldering, like hot ashes from a fire.

He leaned down and kissed her lightly. "You had better get home. I will be meeting some friends shortly. Keep your father and brother in the cottage tonight."

She felt disappointment. She'd wanted to be present at the earl's downfall.

"It's important, Holly."

"Will . . . will I have to witness against him?"

He hesitated. "Perhaps."

A lump settled in her throat. "Then Da will have to know?"

"I think you might want to tell him yourself," he said gently. "Secrets have a way of revealing themselves."

"And then you'll leave?"

He was silent for a long time. "Yes," he finally said.

She bit her lip and lowered her eyes, blinking to keep tears back. *To thine own wish be true. Fight for him.* Two pieces of advice, one ancient, one uttered just moments ago. But how could she fight for something so out of the realm of possibility?

"I'll miss you," she said simply.

"Will you, Miss Holly? I don't think I've ever been missed by anyone before." His voice was sensual, beguiling.

"I . . . don't believe that."

"It is the plain truth, and I thank you for changing that dismal fact, as well as for your help with Gatwell," he said. "And now I think you'd better go."

"You'll let me know what happens?" she asked, unwilling yet to leave him.

"You can be sure of that. I'll not disappear without saying good-bye."

"Be careful."

His finger caressed her cheek but he said nothing. Then he turned around, facing the sea again. "Good afternoon, Miss Hastings."

Feeling abandoned, she stood still a moment, watching him. Then she straightened her back. "Good afternoon, Mr. Savage," she managed to say with no small measure of dignity.

JUSTIN DREW the cloak around him. A familiar excitement shimmered inside as he saw dim lights dancing in the distance. Lanterns, he guessed. Lanterns dimmed by the falling rain and light fog.

Voices were audible, even against the tattering of raindrops and the occasional drum of thunder. He could not have summoned a more perfect night for smugglers.

Would the earl himself come?

Justin wasn't too sure. But he was gambling that the French brandy was too valuable for Gatwell to leave to chance a second time. Gatwell wouldn't have time to create the usual layers of obfuscation around him.

Gavin's gloved hand touched his, letting him know he too had seen the lights. Five men, including the two of them, lay hidden among the jutting rocks above the caves. Five more men were secreted in the cave below. A mile away, more men waited with horses.

Justin watched as the lanterns bobbed closer to them before he and the others ducked out of sight. They would follow the smugglers down to the cave, catching them neatly in a trap.

He heard the sound of wheels. A wagon of some kind. It would have to be left on the cliff above, with at least one man to stand watch.

The sound of boots and voices disappeared where a path led down to the sea. After several moments, Justin motioned to Gavin. The two of them separated, crawling along the ground. Justin looked between two rocks and saw the dark outline of a wagon. Unfortunately, the leader of this band had been smart enough not to leave a lantern burning, and Justin had no idea where the watch might be. If it were him, though, he would seek some kind of shelter.

He listened, then he heard the sound of rocks rolling. Gavin was doing his part, creating a diversion.

A rough voice challenged the sound. "Who goes there?"

Justin managed to get a fix on the sound. Toward the front of the wagon.

"Who goes there?" came the voice again, this time more threatening.

Justin circled to the right, grateful for the rain that covered what small sound his boots made. He saw the outline of a man, and he took the knife from his belt as he inched forward.

Gavin made another rustle, and the man swung slightly to his left. Justin crept up to him, wrapping his arm around the neck and putting the knife to the man's throat.

"Not a sound," he whispered. "Drop that revolver."

The weapon dropped.

"Are you alone up here?" he asked.

The man nodded.

"Gavin," Justin called out. Gavin appeared out of nowhere.

"Is Gatwell with you?" Justin asked his captive. When no answer came immediately, his knife pricked the man's neck. "Is he?"

"Aye," the man said quickly.

Satisfaction flooded through Justin. After tying and gagging the man, he and Gavin gathered the remaining soldiers and started down the path.

The small beach was almost totally awash with waves. Justin, followed by the others, picked his way along the bottom of the cliffs to the opening of the cave. Trying to blend with the dark walls, he moved inside, seeing the flickering lights ahead.

Their men had removed some kegs earlier and hidden themselves toward the back of the cache. Their instructions were to wait until they heard Justin and their lieutenant.

Justin picked out the shadowy forms of five men. No, six. The last man was standing to the side as the others were in various stages of reaching for or carrying kegs.

"Gatwell!"

Justin's voice echoed inside the cave. Several kegs dropped at the sound. Gatwell reached for a pistol tucked in his belt.

"Don't!" Justin shouted.

But Gatwell had already pulled out the pistol.

Justin fired, aiming at Gatwell's arm, and the earl slumped against the side of the cave, his weapon falling to the ground.

"King's men," Gavin announced. "You are all under arrest."

Curses echoed in the cave, and one man reached for a blunderbuss leaning against several kegs.

"I wouldna' be doin' that," a voice warned as men stepped out from behind kegs. The smugglers were now sandwiched between two groups of armed men.

A roar of pure rage came from Gatwell. "Do you know who I am?"

"I know exactly who you are," Justin replied, stepping into the light.

"Savage," the earl said, holding his bleeding arm. "What in the devil?"

"You should have paid the gambling debt," Justin said mildly. "And a few other debts as well."

"What do you mean?"

"One you owe a company of king's guards you sold to Napoleon."

Gatwell's eyes narrowed on Justin, as the earl tried to remember.

"Did you betray so many companies that you can't recall each one?" Justin yearned to kill the man here and now.

"You're insane," Gatwell said. "I'll have you arrested. I heard about this shipment, and I decided to secure it for the Crown."

"In the dead of night?" Justin said. "You told the constabulary, of course?"

"I don't have to," the earl said arrogantly.

"Then you can explain it to a magistrate."

Gatwell shrugged carelessly. "I want a doctor."

"In Polperro," Gavin said, stepping in. "There's a secure gaol there."

"I'll have you cashiered." Gatwell sneered.

Gavin laughed. "Tie them up," he told two of his men.

"My arm," Gatwell protested.

Gavin looked at Justin and shrugged. "He's not going anyplace."

Justin hesitated, and then nodded reluctantly.

In minutes, the five men with Gatwell were tied, including a man Justin identified as the butler who'd admitted him to Gatwell's estate earlier in the day. He didn't look as superior now as he had then.

"What about the brandy?" Gavin asked.

"We'll take five casks as evidence and leave the rest here," Justin said. "The sea will probably take them." And if not the sea, then certainly the villagers, who could use the money.

Waves were beginning to lap at the cave as they left, two of Gavin's men guarding Gatwell, five carrying casks of brandy, and the remainder prodding the other smugglers. Justin, a lantern in hand, took the lead as they started up the path.

HOLLY SLIPPED out of the house and made for the path to the sea. She heard Georgette complain noisily from her enclosure. The goat would continue until she woke someone.

She slipped the latch from the gate and allowed Georgette out. If anyone saw her, she could always claim Georgette had escaped and she'd been out looking for her.

Holly walked slowly at first, allowing her eyes to adjust to the darkness. Rain came steadily and she shivered. By the time she neared the cliffs, her cloak was soaked through.

The rain finally slowed. She looked up at the sky. Her father would call it the devil's sky. A small patch of light had escaped from the shrouded moon, casting eerie shadows across the moor. Her visibility improved and she speeded her steps. She heard the waves smashing against the cliffs and listened intently for human sounds.

Finally, she heard the harsh commands of men, the oaths of others. She looked around her. Georgette was grazing some distance from her, safe for the moment. Holly ducked behind rocks. Men appeared, all of them clad in black. She could tell from their movements that some were bound. Justin was leading the procession. The earl was positioned between two armed men, and she noticed that he was stumbling.

"You're going too fast," the earl shouted, and Justin stopped. He turned back just as the earl, moving more swiftly than Holly thought possible, grabbed a pistol from one of the men guarding him. Gatwell pushed the man aside and backed up, moving toward where she hid.

"You can't escape," Justin said.

"No," the earl agreed. "But which one of you wants to die first? You, Savage?"

"What do you think to gain?" Justin growled.

"I won't go to prison," the earl said. "Or hang. That's what you have in mind, isn't it, Savage? Or should I say Talmadge?"

Holly saw Justin's body tense and heard his curt words. "You know?"

"Once you gave me the clue," Gatwell said, "I remembered you. A boy in uniform with a fool for a brother."

Holly hadn't understood until this second what the earl hoped to gain. Now she did. He was goading Justin—or one of the other soldiers—into killing him.

She realized something else. The earl's pistol was aimed directly at Justin. Gatwell knew *who* had led him to ruin. And now why.

Fear wrapped her heart. She had no weapon except surprise. Yet surprise might well spur Gatwell into shooting.

The earl took two steps back. Then Holly heard something behind her—a loud bleat from Georgette.

The bleat sounded again, and the earl turned toward the noise. He saw what everyone else was seeing: a white blur rushing toward him.

Then she heard a grunt. Justin had taken advantage of the distraction and jumped the earl. Both men fell to the ground, fighting over the pistol.

Holly grabbed Georgette's halter. She held her breath, wanting to do something as the two men struggled and the soldiers stood still, afraid to fire for fear of hitting the wrong man.

A shot rang out, and both men stilled. Her heart stopped beating for an instant, and then slowly Justin rose, shrugging off the earl's heavier body. A growing red stain covered the earl's chest.

The sky rolled again with heavy clouds, and the air was filled with confusion, murmured curses, and stunned cries.

Holly took a tentative step toward Justin. He reached out to her, and she released Georgette and took Justin's hand, feeling its warmth and strength.

"I should turn you over my knee," came the familiar, beloved voice, "but I'd rather just hold you."

With that reluctant admission, he swept her into his arms, holding her tightly against him. "Little fool," he whispered into her ear. "But you might just have saved my life tonight."

A man, stooping over the earl's body, interrupted. "You might like to know that he's quite dead. I do say, you always make things interesting. First time I've seen an earl undone by a goat."

There was a pause, then, "Are you going to introduce me?"

"To the goat?" Justin asked with rare amusement.

Holly savored the sound. She'd seen too little of this side of him.

"Go to the devil," the man said, bowing in front of her. "Lieutenant Gavin Karr at your service, miss. I hope you forgive my friend's appalling manners."

"If you will forgive Georgette's," she said, instantly liking the officer.

"Georgette?"

"My goat. She's named after—"

But Justin's mouth stopped her words with a kiss, a long, lingering kiss that cleared her mind of anything but how much she loved him, how much she'd feared for him, how content she was in his arms.

When he released her, she realized everyone was staring at them. Even in the blackness, she could feel their curious gazes.

But Justin apparently didn't care to explain himself. "Gavin, take your prisoners along, then I would suggest searching the earl's house. I'll join you there later."

Lieutenant Karr bowed again. "A pleasure, miss." Then he turned to Justin. "I want to know the whole story," he said. "Swear it?"

Justin chuckled.

Lieutenant Karr hesitated a moment, gave a snort of disgust, then dispatched two of his men to carry the earl to their horses. His orders came quickly now.

And then they were alone.

Rain fell gently on them, but she was unaware of anything but Justin. He wiped raindrops from her face.

"I thought I told you to stay home."

"You told me to make sure Da and my brother stayed home," she corrected.

"Am I safe from that goat?" he inquired cautiously, but his words were laced with humor.

"At the moment, I think."

"You know, Gatwell's death clears your family," he said. "Tim Bailey and the Conleys are the only ones who know of the connection, and they would be risking their own necks if they talked."

She would have nodded but her head was buried in his cloak.

"There will be a reward," he said. "A large one. You can go to America."

Her heart stopped.

"And I suspect that if some of your father's friends inspected a particular cave in the morning, they might find some casks of brandy."

"But Lieutenant Karr?"

"Gavin will be far too busy with more important matters," Justin said. "And then he'll believe they floated away on the tide. His interest, like mine, was in Gatwell."

She could only stare up at him.

"I've been thinking about America, too," he continued. "Especially now. Too many men heard my name tonight."

"America?"

"America," he confirmed. "Would you . . . consider being courted by a battered cynic?"

Her breath caught in her throat, keeping her from saying the words she so wanted to say. Instead, she stretched up onto her toes and melded her mouth with his. A promise joined with a promise. "I love you," she whispered softly when the kiss ended.

"Ah, Holly," he said. "I'd stopped believing in miracles. And then you came along."

"And Georgette," she added.

"I don't have to love her too, do I?"

Love her too. Holly's heart swelled until she thought it

might burst. Her hand tightened around his, and his fingers clasped hers.

"I'm not used to loving," he warned. "I'm not sure I know how to do it right."

"I am," she said, touching the bottle in her pocket. "I am."

EPILOGUE

*H*ER BODY MELLOW with lovemaking, Holly stretched out beside her husband.

They'd been married two weeks, and she'd never known such joy in her life. He felt it too, for he smiled easily now.

They were on a ship bound for Charleston, then they would head for Tennessee, where they planned to buy land adjacent to her da's.

He had reluctantly accepted part of the reward after Justin explained that Holly and Georgette had accidentally assisted in the apprehension of the earl. Now her da, mother, and Paul were also on the ship, and for the first time in a long while, had some money in their pockets. Even Georgette had been brought along. After all, Justin said, she'd saved his life.

Just yesterday, he and Holly had stood on the deck of the ship and tossed out the silver-trimmed bottle. It would travel thousands of miles and, they hoped, land in the hands of someone who needed it. The message had given Holly courage; perhaps it would do the same for someone else.

Justin had not laughed at the notion; instead he'd handled it with the same reverence as she. . . .

The same reverence with which he now touched her. . . .

Justin heard the small moan in her throat and he moved

on top of her, rejoicing in the sparkle in her eyes, the soft smile on her lips, the instinctive movements of her body that said, as much as words, how much she loved him.

This tender loving was new to him, but she made it easy. Because of her he'd dared to hope again.

Dear God, how he loved her! He felt her opening to him. She had no secrets from him, no inhibitions, and yet she understood his own dark shadows, and her patience was infinite.

Except now. He felt her body moving under his, and he entered her, then moved with her in a dance of love, each movement designed to prolong pleasure, to explore every new and familiar feeling and exploit it until the dance turned wild and uncontrollable, rocketing to places still unknown in flashes of white hot splendor.

The final explosion was pure glory, and he wondered whether they had created life. The thought was humbling, and his touch gentled as he drew her closer to him.

He'd never known feelings like this, the peace of being at one with another, the joining of heart and soul, the joy of sharing simple things, and now the promise of even greater adventure.

She smiled at him when the ship rolled, bringing them closer together.

"I think we might have made a baby," he said tenderly.

"If we haven't already," she replied as she nuzzled his neck.

"Should we call her Joy?"

Her eyes sparkled like a million diamonds. "Mmm, a good beginning."

"Beginning?"

"I want a half-dozen children."

The notion took a moment to penetrate. "A half-dozen?"

"At least," she mumbled happily.

A half-dozen! The notion was overwhelming.

Her fingers caressed his mouth, then moved downward. He felt his body responding to the challenge just as her mouth met his.

A half-dozen sounded just right.

PATRICIA POTTER

PATRICIA POTTER has won the *Romantic Times* Career Achievement Award for Storyteller of the Year for 1992 and the Best Western Romance Author for 1996. Look for her next historical romance, *Starcatcher,* on sale in December 1997, in which a Scottish chieftain kidnaps his ladylove, despite the perilous consequences for their clans—and their future together.

The Unwanted Bride

Suzanne Robinson

CHAPTER ONE

Somerset, England, 1857

TEMPLE STIRLING STOOD beside one of the hundred fountains in his garden, his arm resting on the head of a statue of a Roman river god. Behind him rose the symmetrical facade of Stirling Hall, imposing, classical, an expression of the wealth and power of his ancestors. Temple glanced over his shoulder, up past the ivy-covered balustrade to the rows of windows that formed a glittering backdrop for the garden. Through one set he glimpsed a billowing skirt, then another, and a third. Yet another pack of ladies with eligible daughters in tow had called on his mother this morning. He heard a French door open.

Stepping behind the river god, Temple waited for whomever had opened the door to go inside and close it. Then he left his refuge and returned to his study by the service stairs. On his desk lay the letter he'd almost finished. He'd gone for a walk to clear his head after the strain of composing it.

Never had he expected to write such a letter, for in it he proposed marriage to a woman he'd never seen. No, that wasn't quite right. He'd seen her picture, heard of her tranquil nature, temperate manners, and uncomplicated habits. After nearly six months of evading the traps of ambitious mamas and his own mother's attempts at matchmaking, Temple had found an alternative. He would marry the daughter of the man who had saved his life in the Crimea.

There was a knock. Busy adding a closure to his letter, Temple didn't answer it. After a moment, the door opened enough to admit a wide head with a ruddy complexion and crimson nose. Gray hair lay flat on the head and curled at the ends as it fell from crown to forehead in an outdated Napoleonic style. A gruff, low voice spoke.

"T'ain't going to be much longer before the dowager countess comes looking for you, m'lord major." A career cavalryman, Sergeant Mungo Fidkin had yet to adjust to civilian life. His manners were having an even harder time. "You bean't writing that letter, are you?"

"Go away, Fidkin."

"It ain't fitting." The sergeant slipped into the room, put his back to the door, and shook a stubby finger at Temple. "I didn't spend all these months nursing you and your wounds like you was a sick lamb to have you go marrying some doctor's daughter. Your mum—the countess—will take a fit over this. You got to think of your position. You ain't a wild young cavalry officer no more."

Temple was busy blotting his signature and didn't look up. "It's not my fault Robert fell off his horse and got his neck broken. I was happy being the feckless younger brother that everyone wanted to get rid of."

"Feckless persons don't get given the Victoria Cross by Her Majesty herself," Fidkin replied.

"Don't some of my morning coats need pressing?" Temple asked.

"Is this what you want after being near blown to bits in that cussed Crimea, to marry some doctor's chit? It ain't respectable."

"Fidkin, you're a snob."

Temple ran a hand through soft black hair in a futile attempt to make it stay off his forehead. As he began to fold the letter, glass shattered with a loud report in the hall outside his door. His body jerked, and his hands slipped, sending the letter sliding across the desk. Temple squeezed his eyes shut and tried to fight off the images of men and horses exploding into bloody pulp. He smelled burning flesh, swallowed the dull, bitter taste of blood. Then a voice with the texture of a saw cutting wood broke through the vision.

"M'lord major."

Temple blinked and focused on the sergeant's crimson nose. He glanced down to find that Fidkin had grabbed his wrist. Temple looked at his hand and was surprised to see he was gripping the blade of a medieval dagger he used as a letter opener.

"One of the footmen dropped a tray of lamps. Open your hand, m'lord, slowly."

Fidkin removed the dagger. Two thin lines of blood crossed Temple's palm and fingers. The sergeant pulled a handkerchief out of his pocket and wrapped it around the hand.

"Not too bad this time, m'lord major. You're getting better."

"So you say."

"Was a time you didn't need no noise to push you into one of them visions."

"True," Temple said. "But if I marry one of these society princesses I'll never get any peace. My life will be plagued with balls and drawing rooms and . . ." Temple shuddered. "The Season. Have you had a Season, Fidkin?"

"No, m'lord major."

"You're blessed by Providence. It's a torture worse than any the Russians devised in the Crimea. And if I marry one of the girls my mother has in mind, both families will want me to enter politics. Politics, Fidkin. It's not to be borne. I have to marry or my dear brother Hal will inherit and drink away the family fortune. But I'm going to marry a girl who is quiet and biddable and undemanding." Temple gave his valet a severe look. "And I'll not hear another word on the subject. It's an unconscionable liberty for you to speak of it to me. I don't know why I allowed you to talk me into keeping you as my man."

"You need me, m'lord major. You and me been together

since you was a young pup of a cornet." Fidkin put a hand over his heart, gazed up at the ceiling. Tears brimmed in his eyes. "I never will forget the night you came to that tavern and dragged me back to the barracks before I could be missed. And there was that time when I got the dysentery outside of Sebastopol. I woulda died then if you hadn't took care of me." Fidkin's bloodshot eyes slid sideways to glance inquiringly at Temple.

Temple inserted his letter into an envelope and sealed it. "And for these ill deeds I'm to be cursed with you forever?"

"Yes, m'lord major."

"Then make yourself useful and post this." Temple handed Fidkin the letter. "And on your way, stop at Bywell Park and ask Lady Alberta if I may see her this evening."

"You ain't going to see that widow again. It ain't proper, you being almost ten years younger than her, and her a respectable lady."

"I've never been respectable, Fidkin."

"That's what I mean."

Temple rose and walked around the desk. "I'm going for a ride."

"What am I to say to the countess when she wants to know why you didn't come in to see her lady guests?"

"Tell her I forgot."

"I can't tell her that."

"I don't care what you tell her. She's never approved of me anyway, so one more little sin won't matter."

"You're going to see that woman!"

Temple stopped at the door and half turned, his gaze that of a Roman emperor ready to condemn a gladiator. "To whom do you refer, Fidkin?"

"Er, no one, m'lord major."

"I thought not," Temple said. "Post the letter."

"Don't see it will do much good if you're just going to prowl around the neighborhood hen houses like a loose cock."

Temple sighed as he opened the door. "Do you know, Fidkin, that ever since I inherited, you've become as strict and censorious as the governess of a king's daughter?"

"Somebody has to get you to behave like an earl and

marry a lady of suitable rank. You won't listen to your mother."

Temple slammed the door shut and rounded on his valet. "Rank be damned! My parents were of suitable rank, and they fought like ravenous crocodiles until the day Father died. Savaged each other with their tongues, screaming at each other, trying their damnedest to cause the greatest pain. I'm not having that. If I've got to marry, I'll have a girl who won't argue, who won't create a great noise with her Society friends, one who'll leave me be to go my own way. And I'll allow her to do as she pleases, to a point."

Fidkin was silent for a moment. Then he came across the room to stand before his master, fists planted on his ample waist.

"I see you got it all planned. Very thoughtful, that is. And marvelous. Marvelous that a man who's known as many women as you could conceive of such a folly. These ladies what that countess has proposed, they come from blood like yours. They know what to expect. Some doctor's daughter ain't going to know what's proper, and believe me, she sure as eggs won't like it when you go back to your ways. She won't understand if you take a fancy to a duke's wife, and she ain't going to like it when some precious lady decides she wants you in her bed for the Season while her husband sports with his mistress."

Temple felt a flush rise from his neck to his forehead. It was most embarrassing to be confronted with his private habits by a servant, even if that servant was Fidkin.

"How do you know so much about—Society?"

"Talk, m'lord major. The ranks talk about their officers, you know, and it's the same belowstairs."

"Well, don't do it," Temple snapped. He walked back to his desk, sat, and propped his booted feet on it. "Post the letter at once, Fidkin."

Once the sergeant was gone, Temple sat lost in thought for a few minutes. Then he drew a key from his vest pocket and opened a drawer set in a recess of his desk. Rummaging beneath a stack of papers, he pulled out a black velvet envelope tied with a ribbon. Inside lay a hinged triple frame bearing daguerreotypes of three girls, each with a name etched at the bottom of the frame.

Last year he'd been on an outlying picket, riding ahead with the scouts searching for any Russian approach. It had been so foggy he couldn't see past his horse's ears. That was when he'd heard the artillery. He couldn't remember much else, except waking up in an overcrowded makeshift hospital. Dr. Peabody was bending over him, his spectacles nearly falling off his nose, his hands bloody. He'd glanced at Temple and called for an orderly.

After that, Temple could recall nothing until he woke, fevered and in such pain that he cried out. But the doctors had run out of medicine. There was no relief. Only hours of fever, shakes, and agony. Until Dr. Peabody had come to see him, bringing with him the pictures of his daughters. He distracted Temple and the men near him with tales of his girls. Then another wave of wounded came, and the doctor was gone, leaving the picture frame behind. Nine days of delirium and pain followed, but the worst was hearing the men around him scream and cry. He'd survived by fixing all his attention on the pictures and recalling the doctor's descriptions of his daughters. There was the youngest, who loved horses and nearly broke her neck in a fall from one. There was the one with the biting wit who was determined to save every stray and homeless animal in the kingdom.

And then there was the ethereal one whose presence brought peace and spread tranquillity and gentleness among all lucky enough to be her companions. When the pain grew unbearable, Temple would clench her picture in his hand and stare into her eyes, imagine her serene presence, as soothing as cool blue silk. He would sink into a floating state, wrapped in images of her sitting at a pianoforte playing wondrous music just for him. Once he was deep in the image, it became a dream, and if he was lucky, he slept.

Temple set the picture frame on the desk in front of him and surveyed the three girls. Two had dark hair. Of these, one was barely out of childhood and bore the name Marie-Claire. The other, Madeleine, was older but small, so small that her bell-shaped skirt made her look squat. Temple passed over the slight smile and nondescript face to the third picture, the one labeled Mélisande. This was a slender version of a Baroque angel. He remembered Dr. Peabody's description of her sunrise-golden hair, her cream-and-pink skin, which the doctor compared to that seen only in a portrait by Gainsborough or Reynolds.

He'd come home, still weak, still suffering more from memories of battle than his own wounds. His family had never liked his headstrong nature and no doubt had considered themselves well rid of him when he joined the cavalry. With his father dead, his mother's pride and hopes had fixed on his older brother, Robert. She had little time to nurse a wild younger son who'd lived a scandalous life among the fast set of London's aristocracy. Then Robert had got himself killed, blast him.

So here he was, trapped into having to marry, knowing what hell marriage could be, unwilling to expose himself to the rigors of a Society alliance. That's why he'd thought of Mélisande. She was the solution to all his problems. With Mélisande, known to her family as May, he would avoid the loveless misery he'd witnessed between his own parents. He would spend his life with a peaceful angel, away from war and blood and pain. And Fidkin was wrong. He wouldn't continue to interest himself in Lady Alberta with May for a wife. At least, not as much. There was the possibility that too much tranquillity would grow boring. If that happened, well, he would see. If there was one thing a man learned quickly, it was how to be discreet. No doubt his angelic Mélisande would understand.

SHELLEY AND Wordsworth would have loved the village of Exbridge. Just west of the sprawling London suburbs, it contained a lively market, a street of brightly painted shops, and was surrounded by forested hills, and streams that splashed their way into shadowed valleys. Exbridge also contained a doctor, for when one got sick from food purchased at the market or broke a leg climbing one of the hills.

The widowed doctor lived in a modest house called Ivy Park outside the village with his three daughters, a cook, a coachman, and a lady's maid for the girls. He'd been to the Crimea and survived. A remarkable feat, even for a doctor. And now he was busy marrying off the last of his daughters, or so the village gossips said. Of course, they didn't count the eldest, Miss May, whom the doctor and the village gossips had long ago given up for a hopeless spinster.

The doctor had lost hope when, at the age of eighteen, May failed to attract the attention of an eligible man from among his large number of acquaintances in medical circles or in those of the numerous relatives of her late mother. The Exbridge gossips could have foretold this failure if they'd been asked, the reason for it being illustrated at this very moment.

On this late afternoon, the time of day when the light turns gold and shadows lengthen, a small woman in an old-fashioned housedress handed a few shillings to a peddler on Exbridge's High Street and ignored his attempts to sell her anything else but the small bottle she now held up to the golden sunlight. She had been attracted by the unusual range of colors that seemed to appear and disappear in the depths of the glass. Lit by the deep, soft glow of the setting sun, she caught sight of dark forest colors that shifted into the teal, then lapis lazuli and midnight blues of the sky. These were colors that had always attracted her.

May touched the silver top of the stopper and the bands of it that flowed down the sides of the vessel. She was so distracted by her purchase that she failed to acknowledge the greetings of several acquaintances. Her fingers plucked the stopper from the bottle. She was about to replace it when she saw something lodged in the neck. Using a hairpin, she pried out a rolled scrap of leather, discolored with age. When she unrolled it, she read words in an old style of writing, the age of which she couldn't place.

To thine own wish be true. Do not follow the moth to the star.

"How odd," May whispered. She contemplated the

inscription, but soon decided that some child had placed it there as a game.

May raised her brows. "Moths to stars? What advice is this? Perhaps caution against foolish ventures. Father certainly doesn't want me to go with him to India. What a coincidence." She contemplated her father's approaching journey for a moment, then looked down at the bottle.

"Thine own wish," she said with a faint smile as she replaced the leather roll and stoppered the bottle.

Her wish, what would it be? If she wished for anything, it would be to have enough of a fortune to care for all her charges, keep them safe, fed, in good health. It would take a large fortune, for the need was great, so great that it kept her awake at night contemplating what horrors might be taking place that she could not prevent.

Sighing, May put the bottle in a pocket of her gown. "No use wishing for what Providence hasn't seen fit to provide."

As she settled her skirts and pulled her mantelet straight, a village lad ran up to her and babbled excitedly. May picked up her skirts and burst into a sprint behind the lad, who hopped and capered ahead of her while gesturing wildly and urging her to hurry.

Here, then, are the proofs of why Miss May is not married, which the village gossips beg to present—a habit of unseemly haste, a regrettable lack of attention to personal appearance, and no sense of the impropriety of a young woman rushing about the streets unescorted.

To which proofs May Peabody would reply, "Rubbish and cant!"

That is what she would have said now, if she bothered to stop. But she was in haste, and only paused at the blacksmith's shop to summon Small Tom, the proprietor's massive son. Small Tom emerged from the smithy, wiped his hands on a rag, and set off in May's wake.

May was already near the end of High Street. There she suddenly plunged into the ancient inn after the lad. She had heard the yelping from the other end of High Street, and it was loudest in the old inn yard. Racing across the parlor past the boy, who was one of her scouts, she hurried through the kitchen and out to the yard. There May saw the inn's owner, Mr. Blunt, flaying a coach dog with a whip. May flew across the yard as Blunt raised the whip over his shoulder. She snatched the end of the weapon and yanked hard. The whip jerked out of Blunt's hand as he sought to ply it, sending him off-balance. Blunt wasn't a tall man, but he was wide and built like a beer barrel, so he recovered quickly and turned on May.

"You! I told you to keep yourself out of my inn, Miss. I'll have the law on you, I will."

Blunt tried to snatch the whip back, but May ducked and placed in on the ground. Then she stepped on it, bent the handle, and broke it. Blunt's howl was almost as loud as the poor coach dog's. May ignored him and knelt beside the dog as Small Tom arrived. Blunt was reaching for May when Small Tom wrapped one of his hands around the innkeeper's neck and lifted him off his feet. Blunt hung in the air, strangling and kicking his legs.

May paid him no attention. The coach dog's white fur was dappled with black spots and stripes of red blood. It was a young male, and would have been strong had he been fed. May could see his ribs. She felt his body gently while he lay still and whimpered a bit. Behind her Blunt was making noises like a sick pig.

May took off her mantelet, laid it on the ground, and lifted the coach dog onto it. Wrapping the garment around the creature, she picked it up. The animal was so weak it hadn't the strength to be frightened or to struggle. The dog should have been too heavy for her, but Blunt's treatment had made lifting him easy. Cradling the dog in her arms, May turned to face the innkeeper. His face vermilion, Blunt could only make choking sounds while Small Tom looked on impassively.

May surveyed Blunt, her manner seemingly calm, her voice revealing the turmoil within by its tremor. "Not two days ago I warned you about your cruelty, Mr. Blunt, and you haven't mended your ways. Put him down so that he may speak, Small Tom."

Blunt's feet were allowed to touch the ground. The man

gasped, coughed, and then swore at May. Small Tom's hand closed around his neck, and he flew into the air again to dangle for a few moments before being dropped. Blunt landed on his knees this time, but he stopped swearing.

May said, "You are a poor creature, Mr. Blunt. To beat and starve an animal is abominable. You will not do it. Do you understand?"

"I'll have the law on you!" Blunt croaked.

"No, you will not, Mr. Blunt."

"I will, you bleeding—eck!"

Small Tom cuffed Blunt on the side of his head with a massive fist, and the innkeeper subsided.

"I can see that you're a man whom no one's words will control, Mr. Blunt, and I'm sorry for it."

May nodded at Small Tom, who suddenly acquired an interest in the sky. Walking away from the two, he clasped his hands behind his back and whistled as he contemplated the clouds. When he was a few yards away, May bent down to hiss at Blunt.

"Infamous creature, upon my soul, if you ever seek to own another dog again, I'll see to it that you pay."

"You can't touch me."

"I won't have to," May said in a vicious whisper. "I'm a doctor's daughter, Blunt. I know how to get medicines that will make you puke until your stomach dissolves and slides up your throat." Clutching the dog tightly, May drew close to Blunt's purple ear. "You hurt one more animal, and you'll end up floating in your own bile."

"I'll have the law—"

"Oh, do shut up, Blunt," May snapped. She turned on the smile of a sweet innocent, which made the innkeeper blink. She addressed an imaginary person in a treacly sweet voice. "Upon my soul, Constable, I have no notion what Mr. Blunt can be speaking of." May's smile vanished. "Who will the constable believe, Mr. Blunt?"

"Drat you!"

"Remember, Mr. Blunt, floating in your own bile." May turned on her heel. "Come, Small Tom. It's time for tea."

May handed the dog to Small Tom, who cradled the animal even more gently than she had. Lifting her skirts, she

picked her way back through the inn as if crossing a swine
pen and marched back down High Street. The lad who
had fetched her, Ian, preceded her like a herald, and their
group attracted the attention of the Exbridge gossips.

Old Mother Sneed just happened to decide to sweep the
stoop in front of her daughter's bonnet shop as May went
by. The Honorable Mrs. Horace Pettyjohn and her friend
Miss Prudence Tadgett whispered together in the window
of the sweet shop. The old shepherd Thadeus Twig dug an
elbow into the side of one of his cronies as May swept past
the ancient oak where the old fellows gathered to drink
ale. Newly married Mistress Jane Pattle and her sister Florence whispered behind their gloved hands on the thresh-
old of the draper's shop. May nodded to them politely and
strode past without stopping. She hadn't taken notice of
the whispering since she was a schoolgirl.

Back at home, May led Small Tom to the old stone barn
behind the house. Inside, she had him lay the coach dog on
a long table that had been scrubbed and set up there when
she'd taken over the building years ago. Barks and yelps
came from her various patients and the regular inhabitants
of the barn. There were at least seven dogs of various sizes
and lineages, as many cats, a pony that was nearly blind, a
few ferrets, a family of displaced hedgehogs, and an old
milk cow that was more bone than flesh.

Using medicines and instruments filched from her father's supplies, May set about mending the dog's injuries.
By the time she was finished, teatime had long passed. She
left the dog sleeping in a bed of blankets. Returning to the
house, she was met by her youngest sister, Marie-Claire, at
the door.

"Cook said you've brought another one home," Marie-
Claire said as May headed for the stairs to the bedrooms
on the second floor.

May blew a stray curl of red-brown hair off her forehead.
"Yes, the coach dog from Blunt's." Gathering her skirts, she
mounted the stairs. "I'll wash and dress for dinner."

"Shall I see if the poor thing will eat?"

May paused and smiled at her sister. Marie-Claire
wanted to feed every creature she met, animal or not. "He

should be feeling better by now. You might try broth. If he takes that well, we can try a bit of meat in the morning."

They heard the double doors to their father's library slide open. Dr. Peabody appeared in dinner dress, his tie askew as always, a pipe in one hand and a letter in the other. A man who prided himself on his storytelling and ability to calm his patients with an amusing manner, Dr. Peabody's features were set and unsmiling. May and Marie-Claire glanced at each other while their father glared at the letter in his hand.

"May, a word if you please."

"It's not Madeleine, is it, Father?" Marie-Claire asked. "She's still coming to fetch me?"

Dr. Peabody waved a hand at her. "No, no. Your sister and her husband will escort you to the wilds of America to marry your precious Timothy as we planned, my dear. May, please. A private word."

May came down and entered the library. She took a seat at her father's request while he shut the doors. Dr. Peabody sat opposite her in his heavy leather armchair. He leaned toward her, propped his arms on his knees, and puffed on his pipe in silence for a while. Then he looked straight into her eyes.

"Daughter, it has been my one care in the world since returning from the Crimea to settle you and your sisters."

"I know that, Father."

"And I'm sure I don't know how I'm going to settle you."

"You mustn't mind it, Father. When you leave for India, I'll do very well here on my own."

"There'll be little money once I've provided for your sisters. Not enough to keep going as we have, if I'm in India."

"I'll make do, Father. I don't need a lady's maid and a cook. We'll get a maid of all work, and we won't keep a carriage."

"And who will protect you?"

"Father, we've discussed this. I could go to India."

"It's too hard a journey, too dangerous," said Dr. Peabody. "No, I won't have it." He knocked his pipe against a side table, then emptied ashes into a tray. "No, I shall see you settled, too."

May almost grinned. She was a spinster of twenty-five. Old. Past her prime husband-catching years, if she'd ever had any. The smile that hovered over her lips vanished at her father's next words.

"I've had a most unusual letter, Daughter, and one that comes from Providence, or so I say. A gentleman of my acquaintance has written to me asking permission to marry you, and I'm quite decided that you should."

CHAPTER TWO

*T*HE SHINING BLACK carriage with the Stirling arms emblazoned on its doors turned away from the train station and Long Riding. The coachman and footmen stared proudly ahead, their livery brilliant, as the vehicle proceeded at a sedate walk down the lane. Inside sat May Peabody, her great-aunt Violet, Isis the Siamese cat, Echo the Shetland sheepdog, and Puck, an English springer spaniel.

Isis lay in May's lap while Puck had curled up at her feet. Both were asleep, but Echo sat next to the window, directed her pointed nose at each new sight, and barked madly at it. Echo's favorite occupation was barking. She barked at May. She barked at the entire Peabody family. Echo would bark at strange noises and at noises she heard every day. Echo would bark at a passing carriage, a creaking door, at leaves tossed in the wind. She only stopped when May scolded her.

May's gloved hand stroked Isis's cream fur as she listened to Aunt Violet's chatter. Aunt Violet was a kind woman, but irritating in her silliness. She seemed to think May would be interested in the hallowed Stirling lineage and had been relating all she had gathered from her friends who lived near the earl's family.

"What have I done?" May curled her fingers into the

voluminous folds of her merino traveling dress. "What have I done? I never should have listened to Father."

Aunt Violet shook her head, causing the little corkscrew curls gathered at her temples to bob. "Now, my dear, don't upset yourself again. Your father assured you that the earl is of the finest character."

"But there was no reason for all this haste."

"Nonsense. Your father could hardly leave you alone in that house to embark upon this journey after he'd set sail. As it is, he'll be gone in a few days. And just think of it, my dear. You'll be marrying into a noble family. Not merely a baronet, but a true peer with a title that goes back to the Normans."

"I'm sure I don't care about titles, Aunt."

"Of course not, my dear. But they are nice. Why, I remember when my friend Amelie de Frobisher-Frobisher married Sir Oswell Cheesewright . . ."

May let her aunt chatter while she settled back against the leather squabs and stared out the window at the gentle slopes of hills covered with grass. The carriage passed over a stone bridge and plunged beneath a canopy of beeches. The trip from Exbridge had taken only a couple of hours, and dew was still reflecting off the leaves.

It was September. The air was crisp with the first chill that warned of approaching winter. It was her favorite time of year, but May was too fearful to enjoy it. She regretted allowing her father to accept Temple Stirling's proposal three weeks ago. She was even sorrier she'd been foolish enough to get on the train to Long Riding, and now she was trapped in this carriage with her dear, silly aunt, on her way to meet a man she didn't know and to whom she was now engaged.

Why did this strange fortune have to come upon her? She'd been quite content with her lot, having grown accustomed to thinking of herself as a spinster. Her unmarried state had become a familiar friend, well-known, comfortable, like old boots of good quality. And she'd accepted herself as she was.

From a child her character had been too forceful, her opinions too strong, her ability to hide them negligible.

By the time she had come out, the good families in the neighborhood had already formed their opinion of her—Mélisande Peabody was a fright. May was certain they held it against her that she rescued tortured frogs, otters, and hedgehogs from their sons. Just because she'd often been forced to give the boys split lips and boxed ears.

When she'd stood by the wall at dances while her friends and sisters were partnered, she had been humiliated. But she'd also been unwilling to amend her conduct. Every time she had thought of trying to, she would remember the suffering animals who would get no help without her.

By the time she was twenty, she and everyone else had accepted the fact that she was a spinster. At first May had been ashamed, knowing that her lack of softness, manners, and meekness had been the cause. But then, gradually, she had realized that, without a husband, there would be no one to tell her what to do. This was an excellent thing.

So the years had passed. Her sister Madeleine had married, and May's opinions hadn't changed. Madeleine was governed by her husband. Luckily, he was a good man. However, May knew that had she married him, he would never have stood for her constant animal rescues, the dozens of creatures in residence at the barn, her battles with those whose cruelty she was determined to eliminate. No, a husband wanted a wife who would devote herself to him, who would vanish into his life, his interests, his convenience.

But a spinster didn't vanish. True, she had to endure people's pity and barely concealed contempt for her failure, but the reward was that, as an unmarried woman, she had the same rights as a man. May could do as she wished. Of course, without a fortune, she couldn't really do what she wanted—take in many more lost and starving animals and provide a permanent shelter for them. To do that, she would need to build a special building. Although she would have a small sum upon which to live, she would never be able to afford her dream.

Dreams. Dreams were like wishes. May straightened and shoved aside yards of merino until she located a bulge in the pocket of her mantle. She stuck her hand inside and drew out the green glass bottle. It fit in the palm of her hand.

Holding it up to the light from the carriage window, she watched the iridescent glow of green and blue. Shades of the dark woodland, new meadow grass, and of lichen swirled with the color of the sky before sunset and mysterious hues of amethyst, madder violet, and hyacinth. When she looked into the glass of the bottle, she was reminded of her dreams and wishes.

"What a pretty thing, May."

"What? Oh, yes, Aunt. I bought it from a peddler the day the earl's letter arrived."

"Is it a scent bottle?" Aunt Violet was frequently taken faint and had a large collection of scent bottles.

"No. There is something in it, but not scent." May pulled out the stopper and removed the tightly rolled piece of leather.

Aunt Violet took it and unfurled it. "It's only senseless scratches."

"Look on the other side."

" 'To thine own wish be true. Do not follow the moth to the star.' How pretty, but what does it mean?"

"I don't know," May said. "Possibly some children were playing a game and put the message in the bottle."

"The leather looks terribly old, my dear. Where did the peddler get it?"

"I don't know. I'd just discovered the message when Small Tom's cousin came to me about the innkeeper's dog, and by the time I thought to inquire, the peddler had left Exbridge. I'm afraid I've been upset about . . . Well, I have been thinking about the letter from the earl."

"I understand, my dear."

May barely heard Aunt Violet. She was beginning to feel guilty. She'd been determined to refuse the earl, had been steadfast in her protests to her father. Then, one evening she had retired to her room and was walking past the table where the bottle rested beside her sewing box. Some trick of light from the candle next to it caused the colors to shimmer and shift, catching her attention.

On a whim, she opened the bottle, read the message,

and remembered her own wish, her dream. Temple Stirling had promised that he would study to make her comfortable and happy. To this end he would settle a sum upon her for her own use. The sum named in the letter had been enormous, more than enough to build a refuge for her animal orphans and keep it running forever.

The message had given her the idea, but she'd immediately rejected it. How could she marry a man to get her hands on his money, even if it was to save her animals? How could she, when the earl had proposed based on much finer feelings? He had remembered Father's stories about her, had admired her, and wanted her to be his wife because of what he knew. A dream, that's what she would have called such an occurrence if she'd heard about it. That a man would conceive an admiration for a young lady solely by what he'd heard—but that wasn't entirely true. Temple Stirling, earl of Darent, had her picture. And he still wanted her.

Perhaps this was why she'd accepted. He'd already seen her picture. He'd seen the short little body, the plain brown hair and brown eyes, all working to create the impression of a field mouse in a dress. And then there was that other reason, the one she hadn't allowed herself to contemplate. She would have a home of her own, a family, children. There were many excellent reasons for remaining a spinster, but if she did, there would be no children. And every time she thought about that, she felt a dull, throbbing ache in her chest. Which was why she tried not to think about it.

"You look pained, my dear. You really shouldn't worry about marriage. It all takes care of itself." Aunt Violet had been married for over thirty years when her husband died, and thought that every woman worshiped her husband as she had hers.

"Yes, Aunt."

"And think of it. You'll be a countess."

"Yes, Aunt."

"I think a title does so much for a young woman's character."

May blinked, trying to sort out the logic of this statement.

"You'll go to London for the Season," Violet said, her hands clasped in rapture. Then she leaned toward May and touched her hand while giving a confidential wink. "And best of all, you'll be presented."

"What?"

"Presented. To Her Majesty the queen!"

"Oh, Aunt, do you think that is a reason to accept a gentleman? I—I accepted because Father was so worried about me, and because, because the earl seems a man of good character."

"I'm sure you did, dear."

"I did!"

"I'm not disagreeing."

"Oh."

The carriage suddenly turned off the road, and they passed through a gate formed by huge brick pillars surmounted by a great coat of arms in gilded iron.

"We're nearly there," Aunt Violet cried as she peered out the window. Suddenly she fell back, fanning her face with a handkerchief. "Oh, dear. Oh, dear."

"Are you ill, Aunt?"

"Oh, dear." Violet gestured out the window.

May stuck her head outside and looked down nearly a mile of avenue bordered by ancient oaks and a succession of rectangular pools, the last of which bore a fountain in the form of wildly galloping horses ridden by sea gods. Beyond this lay a broad expanse of emerald lawn from which rose the shining white expanse of Stirling Hall. With an elongated facade surmounted by a balustrade, and statues of Greek deities on a parapet below, the house rose like a temple before her. May swallowed hard, noting the massive central portico with its Corinthian columns. Her gaze traveled along rows of tall, glittering windows.

"Oh, dear," she said.

She drew back inside. Isis had been disturbed by her movements. The cat rose, jumped to the seat beside Aunt Violet, and began to stretch. Puck raised his head and shook it, sending his ears flapping. Echo stood on the seat beside May and swished her tail while watching May and trying to decide whether to risk barking. May paid the animals no heed.

"Oh, dear." She began patting her hair, resetting the pins in her hat, pulling at her veil. "I shouldn't have come. I shouldn't have come. I'm such a noodle."

Aunt Violet had taken a few sniffs from her scent bottle and composed herself. "Nonsense, Mélisande Peabody. You're of good family and a proper choice for his lordship. Your mother was a Seymour, you know. And your grandfather's stepfather was an admiral and a Percy."

"What does that matter, Aunt? I don't know the earl, and look at that house. It's not a house; it's a confounded palace!"

In her agitation, May grabbed Isis and began stroking her. The sudden attention irritated Isis, who began struggling as the carriage neared the house. The vehicle turned down a semicircular gravel drive that would take them to the portico. May glimpsed a long line of servants, footmen in livery, others in formal black.

Then she saw a tall figure at the foot of the entryway stairs. In a brief moment, she glimpsed the face of a man. She perceived angles covered by smooth flesh, glittering eyes like those one expected to see over a bandit's mask, and hair as black as hell ought to be. Her mouth went dry. Was that Temple Stirling?

The carriage bounced. She heard the wheels grind into the gravel of the drive. Time seemed to slow while colors grew more vivid, and the sun grew brighter, sharpening contrasts between light and shadow. Isis continued to struggle in her hands while May stared. This couldn't be the earl. Now she realized she'd assumed the earl of Darent would be much older, more like a stately uncle. Earls were stuffy, pompous, with rounded stomachs and fuzzy whiskers.

This man had no whiskers to mar the clean lines of his cheeks. He looked severe, but not pompous. May glimpsed an exquisitely styled dress day coat, pristine linen, a gold watch chain. That was when the carriage came to an abrupt stop, sending Echo sliding off her seat. Isis lost what little tolerance she had left, spit and yowled before clawing free of May. She leaped to the seat, then balanced on the window while Echo erupted into ear-piercing barks. Then the cat sprang out of the carriage as a footman opened the door.

"Isis!" May lunged for the Siamese and missed.

To her horror, Isis landed in the arms of the black-haired man standing before the carriage. He gasped, fighting off a whirlwind of claws just as Echo hurtled onto him from the carriage. May tried to follow, but Puck scrambled between her feet, jumped, and landed on Echo. The added weight sent the young man toppling backward to land on the bottom stairs with Isis clinging to his chest.

There was a moment of frozen shock. Then everyone moved at once. May lifted her skirts and hopped out of the carriage as the footman rushed to the gentleman. A butler hurried over and tried to shoo Isis away. Isis hissed and slashed at him. The butler cried out and clutched his hand. More servants crowded around while Puck put his paws on a wide shoulder and fell to sniffing every inch of the man's face and neck. Echo stationed herself on the other side of the man's head and uttered an endless series of shrieking barks, wagging her tail the whole time.

The footman shouted. The butler shouted. Maids screamed. One or two covered smiles. May shoved her way through the crowd surrounding the prone figure. Grabbing Puck's collar, she pulled him off the young man.

"Puck, sit!" The springer immediately lowered his bottom to the ground and sat wiggling his tail.

"Echo, no bark." Echo yapped on happily.

May darted over the young man, and gave Echo's long nose a tap with her index finger. "Echo, no bark."

Echo seemed to wake from her frenzied state. Panting heavily, she stood over her victim and waved her tail back and forth in victory. With the dogs out of the way, May turned her attention to the man lying at her feet.

It was then that she noticed the glare. It was a glare that had weakened the knees of battle-hardened cavalry officers. It was the kind of glare that reminded its victims of barbarians threatening the city of Rome, of Mordred's wrath against Arthur, of Satan cast out of heaven. Its owner raised himself on his elbows and spoke for the first time.

"Get this damned cat off me, my girl, or I'll wring its neck."

May gasped. "You leave her be!"

The young man's jaw tightened, and he said through stiff lips, "Then get the bloody thing off me, damn you."

Always ready to take offense at anyone who threatened her pets, May glared back at the stranger, her fears forgotten. When he refused to be cowed by her scowl, she knelt beside him and whispered to Isis. "That's my kitty. Sweet kittykitty. My Isis, my sweetie." She stroked for several moments.

"Are you going to take the whole afternoon?" the young man snapped.

"Hush," May said.

He gave her a startled look, but kept his mouth shut. Slowly, May pulled Isis's claws from the young man's coat. The last was embedded in his shirt just above his vest. When she drew back the paw, the cat's claws came free, leaving behind a tiny pool of blood.

Biting her lip, May folded Isis in her arms and stood. "I'm sorry."

The butler helped the young man to his feet.

"Are you hurt?" May asked.

"Are you hurt, my lord?" the butler asked.

Temple Stirling jerked his coat into place, brushed dust from his sleeves, and replied, "I'm fine."

May felt blood rush to her face. "I'm sorry, my lord. My cat was startled."

The earl finished straightening his clothing and looked down at her. Dark brows drew together. "Who are you, and where is Mélisande?"

PART OF him was standing in front of this strange young woman. Part of him was still trapped in the vision the sudden attack and noise had provoked. While staring at his unexpected guest, Temple fought waves of memory.

Part of him was falling from his horse, hitting mud

mixed with the blood of his friends. A galloping horse splashed more of the reddish-brown sludge in his face. He thrust himself upright, knowing that he had only a few seconds to find a mount with artillery shells bursting and hundreds of men locked in death battles all around him. Temple wiped his face and experienced the nauseating taste of blood mixed with dirt.

A Russian careened toward him, his horse wild-eyed, his saber pointed at Temple's heart. Temple waited until the last moment to jump aside, turn, and fire at the man with his pistol. Then something hit him from behind, and he was thrown to the ground again. Struggling wildly, he shoved the weight from his back. As he came up, he pulled his revolver free and fired—just as he recognized the features of young Corporal Henry Beddowes, Harry. It took him precious seconds to realize that Harry's legs had been blown away and that he hadn't killed his own man.

No! It's over; leave it. Temple wrenched himself back to the present, praying no one had noticed. The young woman hadn't answered him. He was almost certain of it, so he repeated his question.

"Where is Mélisande?"

All at once he noticed that there was a great space around Temple and this young woman he did not know. The servants had retreated with blank expressions. From the carriage an older woman fluttered a handkerchief at a footman to summon his help.

"Well," he demanded again. "Where is Mélisande?"

May swallowed hard. "I am Mélisande Peabody."

Temple flexed his arm, which he'd hurt in his fall. He glanced up, wincing, and really looked at her for the first time. He hoped he wasn't as pale as he felt, for he was still possessed with the vision of Harry's black, staring eyes flecked with tiny bits of dirt.

"You're not May. You're the Pea, the little plain one, Madeleine."

"I am not."

Her cheeks grew red, then paled as blood ebbed from her face, but Temple had no feeling for her. She was the cause of this nightmare of screaming horses, men, and shells. She and her cursed animals and their noise and chaos. He couldn't abide her, for she'd made him weak again.

"I'm May," she said.

His jaw was clenched so tight it hurt. "You can't be."

"I am, I assure you."

"What is this?" he asked, barely controlling his desire to bellow his agony. "I never thought Dr. Peabody would try to get off with me just because I have a lot of tin. But perhaps I wrong him. Have you tried some trick, miss, by replacing your sister with yourself?"

"Ohhh!"

He remained silent. The older woman, who must have been the aunt Violet Dr. Peabody had written about, had left the carriage and joined them in time to hear this last statement. Her handkerchief fluttered wildly. Her plump frame tottered, and the impostor rushed to her side. Holding her aunt's arm, she found the old lady's scent bottle and waved it in front of her nose. The butler appeared with a newspaper and began to fan the lady. The young woman thrust her aunt into the arms of a waiting footman and rounded on the earl.

"Why you pompous, self-important, mannerless wretch!"

No one said anything. Temple was speechless for a moment before his back straightened. His shoulders went back, and he thrust one fist behind his back while his other hand remained white and clenched at his side.

"I do not have rows on the front steps of my house with impostors." He lifted his gaze from the young woman as if she were a vegetable vendor who had had the temerity to present himself at the front door instead of the tradesman's entrance. He signaled to the butler. "Breedlebane, show these . . . persons to the Blue Drawing Room."

A crimson flush had returned to his guest's cheeks. "I shall not enter your house—"

"Silence!"

The roar shocked even him and startled her into obedience. He glared at her, waiting for further transgressions. When none came, he continued.

"You will wait in the drawing room. I shall see you

there in good time. Until then, your animals will be tied
up. Breedlebane will see to it."

Without waiting for her consent, he turned his back on
the young woman and left. He had only to reach his study
before he lost all composure. It wouldn't do to allow himself to give way to his rage, even if she was responsible for
his disappointment and misery.

MAY STARED after the earl, wishing she had one of the
mud pies she and her sisters used to concoct. It would
make a most satisfying splat right in the earl's pretty face.
He was mad, and he'd called her little and plain. Did he
think her so stupid that she would be unaware of her
shortcomings? Oh! She hated the way her cheeks burned,
but she was so humiliated. He didn't want her; he'd never
wanted her. She'd been conceited to think he would. He
was mean, mean in the soul, or he wouldn't have been so
horrible about Isis and Echo and Puck.

She was scowling at the front door and stroking Isis
when a footman approached, his gloved hands outstretched to take the cat. May took a step back. Puck immediately broke his stay, jumped between her and the
footman, and growled. He was a spaniel, but he was a
sixty-pound gun dog with canine teeth the size of crocodile
fangs. The footman stopped in his tracks.

May smiled nastily at him and addressed the butler.
"Breedlebane?"

"Yes, miss."

"I'm leaving."

At that moment the coachman clucked to the carriage
horses and pulled away from the portico. May swore
silently as the carriage retreated and Aunt Violet set up a
chorus of oh dears.

"Breedlebane?"

"Yes, miss."

"Show me to the Blue Drawing Room."

"Yes, miss. And the footman will take the animals to
the stables."

THE UNWANTED BRIDE — 425

The footman reached for Puck's collar. Puck growled and curled his lips up to reveal his teeth.

"No he won't, Breedlebane. My animals will come with me."

"But, miss, his lordship said—"

"Is the earl the one who's going to get bit, Breedlebane?"

"No, miss."

"Then if I were you, I'd make this decision myself."

Breedlebane looked at Puck. He looked at Echo, who was small but quick, and at Isis, who hissed at him. Then he waved the footman away.

"If you will follow me, miss?"

They entered into a long hall with a floor of gray-and-white Italian marble. To the right and left, a double staircase ascended to the second floor, the white balustrades creating a frame for the whole room. Beyond the hall lay a great saloon, visible through open sliding doors. May glimpsed white plaster decorations, Ionic motifs, fretwork of arabesques and garlands. Walking between the two staircases, Breedlebane ushered them into a lofty drawing room that made up a good portion of the front facade of the house.

When she walked into the drawing room May immediately wished she hadn't brought her pets. Paneled in silver-blue damask, the entire room was filled with Louis XIV furniture. The decorations on the ceiling, walls, and around the doors were of ornately carved white plaster picked out in silver, and on the walls hung portraits by Raphael, Holbein, Van Dyck, and Reynolds.

"Confound it," she muttered to herself. "It is a palace."

Finding a place of the floor that didn't bear a priceless Aubusson carpet, she ordered Puck and Echo to a down stay. Aunt Violet subsided onto a sofa of slippery blue damask and indulged in a frenzy of handkerchief waving and bottle sniffing.

May sat down in an armchair that looked strong enough to hold her with Isis in her lap. The cat curled into a ball and fell asleep, oblivious to the disaster she'd precipitated. May hadn't bothered to remove her mantle, knowing she wouldn't be staying long. It was a good thing, because the room was chilly. Her hands and feet were cold. But her face was still hot.

Biting the inside of her cheek, she spoke to herself silently and firmly. *You will not cry. Don't let him see how hurt you are. It will only make him pity you, and you don't want to see contempt in those devil's eyes.*

Degradation permeated her like the heat of a sunburn. She closed her eyes and forced the pain deep inside herself, far behind the superficial mask she presented to the world. She stuffed the hurt down so deep that, with luck and perseverance, she might never have to feel it again. Might never have to acknowledge, even to herself, that she'd showed up on a man's doorstep expecting to be greeted as a precious intended bride and been rejected.

Gradually May felt the heat in her face recede once more. This time it stayed away. All she hoped for was the earl's speedy return. She would ask him to make arrangements for her to travel home on the next train. May's eyes popped open.

"Oh, no."

Aunt Violet stopped flapping her handkerchief. "What?"

"We rented out the house."

"Yes?"

"Aunt Violet, the house is rented." She heard the shrillness in her voice and tried to master it. "We've nowhere to go."

"Oh, dear, oh dear oh dear."

May stroked Isis rapidly while she thought. "We shall take a small cottage in Exbridge."

"There are no suitable houses in the village. Oh, dear."

"There's a cottage," May said. "Old Mrs. Sibthorp's cottage."

"Mélisande Peabody, that place hasn't been occupied in a dozen years. No, miss, we're not taking Mrs. Sibthorp's."

"Now see here, Aunt. I'm leaving for Exbridge, and we have to stay somewhere."

Their argument was interrupted when the door opened to admit the earl of Darent. Taking long strides, he approached May without a greeting, thrust a picture frame at her, and pointed to the portrait bearing the name Mélisande.

"There," he said coldly. "That is Mélisande." He glanced down at May's picture. "You, miss, are Madeleine, the Pea."

May rose and set Isis on the floor. She snatched the picture frame, turned it over, and slid aside the backing to remove the two portraits. Presenting the backs of the daguerreotypes to the earl, she pointed to the names inscribed in ink. Then she turned the pictures over.

"As you can see, my lord, someone has exchanged the pictures so that Madeleine's portrait was placed in the frame with my name on it."

Her announcement was met with silence. She thrust the pictures and the frame into the earl's hands. Picking up Isis, she headed for the door.

"Kindly send for your carriage. I have no wish to remain in your house or near you, sir. Naturally I release you from your promise of marriage, since it was given by mistake. Good day to you."

CHAPTER THREE

*T*EMPLE STOOD IN the middle of the Blue Drawing
Room with the two daguerreotypes in his hands, his cold,
white hands that only now had stopped that cursed trembling. He looked at the frame. When inserted, stiff backing
held the portraits against the frame and covered their reverse sides. The exchange must have happened in the
Crimea when he was fevered. No doubt Fidkin or a nurse
had cleaned the frame and accidentally switched the
photographs. And he had blamed Miss Peabody.

But he wouldn't have been so rude if her animals hadn't
attacked him. The barking, that loud, sudden barrage of
noise—damn that cursed fuzzy, insane mongrel. The pain
had thrust him into a fury, which he'd loosed on poor
Miss Peabody.

Hell! Miss Peabody. She was gone. Temple laid the pictures and frame on a table and hurried into the hall. Miss
Peabody and her aunt were standing beside a bust of the
god Mercury.

"Miss Peabody, please wait."

She lifted the veil from her hat as she turned to face him,
and he almost missed his stride. She had eyes the color of
bourbon and a way of looking at him that was like hearing
the enemy order to charge. She might be the size of a pea,

but she entered a room the way an admiral came on deck. God help the man who married her; he'd never live a peaceful, quiet life.

"Miss Peabody, there isn't another train to London today, and in any case, I'm responsible for you until I can contact your father. You'll remain as my guest until then."

The glance she gave him had less warmth than the marble statue next to her. "My father is leaving for India, as you well know. He's quit the house for London now that my sister Marie-Claire has left to be married."

"And Madeleine?"

"Is married."

"I see." His last hope vanished, but he continued. "I must apologize for my mistake, and for my rudeness."

"I, my lord, have already apologized for my pets."

Temple noticed the animals at her feet for the first time. "But they are in my house."

"They are my pets, not farm animals. They have been trained with house manners."

Aunt Violet interrupted the chilly silence that followed. "Oh, dear, oh dear. We're most grateful for your hospitality, my lord. You see, the house is rented and Dr. Peabody sails day after tomorrow. I really don't know what we're to do."

"We're renting a cottage, Aunt."

Temple noted the implacable tone in May's voice and the way her animals sat at her feet and stared up at her. Their little heads shifted from Violet to May and back as if watching a contest. He almost smiled, then remembered he'd lost his Mélisande and gotten a fury in her place. He was so weary of fighting, any fighting. Suddenly exhausted, Temple stiffened his spine.

"Naturally you will stay here," he said.

Offering his arm to Aunt Violet, he escorted the old lady back to the Blue Drawing Room without looking to see if Miss Peabody was following. He nearly smiled again when he heard the patter of paws behind him.

Miss Peabody stalked into the room and plumped herself down in a chair. "Well?"

He was accustomed to the respect of junior officers and

the men under his command. He was growing accustomed to the respect according him as earl. He would never become accustomed to a girl the size of a pea barking demands at him.

"I shall write your father."

"You'd better hurry."

"I'll do it at once, and you, miss, will take your animals to the stables."

"If they stay in the stables, I will."

"I won't stand this, Miss Peabody. You are the most absurd creature, and I'll not row with you. Ladies stay in the house. Animals stay in the stable."

May Peabody rose and marched over to him. He heard her aunt whispering frantic oh dears as May stopped in front of him, her fists planted on her hips.

"Now you see here. I'm not some silly little girl to be ordered about the schoolroom. I'm twenty-five years old, and if I want to stay in your stables with my animals, I will. I've stayed in the barn at home many a time, and it won't hurt—oh, the animals."

"I beg your pardon?"

Miss Peabody seemed to be staring through him.

"What? Oh, nothing. I just remembered something. Tell me, how big are your stables?"

"My stables? I don't know. They were built by one of my ancestors who had a taste for Thoroughbreds. We don't use most of the stalls anymore. I suppose there are twenty or so."

"Hmmm."

"Miss Peabody, about your animals. Of course there's enough room for them."

"And me."

"Damn it!"

"Oh, my lord." Aunt Violet pressed her hands to her cheeks.

"I beg your pardon, madam." Temple pulled himself up to his full height and glared down at Miss Peabody. "There will be no ladies sleeping in my stables."

He caught his breath as May Peabody suddenly turned on a mischievous grin that reminded him of sweets stolen from glass candy jars and swings that carried one to the treetops. It was the first time in his life that he'd been transfixed by a smile.

"Thank you, my lord."

His brows drew together as he tried to understand what she was thanking him for. Then Breedlebane knocked and entered to say that the ladies' things were now in their rooms.

"Excellent," Miss Peabody said. "Aunt and I would like to rest, if you will show us the way, Breedlebane."

The butler gave Temple a look of inquiry. Still confused by the effects of Miss Peabody's smile, he nodded his consent. It wouldn't have mattered, however, because May was already tripping rapidly out of the drawing room with her animals right behind. She swept into the hall, leaving him to escort Aunt Violet. By the time he got the old lady out of the room, Miss Peabody was halfway upstairs. It was then that he realized that the dogs and the cat were with her.

"I say!"

"Yes, my lord," said Aunt Violet.

He heard the strained note in the old lady's voice and bit back his own irritation. Summoning a footman, he sent her upstairs to rest. He was scowling up at the landing when he noticed a fuzzy, curling plume traveling along the balustrade. The dog Echo appeared on the landing and stood facing him. He could have sworn the cursed mongrel smirked at him. Then it uttered one loud, screeching bark that resounded off the walls and marble floors. Temple started, his heart jumping to a gallop.

"Hell!"

Echo wagged her tail happily and trotted back the way she'd come with her tail held high like a banner. Temple swore again and ran up the stairs, but instead of turning to the right and following Echo, he turned left and stalked through the White-and-Gold Room, the Tapestry Room, the Small Dining Room, the Music Room. He crossed two long galleries stuffed with paintings and antiquities. God, he hated grandeur. It was like living in St. Paul's Cathedral.

At last he reached his own apartments, which had formerly been called the King's Apartments because Charles II had been a guest in them. "Fidkin, Fidkin, where are you, damn you?" He walked swiftly through his sitting room to the bedchamber.

"Here, m'lord major."

"Where the hell is the dowager countess? Miss Peabody and her aunt have arrived." Temple removed his coat and began taking off his shirt.

"She be in her room. Still refuses to meet Miss Peabody."

"Hell." Temple flung his shirt on a chair.

"Yes, m'lord."

"I suppose you've heard."

"Yes, m'lord major." Fidkin picked up Temple's shirt and removed a clean one from a chest. "Never heard of such a dustup afore."

"It's a catastrophe, Fidkin."

"Well, at least you found the mistake afore you married. What if you'd have done one of them proxies like you considered? That would have been rum."

"She's like a windstorm, Fidkin, and she's brought a hound from hell. No, two of them, and a sneaking, spitting feline with claws like razors. Hell."

Temple went to a dresser, where he poured water into a basin. Thrusting his hands into it, he splashed water on his face. He was feeling better now that the effects of the vision had faded. His eye caught a glimpse of a scratch on his bare chest. "Hell."

There would be no chance of quiet and tranquillity with her and her beasts in the house. She and her creatures would constantly provoke his weakness. If Miss Peabody remained in the house, he would exist in a perpetual state of vulnerability, as though the top layer of his skin had been peeled from his body. God, he couldn't abide such a woman.

"I'll write to Dr. Peabody at once and explain the misunderstanding," he said to himself. In the mirror he noticed Fidkin standing behind him. "What are you staring at?"

"Oh, naught, m'lord."

"Out with it, Fidkin."

The sergeant clasped his hands behind his back and rocked on his heels. "Well, since you ask, m'lord major, you appear to have livened up a sight."

"What are you babbling about?" Temple sloshed water over his chest, growing more irritated by the moment.

"You been flitting around the hall like a ghost these past few months. I thought you just needed more rest and quiet, but now I don't know."

"I don't need rest," Temple snapped, "but I do want quiet, and that Miss Peabody is not quiet."

"You got color in your face for once."

"From anger."

"And you got bounce in your step."

"From being startled near to death by her blasted dog."

Fidkin came closer, holding a clean shirt. "And there's life in your eyes, m'lord, where before I was used to seeing something close to death. Seemed like you was looking at all them dead boys back in the Crimea, your friends, the men."

Temple slipped his arms into the shirtsleeves, taking the opportunity to turn his back to the sergeant. Fidkin was too close to the truth. And the last thing he wanted was to talk about the dead. He could still feel their blood splattering him, dripping down his face as he rode on a charge. Temple closed his eyes. No, he hadn't been living with his dead friends for company. Fidkin was wrong. It was Miss Peabody's fault that he'd been thrust into the past again.

No, all he needed was a quiet life here, taking care of his estates. He wanted a life of peace and serenity, not one filled with yapping dogs, spitting cats, and a defiant little whirlwind with bourbon-colored eyes and that interesting smile. She brought chaos, and by her very presence stabbed at old wounds. Temple felt his nightmare threaten, a ravening hyena, snapping at the edges of his composure. All her fault, this whirlwind miss with her defiance, her merry, stubborn character, her smile that seemed to brighten the world.

Temple's eyes flew open. Thinking of Miss Peabody's defiance and sunburst smile had quite banished the threat of the waking nightmare. His breathing eased, slowed. Curious how his thoughts had fastened upon her. True, she had certain good qualities. He liked the way she walked, with confidence, with complete lack of awareness of the way her hips set her skirts swaying. Irritated as he had been, the baser part of him had noticed Miss Peabody's hips, her smile, her curves.

Temple suddenly realized what thinking of Miss Peabody had done to his body. "Hell."

He couldn't want her. She irritated him and was a threat to his peace; he didn't like her. But wanting and liking weren't the same. He'd learned that long ago.

"Hell."

MAY HURRIED out of her room shortly after dawn and went through the Cabinet Room, George IV's Apartments, and the Roman Room. She'd been at Stirling Hall for three days, and had spent most of them trying to have a private word with the earl of Darent. What she hadn't realized was how easy it was for a man to avoid someone in a house the size of the Houses of Parliament.

Luckily, yesterday she'd stumbled upon the library, an enormous room off one of the galleries. There she met the Stirling Hall librarian, Cuthbert Finch, who told her that the earl was in the habit of riding early in the morning, and that he always stopped at the ruins of Castle Darent in the hills behind the house. She had ordered a horse made ready for her, and was determined to corner Temple Stirling where he couldn't easily slip away. She had a small request to make of him.

After all, it wasn't her fault that he'd mistaken her for Madeleine. She couldn't be responsible for his disremembering the character attached to each name. Madeleine was the quiet, restful one. Both May and Marie-Claire agreed that Maddie was the prettiest of the sisters. May emerged from the Gold Dining Room onto the landing only to meet the dowager countess of Darent and the Stirling estate manager coming in the opposite direction.

May faltered, then stopped as they came toward her.

May had been introduced at dinner the first night at Stirling Hall and had come to some conclusions about the earl's mother. The countess, Lady Charlotte, had spent years under the thumb of the previous countess before becoming mistress of Stirling Hall on her own. Now she resented giving precedence and power over to a younger woman, especially one without a title or proper breeding.

May curtsied to the older woman, who passed her as though she were one of the paintings hung on the wall. The estate manager, Mr. Radwinter, goggled at her from behind thick-lensed spectacles. May rolled her eyes when they were gone. Mr. Radwinter annoyed her much more than the countess, because his likes and dislikes, opinions and habits, were exact copies of the countess's. The countess disapproved of families with too many children; so did Mr. Radwinter. The countess disliked peas with onions in them; so did Mr. Radwinter. If the countess had disapproved of heaven, Mr. Radwinter would have also. She was about to resume her progress when Fidkin, the earl's man, came hurrying after the countess.

"Oh, Miss Peabody, your pardon."

May nodded and would have gone on, but Fidkin cleared his throat. She gave him an inquiring glance. Fidkin edged closer to her, glanced around as if he were afraid the ancient portraits might be listening.

"Pardon my liberty, miss, but I got to explain about m'lord major."

"The earl?"

"Aye, miss. You see, we was in the Crimea together. Right brave was the major. Near got hisself killed trying to keep his men safe. Wouldn't take no food his men didn't get. A matter o' honor, he said. When all them officers was off in their tents being served big dinners, he was with us."

Fidkin appeared to settle in for a discourse. "Saved my life, he did. Shoved me out of the way of a Russian saber. Right after that, he took a hit himself. Hurt bad, he was. Had to be sent home. But he's better now, except that he gets these attacks if there's a sudden noise, or if there's a lot of confusion." The slam of a door recalled Fidkin to the proprieties. He pulled on the hem of his coat and cleared his throat again.

"Your pardon, miss. I shouldn't have spoken, only you ain't seen his lordship major at his best."

Having never been presented with a servant who dared to expose his master's most private affairs, May was at a loss. At the same time, the earl's conduct suddenly seemed more excusable.

"Thank you, Fidkin. You may rely upon my discretion."

May hurried on to the stables, and, after making certain she understood the groom's directions, she rode into the morning mist. Puck and Echo came with her. Isis remained with Aunt Violet. Isis did not take walks or rides. Her favorite form of exercise was hunting things and killing them.

It took May almost an hour to find her way through the hills to the valley where Castle Darent lay. The sun had risen when she cleared the trees through which she'd been riding, and the castle appeared to be floating in the middle of a pool of silver water and shrouded by clouds of mist. Cuthbert Finch had told her that the pool was the castle's moat, which was fed by a nearby river.

After watering her horse, she rode across an arched stone bridge and under a rusted portcullis. In what used to be the bailey, she tethered her mare behind the remnant of a wall where she couldn't be seen. Castle Darent once consisted of four massive, round towers connected by battlements, a mountain of a gatehouse, and opposite this, a series of reinforced stone chambers—the great hall and family apartments.

These were shells without floors or roofs, but the towers still stood. Echo and Puck scampered off to explore. May located the one called the Well Tower and climbed its winding stair past several floors with rotting timbers, to a landing. There she found a telescope covered in a dust cloth, a hamper filled with tinned meat, wine and utensils, and a box. The box held books, some of which May had read—the usual Aristotle, Plato, Virgil, and Ovid. She was surprised to see Molière, Alexander Pope, and Mr. Dickens's *Bleak House*. Cuthbert Finch hadn't told her the earl had made this place a private retreat. May shut the lid on the book box, feeling like a snoop.

There was a ladder leading to a door in the roof. She climbed up and stuck her head outside. The sun was beginning to burn off the mist. She climbed out, went to the crenellated battlement, and leaned over the edge. She drew back behind a merlon and peeped around it as the earl rode across the stone bridge.

Now that she'd heard Fidkin, she was disposed to view the earl with much less trepidation. May found herself watching him with shy interest, even curiosity. He had been riding hard and had removed his coat. His cambric shirt was damp and clung to his chest and shoulders.

She remembered her father saying the earl had been in the Heavy Brigade, and now she understood why, for Temple Stirling was too tall for the Light Brigade, and had a build that could easily have borne the weight of the armor his ancestors had worn in this castle. She watched sunlight cause his wet skin to glisten where his shirt opened at his throat. He must often have removed his coat while riding, for the skin there had turned a warm brown.

Her gaze roamed upward to fasten on onyx locks plastered to a straight, determined forehead, then lowered to glimpse a hand resting on a thigh the size of a cathedral pilaster. Then he vanished beneath the portcullis. May came awake from her fascination to find herself in a strange state. She couldn't concentrate. It was hot, and she felt quite odd.

"Compose yourself, May Peabody," she muttered to herself.

She could hear him coming up the winding stair. He was on the ladder. May skittered as far away from the trap door as she could, so that he would be facing away from her when he came out. All too quickly the earl's black cap of hair appeared. Then he was on the roof and walking over to the battlement. Bracing himself against two merlons, he leaned out to gaze across the countryside.

She wished he weren't so large. Even facing away from her he was intimidating. She surveyed a long leg, the shining black boots, pants that had drawn tight over his hips as he leaned. She should speak. It was growing too hot, and she wanted off this roof.

"It's the Pea. What in bloody hell are you doing here?"

May jumped and cried out. His back still to her, the earl straightened and turned. He fixed a glare on her that would have made the stones of the battlements crumble. How could such lovely eyes turn one's knees to custard? War sufferings or not, he was rude.

"Kindly refrain from calling me the Pea, my lord."

"Very well, Miss Pea-body. However, you must admit you're aptly named."

Was the sun hotter than usual? May felt her cheeks burn and pulled off her riding hat. "Perhaps my appearance here has encouraged you to make fun of me, but as I don't call you names like roof beam or Maypole—"

"Maypole?" The earl threw back his head and laughed.

"I fail to understand your merriment," May said stiffly.

The earl grinned at her. "I know."

He was moving! May stirred uneasily as the earl walked across the roof to her side. He stopped an arm's length away, but for her, it was too close. She wouldn't allow him the satisfaction of seeing her shrink from him.

"There is something I want to discuss with you, my lord."

He didn't seem to be listening to her. The earl's gaze appeared fixed at some point below her chin. Annoyed, May sank down until her face replaced whatever had fascinated him.

"Please do me the courtesy of listening when I address you," she said.

Now he seemed to be half asleep. He gave her a slow, half-teasing smile and said softly, "Do you know something? Not seeing something has proved to be no method by which to banish it."

"I beg your pardon?" May stood up.

The earl leaned over and whispered near her ear. "And I love peas."

May darted away from his lips, which were too warm and had a disconcertingly dark rose color. "Nonsense. Now, I wanted to discuss something."

"Did you?" he murmured. "Still, it was a mistake to come here, Miss Pea-body. A mistake."

May suddenly realized she was wary of this man. This wasn't the dignified and elegant suitor of their first meeting, or the wounded soldier striving to maintain his composure. This was a man barely clothed in manners of civilized society. She sensed he'd come here to be something other than what everyone saw in the outside world. And she had intruded, thrust herself in the path of something he kept chained and hidden. She was proved right when the earl abruptly turned away from her and grabbed the stone ledge of the battlement.

"Go away from me, Mélisande."

"My lord, I haven't told you—"

He whirled around and scoured her with a vicious look. "Hell, woman. Have you not understood what is happening? Go away from me." He raised his voice. "Now!"

May gasped and raced for the ladder. She was at the bottom and hurtling down the stairs in moments. Not stopping until she ran out into the bailey, she paused to catch her breath. Then she went for her mare. He had alarmed her, deliberately, the vile ruffian.

"Wretched bully," she said loudly. "Rude, tyrannical know-all."

Holding the mare's reins, May looked around for Puck and Echo but couldn't see them. Then, casting a sly glance at the Well Tower, she put her little fingers to her lips and gave the loudest, shrillest whistle of which she was capable. It bounced off the stone walls and produced a shrieking bark in answer. Echo's pointed ears popped up from behind a pile of stones. Puck came loping toward her silently while the sheltie yapped her ear-destroying yap and bounded over the stones. May welcomed the two, kneeling and wrestling with them when they arrived, which made Echo bark even louder. As they played, the earl's dark head appeared on top of the tower.

"Be quiet down there," he called.

May ignored him and began to scamper around the bailey, allowing Echo and Puck to chase her. All the while, Echo's yammering continued. May was so engrossed in creating more noise that she failed to notice the tall figure emerge from the Well Tower and stride in her direction. When she glimpsed him, he was too close to evade. He lunged at her and grabbed her arm.

It was then that Puck, who had been silent, growled the deep, killing growl of a dog twice his size. From a sitting position several feet away he sprang and landed between May and the earl with Echo barking hysterically. Puck bared his teeth; the hair on his back stood up, and his floppy ears flattened.

Her wrist still imprisoned, May yanked it, but failed to free herself. "Let me go, my lord." She smiled as Puck's growl grew louder.

The earl glanced down at Puck. Raising a brow, he pointed at the dog and bellowed, "Down, sir!"

To May's consternation, this thunderous command made Puck yelp and bolt. He raced around her skirts to hide behind her legs while Echo continued her frenzied yips. The earl bent to her level and yelled at the top of his voice.

"No bark!"

Echo's jaws snapped shut out of amazement. Then she raced around to join Puck behind May's skirts. By this time May's wrist was growing numb from the earl's grip. When he rose and pulled her toward him, she dug in her heels.

"If you hurt me, they will attack," she said desperately.

He stopped tugging on her for a moment to give her a startled look. "Hurt you? Hell, woman, that's not what I had in mind."

May felt him pull on her wrist, a gentle exertion of his strength that sent her flying toward him. She landed in the circle of his arms to stare up at him with her mouth open. Evidently his strength had surprised the earl too, for he seemed frozen, his expression startled. Seeing him lose his composure reassured May. Then she realized that her hands were on his chest, and that one of them was placed on his shirt near the open collar. The earl followed her gaze to join her in staring at her hand. His own covered it,

and May looked up to find him directing a look of mysti-
fied query at her.

A sharp bark made them jump. The earl suddenly closed
his eyes and swore. Then color drained from his face. May
stepped back, alarmed that he seemed so tortured, and she
stumbled over Echo. Her cry made the earl open his eyes
in time to see her fall backward over her dog. Echo yelped,
scampered out of the way, and returned to stand over her
mistress and berate her with a series of shrieking barks.
May winced but was distracted at the sound of a soft
laugh.

"Sweet Mélisande, what are you doing to me?"

To May's astonishment, he took her hand and brushed
his lips against it. This was when two big paws landed on
her shoulder. May grabbed his arm. Temple Stirling pulled
her to him and cursed. For a moment they remained
locked together while Puck bounced in place on his hind
legs. Suddenly he jumped higher, licked the earl on the
cheek, and bounced away to sniffle at his boots. Echo wiggled between them and raced around their feet. The earl
laughed and released May. He caught Puck under the
shoulders and pulled the dog up to face him.

"I take it you approve of me now, sir."

Puck gave him a sniff, and the earl released him. May
watched this display, wishing she understood what had
just happened. Then the earl stood up and took her hand.

"Come with me."

He pulled her after him and didn't stop until they
reached the doorway in the Well Tower. Before he stepped
inside, May planted her feet and yanked on his hand.

"My lord, what are you doing?"

"Pursuing what you began, Miss Pea-body."

"What are you implying I have begun?"

"Don't pretend you didn't set out to gain my attention
with your display of noise."

All the pleasant feelings that lingered in her body vanished in a heat storm of fury. May yanked her hand from
his and whirled around to leave. The earl caught her arm,
and before she knew it, he planted his arms on either side
of her. She was caught against the stone wall of the Well

Tower by a body that definitely belonged to a cavalry officer in the Heavy Brigade. His nearness and heat provoked a tingling tension even though he hadn't touched her. At this thought, May gave a little cry and shoved.

Of course he didn't move. She doubted if he even noticed, so slight was her weight compared to his. That was when she lost what little composure she had left. May slid down the wall, scooted to the side, and sprang free. Not daring to look behind her, she raced for her mare, jumped into the saddle, and kicked the horse into motion.

Echo and Puck raced alongside. As she headed for the gatehouse, she glimpsed the earl standing with his legs apart, his fists on his hips and an evil smile on his lips. As she rode under the portcullis, she heard him call after her.

"Miss Pea-body, come back and I'll let you call me Maypole."

To her chagrin, the clatter of the mare's hooves didn't cover the sound of his laughter.

CHAPTER FOUR

*H*E WAS DREAMING. He was near the boathouse in the park at Stirling Hall looking out on the lake just past the hundred fountains. It was a blue glass mirror set in the landscape. On the river floated a small white rowboat, and in the boat was Mélisande. She wore a loose gown of some misty, transparent fabric and he saw her through a haze of swirling jewel colors—teal, darkest green, amethyst, and purple. The boat floated toward the shore, and as it drew near, Mélisande held out her arms to him. Her gown fell from her shoulders . . .

The world was shaking. Temple groaned and burrowed deeper under a pillow in search of the image of Mélisande, but the pillow flew off his head. Sunlight turned the insides of his eyelids red. The shaking began again.

"Come, my pretty. Out of bed with you."

He opened one eye. Lady Alberta, his sometime mistress, was standing over him fully dressed. She was the kind of woman whose attention started fights among regimental officers, the kind of woman who attracted entourages of young men at balls and thus gained the enmity of every eligible young lady in society. It didn't matter that strands of gray streaked her ash-blond hair. Her suitors didn't care that fine lines etched the corners of her eyes.

What kept them enthralled was her deep, rough voice, her direct gaze that probed a man's sensuality, and her daring.

Temple held out his hand to her. Alberta took it, but instead of joining him, she pulled him upright and ruffled his hair. He sighed and sat up. Alberta kept hold of him and sat on the edge of the bed. Taking his hand in both of hers, she paused to run her gaze over his bare skin. Then she kissed his cheek and spoke in a confiding manner.

"You must go, pretty one."

"There's no hurry," Temple said. He didn't want to go.

"No. I mean you must go from me, Temple my darling. When a man comes to me, desperate to make love, and then stops before he attains what he clearly desires, I know it is time to part."

Temple looked away from Alberta's calm gaze. "I don't know what you mean. I was troubled, that's all."

"I agree. You're troubled, and you won't settle your troubles with me, much to my sorrow. I knew you would go from me someday, but I didn't think it would happen so soon."

Temple jerked the sheet higher over his hips and stuck out his chin. "Hell."

"She has you stirred and fizzed." Alberta gave him a sad smile. "I regret I wasn't the one to banish the ghosts in those eyes, but I'm glad they're gone."

"Alberta, I don't know what you're talking about."

"You do, or you wouldn't have come flying here in such urgency. But I don't involve myself with men who love elsewhere, and I won't break my rule, even for your beautiful self. Good-bye, my dear."

Temple bathed and dressed and was on his way back to Stirling Hall in less than an hour. May had left him in a painful state yesterday morning at Castle Darent. For days now he'd struggled to rid himself of this unexpected desire for her, had tried to free himself of it by keeping away from her.

His household had foiled his efforts by reporting Miss Peabody's ill conduct. He'd heard from the housekeeper how Miss Peabody had returned from a walk with a stray dog, which she insisted upon nursing in the kitchens. The bootboy lodged a protest with Breedlebane that he had been set to feeding a wounded hedgehog. His vexation had turned to laughter when Fidkin burst into his library, his chest heaving with indignation. He was holding up a bandaged hand and pointing at it.

"Look here, m'lord major, just look here!"

"What happened?"

"She wouldn't listen. Never saw a lady with such a passion."

Temple lifted a brow and smiled. "Indeed?"

"It's Miss Peabody."

The smile vanished. "Be careful of your language, Fidkin."

Fidkin rubbed his red nose and began to commiserate with himself. "Won't you feed my spaniel for me, she says. Dear Mr. Fidkin, she says. I must place this baby robin back in his nest, she says, and I don't want Puck to miss his dinner." Fidkin groaned and cradled his injured hand as though it were a terrible war wound. "How was I to know he don't like nobody petting him while he's at his dinner?"

"You petted that dog while he was eating? Fidkin, you're addled. Let me see your hand."

Temple unwrapped the thick wad of bandages, expecting to encounter blood. Layer after layer was removed without a spot of red on it. Finally, Temple revealed the wound. Fidkin had squeezed his eyes shut and turned his head away.

"Will I lose me hand?"

Regarding the small scrapes and nicks, Temple thrust Fidkin's hand away. "You coward. He only nipped you."

"I was bleeding! Miss Peabody had to take care o' me herself. She give me a recipe for a poultice and—"

"Damn you! She goes about taking care of helpless creatures, and you take advantage of her sympathy. You're not to exploit her too-soft heart. Do you hear me?"

Shaking his head, Temple turned his attention to his horse. The morning was fine. Just the sort of day Miss Peabody would like, excellent for hunting wounded or lost animals.

The day she arrived he'd sent word to Dr. Peabody, but the doctor had left for London. Then he'd sent to London, to the respectable hotel at which Dr. Peabody was to have stayed, only to receive word that his message had just missed its intended recipient. He had sent a servant to London, hoping that the doctor had merely changed hotels. Now all he could do was wait and endure the confusion wrought upon him by Miss Peabody.

How could he find himself growing attached to this— this disturber of tranquillity? Finding her in the Well Tower had brought unexpected pleasure. Not simply because he'd suddenly found her desirable, but because he learned that in her company, his waking nightmares lost their power. True, that little beast Echo was an irritant, but putting up with her had brought the reward of glimpsing an escape from his misery. He owed it to Miss Peabody. But after she'd run away, he'd fled, unwilling to face what Alberta had just forced him to acknowledge. His world of order and tranquillity had been invaded by a contentious little whirlwind and her noisy, troublemaking pets, and he had conceived an attachment.

It was like growing fond of hemlock. Miss Peabody was death to his peace, and he still desired her. Why? All these months since he'd come home seemed a drugged nightmare from which May had jolted him awake. With May defying him, forcing him to care about things, refusing to be bound by anything but her greathearted love of her family and animals, he was beginning to love life again.

Temple reached down and stroked his horse's neck as he envisioned May's startled reaction to him at the ruins. Now he was as frightened as she had been. He'd never felt like this, never found a woman invading his dreams, possessing his thoughts, challenging him, commanding his admiration for her courage and gentle heart.

She had responded to him. She was attracted to him; he'd assured himself of that, almost out of habit. He'd done that to many women and released them, but this time, he didn't want to let her go. Kicking his horse into a trot, a canter, and then a gallop, Temple raced toward Stirling

Hall. He had to find Mélisande. He'd need all his persuasive skills to soothe her anger at his behavior at the castle.

Upon reaching home, he asked Breedlebane where Miss Peabody was and was told she'd gone to visit Cuthbert Finch in the library. Cuthbert, however, was alone when Temple found him. He wanted to continue his search for Mélisande, but Cuthbert was insistent upon giving him news that made the old man quiver with excitement.

"Look, my lord. This was between the pages of the family's copy of the *Domesday Book*." Cuthbert pointed to a yellowed sheet of parchment that lay on his desk. "It's a drawing of the old keep that Castle Darent replaced."

"Very nice, Finch old fellow. Did Miss Peabody say where she was going?"

"Miss Peabody seems as interested in the castle as you are, my lord. She wanted to know all about the Well Tower. A well-read lady, is Miss Peabody. Did you know that her father educated her? She has read the classics."

This distracted Temple. "She has? Well, I knew she was intelligent." The absent-minded Cuthbert had returned to examining his find. Temple placed his hand over the parchment. "Finch, damn you, where did Miss Peabody go?"

"She said she was going to join her aunt in the Blue Drawing Room, my lord."

Temple hurried out of the library. When he reached the landing above the hall he saw Mélisande and her aunt donning mantles in preparation for a walk. That monster-dog with the earsplitting bark was yapping madly at them while the spaniel lay watching in calm silence. Temple grinned at the picture before him.

"Miss Pea-body," he called.

Mélisande turned to look up at him. He held her gaze, put a hand on the banister, and descended the stairs. He was concentrating on binding her to him with his eyes or he would have seen the cat.

Isis was lurking between the support posts beneath the banister in search of amusement. As he passed, her paw darted out, and she clawed his trouser leg. Her claws stuck in the material. His leg dragged, and he tripped over the cat. Falling, he managed to slow his momentum by grabbing a post and rolling on his side. As he landed near the bottom of the steps, he heard Aunt Violet scream.

"Hell!"

Suddenly Mélisande was bending over him. Her hands fastened on his shoulders as he began to feel the pain in his back and legs.

"Are you all right?"

His spirits lifted; she was afraid for him. He was tempted to kiss her, but suddenly his body let him know he'd banged it against something hard, several times. "Hell! No, I'm not all right, woman." He sat up. "Where is that bloody cat?"

Mélisande released his shoulders, turned, and scooped up Isis. As Temple got to his feet, she hurried back down the stairs. He came after her, limping a bit.

"Give me that cat," he growled.

She rounded on him, the cat held tightly in her arms.

"No."

"I'm going to—"

He stopped because Mélisande suddenly thrust Isis at Aunt Violet and faced him. She seemed to grow to double her height. Her eyes glittered and she took an aggressive step toward him, raised her arm, and pointed at him. Her voice boomed around the hall.

"You stop!"

The plaster on the walls should have cracked. Temple felt his jaw loosen and come adrift. Mélisande's roar dwarfed any he'd imagined could come from that small body.

"You hurt my cat, and I'll pull your spine out your throat and make you eat it." She planted her hands on her hips and marched up to him. "She's only an animal. She didn't understand what would happen."

This was too much. He was the injured one.

"Didn't understand? That bloody cat knew exactly what she was doing. She tripped Breedlebane like that yesterday. She enjoys lurking about and ambushing people. The day before that I saw her hurtling in a circle around the hall and saloon like some crazed miniature racehorse. She broke three antique vases and a statuette. I should have skinned her right then!"

That was a mistake. He knew it as the words left his mouth. Mélisande's color faded. Her brows drew together, and she looked at him as if he were the Inquisition's most enthusiastic torturer.

"My lord, I can no longer remain under obligation to you for your hospitality. My disgust with your character forbids it."

"Disgust, is it, Miss Noble Heart? I'd like to hear your comments if that bloody cat had nearly broken your neck. I'm quite weary of being accused of possessing bloodier appetites than Caligula, and I've some news to impart to you." He waved a hand over her head. "You see? There's no halo there, so kindly refrain from acting as if your sainthood has been ordered and is expected any day."

He backed up, his wrath spent, satisfied that he'd put Mélisande in her place. Then he saw her eyes, those bourbon-colored eyes. They'd turned glassy from unshed tears. Two bright crimson spots burned in her cheeks. She said nothing to him. Taking Isis from her aunt, Mélisande walked in a wide arc around him and up the stairs.

Echo bounded after her, and Puck rose quietly to follow without giving him so much as a sniff. He watched her vanish, and then Aunt Violet paused beside him on her way upstairs.

She fanned her face with a handkerchief. "I'm afraid you've done it, my child. I don't know what can be done now, I'm sorry to say. Too bad. Too bad. She was enthralled, you know. I've never seen her like that. A pity. Such a great generous heart to give, and the only time she entrusted it, to a man that is . . . Oh dear, oh dear."

Temple found himself alone in the hall, staring up at the landing. He rubbed a sore spot on his arm, winced, and stopped. A great generous heart, entrusted to him.

"Hell."

He was prevented from going after Mélisande by the appearance of Breedlebane and Fidkin.

"My lord, a word if you please," said the butler.

"Not now."

"Beg your pardon, m'lord major, but there be something you got to see."

"I said, not now." He mounted the bottom stair.

"It concerns Miss Peabody," Fidkin said.

They took him to the stableyard, where he found a caravan of six wagons and carts arriving. Each was stuffed with yelping, baying, squawking animals. A giant hopped down from the first wagon, pulled his cap from his head, and introduced himself as Small Tom.

"I brung Miss May's critters."

"You've brung—brought Miss Peabody's—these are all Miss Peabody's animals?" Temple heard his voice climb almost an octave.

"Yes, my lord."

He saw a cow with pelvic bones sticking out like fence posts, a donkey that appeared blind, and cages. Cages full of hedgehogs, ferrets, cats, dogs, more cats. There was an ailing coach dog nestled in a large basket full of blankets. This privileged creature rested its chin on the edge of the basket and flopped its tail back and forth in contentment. In a separate cart he saw parrots, larks, sparrows, robins, budgies, and every last one of the animals was barking, braying, squawking, yowling, or racing around its cage as if lightning were chasing it.

"Dear God," he whispered. Then he looked closer at one of the cages, at an animal that seemed part cat, part dog, and had ears so large the creature could have used them for umbrellas. He raised his voice so that it could be heard over the din. "What is that?"

"Fennec, my lord," said Small Tom. "Miss May rescued it from some daft old besom what bought it off a gentleman who'd been in Arab parts. It's a fox, she says. Miss May wants to find someone to take it back home."

Without warning, the ancient cow kicked the donkey. The donkey kicked back, and the dogs renewed their furious barking. Temple watched the fennec burrow under its bed of straw. He went to the wagon and lifted its cage. As he brought it out, a giant parrot sitting in the cage beside the fox let out a screech that shot like shrapnel through his head.

Temple cried out, and was hurled into the midst of battle.

Shells screamed around him. His friends exploded, and he rode over the remains of their bodies before he could turn his horse. Then something soft and cool touched his cheek, and a voice like sunbeams shining through mist called him back to the present. He opened his eyes to find Mélisande in front of him, his face in her hands. He was kneeling beside the wagon. His arms clutched the fennec's cage.

Mélisande gently took the cage and handed it to Fidkin. Then she clasped his hands in hers, holding them tightly. He was half in the vision and half out until she pulled him nearer and said his name. It was the first time she'd used his given name. He latched on to her summer-meadow voice.

"Temple, you're safe. Temple, you're at home now. There's no danger."

Using her voice as a shimmering tether, he dragged himself back from the nightmare. He opened his eyes to find her kneeling beside him, his hands in hers. He tightened his grip and almost whispered something to her, something pitiful. He stopped himself in time, but could not endure the thought of how exposed and weak he must appear to her. And someone had told her of his condition!

She must have seen his discomfort, because she released him and asked how he did.

"I'm fine," he said. He glanced around to find that Breedlebane, Fidkin, and Small Tom were all looming over him. He scowled at them, stood, and helped Mélisande up. "I'm fine, damn you, Fidkin. Help the grooms see to these animals." Then he turned to Mélisande. "Small Tom tells me that these are more of your blasted animals, Miss Peabody. I want to speak to you, in private."

May looked at him and widened her eyes. "I tried to tell you about them."

"Now, Miss Peabody." He came toward her.

She began to retreat. "I did! Several times, but you were so rude."

She edged her way down the path that led from the stables to the house with him matching her steps.

"Come here, Miss Pea-body."

Eyeing him, she shook her head. "Don't touch me. It's

all your fault. I was trying to tell you about my orphans at the castle, but you behaved like a—a . . ."

"Lover?"

May gasped and blurted out, "Madman!" Then she ran. Temple swore and launched himself after her. She was small, but quick, and she vanished into a glade of trees. Luckily, he could hear her footsteps on the dead leaves that carpeted the ground. He chased the sound and saw her break out of the trees. He closed the distance between them as she sped down a grassy slope beside the lake. Then she made the mistake of looking back and tripped over her skirt.

May went down, and he nearly ran over her. Dodging to the side, he sprinted after her as she rolled down the slope. He managed to get ahead of her and stopped her by blocking her with his body. They collided with a jolt, and he fell on top of her. After a moment, a small hand pounded his ribs. He sat up. She sucked in a deep breath and let it out.

"You nearly crushed me," she said while she panted.

"Don't snap at me, you little beast. I saved you from a broken neck."

"And then you nearly crushed me. I'm going in."

She stood, but Temple simply grabbed a handful of skirt and yanked. Mélisande toppled to her knees, hissing and trying to pull herself free. He tugged hard, and she fell on her back. Before she could get up, he put a knee on either side of her legs and pinned her skirts to the ground. He watched her eyes widen in alarm as he slowly lowered himself on top of her.

"Miss Pea-body," he said when their lips almost touched. "I would like a word with you in private."

MAY WAS struggling with two urges, to pull Temple's mouth down to hers, or to spit at him. This man had aroused the most wondrous feelings in her only to suddenly thrust her away and shout at her. Why had he barked at her to go away from him? That was the question she'd been asking herself since their encounter at the castle. What tormented her was that she already knew the answer. He had been willing to kiss her, but he'd stopped himself for fear of the consequences. Temple Stirling might entertain himself with her, but he didn't want to commit to her. Hadn't he already made himself clear? Why had she been so stupid as to forget?

Because he's the first man who ever paid attention to you in that way. Because he turns your body into one big searing flame. Because you've fallen in love with him. You, an old silly spinster.

She'd seen his pain. Indeed, he'd seen so much blood and suffering that his family and Mr. Fidkin had feared he'd never recover. Just now, he'd been thrust into some terrible memory. She had wanted to take away the pain.

But now he was acting like a wretch, tempting her when she knew he would never risk committing himself to her. May turned her face aside so that he couldn't kiss her. She planted her hands on his chest and shoved. He didn't move an inch. She was never going to escape by using her strength, so she would use the truth.

Turning to look at him, she tried not to let those emerald eyes distract her. "You may as well let me up, my lord, for I know you won't risk having to marry me by seducing me."

"What?" He went still and gaped at her.

"Temple! Get off that girl at once."

May looked over his shoulder to find the dowager countess and Mr. Radwinter standing over them. She heard Temple sigh. He rolled off her, stood, and helped her up.

"Hello, Mother."

"Humph. I'll speak to you later. Miss Peabody, my entire household is in an uproar. Your aunt is beside herself and cannot be calmed. She keeps bleating about someone with the odd name of Isis. She says Isis is lost. Please return and settle your aunt."

AUNT VIOLET was in the Blue Drawing Room on a sofa, moaning and sniffing her scent bottle. With Temple, the countess, and Mr. Radwinter standing by, May managed to get her to make sense.

"I can't find Isis anywhere. The servants have looked and looked. Oh, dear. We can't leave without Isis. Oh, dear."

"Now, Aunt, you know how she is. She goes her own way, but never for long."

She felt a warm hand envelop hers and looked up in surprise to find Temple smiling at her. "Rather like her mistress, wouldn't you say?"

She met his gaze, and almost forgot to breathe. Then she furrowed her brow and said in an accusing tone, "You aren't angry."

He bent down and placed his lips close to her ear. "I didn't say I was, Mélisande."

She jumped when the countess barked, "Temple. I thought Miss Peabody was leaving."

"What is that curious sound?" Mr. Radwinter asked.

"What sound?" the countess demanded. "I hear nothing."

There was a bang, and then the sound of baying mixed with yips and barks and the patter of dozens of paws. It was growing closer.

"Oh, no," May said. She rushed into the hall with Temple behind her.

Through the arch between the saloon and the hall rushed a white-and-cream ball of fur. In close pursuit were Puck and Echo, leading a band of happily barking mongrels. The fennec bounded toward May and Temple, saw them at the last moment, and dashed into the Blue Drawing Room. The dogs skittered into a turn and scrambled after it. May and Temple exchanged horrified stares.

"Dear God," Temple said.

"The poor thing."

Grabbing her hand, Temple said, "Come on."

They rushed back into the room in time to see the fennec jump onto the fireplace mantel, toppling delicate porcelain and precious silver. The countess screamed. Aunt Violet screamed, and Mr. Radwinter shouted. Hurtling around the room, the dogs jumped for the fox, but it sprang from the mantel to the top of a tall armoire where it stayed, panting. Puck stood on his hind legs, bounced in place, and barked incessantly. All around him his other hunting fellows wiggled, danced, jumped, and yipped at the same time.

"Stop this," the countess screamed. "Stop this at once."

May was busy trying to grab dog collars. "Don't shout. You'll only get them more excited."

Breedlebane, Fidkin, and Small Tom came to help. One by one, she and Temple captured the dogs, and the three men took them away. Once the fennec was caged, Mr. Radwinter was asked to conduct Aunt Violet to her room so that she could lie down.

Temple set the fennec's cage down on a table beside the fireplace. May removed the shawl she wore fastened to her gown with a brooch and covered the cage with it. Then she and Temple surveyed the ravaged drawing room. The dowager countess was standing in the midst of broken porcelain in front of the fireplace, her whole frame rigid. May reddened at the distaste she met in the woman's stare. She cast a shamed glance at Temple, but he was smiling at her and appeared not to have noticed his mother.

"Do you know I've never seen a more ridiculous sight than that daft springer of yours bouncing in place in front of my armoire on his hind legs like a jack-in-the-box, with his ears flapping, his tongue hanging out, and his nose pointed straight up at that fox." He leaned toward her and touched the tip of her nose with his finger. "Except perhaps you trying to outrun me and tripping over your own skirt."

May felt her insides begin to tingle at the look in his eyes. She was warm and cold at the same time, and she just knew she was grinning like a clown.

"Temple!"

May started at the sound of the countess's hunting-horn voice. Temple raised his eyes to the ceiling before addressing her.

"Yes, Mother?"

"I cannot have that creature in my house."

"It's only a fox, Mother."

The countess closed her eyes for moment before answering. "Not the animal. That creature." She nodded at May. "Never have I seen such a mannerless, indelicate person. Miss Peabody, I find myself unsurprised that you are, and will no doubt remain, a spinster."

Silence invaded the Blue Drawing Room. Shame drained the strength from May's body, and she dared not look at Temple. Spinster. She had been exposed for what she was—unappealing, indecorous, lacking in the gentle ways that Temple so desperately needed to assuage his battered soul. She didn't dare look at him. She couldn't bear to see the distaste in his eyes.

"Miss Peabody, you will take yourself out of my house at once," the countess was saying.

"Mother, shut up."

May felt her mouth drop open. She looked up to see Temple glare at the countess.

The dowager gasped, then said, "You forget yourself, Temple. It's all this upset. You need quiet, and peace."

"Mother, I think you need quiet and peace. I'll arrange for you to take a house in Spain for the winter. It's much warmer there."

The countess was so rigid she began to resemble one of the Corinthian columns on the portico. "And Miss Peabody?"

"She isn't leaving, Mother, you are."

"Temple!"

"It's time for you to dress for luncheon, Mother."

Without another word, the countess swept out of the room, her head held high. Surprise and confusion robbed May of speech. She clasped her hands and stared at the tips of her boots, all at once afraid to look at Temple.

"Miss Pea-body."

"Yes," she whispered.

"*Now,* may I have a private word?"

May's head shot up, and she found him standing in front of her, his arms folded over his chest, his eyes glittering.

"I'm sorry about the dogs and the fox. I'll pay for the damage, although it may take me a while. I really did try to tell you my orphans were coming. I forgot in the confusion when we first met, and after all, you were terribly mean to me."

"Mélisande, shut up."

He was coming toward her, and he was looking at her as if he was planning something dangerous. Perhaps he was angry after all. May backed up, but hit the armoire. His arms came down to either side of her and blocked her escape. She tried to duck under his arms, but he captured her wrists and held them against the armoire. His body pressed against hers, and she felt his breath disturb the fine curls at her temple. Then she heard his low, hoarse whisper.

"At last, a private . . . word."

The world grew dark as he lowered his mouth to hers. She sank into that hot, misty place to which his touch always sent her. His lips lifted for a moment.

"Mélisande, would you mind very much if I retracted my retraction?"

"What?"

He moved back so that he could see her face. "I'm asking you to marry me, little pea."

"I will accept if you'll promise never to call me a pea again."

"I promise."

She freed her hands and wrapped them around his neck. Temple lifted her against him and kissed her, but his lips formed an O and he gasped as May heard a ripping sound. She looked down to see Isis sink her claws into Temple's trouser leg. The black material ripped again as the cat pulled on it and arched her back. This time Temple cursed and snatched the cat by the scruff of her neck. Alarmed, May almost protested, but Temple lifted the cat and stuffed her into the crook of his arm. He stroked her flat little head until she purred.

May watched the two for a while, but her patience gave out. She grabbed Isis and held the cat so that she could look into her blue eyes.

"That's enough. He's mine." She set the cat outside the door.

As she closed the door, the swirling colors of the little green bottle came to mind, and with them, a reminder of her dream, her wish. She'd pursued her dream, and it had come true in an unexpected way. Setting her back to the portal, she took note that that glittering look had returned to Temple's eyes.

"Now, my lord. You wanted a word in private?"

SUZANNE ROBINSON

SUZANNE ROBINSON is the award-winning author of such bestselling historical romances as *The Engagement, Lord of the Dragon,* and *Lady Dangerous.* She is also an acclaimed mystery author under the name Lynda S. Robinson. Watch for her next thrilling romance *The Rescue,* on sale in February 1998.

EPILOGUE

Jane Feather

EPILOGUE

*H*E WAS WAITING for her when the girl walked slowly into the village as the faintest gray lightened the eastern horizon. He stood just within the village walls, the dogs pressed to his sides.

The girl stopped beside him. She stroked the nose of the laden donkey and ignored the dogs who sniffed and slobbered around her ankles.

"Where have you been?" he demanded, a taut whisper in the predawn stillness. "I've been waiting for three hours. Would you force me to leave you without one last farewell?" His voice was anguished. "The elders have decreed I must be gone by dawn. They will kill me if I'm found within five miles of the village."

"There was something I had to do," the girl replied. She raised a hand, pushing it beneath the hood of her cloak to touch the back of her neck, which felt cold and exposed and slightly prickly.

"What have you done?" His voice was suddenly harsh with shock. Roughly he threw back her hood and then stared in dismay. "What have you done?" he repeated. "Your hair . . . your beautiful hair. What have you done?"

"I sold it." She smiled suddenly and the solemnity vanished from her face. Her eyes glowed and showed him again in all her joyful beauty the girl he loved, the girl for whose sake he was now banished from his home.

"I sold it for an answer that wasn't forthcoming." She lifted her hand and touched his face. "It was foolish of me since I had the answer all along."

He didn't understand what she meant. He could think of nothing but the consequences of what she'd done. "What will they say in the village when they see you shorn?" His hands raked through the short jagged silvery cap. "You look like a shaved harlot," he murmured in distress. "No man will take you to wife with the shaved head of a whore."

"But will *you*?"

He stared down at her. "I will not condemn you to share my exile. I have said so."

"But if you leave me, you will condemn me to the judgment of the elders. As you say, no virgin has a shorn head." She continued to smile at him, her face radiant with the knowledge that the die was cast. "They will say that the loss of my maiden hair proves that I was not innocent. They will say that I share your guilt, as they suspected all along."

She hadn't realized it when she had sought the druid's help, but the very act of seeking that help had confirmed the only decision she could possibly make. By selling her hair, she had burned her bridges. And some part of her had known exactly what she was doing.

The decision was now irrevocable. She was going with her love into exile. And he could not now refuse her.

"They will be right," she continued softly. "If there be guilt in loving you, then I am guilty."

"No," he whispered. But beneath the syllable of protest and denial stirred the beginning of hope. The beginning of an acknowledgment that there could be another future than the one he faced alone.

He caught her to him, pressing his lips to her broad forehead. He had wanted her to stay safe in the village, to live the life that was her due as the daughter of a chief. He had taken upon himself the punishment for an illicit love, strengthened in his resolve by the conviction that the woman who held his heart must never suffer for his love.

Beyond the walls of the village, denied all kinship support, their prospects were bleak. But as he looked into her smiling eyes and read the strength and power of her love, a surge of optimism thrilled him.

"We will go to the sea," he said. "I've heard it said that seafarers accept strangers into their villages more readily than farmers."

"I have always wanted to see the sea." She linked her arm through his, turning with him toward the village gates.

She was smiling to herself, thinking, *We will follow the druid's green bottle down the river and see where it leads us.*

A cock crowed its arrogant, jubilant greeting to the morning as the man lifted the girl onto the donkey's back. She glanced once over her shoulder to the village that was all she knew of the world, then she turned her face to the future that she had chosen.

THE WOMAN STOOD trembling, breathless, on the corner of a narrow fetid lane running up from the river. Her heart was beating so fast every dragging breath was an agony. Her bare feet were bleeding, cut by the jagged stones along the quay, and her thin cloak clung to her back, wet with sweat. Her hair hung limp around her white, terrified face, and she clutched her babies to her, one in each arm, their little faces buried against her shoulders to stifle their cries.

She looked wildly up the lane and saw the first flicker of the pursuing torches. The voices of the mob rose in a shrill shriek of exultation as they surged toward the river. With a sob of anguish, she began to run again, along the river, clutching the babies, who grew heavier with each step. She could hear the footsteps behind her, a thundering pounding of booted feet growing closer. Every breath was an agony, and slowly, inexorably, the despair of resignation deadened her terror. She could not escape. Not even for her babies could she run faster. And the crowd behind her grew, augmented by others who joined the chase simply for the pleasure of it.

With a final gasp of despair, she turned and faced her pursuers, the babies still pressed to her breast. She stood panting, a hart at bay, as the crowd with their mad glittering eyes surrounded her. Every face seemed filled with hatred.

"Abjure . . . abjure . . ." The chant was picked up, and the words battered against her like living things. The mob pressed against her, their faces pushed into hers as they taunted her with a salvation that she knew in her heart they would deny her. They were not interested in a convert, they were interested in her blood.

"Abjure . . . abjure . . ."

"I will," she gasped, dropping to her knees. "Don't hurt my babies . . . please, I will abjure for my babies. I will say the *credo*." She began to babble the Latin words of the Catholic credo, her eyes raised heavenward so that she couldn't see the hateful faces of the men who would murder her.

The knife, already reddened with Huguenot blood, swiped across her throat even as she stammered to an end. The words were lost in a gurgle as a thin line of blood marked the path of the knife. The line widened like parting lips. The woman fell forward to the cobbles. A baby's thin wail filled the sudden silence.

"To the Louvre . . . to the Louvre!" A great cry came over the rooftops and the mob with one thought turned and swept away, taking up the clarion call, "To the Louvre . . . to the Louvre," like so many maddened sheep.

The black river flowed as sluggishly as the woman's congealing blood. Something moved beneath her. One of the babies wriggled, squiggled, wailed as she emerged from the suffocating warmth of her mother's dead body. With a curious kind of purpose the little creature set off on hands and toetips like a spider, creeping away from the dreadful smell of blood.

Ten minutes passed before Francis found his wife. He broke from the lane, his face white in the sudden moonlight. *"Elena!"* he whispered as he fell to his knees beside the body. He snatched his wife against his breast, and then gave a great anguished cry that shivered the stillness as he saw the baby on the ground, gazing up at him with almost vacant eyes, her tiny rosebud mouth pursed on a wavering wail, her face streaked with her mother's blood.

"Sweet Jesus, have mercy," he murmured, gathering the infant up in the crook of one arm as he continued to hold her mother to his breast. He looked around, his eyes demented with grief. Where was his other daughter? Where was she? Had the murdering rabble spitted her on their knives, as they had done this night to babes all over the city? But if so, where was her body? Had they taken her?

Footsteps sounded behind him and he turned his head with a violent twist, still clinging to the child and his dead wife. His own people raced from the lane toward him, wild-eyed from their own desperate escape from the massacre.

One of the men reached down to take the child from the duke, who yielded her up wordlessly, bringing both arms around his wife, rocking her in soundless grief.

"Milord, we must take milady and the child," the man with the baby said in an urgent whisper. "They might come back. We can take shelter in the Chatelet if we go quickly."

Francis allowed his wife to fall into his lap, her head resting on his knee. He closed her open eyes and gently lifted her hand. A gold pearl-encrusted bracelet of strange serpentine design encircled the slender wrist. A single charm swung from the delicate strands and his tears fell onto the brilliant emerald cut into the perfect undulating shape of a swan. He unclasped the bracelet, his betrothal gift to Elena, and thrust it into his doublet against his heart, then he raised his wife in his arms and staggered to his feet with his burden.

The baby wailed, a long-drawn-out cry of hunger and dismay, and her bearer hoisted her up against his shoulder and turned to follow the man and his murdered wife as they vanished into the dark maw of the lane leading away from the river.

Dover, England, 1591

IT WAS THE *most extraordinary likeness*.

Gareth Harcourt pushed his way to the front of the crowd watching the troupe of performers who had set up their makeshift stage on the quay of Dover harbor.

Her eyes were the same cerulean blue, her complexion

the same thick cream, and her hair was exactly the same shade of darkest brown, right down to the deep reddish glints caught by the sun. There the resemblance ended, however. For whereas Maude's dark hair hung in a cloud of curls teased daily from curling papers and tongs, the acrobat's crowning glory was cut in a short straight fringed bob that owed more to a pudding basin than the more sophisticated tools of feminine coiffure.

Gareth watched with considerable enjoyment as the tiny figure performed on a very narrow beam resting on two poles at some considerable height from the ground. She was treating the six inch width as if it were solid ground, turning cartwheels, walking on her hands, flipping backward in a dazzling series of maneuvers that drew gasps of appreciation from the audience.

Maude's frame was similarly slender, Gareth reflected, but there was a difference. Maude was pale and thin and undeveloped. The acrobat, standing on her hands, her bright orange skirt falling over her head, revealed firm muscular calves encased for decency's sake in skin-tight leather leggings, and he could see the strength in her arms as they supported her slight weight. She released one hand and waved merrily, before catching the beam again with both hands and swinging sideways, tumbling over and over the beam, her hands changing position at lightning speed, her skirt a blur of orange as she turned herself into something resembling a Catherine wheel.

At the top of the arc, she flung herself backward, turned a neat somersault, landed on both feet, flipped backward, her body curved like a bow, then straightened, her skirt settling around her again as she swept into a triumphant bow.

Gareth found himself applauding with the rest. Her face was flushed with exertion, her eyes alight, beads of perspiration gathered on her broad forehead, her lips parted on a jubilant grin. She put two fingers to her mouth and whistled. The piercing sound produced out of nowhere a small monkey in a red jacket and a cap sporting a bright orange feather.

The creature dragged off his hat and jumped purposefully into the crowd of spectators, chattering in a manner that sounded vaguely obscene to Gareth, who tossed a silver penny into the outthrust cap, receiving a simian salute in response.

The girl began to turn cartwheels as she waited for the monkey to return from his fee collection.

A trio of musicians had just taken the stage, with flute, hautboy, and lute, and he was about to turn away when he saw the girl again. She was sidling around from behind the musicians, something in her hand. The monkey was perched on her shoulder and seemed to be imparting news of grave importance into her ear.

Gareth paused. The girl's air of mischief was irresistible. The musicians played a few notes to establish pitch, then settled into a lively jig. The monkey leaped from the girl's shoulder and began to dance to the music. The crowd laughed and were soon tapping feet and clapping in rhythm.

Gareth watched the girl unobtrusively position herself just below the musicians. She gazed up at them and put something to her mouth. It took him a minute to realize what it was. Then he grinned. The imp of Satan! She was sucking a lemon, her eyes fixed on the flautist. Gareth waited in almost dreadful fascination for what he knew was going to happen. The flute player's notes began to dry up as his mouth puckered, his saliva dried, in response to the girl's vigorous sucking of the lemon.

With a sudden bellow, the flautist leaped forward, catching the girl an almighty buffet across the ear. She fell sideways, promptly turning her fall into a cartwheel with all the expertise of a professional entertainer, so that the crowd laughed, believing the entire byplay to be part of the amusement. But when she fetched up at Gareth's feet, righting herself neatly, she had tears in her eyes.

She rubbed her ringing ear ruefully with one hand and dashed the other across her eyes.

"Not quite quick enough," Gareth observed.

She shook her head, giving him a rather watery grin. "I usually am. I can usually run rings around Bert, but I was distracted for a minute by Chip."

"Chip?"

"My monkey." She put her fingers to her mouth again and whistled. The monkey abandoned his dance and leaped onto her shoulder.

She had a most unusual voice, Gareth reflected, regarding her with frank interest as she continued to stand beside him, critically watching a group of jugglers who had joined the musicians. It was an amazingly deep voice to emerge from such a dainty frame and had a lovely melodious ripple to it that he found very appealing. She spoke English with a slight accent so faint as to be difficult to identify.

The monkey suddenly began a frantic dance on her shoulder, jabbering all the while like some demented Bedlamite, pointing with a scrawny finger toward the stage.

"Oh, sweet lord, I knew I should have made myself scarce," the girl muttered as an exceedingly large woman hove into view. She was wearing a gown of an astonishing bright puce shot through with scarlet thread; her head seemed to ride atop a massive cartwheel ruff; the whole was crowned with a wide velvet hat tied beneath several chins with silk ribbons, gold plumes fluttering gaily in the sea breeze.

"Miranda!" The voice emanating from this spectacle suited the grandeur of its appearance. It was a massive, heavily accented, throaty bellow that was promptly repeated. *Miranda!*

"Ohhhh, lord," the girl muttered again in a long-drawn-out sibilant moan. The monkey took off, still chattering, and the girl dodged behind Gareth. She whispered urgently, "You would do me the most amazing service, milord, if you would just stand perfectly still until she's gone past."

Gareth was hard pressed to keep a straight face but obligingly remained still, then he inhaled sharply as he felt a warm body slip inside his cloak behind him and plaster itself against his back. . . .

If you liked BEWITCHED, you'll love

The Assassin

by Elizabeth Elliott

on sale in March 1998

Avalene de Forshay was furious. The best and bravest knight in the whole of England was a fraud, an imposter who wasn't even English! The man he had pretended to be was the stuff of legends; a knight kind and courteous, handsome in form and face, sworn to keep her safe from all dangers. The cur had wooed her with lies and deception. Her cheeks burned each time she recalled her lovesick antics, the long riband she had dyed a shade of deep emerald green to match his eyes, and how unworthy she had felt when he'd accepted the token of her favor. That simple act had declared him her champion, a knight forever chaste in his adoration, fiercely dedicated to the protection of her virtue and honor.

Life had seemed so full of promise, his chivalrous act a sure sign that God would reward her long years of penance. Even the morning she had awoken outside the walls of Coleway Castle, she had believed every lie he'd told her and trusted him completely. She should have heeded her conscience, those small warnings that he was too good to be true.

Yesterday she had learned too late that her perfect knight was nothing more than a common thief. He had carried her away from her home in the dead of night and left behind the one prize he didn't want. Her heart.

Now he had the gall to remind her of his betrayal. She looked him squarely in the eye. "You will never be my champion, Sir Liar."

"I carry your favor," he said in that deep, silky voice she

had once adored. The sound would have no effect on her at this late date if he had thought to steal an extra horse. Instead he had seated her like a common strumpet across his lap, trapped within the strong circle of his arms.

Her mind could ignore the inescapable intimacy, but her traitorous body refused to accept his betrayal. She had faced that sad fact an hour ago when he reined in the horse to avoid a muddy section of the road and his arm had accidentally brushed against her breasts. The shock of unwelcome desire eventually passed, but she still felt a ridiculous urge to rest her head upon his broad shoulder and let her pulse race unchecked. Instead she kept her arms folded tightly across her chest, determined to ignore the few pleasing qualities he still possessed and their seductive effect on her senses.

Her captor seemed unaware of her discomfort. He placed one hand near his heart. "You insisted that I wear the token of your favor in the next tournament."

"Thieves cannot participate in the sacred trial of combat," she shot back. "Even if you were a knight, the lists are closed to those who break their vows of chivalry."

"Indeed?"

"You prove my point. An *honorable* knight would never speak to a lady in such a sarcastic tone." She lifted her chin and mimicked his air of superiority. " 'Indeed.' "

His expression rarely revealed his thoughts, and now proved no exception. The long silence that followed gave her ample time to recall her situation. Her fate lay in the hands of this stranger, and she had just reminded him that he was a man without honor, the sorry sort of rogue who ravished fair maidens and visited unspeakable cruelties on the defenseless. Her throat constricted and she tried to swallow past the lump of fear. "Do Italian knights take different vows of honor?"

"Are you hoping for a vow to protect damsels in distress?" His smile made her forget much of her fear, yet its breathtaking effect was enough to distress any damsel. Whatever he saw in her face made him chuckle. That, too, had disturbing consequences. Impulsively, she smiled back at him.

"That would be nice." Her voice sounded hopelessly giddy. She cleared her throat and attempted a more dignified tone. "Do Italian knights swear to uphold the rules of chivalry?"

"The vows are similar," he admitted, "although the English chose strange ways to interpret them. I suspect you would create a special order and knight me yourself, if I agreed to follow your own notion of the rules."

She thought that over for a moment. "Then you are not a knight, even of a foreign order?"

"The spurs are mine," he said, "earned fairly in battle." His expression turned somber as he brushed his fingertips over her cheek, then lower to the soft skin beneath her chin. He seduced her with his eyes. "I hold your favor, and I am indeed your champion. In more ways than you can imagine."

The intensity of his words frightened her. This was not the noble knight who had sworn to defend her honor and virtue. Lord knew what fate he intended for her heart. It was a bad time to realize that he had stolen that prize as well. "Do you swear to protect my . . . my honor?"

" 'Tis my duty." His answer made her breathe a sigh of relief, but the glint in his eyes made her suspicious. "Of course, the Italian rules of chivalry are not so restricting as your English rules." He leaned closer, until his lips were no more than a breath from her own. "I took no vows of chastity, sweet Avalene."

Be sure to watch out for

STARCATCHER

The dazzling new historical romance
from national bestselling author

PATRICIA POTTER

on sale in December 1997

WITH HER HAND held securely—nay, tightly—in Patrick's, Marsali allowed him to lead the way toward the other side of the secret grotto, where a high pile of rocks and a thicket of hawthorne would provide them some privacy.

Hours ago, she had been dreading a ceremony that would bind her to a man she distrusted. Sick with dismay and terror, she'd prayed hopelessly that Patrick would come to rescue her. And here he was. The man she'd loved all her life.

He had changed. Her handsome prince was a man now, one whose face bore physical scars, and his soul scars of another kind. Yet his glittering green eyes, as vivid as emeralds, softened each time they looked at her.

As they walked, Marsali studied the man who held her hand as if he were afraid she might escape, and for a moment, she was seized by uncertainty. More than twelve years separated the boy she had known and the man she had just met. There was a hardness to him now, an aura of danger, that she did not remember.

She wanted to put her arms around him, feel *his* arms around her. She wanted the comfort of his closeness. But their clans were at war. And while she told herself he was still Patrick, her Patrick, her senses told her something else. Her father had been willing to trade her to achieve his own ends. Her brother Gavin had supported him. So would not Patrick want to use her, too? Did not all men think of women as weapons to be used to wage their bloody wars?

She would be a fine trophy to flash before Gregor

Sutherland. It would please the marquis greatly if his heir were to bring home a Gunn hostage. And she knew her father well enough to realize he would never give her up to a Sutherland without a fight.

Marsali's head was filled with both longing and doubts. Still, her hand tightened in his, clutching a few moments of fading dreams. Her love. Her starcatcher. She had looked for that star every night and prayed for his safety. As long as it hung bright in the dark sky, she had known he was safe.

Patrick pulled her to a halt beneath an old, gnarled oak. Suddenly his arms crushed her to him as if he needed her as much as she had needed him. No man had ever held her like this, so close, so . . . intimately. So that she could feel every inch of his lean, hard body pressed to hers. He was so tall and strong, and for an instant, she was afraid.

Then she looked up and found him regarding her, his green gaze familiar and filled with hunger. She had never hoped that he loved her. It was enough that she loved him, and that he'd consented to their betrothal. Yet as she grew accustomed to his tight embrace and, indeed, relished it, she realized she wanted everything. Everything, including love, that Patrick could give her.

When his head lowered, her heart started to race. She felt his hand at the small of her back tremble, and it astonished her to see a trace of uncertainty flash in his eyes, locked with hers. Surely this confident man who held her so boldly couldn't be waiting for her permission.

Still, she gave it, whispering his name. "Patrick . . ."

An instant later, his lips seized hers.

It wasn't the first time he'd kissed her. Six years ago, saying goodbye, he'd held her hands and touched his lips to hers in a sweet parting. A gentle kiss. A passionless kiss. A kiss that was nothing at all like this.

Before she knew what was happening, fire was raging between them. The joining of their lips contained an energy so intense she thought she would be consumed by it. It was an energy filled with longing. And desperation.

All doubts sank to the recesses of her mind as the fire intensified, and a need she'd never known exploded into raw hunger. This was Patrick. He was kissing her as she'd dreamed he would for so very, very long. Until that moment, she'd never realized how much she'd feared for him, how much she'd needed him, how deeply her spirit had yearned for him.

She knew it was madness to stay here, kissing Patrick, when the result could be his death. Yet she couldn't push away, couldn't forgo the shelter of his arms. Nor could she force herself to end the heated flow of desire between them.

A deep growl rumbled in his chest. "Sweetness," he whispered into her hair. "I dreamed of this."

SUZANNE ROBINSON

In the style of her highly popular THE ENGAGE-
MENT, a sparkling new romance bound to
capture you in the first pages . . .

THE RESCUE

on sale in February 1998

THE STRUGGLING CEASED, but he counted to twenty before he opened his eyes. She was staring up at him with her eyes wide. That tight little bun she wore had come loose, and her hair had fallen about her shoulders and across her cheeks and temple. Some of the strands were pale gold, others a darker, old-wheat color, some light amber, and some the color of bleached almonds. He'd never seen so many colors in a person's hair. When he found himself trying to count them, his anger returned. It didn't help that she was breathing so hard that her chest kept pushing his. It was like being teased by an experienced and talented harlot. Nightshade kept his grip on the old maid's wrists, but he shoved himself up on his elbows so that there was enough distance between them for him to keep his sanity.

This measure gave him a chance to really look at her for the first time. Primrose Victoria Dane hardly resembled the sketch he'd been given. The sketch must have been taken from a portrait done about ten years ago, for her cheeks no longer puffed out from childish plumpness. No, the sketch had been bad. Beneath him lay a young woman who would never be called beautiful, but who with age had acquired a neatness of feature that pleased him. He liked her eyes, the rings of teal surrounding a burst of gray-green. He liked the way, if one looked closely, her nose seemed just a tiny bit off center. He especially liked her generous breasts. Too bad he didn't like her.

He growled at the cause of all his grievances. "Are you

going to behave yourself, or shall I throw up your skirts and paddle your bottom till it's as red as that lobster you threw at poor Badger?"

"Infamous creature!"

"That's not a promise," he said lightly as she began to fight him again. He let her struggle until she wore herself out and lay beneath him panting and defeated. "Now, do you admit defeasance?"

She frowned at him. "I beg your pardon?"

"D'you admit defeat, defeasance?"

"I shan't throw anything at you if you will release me."

Nightshade got up, discovered that he wasn't presentable, and turned away from her while he got himself under control. When he faced her again, she had put the collapsed bed between them and was gathering hairpins from the floor and blankets. She stopped when he moved. Her hand clenched around the pins as if she might use them as a missle should he threaten her again.

"Never heard of no lady who preferred the noisome stews and dens of the East End to a toff's house."

"What are you talking about?"

"Oh, never mind, Miss Primrose blighted Dane. I don't care why you're here. You're going home to Lady Freshwell's, so don't throw nothing else at me."

Miss Dane's tongue appeared at the corner of her mouth, and she appeared to be confused. Then her expression grew contemptuous. "I understand. That man Fleet has finally realized he must question me before he kills me. I did not credit him with the intelligence, but perhaps his master issued the decree."

"Fleet?"

Nightshade's thoughts went blank. The name meant more to him than she could know. Mortimer Fleet was as black a soul as the rookeries had ever produced, and Nightshade owed him much—curses, plagues, all manner of evil. He thrust aside his hatred as he realized something he'd have noted sooner if he hadn't been distracted by a pink mouth and multicolored hair. And flying lobsters.

"Choke me dead, Miss Primrose, you ain't lost. You're hiding. From Mortimer Fleet."